FIRST AMONG MEN
A STORY OF THE INVASION OF ATTU ISLAND

Jerry Coker

Pocol Press
Clifton, VA

POCOL PRESS

Published in the United States of America
by Pocol Press
6023 Pocol Drive
Clifton, VA 20124
www.pocolpress.com

Publisher's

Cataloguing-in-Publication data

Coker, Jerry, 1950-.
   First among men: a story of the invasion of Attu Island / Jerry
   Coker.
   p. cm.
   ISBN 978-1-929763-55-9
1. World War, 1939-1945 --Campaigns- --Alaska --Attu Island --Fiction.
2. World War, 1939-1945 --Campaigns & battles --Alaska --Attu Island
--Fiction. 3. World War, 1939-1945 --Military personnel --American --
Alaska --Attu Island --Fiction. 4. World War, 1939-1945 --Naval
operations --American --Alaska --Attu Island --Fiction. I. Title.

PS3603.O39963 F57 2013
813.6--dc23   2013906435

Library of Congress Control Number 2013906435

Cover art by Victor Pietrzak.

For my father

Acknowledgements

To get a feel for the Pacific scale and incredible terrain on Attu Island, Michael Lane of Lane Geographics, out of The Sea Ranch, California, produced numerous Geographical Information Systems (GIS) and satellite images for me to study. His fine work and our many meetings at the Lodge over wine were fun and invaluable. Many of these images were the basis for the accurate reconstructed maps produced by Jeanne and Victor Pietrzak of Graphic Gold Design in Davis, California. I thank them both for the short turnarounds and quick understanding of my requirements. Joseph Hetrick provided thoughtful suggestions and editing, both necessary and appreciated. Last, I want to thank my wife Jan, for her patience and love.

The cherry is the first among flowers,
As the warrior is the first among men

-Old Japanese saying

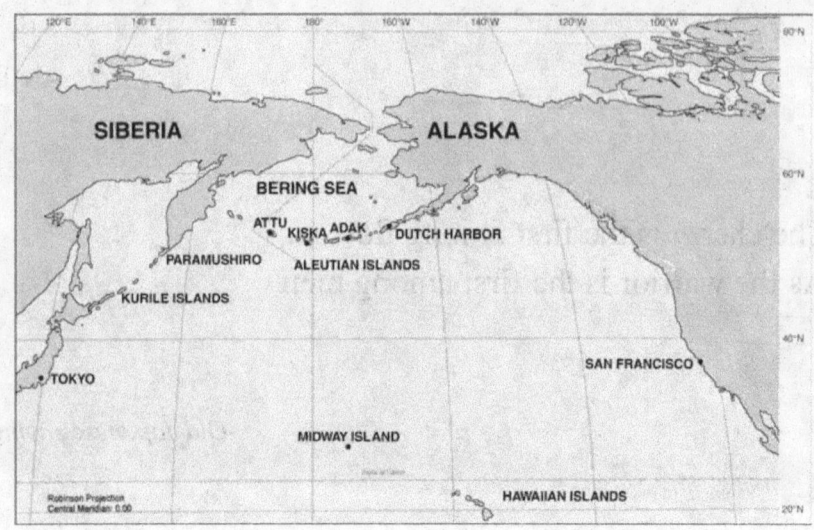

Figure 1: Pacific Theatre Map

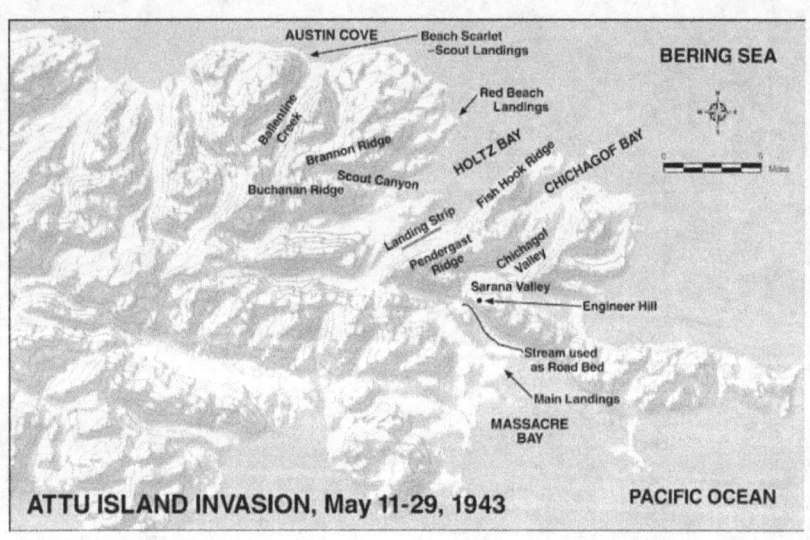

Figure 2: Attu Island Invasion Map

PROLOGUE

This book is a work of historical fiction. I tried to be accurate and true to the dates, general events, and the military ground units and ships participating as much as possible. The characters and their experiences, although based on those general events, are mine alone and are drawn from my imagination. Some military historians may determine broad similarities from my characters to real individuals who actually lived and served during the campaign. Such similarities were necessary in some instances to maintain historical accuracy, but the characters themselves are composites and entities of fiction. For the sake of consistency, I also used the names of some locations for the action throughout the narrative. In reality, many of the scenes of battles, such as Engineer Hill and some of the high-ground ridgelines and so-called "hogbacks" were renamed during the course of the battle, or after the campaign.

In historical retrospect, the battle for Attu Island and really the entire Aleutian campaign could be called "The Last Campaign for Honor". Some students of military history might balk at such a characterization, but I draw the suggestion from the unique time and place the campaign occurred in the apocalypse of World War II. In the spring of 1943 the outcome of the war was uncertain. Even with the primary emphasis of the Joint Chiefs the war in Europe, a number of positive events gave the first indications the Imperial Japanese war machine was not unstoppable. The summer before, early June of 1942, Admiral Isoroku Yamamoto was defeated at the battle of Midway. By late August of the same year the 1st Marine Division was landing on the South Pacific island of Guadalcanal in the Solomons. This highly contested battle was a series of defeats for the U.S. Navy and almost the decimation of the 1st Mar Div in those early months. The eventual triumph in Guadalcanal is storied history, the end of the Japanese drive to the south to invade Australia, the beginning of the first steps up the two-pronged climb for Allied forces from the South and Central Pacific to the heart of the Japanese homeland.

The real story though was how other events aligned to allow for the eventual success of those two watershed campaigns. In the spring of 1942 Admiral Yamamoto wanted to draw the remains of the shattered U.S. fleet, especially the three carriers, away from Midway so Yamamoto could successfully invade the island. To do so he launched a large amphibious force called the "Northern Fleet", including two light carriers, towards the Aleutians under the command of Admiral Boshiro Hosogaya. On June 3rd and 4th, carrier aircraft from Hosogaya's carriers attacked the U.S. auxiliary submarine base at Dutch Harbor, far up the Aleutian chain, and sent a small amphibious group to capture Adak. Not a lot of damage was done, but the ruse was designed to give the clear impression the Japanese intended on invading and capturing Dutch Harbor and other U.S. military installations in the Aleutians, which represented U.S. soil. Yamamoto's feint, he reasoned, would draw the U.S. carriers and task force north while his main fleet assaulted and captured Midway. When the U.S. carriers realized what was happening a day or so out of Midway, they would turn around and rush southward back to Midway. Yamamoto had another task force, mostly battleships and heavy cruisers, waiting to intercept and sink the U.S. task force, essentially decapitating the offensive capability of the U.S. Navy.

Unknown to Yamamoto, Admiral Chester Nimitz, commander of the Pacific Fleet, was aware of his plans since the U.S. Navy broke the Japanese codes by May 21. Timing couldn't have been more perfect. Nimitz held his carriers for the battle of Midway, with the eventual loss of four of Yamamoto's big deck carriers on June 4th and 5th. This critical defeat was never released to the Japanese public until after the war was over. Yamamoto then ordered Admiral Hosogaya to invade Attu and Kiska Islands immediately with his Northern Fleet, releasing this information back to Japanese high command and to the Japanese public. Both landings, on June 6th and 7th, were touted as great victories, when in fact the landing forces of naval infantry and engineers encountered zero resistance. On Attu they captured two Americans, a man and his wife in their sixties plus 60 native Americans; on Kiska a 10-man U.S. Navy radar team.

What was done as a face saving maneuver by Yamamoto created some confusion for the U.S. Joint Chiefs. With the Japanese code broken, the ruse for the earlier attack on the Aleutians to draw the U.S. carriers north away from Midway was understood. But the battle was lost on June 5th. Why would Yamamoto then land troops 1,000 miles to the west on Attu and Kiska two days later?

The conclusions for armchair strategists in Washington D.C. were obvious to themselves based on geographic review. Drawing an arc line from Northern Japan up through the Kurile Islands near the Russian coast placed Attu Island, the western most of the Aleutians, 750 miles away. From Attu to mainland Alaska was a 1,100 mile journey up the Aleutian chain of islands. Mainland Alaska is part of the North American continent, the strategists mused, the Japanese must be planning a potential invasion route to the U.S. West Coast from a different direction. Historically, it appears there was some support to this theory among the Joint Chiefs, as a sizeable force, including naval, air and ground forces were retained in Alaska throughout the war.

On the other hand, it appears Yamamoto believed there was some potential the Allied forces would use the Aleutians as a stepping stone to Japan, possibly through Russia. Only the evidence remains to draw the conclusion, as the Japanese, like the U.S., maintained significant ground forces in reserve through their Imperial Northern Army and the Northern Fleet throughout the war, forces that could have been directed south to support the embattled forces in the South Pacific, men and material that might have made the difference in New Guinea or Guadalcanal.

Perhaps the U.S. Joint Chiefs chose to listen to those who actually knew what the Aleutians were about rather than the armchair strategists. Flying or sailing the Bering Sea was just about the most hazardous duty imaginable. Ground forces stationed there, dealing with the cold, wind, rain and snow through much of the year would have had plenty to say about the feasibility and logistical practicalities of a land invasion via the Aleutians.

All we have nearly 70 years later is the evidence to ponder. Neither side, Japanese or Allied, had the resources to seriously pursue an Aleutian island chain northern invasion option. Neither side was apparently willing to categorically rule out, however, the potential of the other side *trying*. In early 1942, evidence, hard real-time on the ground intelligence, irrespective of breaking the Japanese naval code, was hard to come by in the Aleutians. Neither side knew for certain what the other side was planning. Air surveillance was spotty at best with the weather and constantly changing visibility. Both sides built airstrips within patrol range to sortie aircrews every opportunity on monotonous, high-risk reconnaissance missions, looking, searching for clues of large forces moving about.

Also evident were the priorities required by leaders like Admiral Nimitz. His operational sand table spread from Australia, south, to the Aleutians, north, and all east-west points from the coast of China to the West Coast of California. He had only so many resources. With the shortage of shipping tonnage, platforms for gunfire support and amphibious infantry landing craft, first priority had to go to the South and Central Pacific invasion fleets. One can only imagine what little enthusiasm he had for diverting critical cargo and fighting ships to an invasion of a tiny, fog enshrouded frozen rock inhabited, reportedly, by 500 Japanese troops.

The decision to retake Attu and later Kiska Island was, therefore, on first take, one of necessity to secure a backdoor, nothing more. A second look at the decision, however, suggests something a little different, something less tactical. The United States West Coast was suffering from a rash of hysteria over a potential invasion from Japan. There didn't appear to be anything the government could say to change this public perception, especially with the repeated attempts by the Japanese to take U.S. soil (Midway being the most recent example). Reports of exploding balloons or Japanese submarines surfacing to fire on U.S. shore installations with their deck guns (some of them turned out to be true) were played down or flat out buried. The possible suggestion in the media that there were Japanese forces on *U.S. soil in Alaska,* and the U.S. was not doing *anything about it,* was one the Joint Chiefs was not willing to accept.

The Japanese Imperial Navy landed troops on Attu and Kiska initially to save face after the loss of Midway. They chose to remain on both islands until it became tactically imprudent to keep forces there. In the case of Kiska, the entire force of approximately 10,000 slipped out under the cover of darkness and weather three weeks before the U.S. Allied invasion D-Day, August 15th.

For the garrison at Attu, there was no such option. For the first time in the war, a sizeable force of Japanese troops were ordered to hold and fight in place with no hope of escape. Since the troop withdrawal from Kiska came after the Attu battle, it could be suggested the garrison was abandoned because there was no other option at the time. The Battle of the Komandorski Islands on March 26th, where a U.S. Navy blockade encountered a large resupply force for Attu and Kiska commanded by Admiral Hosogaya, was decisive in that it forced Hosogaya to turn around and not land his supplies. The only resupply after this battle was by submarine.

It would appear the Joint Chiefs wanted yet another quick decisive win, a simple one with ostensibly a single objective: kick the Japanese off U.S. soil and tell the world about it. With only limited resources available for a few months, Kiska, with what U.S. intelligence believed was a much larger defending force, would have to wait. Attu became the specific target. With initial intelligence reports of only 500 defenders, it was determined the assault troop requirement would be a reinforced infantry regiment. The tactical requirement to clear the island was estimated to be three days. Therefore a decision was made to transport the troops to the Aleutians without arctic cold weather gear. They issued instead the normal stateside cold weather clothing (cotton field jackets instead of parkas), and the new high-top all leather combat

4

boots instead of the waterproof and lined snow pak boots. This decision of expediency would cost the men of the 7th Infantry Division dearly.

The less public objective for the U.S. Army was to establish a knowledge base for future amphibious operations, both in the Pacific and for the European theatre. The fast-expanding U.S. Marine Corps would carry much of the load for the island-hopping campaigns up through the Central Pacific, but the Allied South Pacific push under the guidance of General Douglas MacArthur, up through New Guinea, Borneo and the Philippine Islands would be almost entirely a U.S. Army effort. The Army looked forward to this small, limited assault to work out the kinks of what is reputed to be the most difficult of military operations to coordinate well, amphibious landings on a hostile shore.

By the time the 7th Infantry Division was loading onto attack transports in San Francisco in April of 1943, aerial intelligence was starting to give hints there were more than 500 Japanese defenders on Attu, perhaps three times that number. The operational assault troop requirement was raised to include both infantry regiments assigned to the Seventh, the 17th and the 32nd, and the 4th Infantry Regiment was included as a tactical reserve. The troops themselves, freshly trained in amphibious assault operations, went aboard with tropical gear. To the man, most expected the next stop to be Honolulu on their way to the South Pacific.

The commander of the Japanese garrison was keenly aware an invasion was imminent by April, with no hope of a troop withdrawal. The naval battle of the Komandorski Islands in March as noted earlier also ensured the ration supplies, dwindling rapidly, would at some point be gone. At this juncture in the war most of the Japanese troops operating independently on island commands were very good, well equipped and with high morale. The tactical limitations of long-range amphibious basing was just becoming felt, as the Imperial Japanese Navy's sea-going supply chain was being systematically eliminated by sinking. The same ships providing needed fresh supplies of food and ammunition were also the tonnage needed to move troops around, either for other assaults or for withdrawal. There was no hint at this point in the war in the Pacific of Japanese forces being ordered to sacrifice isolated garrisons wholesale. There was certainly no uniform Allied understanding of the Japanese warrior culture as nurtured by their government in the thirties and forties. The Australian Imperial Army (AIF) in New Guinea and U.S. forces in the Solomons encountered isolated Japanese units that held their positions to the last man, or attacked Allied positions against overwhelming firepower only to be decimated. In the same token, large numbers of Japanese troops, both in New Guinea and in Guadalcanal, were skillfully withdrawn virtually overnight when transport was available and it was tactically prudent to do so.   It was certainly the case two and a half months after the battle for Attu when the U.S. forces amassed a large Allied (Canadian troops were involved) force to assault and recapture Kiska only to find the island completely deserted.

It would never be easy for westerners to understand how the Japanese government managed to transform an ancient, once outlawed feudal knight warrior code, the Bushido, into an everyman code for all living subjects, but especially those in uniform.   But as a country Japan at the time was perhaps the most militaristic society on the planet.   The code as practiced in the Imperial Japanese forces was identical to the samarai code of the shoguns, so severe in its interpretation you begin to recognize the code mostly for what is omitted.   Honor is interchangeable with winning.   There is no other option.   Offense is defined as attacking until the enemy is destroyed.   Defense, which has little emphasis, is inflicting as much pain as possible on the enemy. Strangely, the types of weapons used seem to be of less consequence, although there is a strong emphasis on individual initiative and action ensuring focus on the primary goal, which is to gain honor by winning, by vanquishing the enemy.   Such a simple philosophy assumes the enemy warrior shares some of the same goals and values as yourself. You will kill him or he will kill you.   The concept of a prisoner, a warrior surrendering, is not in the code.   There is no honor in surrendering in defeat, so neither the concept of surrender nor the prisoner would be recognized.

The Japanese Imperial forces took the philosophy of no surrender one step further, implying directly an act of surrender would dishonor your family, who would suffer public humiliation.   Loyalty—blind loyalty to western thought—is the most important of the virtues.   It became the ultimate tool for social discipline.   Loyalty to the emperor or to your leaders at all costs, including your life.

American troops, when they began to encounter Japanese forces unwilling to surrender, didn't spend a lot of time mulling the issue. They recognized instantly an enemy who fought to the death, so whenever a Japanese soldier, wounded or otherwise presented himself, he was shot to death on the spot.   Most Americans in World War II were from European heritage and perhaps would understand a feudal knight code of conduct.   But American combat soldiers lived in a free society where if there was a code of honor, it was the code of Tom Mix, Gene Autry, or Gary Cooper.   You shot when fired upon, and quit shooting when your opponent was down.   Only rattlesnakes pulled out

6

belly guns to shoot people in the back. The troops were appalled when encountering a social code leaving no option other than death when the adversary was cornered and trapped. The social code was a two-edged sword as it left no option for surrender, therefore leaving no option for your opponent.

Little did the planners for the Attu invasion know how the battle would foreshadow the behavior of isolated, cut-off Japanese troops in future campaigns. A war of attrition does not lend itself to the characteristics of the offense, unless defense is recognized as just another way to hurt the enemy. Unlike later battles such as Tarawa, six months later in November of 1943, the invasion forces on Attu encountered no resistance on their landing. Tiered defensive positions taking advantage of the terrain approaches the assault troops must use were dug in two miles from the beach. Despite the excellent defensive preparations the Japanese garrison already knew they could only last so long. The troops were on half rations on the day the invasion began and most units were completely out of food by the end of the campaign, two and a half weeks later. With a clear understanding of their tactical situation, westerners cannot comprehend the command decisions once the outcome was clear and the survivors were surrounded.

My father, who served during this campaign and was decorated for his actions on Fish Hook Ridge, felt that at this stage in the war the Japanese arguably fielded the best light infantry soldier in the world. He meant this in the pure sense of what it meant to be a soldier. Not necessarily the best equipped or even the best led, but highly disciplined, highly trained individuals with enormous endurance and driven by unflagging loyalty. Perhaps these characteristics blending with the culturally woven fabric of the Bushido could explain how these men, once the hopelessness of their situation was clear, could embrace *gyokusai,* the spirit of glorious death. Not only for themselves, but for those who were helpless, their wounded lying in their hospital beds.

Over the years before his death when I could get my father to talk about his experiences in the Pacific war, he would often return to Attu. It was almost as if Attu, being his baptism to fire, was his touchstone to reground himself. That early in the war, he said, things were different and there was a lot of excitement to the training and the finality of loading on the ships in San Francisco. There was a clear sense of adventure and romanticism about it that was never present again, certainly for him or any other combat veteran. There were no combat veterans with the 7th Infantry Division then, so even the old Army cadre training the draftees could only guess to what was in store for them. Of course, they thought they were going to the South Pacific.

7

The horrors of that two and a half week campaign came out in bits and pieces. My father's feet were always sensitive to being cold. He told me more than once he still couldn't understand why he didn't get frostbite, since his feet were constantly wet. When men were wounded in such conditions, they often commented the first warmth they felt in days, fleeting as it was, was their own warm blood seeping across their body. The cold wind, constantly blowing snow or rain across the terrain, changed the way you heard things. The muzzle blasts from Japanese machine guns or rifle fire may not be heard, simply blown away, but the unique sound of the arriving bullet when it punctures a steel pot helmet when someone is still wearing it never went away. Nor would he ever forget, near the end of the campaign, the sickening sound when a hand grenade is tucked against a man's stomach and exploded. When American troops closed in on some bunkers, not a sound could be heard of firing, just the muffled explosions as the suicide grenades went off.

My father did not harbor any ill will towards the Japanese soldiers he fought against during this campaign and others after it. After my own service twenty-five years later as a U.S. Marine infantryman in South Vietnam, he asked me if I hated the Vietnamese. I had to think about it, and truthfully told him I didn't think so. They had a job to do and believed in what they did. Were they good soldiers, he asked, those enemy soldiers, those Viet Cong and what you call them, the NVA? Yes, I said emphatically, they were damned good soldiers.

He looked at me for a moment and then nodded his head. Yep, he said, that was my experience too. Men who did what they had to do, and they were damned good soldiers. Just like you and me.

This story then is for them, all of those damned good soldiers on both sides who found themselves on that cold, frozen black rock in the middle of the Bering Sea in 1943. Records reveal about 11,000 Americans were involved in the ground invasion, resulting in one of the highest overall casualty rates of the war, with nearly 4,000 dead or injured, including over 1,000 from cold exposure. For the Japanese Imperial forces, the losses were catastrophic. It was estimated there were 3,000 Japanese defenders on the island. The U.S. Army buried 2,351 dead, but it was assumed hundreds of others were buried by the constant bombardments from ships, airplanes, and artillery. Only 28 prisoners were taken.

8

CHAPTER 1

0830 Hours, May 27, 1943, D-Day Plus 16, Fish Hook Ridge

Ray Craymer was so cold he knew he would freeze if he didn't move. But he felt no warm, tingling numbness the medical officers had warned about on the ship. He was in goddamn pain and every muscle ached to the bone. The company had been losing men steadily to frostbite and immersion foot, more than bullets or artillery shards and Ray had never felt such misery. *The Japs can have this place*, he shivered, *every bit of it*. The landscape was muted grey to black all around him, an eerie colorless twilight revealing not a sprout of green. The light of the arctic spring was neither bright nor dim, and the thick, damp fog offered no hint of a sun far above as he lifted his helmet to peer up the slope.

The fog raced uphill in long, roping tendrils, twisting and spinning with a wind that brushed snowflakes into their ditch. He could only see about 50 yards but the slope clearly increased in angle and between gusts of wind, the fog split farther up the valley hinting at the steep rocky incline to the ridgeline a couple of thousand feet above them. Far up the slope line, companies of the 17th Infantry engaged the Japanese in fighting holes and caves high up on both sides of the curved bowl forming the ridgeline. The attacking troops clutched to rocks with no cover and were also being pounded by the Japanese on the ridge pouring machine gun and mortar fire down into their exposed positions.

Ray crouched on the balls of his feet, squeezing the canvas shelter half around his body as he gripped his knees. He considered pulling his single wool blanket from his pack before shaking his head. He'd get it wet and he needed it later to sleep. Other squad members laid down together, finally, in sheer exhaustion on the wet, ice cold ground and hugged one another like muddy, boot-clad lovers enclosed under the shell of their shelter halves and wool blankets. It was all they had. There were no sleeping bags waiting for them when they unloaded on the beach, one day after D-Day, so they moved out without them.

Two weeks earlier they were on the APA attack transports, the *Grant* and *Chirikof*, ten steaming hours away from the two beachheads to avoid air attacks from Japanese bombers or torpedoes from submarines.   The 32nd Infantry had one battalion on the ground on the initial beachhead with the 17th Infantry, but two battalions were held in reserve.   On May 11, D-day plus four hours the word came back the defenders were three to four times the anticipated, the assault troops were pinned down, close air support was impossible due to fog, and to release the ready reserve force.   Within the hour Ray's 3rd Battalion on the *Chirikof* was on its way to the northern beachhead, so-called Red Beach.

He remembered stepping into the cold surf from the ramp of the Higgins boat, negotiating the packed narrow beach in the semi- twilight. The beach could only handle two or three of the little boats at a time. After a four-hour working party unloading supplies transferred from an LST, Ray and his company stumbled, exhausted, into a chow line in the rain at 0200 in the morning.   After eating they forced marched in the freezing rain off the beach towards some unknown destination.   Ray was glad to get away from the tiny beach.   It felt like a trap with high cliffs on two sides.   Fortunately there were no Japanese snipers or machine guns on those cliffs, they could have stopped the landing cold. The *CRUMP CRUMP* of artillery was constant somewhere ahead. He couldn't tell whether it was incoming or outgoing.   A few incoming rounds had landed near the beach scaring the hell out of everybody, but the unloading never stopped.   It never really got dark.   Once off the beach they encountered the spongy, bog-like growth known as muskeg, a substance virtually impossible to walk on with a heavy pack this time of year.   It supported no weight and in places, men sunk up to a foot or more into icy water pockets underneath. Mostly, it was slimy and slick. Now Ray understood why dozens upon dozens of heavy trucks, jeeps and every other piece of motorized four-wheel gear were parked off slopes from on the beach.   Muskeg was impassable.   He and the other soldiers, already exhausted from the work detail, stumbled and fell constantly, the slime sucking at their leather boots and canvas and cotton gear, soaking them to the bone.

The next 10 days were hard to recall because when he considered events, the days ran together and he couldn't state if something had happened the first day or yesterday.   He was constantly wet and cold. The first two or three days they may have moved some 500 yards inland, or more geographically correct, stumbled around Holtz Bay.   The fog was so thick they had not seen the water, yet they knew it was there because they could smell it.   The combination of fog, rain, and muskeg was maddeningly slow to negotiate and navigate, and after a frustrating hour where two companies were completely separated, the order came down to reach up and grasp the soldier in front by his cartridge belt and hang on. The exercise did little except to create more confusion as men now stumbled in pairs and in groups to fall to the side of the trail, cursing, ranting and exhausted.

The lead company of the battalion in contact with the 17th Infantry up ahead encountered pockets of Japanese resistance, adding to the anxiety and fatigue of the companies bringing up the rear. The Japanese, they heard, were hidden in tiny holes all along the pass. A Nambu light machine gun would erupt ahead and there would be a furious fusillade of rifle and machine gun fire in return. Small mortars, the little 50mm tubes the Japanese carried with each infantry squad would *WHUMP* up ahead in the gray gloom, then just as suddenly the firefight would die out. The soldiers picked themselves up from the mud and slime, cautiously coming erect to shift their transport packs up and on their backs. Some soldiers looked at others for some idea of what was going on, but most shrugged indifferently and moved forward only when the man ahead moved.

Being just behind the fighting was about the same as being five miles away. It had no impact on them other than the constant delays when lead units stopped to engage the Japanese and wipe them out. Ray saw his first dead Japanese soldiers about an hour after a 17th Infantry company had cleaned out a pocket of spider holes and machine gun positions. The fighting positions were very well constructed and positioned, impossible to see until you were standing next to one. The top of each spider hole, a one man sniper pit dug directly into the hillside of the little pass they were in, had been torn away to reveal the small, damp hole the enemy had lived and died in. Each of the corpses had been dragged out away from the hole and shot repeatedly at close range.

For Ray, the dead men were a curiosity. They were foreign looking, small men with many of their human features removed by ghastly wounds. He did notice how well equipped they were for the arctic environment, as all of them had what appeared to be camouflaged white wool-insulated boots, gloves, jackets and headgear. Some of the articles of clothing had been removed from the bodies then abandoned. Ray figured the soldiers ahead probably tried the gear on and found them too small. Manny Torre from Ray's squad, a man of small stature himself, pulled a blood-free wool/leather helmet from a corpse and put it on his head. Clearly too small, he tossed it aside before jerking the woolen gloves off the body. They seemed to fit. Torre grinned up at Ray who said nothing. *What he wouldn't give for some dry, insulated hunting boots instead of the sodden leather boondockers now freezing on his feet.*

This was the way it was for the first few days, rear guard stuff as the 17th Infantry and the lead company of his battalion continued to plod forward, cleaning out Japanese positions every time they reached higher ground. King Company seemed to always come up on the scene of a fight 15 minutes after it was over. Serious cases of frostbite or exposure were going away as casualties now on a regular basis, with enemy corpses no longer found with their winter clothing. Ray could not comprehend why the Army planners did not include arctic winter clothing for the assault troops. He had heard rumors winter gear was on some of the transports, but the transports were not loaded properly and if the clothing was available, it was now miles away in the harbor, or more likely, the transports had been sent away to be out of range of the patrolling Japanese bombers and submarines. Ray thought about the sleeping bags that were supposed to be waiting for them when they unloaded on the beach, shaking his head.

Nothing seemed to be working as planned, as rumors circulated on the ship the operation would be over in three days. The main landing to the south at Massacre Bay was obviously bogged down early to require the reserve force so soon. The weather, well, the weather was predictable in its unpredictability. Ray occasionally heard aircraft overhead, even the whining turbines of fighters. He couldn't see them at all. One day they were threading through a large cluster of dead and wounded 17th Infantry soldiers at a hastily constructed aid station. Strafed by American fighters by accident 20 minutes before King Company walked up on them, the medics moved about the torn bodies with infinite tenderness.

To Ray it was unworldly, the sudden patches of pure white gauze spotted with bright, bright red, the wounded staring dully into nothingness. The dead were left where they fell for now, six or seven close together in groups on each side of the trail as they had been walking, blown apart by .50 caliber machine guns by young pilots who may or may not know what they had done. The fog and cloud cover came and went so quickly, the decision to shoot was based on a target of opportunity. For King Company, it was a terrifying realization of how vulnerable they were.

After what had to have been five or six days, the fog and rain lifted enough for them to see Holtz Bay to their left, and what appeared to be some very high mountain ridges across the small bay, the tops hidden in the clouds. They heard the 17th broke through and made contact with the Scout Battalion that had landed to the west of them. With the strongpoint destroyed the next step was to cross Holtz Bay and climb the eastern mountain range. *That's where the Japs are,* somebody said. *That's where we're going. Jesus H Christ, how high are them sons of bitches?*

Five minutes after the sky had cleared, Japanese mountain artillery bracketed the lead units of the 17th Infantry. Six or seven deadly rounds of 75mm HE landed up ahead, and about 30 seconds later, the next bracket landed right behind King Company. The observers had to be on the high ground somewhere and sure enough, Ray heard the Army 105 counter battery fire going out from the beach almost a minute later. He hugged the mud as the friendly HE flew overhead to impact on the ridges across the bay. The calls for medics echoed behind them now. After a minute or two the only artillery fire was the outgoing 105s. Ray lifted his head and peered around, finding other frightened eyes just below mud-covered helmets doing the same thing. They'll be calling for litter bearers pretty soon.

It was horrible, exhausting duty relegated to men not assigned to perimeter watch or patrol duty whenever the company slowed down and dug in. It didn't matter whether it was day or night because there was light enough to see and the wounded kept coming. There was no other way to get the wounded back to the beach and onto the transports. No jeeps or trucks could make it very far off the beach, and it took four-man litter teams carrying one man about a day to get to the beach and back. So far King Company had been lucky.

After nearly two weeks the lead units of the 17th Infantry hooked up with the sister battalions coming up from the southern invasion beach at Massacre Bay. With Ray's battalion from the 32nd in tow, the combined battalions curved around Holtz Bay to begin the climb up into the curving ridges on the eastern side of the bay, Fish Hook and Pendergast, leading to the Japanese stronghold at Chichagof Harbor. The Japanese troop concentrations were up and down those ridges. The muskeg gradually disappeared as they started uphill on rocky soil. They were relieved for a brief time until the slope gradient increased alarmingly and the rain again turned into light snow.

Far up the slope the tinny crackling of small arms fire bounced about remote and unthreatening. Those who bothered to look found only grayness and no flashes. The Japanese were using smokeless powder that really did work—no flame or muzzle flash. The *WHUMP* of a grenade or a mortar round smothered in wet earth would echo, simply becoming background noise after awhile. Their eyes would turn

13

up automatically as a flight of radar-controlled incoming 14 inchers from one of the three ancient off-shore battleships slowly arced over them to erupt high above the ridge. The sound was too unique to ignore, something between a ripping canvas or a train working up a grade. If the sky was clear Ray noticed you could just see the dark dots of the giant projectiles as they hurled past. But the sky rarely cleared. Even the mighty HE from the battleships thumped their ears like distant thunder as the huge projectiles exploded on their targets, no flashes to be seen in the fog above them.

For the third or fourth time in the last half hour, Ray pulled the charging handle on his M1 back an inch to ensure the action was not frozen. There was not a spot of oil on any of the squad's weapons as their squad leader, Dan Cooley, inspected them all the last night on the transport, insisting they kept them dry. Feeling the panic of not being able to open his bolt after some freezing rain convinced Ray it was a sound move. Sensing movement he turned to see Dan stand up stiffly as their company commander, Captain Stinson, stumbled down their ditch bent down with their platoon commander, Lieutenant Bowles. This had to be it.

Stinson called for company officers and NCOs to his CP earlier to brief them, but he had the habit of personally briefing the men before an important exercise. This was their first real combat assignment since arriving on Attu. Arriving late and following in the footsteps of other assault troops didn't count. It annoyed the platoon sergeants and other NCOs to no end for Stinson to repeat to the men what they, the NCOs had already told them, but the men respected Stinson for the most part, finding his teacher-style reassuring. Ray got up, kicking the men huddled in pairs on each side of him to wake them up, marveling at their willingness to lie on the wet, freezing ground and simply give in.

Stinson waited until the squad stood up and shook themselves from their blankets and shelter halves. They replaced the blankets with their rubber ponchos. Shivering and plastered with caked-on wet mud, the men looked exhausted and pathetic to him. A tall, thin man with rimless glasses he was always adjusting on his face, he nodded grimly, pointing at their rifles.

"If you've been lying on the ground, check those weapons to make sure you didn't plug up the muzzles." Every single man had rolled his M1 Garand in his arms under his shelter half to protect it, but they took it as an order, going through the motions of examining their rifles. Satisfied, Stinson gripped the wrist of his right hand as if to support it, peering down at his boots as he did so.

14

"It's pretty rugged, ain't it?" He asked to no one in particular. "I know you're tired, but the situation ain't too good up there on the ridge. The 17th Infantry is getting the shit kicked out of em' up there on the southern side of the slope, so they've asked us to come up the southern side, let the 17th shift over to the northern side a bit and get on up there and finish the job on that side of the ridge. They got lots of wounded up there and they can't get them out until we can take control of the southern rim and stop that fire right down on them."

Stinson looked up wearily. "Any questions at this point?"

Manny Torre took his helmet off to adjust his knit hat underneath, glancing to his left and right. His large nose was strikingly red today, as if he had a cold or recently fallen on his face. He rubbed it unconsciously as he raised his hand. Stinson stared at Torre's nose curiously before acknowledging the hand with a nod. Manny cleared his throat.

"Don't look like there's much cover up there, how we gonna do any better than the 17th Infantry, sir?" There was no real challenge to his tone, but Stinson seemed irritated by the question nonetheless. He grimaced with unconcealed distaste, staring at Torre long enough most of the other men looked at Torre too.

"I don't know, uh, Torre," Stinson exhaled. "The 17th have been up there a day and a half and they've been flushing the Japs out of little holes and caves, so they've got to be fewer of them left. But I ain't sugar coatin' this thing, they got the ridge, the high ground, they're hidden in the fog and you'll be on a open rocky slope visible from three sides. They ain't but one way to survive up there, and that is get up on that ridge and keep moving up, flushing them out." No one said anything when he finished.

Ray noticed the snow was sticking now and most of the squad ponchos were turning white. Maybe we'll blend right into the rocks, he thought. Stinson had stepped forward and put his hand on Ray's shoulder startling Ray for a second, until he realized Stinson was looking at the other men as he spoke. Torre had put his helmet back on, slumping his shoulders before closing his eyes. When he opened them a few seconds later he met Ray's stare with a wink.

"Okay, I want to talk to the rest of your platoon, so get your gear squared away and prepare your combat load. The platoon sergeants know what we need, but I'll say it again so there's no confusion. We got a tough climb ahead. Just combat packs with your shovels. That slope is about 40 to 50 degrees in some places, damn near straight up. And the Japs have taken that into account in their defense of the ridge.

15

They've had a lot of months to prepare for us. So you'll be climbing, probably on your hands and knees. It's snowing and the wind is blowing, as you can see. You got about a 2,000 foot climb or better to get up to that ridge. Carry all the ammo you can, with plenty of frags. You're completely exposed up there and there is no night here as you have found out." Stinson pinched his glasses off and looked at them with narrow, and very tired eyes.

"These sons of bitches, these sons of Nippon don't surrender and they don't expect you to either. We've all heard they'll bayonet a wounded man on either side without blinkin' an eye. The only stoppin' is going to happen when we kill all of them. King Company is going on up and getting this done. First and Second Platoons are going up on line, I'll hold Third in reserve until we get a feel for what it's like up there." Stinson squeezed Ray's shoulder firmly without looking at him before turning abruptly away.

As Stinson and their lieutenant moved down the ditch, Dan Cooley walked over to Ray and lit a cigarette. Ray was the assistant squad leader and the only other regular Army (RA) soldier in the platoon other than their new platoon sergeant, so Cooley and Ray got along most of the time. The 7th Infantry Division, which both the 17th and 32nd Infantry were sister regiments, was comprised almost entirely of draftees since 1940. A small cadre of regular Army veterans was sprinkled here and there, but by and large, the division was filled with troops who had been in the Army little more than a year.

A southerner like Ray, Sergeant Cooley's Kentucky drawl and dark moods terrorized the mostly big city draftees, but Ray found Cooley competent and fair.

"The CO wants each platoon to go up the slope with a radio, so you carry the reel and handset since Lieutenant Bowles will be on our side of the flank, okay?" Ray nodded realizing he'd be close to Lieutenant Bowles. The snipers would zero on him pretty quickly and his radioman. The look on his face told the story and Cooley patted Ray on the helmet.

"I can't trust these fuckin' shitbirds to do anything but sit down and shit in their pants up there, so that's why I got you on the radio." Ray nodded grimly and looked up the slope. He turned to retort but Cooley had already walked away. Ray felt a tug on his arm forcing a glance into the hooded face of Manny Torre.

"Cray," Torre grinned, "I kind of pissed off the skipper, huh?" Ray shrugged and started to go but Torre held onto his arm.

"I gotta tell ya, I ain't never been so cold in my life, and skipper wants to go straight up the side of this fuckin mountain into the snow."

16

Torre danced on his feet to emphasize his condition while stepping in closer. Ray shrugged again and tried to slip out of his grasp. He needed to work on getting a field telephone and wire reel from the CP. Torre blocked his path and Ray finally stopped, this time annoyed. He liked Torre but sometimes he acted like such a first-class goldbrick. Torre's eyes glittered with merriment, his audience captured.

"I'm so fucking cold I can't feel my hands and feet, I ain't kiddin. My fingers are so numb I can't load my rifle, even with the Jap gloves." To prove his case, Torre hoisted his M1 up to his chest and fumbled with the charging handle, which he could not budge, apparently. He made a "what the fuck?" look with his face and slyly smiled.

Ray turned to face Torre, abruptly yanked the rifle out of his hands. He inspected the action closely before flipped it over and pulling the charging handle back firmly, locking the bolt to the rear. He released the eight-round clip and pulled it out, running his index finger along the bolt slide grooves looking for signs of oil. He placed the clip carefully in Torre's hand. Ray held Torre's gaze before handing him the rifle back.

"In a couple of hours it won't much matter how cold you are, you will either make that rifle work or a Jap will put a bayonet up your ass." Torre stared at Ray as he shook his head.

"I'm counting on you Cray, we're all counting on you. We don't know what we're doing here." Ray glanced back at Torre as Torre dropped the loaded clip back into the breach of the M1 and released the bolt. Torre grinned and continued his cold weather dance to some unknown tune as Ray gave him a middle finger salute and smiled.

It took over two hours of steady climbing to get within sight of the 17th Infantry positions. If they were exhausted before, they were numb now. It was snowing constantly and growing colder. They were often forced to climb hand over hand, the open field of rocks loose as scale. Lieutenant Bowles stopped frequently to report their position back to Captain Stinson at the base of the slope. Bowles would wiggle his finger towards Ray and Ray would scramble over to the lieutenant's position with the field telephone and reel as quickly as he could. He cranked the handle on the box to alert the battalion comm switchboard, which had all the company telephones hooked together, before handing the handset to Bowles. At the first opportunity, Ray would drift away from the lieutenant to keep his distance.

It was eerie to climb into the fog. After the first hour voices could be heard above them, sometimes quite clearly, both American soldiers and Japanese. What was weird to Ray was the Japanese called out in what appeared to be clear, heavily accented English most of the time. It wasn't some jabber, it sounded like—American words. He listened hard and just couldn't quite make them out. 17th Infantry guys would yell back. Then just as quickly the voices would recede as if the volume of a radio was turned down.

Lieutenant Bowles stopped every 10 minutes to take a compass reading. He adjusted the platoon's direction slightly every time, trying to keep both squads on line. Somewhere on the far right in the mist Second Platoon was doing the same thing. Staff Sergeant O'Hearn, the recently transferred platoon sergeant, stayed out of sight with one of the other squads. His voice could not be heard anywhere.

At some point where the slope seemed to point straight up, Lieutenant Bowles declared the platoon was within 100 yards of the 17th Infantry positions. Nobody could see them, so to Ray it didn't mean anything. Besides, it's the Japs he was worried about, not the goddamn 17th Infantry. The climb was too steep to bring along a .30 caliber machine gun team, so the heaviest support weapon they had was the Browning Automatic rifle, the BAR, a 20-pound fully-automatic, magazine-fed light machine gun, one assigned to each squad. Two or three of them could be heard up above them, their heavy, short bursts a little reassuring. A group of large black boulders emerged out of the gloom so Ray started crawling his way towards them. He pulled himself from rock to rock until suddenly he realized one rock he had grabbed was too light. On examination he found to his horror it was a severed human head. He gasped, instinctively released the sticky, hairy object to fall backwards several feet right into Dan Cooley, who in turn lost his footing. The two them slid down, yelling, until they were stopped by two of the privates below them. Ray somehow managed to end up with his head pointed downhill and his rifle and sling wrapped around his left foot. He lost the leather case for the telephone and the wire reel. Cursing, he found he could not lift himself upside down on the slope. The two privates who caught him, both from Second Squad, propped him up and got him turned around, which was not an easy thing to do. Both men laughed as he fell again and slid, painfully, on his back across a sharp rock escarpment.

One of the privates, a large boy with a small head, stood up and started to scramble down to give Ray a hand. As he got to about five feet from Ray the front of his face exploded outward, showered Ray with bone and sticky plasma. As the body fell forward, two more bullets punched into his chest twisting him sideways and onto Ray. The Nambu muzzle burst from the unseen gun position was a foot-long gray blur almost within arms reach of Ray. Deafened by the machine gun's

18

bark, Ray could not hear the bullets zipping right above him and thumping into the lifeless body on top of him, but he could *feel* them.

Suddenly quiet, Ray was close enough to hear the gun crew release the magazine of the Nambu and reload.   Voices, American voices, were yelling just a few feet away as the gun opened up again, the muzzle blast hurling small bits of rock and debris into his face.   His exposed right hand, stung from the heat of the muzzle blast and bits of flying rock, jerked involuntarily.   The gun team spotted the movement instantly, depressing the muzzle while slamming nine or 10 bullets directly into the soldier's body pressing down on him.   None penetrated to Ray, but more blood and bone sprayed his face as warm fluids soaked his chest.   He flattened his exposed hand, letting it lie still.   He heard the gun crew reload again with the next burst right above him, the sudden steady screaming of a man his clue the gun crew had moved to another target.

Ray knew he could not move as the only thing keeping the Nambu from killing him at point blank range was the soldier lying on top of him.   The dead boy was large and heavy, the weight of his body on Ray's chest suffocating him.   Bullets were striking *below* and *above* him around the gun emplacement from returning fire.   The flameless muzzle blast from the Nambu spun across his legs, the searing heat of the burst confirmed the gun crew was now shooting downhill.   Any moment grenades might be thrown at the gun emplacement, and with the gun port being well hidden and shielded, most would fall harmlessly back from the gun port and explode exactly where Ray was lying.   Since everyone would assume he was dead anyway, what difference would it make? *Oh Jesus!*

For whatever reason the grenades did not come.   Instead a strange rhythm started to play out.   Ray heard the slow jackhammer bursts of a BAR slightly above him, seemingly coming closer and closer, the bullets striking all around the gun position.   The Nambu would return fire just as regularly, occasionally switching its fire downhill to the approaching troops, the muzzle blast searing Ray's legs.   The gun went quiet and Ray heard the quick motion of the crew reloading the Nambu when suddenly right above him a BAR opened up, the gunner holding the trigger down until all 20 rounds were expended.   A half a second later a deafening concussion bounced Ray and the dead boy off the cold rocks. When Ray opened his eyes he found himself looking up at gray sky and Dan Cooley's back.   Cooley reloaded the BAR he was holding, expending another magazine into the firing slot of the gun position. Cooley stepped forward to peer into the torn-open position before turned

19

away.   At that point he noticed Ray staring up at him and the surprise and delight in his eyes were unmistakable.

"Shit, boy!   I figured you were done for!"   He stooped down to examine Ray's bloody face, letting his eyes drop to where he expected other wounds.   "Where you hit?"   Ray pushed himself up warily, his ears ringing.   He looked at his hands, bloodied and bruised, then examined his field jacket and legs for wounds.   The jacket sleeve of his right arm and both of his lower trousers were burnt black in places.   His body was sticky with blood, as if he had done a full shift in a slaughterhouse.   He stared at Cooley as Cooley stared back.

"I figured you as done for, boy," Cooley repeated.

"Me too, sarge."   Dan looked away to notice for the first time a number of bodies directly below him, American soldiers.   They were partially covered with a two or three inch coating of snow.   It was only the contrast of the clumps of bunched up uniforms against the strangely uncoated black rocks that helped him distinguish them as men.

"17th Infantry guys," Cooley noted flatly, following his eyes. "Japs must of let some of the early scouts get past, and then mowed the guys down right there in front of em'.   Didn't have a chance.   Bunch more of them up here to the right.   Probably killed by the gun up the hill supporting this one.   That crew is dead.   You was lucky, boy."   He dipped his head with finality before started up the slope.   He pointed up towards the rocks without looking back.   "Your rifle's up here and so is the telephone and reel.   Bowles is looking for us so he can report what just happened, so get a move on."

After retrieving his rifle and telephone satchel, Ray followed Cooley towards another group of rocks where they found Lieutenant Bowles squatted down staring at a map.   There were fresh splatters of bright red on virgin white snow a foot from Bowles legs, but Bowles appeared uninjured.   Ray could hear the whimpering and sobbing of wounded men to his right, but all he could see was another dead soldier 10 feet away, his left hand missing and the forehead strangely deflated. His eyes were closed but his mouth was open.   Ray did not recognize him.

The machine gun encounter had stopped the advance as men checked out other potential gun positions.   Unwounded men were crunched down close to whatever cover they could find.   Feeling suddenly exposed, Ray crouched down as Lieutenant Bowles waved him over impatiently to come closer.   Bowles was angry but his eyes grew wide with wonder as he looked at Ray carefully.

"Are you—hit—Craymer?" Ray shook his head as he cranked the handle and passed the handset to Bowles. Bowles, a large, athletic-looking young man, wrinkled his nose and squinted at Ray's blood-soaked uniform and face.

"I'm okay, sir. The other fella from Second Squad—that big kid, the one from Indiana..." He never completed the sentence, leaving it hanging. Bowles stared at Ray waiting for him to finish. He rubbed his upper lip with two fingers as though he was stroking an imaginary moustache, reminding Ray suddenly of his younger brother, Orin, who did the exact same thing when he was nervous. A long time since Ray had thought about Orin, and a couple of years since he laid eyes on him. He would be about the same age as Bowles.

Bowles rolled the telephone handset upright, curling it under his chin. Sensing Bowles was through with him, Ray slid a couple of feet to the side, stretching the handset cord as he leaned back on the nearest large rock. He hurt, the grenade explosion killing the gun crew injuring his back somehow. He couldn't stop his body from shaking, so he forced himself to sit up again to examine his rifle to ensure the muzzle or action weren't jammed with dirt or ice. No one seemed to notice him. He could hear Bowles tell Captain Stinson about the hidden gun positions and matter-of-factly report three dead and four wounded. Ray looked at the blood of the big soldier on his field jacket. The blood had soaked through and the warmth was long gone. He shivered from the wet chill. It was clear from the one-way conversation Stinson wanted the platoon to get moving again, as Bowles was interrupted a lot.

Ray watched Dan Cooley hand the BAR back to the BAR man he had taken it from. Cooley picked up his carbine and crouched down as men from Third Platoon came up to take the wounded down the slope. The dead, including the boy from Indiana, would stay where they fell until the assault was over.

"King six, King one, wilco, out." Bowles grimaced and shook his head to himself before waving Ray and Cooley over. Bowles proffered the handset to Ray as he joined them in a half crouch, warily watching the slope.

"Skipper says it's clearing on the ridge with a break above, and the minute it does, the Navy flyboys from the *Nassau* or the Army P-38s from Adak are going to pound the ridge." All of them were staring up at the solid gray wall above them without a hint of yellow. The snow was blowing thick and it was getting colder. Bowles cracked a sad smile. "Any minute now."

21

Captain Stinson was in contact with the 17th Infantry companies above them and as planned, the 17th Infantry moved laterally to the right towards the north as King Company moved up to replace them. Every 50 yards revealed an increase of the slope and fewer boulders to find cover. You had to look for it as the slope was mostly white and features blended into a blur of *maybe* shadows. Many of the clusters of boulders first seen turned out to be more dead American soldiers, dozens of them, piled together as they tumbled backwards in groups slain earlier by unseen weapons above them or to each side. They could hear furious fire far to their right—to the north—as the 17th Infantry immediately attempted another assault on the northern side of the ridge. For King Company in their little gray bowl, it was very quiet, slowing the men down, making them cautious of another ambush.

"Keep moving, Keep MOVING!" Lieutenant Bowles was growing hoarse from all his yelling and Ray, like the rest of them, alternated between slinging his rifle so he could climb hand over hand, or carrying his rifle in one hand and attempting to climb with the other. He had flung the telephone satchel and wire reel carrier over his back, looped over his head. Both kept banging around and falling off his shoulders. After about 45 minutes of exhausting climbing in the thick mist, Ray did notice the sky directly above was lightening and the snow had stopped.

CHAPTER 2

1700 Hours, April 28, 1943, D-Day Minus 17, Dutch Harbor, Unalaska Island

"I still can't believe my luck in finding you here, Ed."

"I still can't believe they stuck me on this fuckin' tub instead of a cruiser or one of the battlewagons with the rest of the intelligence staff." Captain Edgar Ridgeway, a heavyset man of middle height, leaned over the railing of the transport to flick the ash from his cigarette to the black and oily water below. He smiled at his younger companion, as they surveyed the dismal scene from the ship to the dock. Both men wore rubber ponchos over their field jackets as the rain pelted their helmets. Dutch Harbor was a small, obscure submarine base that had been on the receiving end of a brief but violent air attack by a Japanese task force nearly one year before. As far as the two officers could determine in the fog and rain, not much damage had occurred. Row upon row of white, wooden, two-story saltbox military temporary buildings were all they could see from the wharf. If there had been damage, it had been repaired. Few people could be seen at all, as if the inhabitants had simply abandoned the place to the elements or lived underground. Ridgeway couldn't imagine being stationed at such a remote, cold and barren location.

Sharing the same thought, both men shook their heads in wonder.

"You would think the brass would just write this one off, wouldn't ya?" Ridgeway mused. But they both knew—now—the U.S. government was not going to allow the Japanese to inhabit American soil. Not here, not Kiska, and not the windswept 35 mile by 20 mile chunk of mountainous black volcanic rock 1,000 miles to the west of them known as Attu. Orin Thomas Craymer, OT to his football buddies in college, knew the target island by heart. For the life of him he could not comprehend why the Joint Chiefs would consider Attu to have any strategic value at all. Two nights before when Orin questioned it, Ed, in the oblique way of intelligence officers who knew much and could say little, merely nodded and sighed before noting "there was much to be learned" from such an exercise.

"Are we still on schedule?" Orin asked, lighting his own cigarette, waving vaguely towards the rain. "I mean, the subs are not even here yet."

23

"More or less."   Ed turned slightly towards Orin, a sardonic curl forming on his lips.   "Getting nervous?"

Although technically a superior officer, Ed was a friend and Orin knew the comment was not a jibe.   They had been friends for over three years, from the first time Orin reported to his ROTC unit and encountered Ed, then a first lieutenant instructor at the University of Oklahoma.   Orin, a freshman scholarship athlete and Ed, non-athletic intelligence and language specialist who never kept his trousers pressed to Army standards, would not be expected to get close.   But Orin liked Ed's wry, razor sharp wit and Ed appreciated a cadet who actually listened to what he had to say and had a brain to boot.

The lockdown on the information regarding the invasion and where it would be was one of the most effective Ed had ever seen.   The 7th Infantry Division troops, now cooling their heels shoulder to shoulder in the airless holds in transports both at Dutch Harbor and elsewhere zig zagging aimlessly to avoid submarine attack, were plucked from their desert training at Camp San Luis Obispo in California and redirected from the African desert to the Pacific. Guadalcanal was a victory hard won and the campaigns in New Guinea and the Solomons were spooling up.   It was pretty obvious to any man in khaki wearing the red and black hourglass patch of the 7th Infantry Division where they were going once Africa was taken from them.   It had to be the South Pacific.

The U.S. Marines send officers down to Ft. Ord near Monterey when the division was moved from Camp San Luis Obispo.   An accelerated amphibious assault training schedule was developed to be implemented under their guidance.   Not one word was mentioned during this training schedule about the North Pacific or the Aleutians. No issue of cold weather gear occurred.

Two days out of San Francisco where the transports and troops were loaded, room was made in wardrooms and in the airless troop holds for relief maps and small sand tables, revealing the final destination. There was a lot of scratching of heads.   Each transport had intelligence officers from G-2 (division intelligence) and S-2 (battalion intelligence) on board to give these briefings.   In the wardroom of his transport, Orin, as one of the officers in the Scout Company for the division now attached to the Scout Battalion, was given a special detailed briefing by Ed.   Both were surprised and glad to see the other, as Ed had been reassigned from his ROTC duties to a regular Army intelligence unit six months after Pearl Harbor.   It had been almost a year.

There wasn't much privacy on the transport, but as officers they were not stacked five-high in the hold or restricted to remain below decks like the enlisted men.   The first opportunity after the briefing he could find, Orin looked Ed up.   They did a little catching up and in the tiny stateroom Ed shared with three other officers, he poured them both a small dram of scotch from his private stash.   When the other officers went to chow, Ed answered Orin's questions carefully, a wry grin and a raised eyebrow the only response to the ones he could not answer. What he did state, repeatedly, was the nature of the "firsts" the invasion would provide.   The *first amphibious assault* handled entirely by the U.S. Army.   The *retaking of U.S. soil, the first captured* since the War of 1812.   Orin found this historical perspective irritating, especially since the actual assault had not occurred yet, and to his mind, the outcome was not assured.

"With the fighting going on in New Guinea and the Solomons, and from what I hear the Guadalcanal thing was not a sure bet right up to the damned end, why are we tying up ships, troops and resources way the fuck up here in the Aleutians?   I mean, who gives a shit about these islands anyway?   Sure it's U.S. property and all, but we got them from the Russians…"   Orin blurted in frustration.   Ed held up his hand and nodded in agreement.

"You know all about Midway, right, it was in all the papers? Well, this could have gone a couple of different ways, but as you know Nimitz read the tea leaves correctly because the Japs attacked Dutch Harbor specifically to draw Nimitz's carriers away from Midway. They wanted us to think they were going to invade Alaska, and once our carriers were on the way to Alaska, the Japs would have hit Midway and when we realized what was going on, turn the carriers around and come back.   Yamamoto was going to set a trap for the returning carriers and sink them at sea."   Ed paused to refresh their glasses grinning at Orin who simply stared back.

"Well, the carriers stayed put and we kicked the shit out of them at Midway and the tide is turning, but the Japs established bases at Kiska and Attu.   Everybody is trying to save face here.   Remember the map of Alaska I used in the briefing?   Sure, Attu is the absolute END of the Aleutian island string that stretches out a thousand miles from Unalaska to Attu, but Attu is still part of that string attached to Alaska and Alaska is part of the North American continent.   Attu is only 750 miles from the Kurile Islands of Russia, and the Japs have supply bases in the Kuriles.   That, my friend, is a potential bridge to the good old U.S. of A."

"But how did we know Yamamoto was just setting a trap for our carriers?   And you just said the Japs have established bases at Attu and Kiska, why would they do that if it was just a ruse and those troops could be used elsewhere?" Recognizing his mistake, Ed sighed while nodding his head. He reached out to clink his glass with Orin.

"You ain't too dumb for a football player, OT. All I can say is that we knew, and the Japs have punted the ball as they decided they were in a good position, with the situation changing, to block us if WE decide to attack Japan from Alaska." Orin contemplated this for a moment, then shook his head in disbelief.

"They're stretched thin and we're stretched thin," he considered slowly, "and we don't think they're going to attack us from Alaska, and from all I can gather from our current strategy—and looking at the climate, tactical and logistic situation up here—there ain't no way we could mount an attack on Japan from the Aleutians." Orin sat up too quickly in the lower bunk he was sitting on and hit his head on the railing above him. Grimacing, he rubbed his head before pointing his finger at Ed accusingly.

"*Dammit!* What the fuck are we doing here, Ed? I'm going to paddle ashore in the middle of the night with the Scout Battalion and risk my life on a god-forsaken frozen barren rock for what? Are there really only 500 Japs on Attu?" Ed assumed the wry smile and raised eyebrow of a no-answer-possible answer. He patted his knee with finality before standing up. The discussion was over.

Orin dropped his cigarette straight down into the water, watching it float for a few seconds. The assault plan had been reviewed again and again in unit briefings. He knew it would be drilled repeatedly once they were on the submarine. If the scouts were anything, they were thorough, but there was a point where the preparation and practice would run hollow and it would be too much. He also looked at Ed with new found curiousity once Ed revealed, rather casually the night before, the fact he would be coming along on their pre-invasion insertion. The Division Scouts had trained for weeks in the surf off of the California beaches of Monterey and San Clemente Island on the big 10-man raider rafts, so Ed would be joining them clean and untrained. Orin didn't even know if Ed could swim. He clearly had no idea what he was getting into, Orin decided, as Ed seemed just as calm and nonplussed as ever.

"You know," Ed drawled, as though he was reading Orin's mind, "I wasn't even issued a weapon before we left. I guess I should see about getting myself one, at least a pistol or something."

"The Army, in all of its wisdom, for once knew what it was doing." Orin smiled as Ed nodded sadly.

"I'll admit I haven't qualified with anything in years." He turned suddenly to Orin, looking up the passageway for bystanders before adding, "and we really don't know how many Japs are facing us. Everything is an estimate. The activity level, picked up by air reconnaissance when the weather allows for it, between Attu and Kiska gives us the clear impression Kiska definitely has the big population. Which is why we're going for Attu instead of Kiska. But knowing the Japs, well, we will find out soon enough. We might be surprised."

They turned to go back below as the rain pelted them harder with the increased wind. "By the way, OT," Ed leaned in close to Orin to look at his face carefully, "I knew you were in this division because I was skimming the rosters for friendly faces a few weeks back. I wanted to be in on your battalion briefing. But just so you know, before I found you I came across another Craymer, a Raymond Marion, a PFC in the 3rd of the 32nd. I forgot which company—King, I think. You had mentioned you had a brother in the regular Army, and I thought you said Ray or a Raymond. Is that your brother? Because if he is, he's part of the invasion force, but he's in the tactical reserve and they'll keep them offshore unless they're needed. Thought you'd want to know."

Orin did want to know and was impressed with Ed's prodigious memory. He didn't even know Ray was in the 7th, it had been so long since he heard from him. Later sitting by himself in his stateroom, he wondered if he would ever get a chance to see his brother. He wished he could tell his parents if nothing else, but there would be no mail or any communications of any kind to the outside world for awhile during this invasion, unless of course, he managed to get himself killed or wounded. Orin rubbed his face, recognizing a strong emotion tugging at his heart when he thought of his older brother. At one time they had been very close, although extremely competitive because of their athletic abilities. Their father was a farmer, but the Great Depression was kind to some farm families as long as the land would support the crops. At least they could eat regularly. Both Ray and Orin were bright boys besides being athletic, so they tied their future fortunes to sports and a college degree. Ray encouraged his younger brother, never stifling his progress in any way. Orin always remembered that.

At the University of Oklahoma Orin found his path well prepared when he reported to his coaches because of his brother Ray. Ray, who set school records as a freshman, and Ray who was one of the few Oklahoma freshman to be offered a varsity position in the pre-season before his sophomore year. Also the Ray who left mid-way the same year with an outstanding record in football but failing grades in his

27

studies.   Ray left with the option of returning if he could bring his grades up at some lesser school, but he never came back to campus nor did he come home.   He took whatever odd jobs he could with the state of the economy, kept his pain and shame to himself to eventually find steady work at a CCC camp back home in Missouri.

The rest of the story Orin knew well, although the family didn't say too much about it at first.   Their father just couldn't understand how Ray could walk away from it all like that, especially without consulting the family and their father specifically.   It created some bad blood.   In 1940, recruiters came to Ray's camp to persuade him into the National Guard.   Three months later he joined the U.S. Army as a regular in a cavalry unit.   As those cavalry units were transitioned into infantry organizations it was hard to track Ray.   During those years Ray only came home twice.   In both cases there were arguments with their father and Ray left.   In the fall of 1939, Orin won his own football scholarship to Oklahoma, arriving on campus to find his coaches asking out loud if he would follow his brother's path and *choose to fail*.   Orin, embarrassed, vowed to never quit.   He did receive occasional letters from Ray during those years, letters with return addresses of Army posts from Texas to California.   His brother seemed very interested in Orin's sports career and his academic achievements.   He reminded him to always study hard.   *Study hard.*   At some point the letters stopped coming.

When the Japanese attacked Pearl Harbor after the end of the football season in 1941, Orin left Oklahoma to enlist in the Army instead of waiting another year and a half to graduate.   He had a plan though. With his college and ROTC credits, the Army offered him a slot in officer candidate school.   His parents were not pleased, but Orin was hardly alone and the patriotic fever of the time swept the campuses of the country.   Unlike his brother, Orin reasoned, he had every intention of returning.

Now Orin could only think of Ray as a regular soldier in the division, another obscure dogface under a OD helmet shoved below the decks in stifling heat and dead air waiting for the moment they would be allowed to come up on deck and then down the cargo nets into the Higgins boats for the assault to the beach.   His big brother Ray with his large strong hands and the easy, steady smile.   Orin wanted to cry out.

CHAPTER 3

1030 Hours, May 27, 1943, D-Day Plus 16, Fish Hook Ridge

The sky did clear at least partially, very suddenly. Large patches of blue appeared above King Company with the fog evaporating on the slopes except right on the ridge above them. *Holy shit*, Ray thought, *we can't see the Japs but they sure as hell can see us*. He instinctively pressed down on the rocks just as the fog line at the ridge erupted with noise, cracking and popping from one side to the other, the dozens of bullets from *aimed* fire arriving a split second later. *ZIP ZIP ZIP ZIP ZIP BEE-OW BEE-OW BEE-OW* filled his ears as the machine gun and rifle fire scythed through their position, careening off rocks, puncturing pot metal steel helmets and sodden cotton field jackets with sharp *thwacks* and sickening dull *thumps*. *Ah shit, ah shit*, Ray gasped, as bullets tugged at his combat harness, jerked at his boot heel and spit stinging rock shrapnel into his hands, cheek and exposed neck. He heard a sharp cry of pain close by, then from another place a long, low groan. He didn't dare look up.

THUMP THUMP THUMP THUMP THUMP came a quick series of reports Ray recognized, a former mortar man, as big tube mortars fired somewhere up on the reverse slope behind the ridge. These would be high angle taking many seconds to get to them, so Ray pressed his face even harder against the cold rocks. *Incoming!* Some one howled.

The whistling whoosh of the mortars sounded their arrival. All five rounds detonated behind him, the closest concussion bouncing him straight up off the rocks, flipping him over like a hooked fish. Deafened by the yellow and black flashing explosions, he stared up at the sky too stunned to move.

Numbness gripped both thighs and buttocks as his upper left arm burned with pain. The *THUMP THUMP* of more mortar rounds jerked his senses so he quickly rolled over. Miraculously, he had been hurled almost a foot yet somehow held onto his M1. His helmet was nowhere in sight, but without it he could look straight up at the ridge as more mortars screamed in exploding 15 yards behind him. The noise from the ridge and the zipping and popping of nearby bullets were so numerous he expected to be shot any second. The steel and rock shards from the surface detonated mortar rounds whizzed past without touching him.   Dully he realized the indirect fire angle for the mortars fired behind the ridge was probably at the highest possible angle due to the steepness of the slope they were on.   He and the other soldiers up on the leading assault line survived the last string of mortars because they were inside the parabolic arc of the zone of fire.   That had to be it. Whatever it is, it could be a temporary thing and a slight adjustment would end it. He peered over his shoulder, noticing at least five soldiers directly below him, motionless, their limbs splayed and twisted exactly as they fell.   Ray wiggled his toes and gratefully found his legs leaden, but responding to his commands.   He knew he was hit but he had to move. *Now.*

On his right Dan Cooley, recognizing what Ray had about their situation, lifted himself off the rocks to motion with his arm for the squad to move forward.

"Come on, First Squad," he croaked, "let's get the hell out of this kill zone and up this slope!"   Cooley pushed to his feet, spotting Ray, pointing forward. "Let's move it, Craymer, get those men moving!"

Manny Torre appeared on Ray's left with another soldier from the squad, a young miner from Pennsylvania named Drexel who carried the Browning Automatic Rifle.   Drexel looked dazed but Ray noticed Torre had Drexel's arm in a tight grip.   Torre's face was bleeding from numerous small puncture wounds.   He casually picked rocks and small metal shards from his cheek with his fingers as he turned towards Ray.

"We going up or what, Cray?"   He said matter-of-factly.

Ray stared blankly at Torre before pulling himself up a few inches to follow Cooley.   The slope was so steep you didn't stand erect, you leaned up away from the ground is all.   The push up made his left shoulder throb.   He could feel something foreign stabbing into the muscles of his bicep, grating against the bone.   He pulled at his sleeve as Torre slid over for a quick check.   He lifted a torn, bloody flap from the field jacket before poking around.   Ray grimaced from the painful probe, watching Torre's face.   Torre pushed the flap down, shrugging his shoulders as he crawled past him.   The company medics were behind them and busy. *Medic! Medic!* Was filling the air.

"Don't look so bad, Cray.   Somethin' in there, but ain't bleedin' too bad."   They glanced up the slope as Dan Cooley threw himself down behind a cluster of boulders thirty or forty feet away. It offered a tiny defilade from the machine gun fire coming from the ridge.   At this moment the guns on the ridge were shooting over their heads to the troops climbing behind them. Ignoring his wounds, Ray with Torre and Drexel in tow dashed forward to join Cooley. Two other soldiers from the First Squad rose and scrambled up with them.   Ray dragged his leaden legs like a crab and somehow neither he nor any of the others were hit in the short climb. The mortars continued to pound the platoons below them. The rifle and machine guns lowered their sights again, the bullets howling and whining off the rock shelter as they probed for them.

"YOU DIE AMERICAN DOG!" The screech sounded like it was only 20 feet away, although the ridge was more like 35 or 40 yards above them. Ray looked up instinctively towards the high-pitched voice as did most of the others, rewarded with a long, tracer-filled fusillade of bullets from the Nambu machine guns raking their position.

"YOU MISSED ME, YOU FUCKIN FISH HEADS!" Screamed Manny Torre practically in Ray's ear. He raised his head three or four inches when he yelled, shrieking a second later when a single bullet slammed into the top of his helmet, jerked it from his head like it was a cotton rag, tumbling and careening down the slope. "JEEESUUZZZZ...." he gasped, clutching his wooley cap as Ray grabbed his head to push him down. He stared back wide-eyed at Ray for a moment before fracturing into a stupid grin, his head bobbing up and down.

"FUCKER HAS ME ZEROED, CHRIST O MIGHTY!" He howled, rubbing his scalp repeatedly, not really believing he was unhurt. "He *blew my fuckin piss pot off*, can you believe it! Did you *see that*? Did you *see that*, sarge?" Cooley ignored him pulling a fragmentation grenade out of his field jacket pocket. Cooley made the squad members tape the O pull-ring and spoon handles down so they wouldn't hook and trigger by accident when they pulled them out of their pockets. He motioned for everyone to pull out a grenade and remove the tape. Ray looked up the slope and figured they were too far away to throw grenades, knowing they had to get closer.

"COME TO ME, AMERICAN DOG! I HAVE PRESENT FOR YOU!" The Japanese soldier called down, and Ray heard the *clump clump* of something falling down from above them and he looked up to catch a glimpse of a bouncing grenade then another, tumbling down the slope towards them.

"GRENADES!" He yelled, rolling his arm around his helmetless head as one grenade exploded about 15 feet away from the rock shelter. Metal and rock shrapnel whizzed over them harmlessly. Then they heard the *clunk* of the other grenade slam into the lip of the rocks they were hiding behind. Ray listened to it careen down the left side of the rocks on it's gravity journey to the side he was on before it rolled right past him, bouncing and bouncing to disappear somewhere below them. It never went off. *A dud.*

31

Ray looked into the saucer eyes of Torre and Dan Cooley just as they heard the *clump clump* of more grenades coming down the slope. Everyone hugged the rocks as Torre let out a frightened animal howl they all felt and shared. Both grenades exploded mid-way down the slope, the shrapnel whining around them. Ray still gripped his grenade as he tried to control his breathing. He was dizzy because he was sucking in air so hard. He knew he was seconds from dying, maybe the next shower of grenades or the one after that. One of them would bounce right over the rocks and that would be all she wrote. Fucking corpses like the sorry sacks of shit down the hill. Nowhere to go. *Oh motherfuckin' Christ...*

"Hey, look at that, will ya!" Screamed Torre, pointing to the east. Ray and the others turned as the Nambu MGs resumed the staccato lead tattoo on their position, raking the rocks. Despite the fire, they all saw the carving turn of the pale, dusty blue Navy F4F Wildcats arcing across the clouds outlined by a patch of blue sky, lining up for a strafing run on the ridgeline. There were four them, mated in pairs, now widely separated line astern as they hurled down on the ridge following their leader. Black spots of smoke were erupting in the sky around them from the anti-aircraft guns on the ridge, but the first of the Wildcats, his wing gun ports sparkling, was already hammering the ridge with .50 caliber slugs, screamed over and was gone. Four or five seconds later, the second Wildcat strafed the ridgeline, followed by the remaining two. As the Wildcats climbed up to come back around for another firing pass, the machine guns on the ridge resumed their fire down on King Company, although the volume of fire was significantly reduced. Cooley tapped the soldiers on the left and right of him to catch their attention, before pointing at Ray.

"Craymer," he drawled, "we're going to let these Wildcats do another firing pass, and then we're gonna take out those guns. Everybody give me their unwrapped grenades." He grabbed the grenades and gave three of them to Manny Torre. If Torre was hesitant or questioned what was being asked of him, he didn't show it.

"You're hit, Cray," continued Cooley, as if to relieve him of the responsibility, "so you, Drexel with the BAR and the rest of you will put down a good base of fire on those guns so we can get close enough to lob some grenades over that ridge. We're too far away right now, so you got to get their heads down. Torre and I will come from both sides and toss what we got and scoot back down here, okay? Clear enough? If we knock em' out, I'll give you the wave up and come up shootin!"

They waited until the next to the last Wildcat finished his second firing pass, then Torre and Cooley slung their weapons over their shoulders and clutched their grenades to their chests, preparing to roll out from behind the rock shelter. The tail-end Charlie Wildcat started firing farther out as the pilot held the trigger down, wiggling his rudder pedals, forcing the nose of the Wildcat to wave left and right. The heavy bullets sparkled and chewed up rock and snow on the ridgeline right down to the rock shelter but the Wildcat kept on coming, lower and lower and then with a ear splitting roar, screamed right over the ridge.

"JESUS FUCKIN CHRIST!" Howled Torre as they were showered with rock fragments from the strafing run. As the rocks careened around them, Dan Cooley had stood up to start climbing up the loose rock face on the right side of their rock shelter, pulling the O-ring cotter pins from two of his fragmentation grenades, gripping the spoon handles so the fuses wouldn't light. Manny Torre, after a second's hesitation, scrambled around from the left side and started up the slope, crablike, looking up at the ridgeline fearfully, clearly expecting to be shot any second. The snow on the surface looked crusty and pure, but as the two men climbed they encountered an apparent shelf of deep, sticky snow, which immediately slowed them down.

"FIRE!" Screamed Ray, shooting his rifle as the others stared frozen in awe, watching Torre and Cooley continue to climb up the slope totally exposed. "FIRE ON THE RIDGELINE, KEEP FIRING ON THE RIDGELINE!" A split second later Drexel's BAR hammered a long burst right into the gray mist at the top of the ridge. Ray fired the last round of his eight round clip as he heard the steady firing of the two other soldiers on his right. He reloaded and kept shooting, terrified as he watched Cooley break away from the deep snow to climb hand over hand as fast he could using his elbows, a live hand grenade in each hand. The ridgeline suddenly erupted with rifle fire and Ray and the others instinctively ducked down for a second before realizing the enemy was shooting at Cooley and Torre. The BAR hammered another long burst right along the lip of the ridge, abating the torrent of fire temporarily. Out of the corner of his eye Ray watched Cooley jerk involuntarily as he was hit in the thigh. Ray estimated he was no more than 15 yards from the ridge top. Cooley rose to prepare to throw one of the grenades when he was hit again in the shoulder, spinning him around. He fell backwards, tumbling head over heel back down the slope.

Torre, seeing Cooley fall and sensing the rifle fire turning to him, flung himself from the side of the slope and rolled down as quickly as he could, accurate rifle fire following him all the way, throwing geysers of snow all around him. He scrambled back into the protection of the rock shelter covered in snow, wild-eyed with his chest heaving as he sucked in giant gulps of air. One Nambu had resumed firing on them,

33

although it was not as accurate as before because of Drexel's continued cover fire.

Dan Cooley stopped his downward slide about 20 feet short of the rock shelter, on his back, his head down the slope. Ray wriggled over to the right side of the shelter, pushing the other two soldiers over to the left. He peered over the rock edge until he could make out Cooley. He noticed Cooley still had the grenades in his hands.

Ray had seen Cooley pull the O rings as he climbed up. At this moment, the gunners seemed to ignore Cooley, fully exposed to their muzzles, practically point blank range for a Nambu, because he was motionless.

"Dan," called Ray quietly, "Dan, can you hear me?" Between the hammering BAR, the Nambu and the other rifle fire, Ray knew both of them were practically deaf. He heard no response, but he could see the grip on Cooley's left hand tighten for a second, which was a good sign. Then watched in horror as the hand relaxed and the grenade slipped from his fingers out of sight. *Oh no, oh no.* Ray had no choice but to duck, as he was too close.

The grenade exploded with a muffled *BANG*. Ray brought his head up just as Cooley's body turned over from the blast hurling shrapnel to whine over their heads. Ray knew Cooley had to be lying on the second grenade, with no hand gripping the spoon safety handle if he was unconscious or dead. There was a muted pop as the handle flew off, lighting the fuse. That was his answer. Ray dodged his head below the rock rim as the grenade detonated with a stomach churning *WHUMP*. They could feel the ground concussion from this one.

"What the fuck just happened?" Screeched Torre, staring at Ray. *"What the fuck just happened?"* He repeated, but he looked suddenly sick. *"Was that Cooley?* Cray! *Was that Cooley?"* Ray ignored him and slowly pressed his face against the snow.

"Ah, SHIT," moaned Torre, "his own grenades, right?" His face creased with sudden anger as he glanced up the ridge. "The mortars got knocked out, they haven't fired a round since the air strike. We got to get out of here, Cray, take our chances, roll down this hill the way I just did." Ray lifted his head from the snow to look at Torre, his lips curled in pain and anger, before peering over his shoulder down the slope below him. From his narrow view most of the slope was out of sight, it was that steep. No other members of the platoon were visible to his left or right because the blue sky had disappeared and it was snowing again, hard, with a strong wind. Without his helmet his knit cap was crusting white in the minutes since it had started to snow. He was suddenly very cold. Torre slapped Drexel, who had stopped firing, on the shoulder, before reaching over to tap the other two soldiers, now hunkered down under the lip of the rocks watching Torre. They both looked very frightened and confused.

"Follow me," said Torre, "I'm gonna take us out of this fuckin place. You just do what I do, we're gonna roll down this hill and pull back. Cooley's dead." Torre started sliding backwards with a come-to-me motion with his hands. The other two soldiers instinctively followed.

Torre grabbed Ray's leg to pull him back but let it go as Ray kicked the hand away roughly.

"Get your hands off me, Torre!" Ray growled, rolling on his side painfully as he spun his rifle's muzzle in their direction. His eyes grew dark and small as they bored into Torre, then to the others.

"Cooley's dead, *I'm taking over*. Anybody tries rolling out of this hole and back down this hill before I tell 'em to, *I'll shoot dead*. You understand?" Drexel and the other two soldiers simply stared at him blankly, but Torre, after a pause, sighed loudly before shaking his head. The other soldiers glanced at Torre, who stopped moving backwards. Torre opened his mouth to speak, then closed it.

"Okay, Cray," he sighed after looked at Ray's face, "whatever you say."

Ray let his fury pass and slowly brought his rifle around to point uphill again. He and Torre locked eyes before Ray hefted the grenade in his hand. He held it up so all of them could see it.

"All of you, get your asses back up here. Pull out your grenades, we're going to try this again."

CHAPTER 4

0500 Hours, December 23, 1942, San Francisco

Ray woke up from the dream, the exposed left side of his body chilled to the bone. He shivered as he loosened the sheet wrapped around his other foot, stopping when he felt Linda's warm thigh and hip moving as he tugged. He slid next to her warmth momentarily, slipping his fingers under her leg to free the sheet. It was unseasonably warm for December, the humidity high with the low clouds, so they left the third-story window open a four inch crack when they fell asleep. It was freezing now, so Ray made the three-foot distance to the window in one cold wooden floor bound and back to bed. He wished he had some pajamas to slip on, accepting instead the cotton flannel sheets and thick comforter he pulled up to their shoulders, and Linda's soft warmth.

It was still dark, infinitely quiet for San Francisco. The fog and low clouds seemed to muffle the sounds of the city, stuffing the raw edges and open wounds with cotton. The dream was still with him, lingering, a cool clutch of shadows he really didn't understand or wish to explore at all. It was, he believed, the third time he'd had the dream, always coming on the last half hour or so before he woke. It didn't make a lot of sense to him because it was a dream of a place he had never been before. It was dark, cold and gray, with black rocks and icy water with high vertical fiords. A Viking dream, he thought idly. He was aware in the dream, somehow, this place wherever it was was the way it was for eons and eons and would never change. San Francisco had some of those physical characteristics, he admitted. It was a city both beautiful and light in the sunshine, yet under the right circumstances so damned cold and lonely. More than once he had declared he would never come back. But he knew in the dream he wasn't in San Francisco.

Ray rubbed the frozen left side of his body before carefully, slowly turning to face Linda without pressing his icy skin against her warmth. She moaned gently, wriggling closer, almost like spoons, a charming thing she did he liked a whole lot, endearing her to him more than he was willing to admit. He could barely make out her eyelashes in the dim light, long and dark, concealing for the time her soft brown eyes. They were what caught his eye and drew him to her in the first place, those brown eyes, and her shy, downcast glance when he had first seen her. He laid there quietly next to her, not wanting to disturb her, enjoying this best time of the day anywhere. Best time of day to sleep, to make love, or to reflect on where you were that day, that time in your life. The room was lighting up in the high corner of the window, where the steep roofs of the houses were left behind and there was nothing but sky. He loved her room, neat and tidy with clear feminine touches revealing a world and perspective so foreign to men. It smelled clean and fragrant. He just couldn't believe how quiet it was here in the dead center of the city. It was like being on an island, a still spot in the middle of a violent ocean, eye of a storm. The stillness would not last.

Ashbury Street was straight, steep and narrow, with big, well-maintained homes on each side. A perpendicular block away on each side crossing the "I" were Haight and Frederick, noisy and bustling during the day, with even noisier Masonic parallel to the east. He could hear none of them right now, only the sudden chattering of some morning sparrows on the broad limbs of the old oak in the narrow yard to crack the stillness. It was so different from the usual haunts for soldiers and sailors in the city, far from the water, the wharves and the constant hustlers. Taxi drivers, quick to spot a group of servicemen in fresh uniforms near the bus terminals, would try to beat the better advice of the guys who knew the city and the tramlines.

Where ya wanna go? The aggressive ones barked, half out of their cars, opening their back doors with their arms waving them in. *I can take four—no five—if you're all together! Where ya wanna go, eh? Bars, girls?*

It really didn't matter what you said, you were going to get dropped in North Beach or Chinatown, maybe Broadway and Columbus, two bucks each for a six-minute ride. The hawkers, selling just about anything, were in your face before you were even out of the taxi. The voices were loud, addressed to you personally because they were standing in your way, but their eyes were constantly shifting from guy to guy, looking for a hesitation, an invitation for a sale.

For a kid from a small town who first encounters this big city stuff, there was the momentary sense of guilt of being impolite if you didn't at *least listen* to the spiel. But a few experiences watching a hustler continue his pitch until a young fellow finally says no a couple times, and then gets shoved roughly aside for his politeness, sets you straight. You didn't count so they didn't count. Ignoring people becomes a way to get around. But you learned pretty quickly no one's feelings were getting hurt. It was a numbers game for the hustlers. From the north and the east the buses came bearing soldiers and airmen from Hamilton, Travis, Mather and McClellan Fields; from the Bay Area alone thousands of shore-based sailors made the journey into the

37

city most nights of the week and every Friday, to mingle and fight with the thousands on liberty from the dozens of ships tied up on the Embarcadero. The few hundred soldiers who made the journey up from Fort Ord, like Ray, were absorbed like so many peanuts in the peanut butter. Time was short, there was a war on and money needed to be spent. Only a fool concerned himself with the niceties with so much fresh meat, you worked your marks or you moved on.

For Ray, the city lost its luster after the second or third trip. When the 7th ID was still at Camp San Luis Obispo and they weren't in the desert training for Africa, weekend passes meant long bus rides into southern California. The reassignment of the division to the Pacific threatre of the war moved 11,000 men from a sleepy, central California college town near the beach to Fort Ord, a bustling new Army base near Monterey, California. Monterey—and Seaside, Pacific Grove and the tiny village of Carmel—was another sleepy, central California town near the beach, a hundred miles up the coast. Weekend passes, if you could get them after five days of trudging around cold sand hills with rifle and pack, or practicing amphibious landings by circling around and around in bouncing flat-bottomed Higgins boats were always a ticket to far away, i.e., *anywhere but here.* Monterey, with its perpetual cloud of gray extending over Fort Ord, quickly lost its charm. Seaside was virtually right outside the main gate, so no place to be unless you only had enough nickels for a few beers.

Ray was a friend of the company clerk, a California-born graduate of San Francisco State College named Larry Lawrence who was drafted and found himself in the Seventh ID. Once Lawrence discovered Ray liked jazz music and had a small portable record player, Lawrence would lend Ray records and even helped Ray store his record player in the company orderly room. One weekend Lawrence invited Ray to accompany him to a party of his old college classmates in San Francisco. Ray balked, but Lawrence explained his plan of renting a cheap hotel room for two nights so they could get rid of their uniforms and be "civilians" for a couple of days, and his friends included girls.

"I've done this before when I had buddies still living in the city. It's so much better in civilian clothes. People treat you better, and you feel normal, you know?"

Once they were in civilian clothes Ray had to admit it was better, much better. Lawrence knew the city like he lived there all of his life, taking Ray to restaurants and bars where there wasn't a single uniform in sight. The cost of splitting a hotel room in the city, which was hard to get in the first place, was a hardship on Ray on his PFC pay. Lawrence eased the burden, however, explaining he knew the desk clerk

38

at night and there would be a 'special" discount. The special discount turned out to be a real boon though, as the night clerk gave them a room regularly reserved for an airline pilot who flew back and fourth from the Hawaiian Islands. The airline had called and said the pilot would be delayed one day due to weather. The room was paid for in advance by the airline, never rented out.

"We won't even sleep in the sheets, he'll never know we were there," said Lawrence, delighted with their luck. Ray and Lawrence took the room for the first night, gambling they would find another "deal" the second night. They took a cab to the upper part of Market Street, a residential area called Eureka Valley where the street had been widened and moved, displacing Merritt Street long ago. The tall, narrow home they entered had a tremendous sidewalk view straight to the downtown and across the bay to Treasure Island. Ray, a little nervous about re-entering mainstream American life after over two years as a regular soldier, lingered a bit to enjoy the view. He was heartened a little by the warm laughter and familiar jazz music coming from inside the house.

"Come on, Ray," Lawrence ribbed watching his friend hesitate, "you act like a freshman at your first sorority mixer—there are some real girls here!" Ray, embarrassed and uncomfortable as the hostess gave Lawrence a big kiss but kept her large, blue eyes on Ray, sighed and stepped through the threshold, determined not to make a fool of himself.

He followed Lawrence like a puppy dog as Lawrence hugged and kissed his way around the house, stopping each embrace with a sudden jolt to turn suddenly turn around to introduce Ray. Ray realized it must have been some cute mannerism Lawrence had picked up when he was in college with these young people, as they all seemed charmed by it and grinned broadly towards Ray. Ray was introduced as "a good friend and University of Oklahoma football player". He had to assume most of them knew Lawrence was in the Army, so it wouldn't take much to put two and two together and assume Ray was a soldier too, but no one said anything about it directly.

Small talk introductions were followed by *what position did you play? I played baseball (or tennis, wrestling, fencing or whatever) myself.* This went on for 20 minutes until they managed to walk up and down three of the four levels of the house and engaged every person at the party. After another 10 minutes Lawrence drifted off with a couple of old friends, laughing and joking. Ray went back up another level to the kitchen to get a bite to eat. The kitchen had a small, glassed in alcove overlooking the tiny back yard, two stories below, and the back yards and porches of several of the homes facing the other side of the

39

block. He turned away from this view to notice Linda for the first time, assisting another young woman in preparing a platter of food.   Linda's medium length dark hair fell forward and she smoothly pressed it back with her slim hands and held it, turning her head when she noticed Ray looking at her. Her eyes, soft and brown with her long natural lashes, seemed to widen and smile a split second before her lips curled up gently, demurely.

Linda was wearing a black cocktail dress, loose fitting yet every curve in her hip and breast was evident as the thin cloth draped down. She was the most beautiful Asian girl he had ever seen. He smiled, immediately aware he was staring but not wanted to break off their first electric contact.   He walked straight towards her, taking two steps before stumbling over the raised wooden floor of the kitchen separating the alcove. His carefully planned, sophisticated approach destroyed, he cursed and stood up, attempting to regain his dignity by standing taller and smiling.

"I'm Ray," he said lamely.   She smiled thinly and nodded in affirmation.

"I know," she said quietly, "the football player. We met about 20 minutes ago in the living room.   I'm Linda if you've forgotten. Linda Wong."

He had forgotten her name or even if they had met.   He couldn't believe it. For some reason her lovely face had simply blended with the dozens of other faces Lawrence had propped up in front of him during the introductions.

"I—I was—sorry," he said finally, feeling foolish.   He glanced down and then back at her, opening his mouth to explain, then stopped. He looked into her eyes again and couldn't help the reflex action of rubbing his hair in frustration. It was at that moment, she said later, she decided to continue their conversation.   He really wants to talk to me, she had thought.

Ray watched the sky grow lighter and lighter, the dim shadows in Linda's room disappearing. He turned onto his side so he could look at her, placing his hand gently on the small of her back. She purred softly at his touch, her hand reaching to find his.

In the years since he left the University of Oklahoma his life had turned decidedly blue collar. There was nothing in the CCC camps or the U.S. Army remotely like the world he knew as a student athlete. It was a shocking reminder of what he once was, a perspective recognizing the pampered life of a student or a college athlete is a child-like world where *you* are important, *your* opinion matters, and frivolous, useless, completely self-centered behavior is perfectly okay, for awhile.

His father had been right. As were his coaches. They all said the same thing, saying what they felt would inspire and redirect a young man with potential. *You pissed it away, son.* What they thought was a pep talk to turn a kid around he had embraced as a mantra. He knew he was wrong, they were right. But he walked anyway, walked away from a scholarship, a good education and a future.

In the Army, he found you can find success and advancement without thinking too hard if you simply do what you are told to do, and do it well. Early in his enlistment someone noticed Ray would do just that. But they noticed quickly he would only have to be told once. Ray was very competent around complex weapons and found himself in the weapons platoon within six months after joining the regular Army. Within the first year he was promoted to assistant section leader for the mortar section with the corporal stripes to go with it. Unheard of in the old Army, but the war was coming, and the platoon commander was an Oklahoma grad who discovered Ray's background.

"When this war comes and we fill out to our full TO, this rating is for a sergeant. We won't bring somebody in if we got you around, even though you don't have much time in grade." The lieutenant, who would soon be promoted himself to captain and take over his own company, clapped his hand on Ray's back, his voice lowering as he stepped in closer.

"Us Oklahoma boys need to stick together, eh? Once this here war is on, anybody with three stripes can find himself leading a platoon in a heartbeat, you know what I'm saying, Craymer? But you got some college, you're prewar. You're going to come out of this a commissioned officer, I bet my bottom dollar on it." Ray had just received a forwarded letter three weeks old from his younger brother Orin, a long, breezy letter explaining how he was going to join the Army and was guaranteed a commission if he could get through OCS. Ray had written two or three letters back to Orin, one congratulating him, another encouraging his talented baby brother to stick it out and stay out of the military as long as he could. None were ever sent. What he did do within two weeks of this promotion was to get busted back down to private and kicked out of the Weapons Platoon.

One night he went out on an overnight pass with some buddies from Camp San Luis Obispo. Someone had access to an old Buick sedan and they managed to get to Santa Barbara in one piece. They parked the car on a sidewalk before proceeding to get thrown out of three or four bars in succession. The group broke up and Ray and

41

another friend finally settled down in an open air bar with a nice ocean view, sitting by themselves, conscious after while some of the other patrons were staring at them in their uniforms. Ray was quiet most of the evening, drinking steadily but mostly minding his own business until a young navy ensign sitting at the adjoining table stood up and proceeded to take an extra chair from Ray's table. Ray happened to have his left leg and half of his body casually extended across this spare chair. The ensign, a large young man who was about as drunk as Ray, laughed as Ray tumbled to the floor as the chair was removed.

"Sorry about that, soldier, need this chair!" The ensign laughed with his buddies and was in the process of sitting down in the newly acquired chair when it was jerked from underneath him. The ensign, off balance and drunk, sank to the floor hard. Ray, standing right behind him, spun the chair back under his table, his eyes black and narrow.

"Sorry, sailor, this chair is being used," he said icily. The three naval officers with the ensign were stunned, with at least one getting to his feet.

"See here, soldier..." he said in astonishment.

The ensign glanced up at Ray over his shoulder before suddenly pushing himself straight up off the floor, turning and swinging at Ray at the same time. Ray, already balanced on the balls of his feet, simply stepped back, pushing and deflected the punch. Almost instantly the big ensign swung up with his left, his fist thumping Ray's right shoulder hard, missing Ray's chin by inches. Instinctively, Ray jabbed the youthful face with his left and right fists. The solid *THWACK THWACK* of his punches hitting the ensign's mouth and nose were sharp and distinct, as were the gasps and fearful moans of the other patrons as the officer dropped straight down to the floor.

The only thing that saved Ray later was one of the naval officers with the ensign, a full lieutenant admitted Ray had not swung first. As it was the bar owner called the police and Ray was promptly arrested for assault and battery, and being drunk and disorderly. The U.S. Navy was threatening to add military charges of assaulting a superior officer. Ray's platoon commander, the same lieutenant who had intimated his prediction Ray would be an officer before the war was over, showed up with Ray's company commander, Captain Stinson. Once they met with the naval officers involved and it was determined Ray had, in effect, defended himself when the ensign had swung on him *twice,* all the charges were dropped. After a week in a squalid Santa Barbara jail, Ray was brought back up to Camp San Luis Obispo and told to report directly to the company commander.

Ray knew what to expect. Captain Stinson's interview was very brief. The only people present included his platoon commander, the company first sergeant and Stinson. Ray lost his rating and corporal chevrons as an assistant section leader for mortars and would be transferred to an infantry platoon as a private. Stinson exchanged glances with the Weapons Platoon Commander after declaring the decision. He stood up to his full height before approaching Ray, standing at attention in the middle of the office.

"You had an excellent record, Craymer," he said quietly, "what the hell's the matter with you?" It was more of a statement than a question, but Ray was torn whether he should respond or not.

"No matter what the circumstances regarding this—incident— might have been to precipitate your actions, you seem to have forgotten who the hell you are." Stinson, his voice rising with every word, suddenly sighed. He seemed to regain control of his temper, his shoulders slumping as he turned to peer directly at Ray.

"You haven't been in the Army that long, Craymer, but you are a regular soldier and this division needs a solid cadre of prewar soldiers to instill discipline and professionalism in these draftees. You had a hell of a lot of promise, but this incident—this arguing and fighting in public with *a commissioned officer* is something the Army will not tolerate. All I can say is you are damned lucky that navy lieutenant was an honest man and said what he said. You were not only drunk, but you were drunk in uniform when it happened! You did not have any friends other than your other drunken buddy to stick up for you. Any other situation there would have been no mercy, you would be on your way to *ten years* in Leavenworth—after maybe three months in the damned stockade!" Stinson said this last sentence with complete disgust. He abruptly turned away from Ray before returning behind his desk.

"What saved your ass was that ensign was dumb enough to swing on you with two dozen witnesses around. I know he just looked like what he probably was, a dumb ass football player used to *getting his way*." Stinson said this with particular venom. "But he got himself commissioned, and that makes him your superior officer, period. It doesn't matter what *you think* of him personally, but in the armed services you *respect the rank* or pay the consequences, is that clear?"

"Yes sir."

"Dismissed. Get out of my sight."

After they had gotten to know each other better, Ray had confessed to Linda he was a soldier, a common infantryman. She seemed genuinely puzzled by this although Ray knew why. Larry

43

Lawrence was a college graduate and was only a PFC, but Linda knew enough about the Army to know draftees did not get commissions. Ray was a regular soldier, but, as she explained carefully, trying not to insult him, he was *too smart* to be a common soldier. *I suppose,* he had said.

The two of them found common ground in the strangest places. The first time they met, at the party on Market Street, they had talked until very late. Laurence had disappeared with some of his friends, so Ray had walked the several blocks with Linda from Market, up and down until they arrived at the big house on Ashbury. She wouldn't let him come up or let him kiss her, but she did agree to meet him for lunch in Golden Gate Park on Sunday. Linda made a big picnic basket of deviled egg sandwiches, a chicken salad, and cold beer. Surprised she was not offering more traditional Chinese food, whatever that was, he was even more surprised to find out she was a fourth generation Chinese-American, and her parents lived in St. Louis. When he admitted he was from Southern Missouri but had never been to St. Louis, it was her turn to be surprised.

"We did the opposite of Western expansion," she giggled, "my ancestors arrived from China just before the California Gold Rush, stayed in the West for about 20 years, then migrated East. First in Denver, and then some of my relatives went north to Chicago and my family went to St. Louis. I still have some relatives here in California, including my aunt who lives in Richmond, right across the bay here."

Ray looked at her in wonder. He had never seen an Asian face except in the movies until he joined the Army. He saw Asians, either Japanese or Chinese, in the train station in Kansas City on a connection on his way to Fort Riley. They stayed together, spoke quietly in their respective, strange language, and made little eye contact with the other American folk sitting all around them. He tried not to stare, but eventually his constant glances earned him a piercing, long glance from one of the elders of the Asian clan.

"I'm a schoolteacher," she responded to his inquiry, "third grade, at a private Catholic school here." He found out she had attended private Christian schools from elementary to high school, coming to California to attend San Francisco State College.

"It was for adventure—and maybe because my parents thought it was a bad idea!" She laughed, her eyes twinkling. "I graduated and wanted to stay, so I took a position at the Catholic school. I like it here."

Larry Lawrence seemed to look at him differently that first weekend as they waited for their ride back to Fort Ord. Lawrence knew Ray spent the first half of the day with Linda in the park. He couldn't get anything else out of him at all. When Lawrence eventually got to the hotel room Ray was already asleep. When he woke up Sunday morning Ray was gone, with a message he was "having a picnic in the park with Linda" and would meet up with Lawrence in the early afternoon at the bus station. Lawrence, more discrete than most, tried small talk with Ray for a few minutes, getting nothing but grunts before dropping it in sudden frustration.

"Goddamn it, Cray," he said in exasperation, "how was it?"

"How was what?" Ray answered innocently.

"Look, I didn't know you liked that kind of stuff, and it is kinda different, isn't?" Ray turned his head fully around, his eyes black coals. Any hint of humor evaporated from his face as he laid his large hands flat on his thighs.

"What kind of stuff," he said slowly, "are you talking about, Lawrence?" Lawrence raised his hands in surrender, recognizing something he had never seen before in Ray Craymer.

"Sorry, Cray, I mean Linda is—you know, Chinese. I didn't mean anything by it." Ray stared at Lawrence for a few more seconds before nodding perceptively. He turned away to glance down at his feet.

"She's a sweet kid. She's even from Missouri, my home state. Although she's from the upper state near the Illinois border, I'm from the southern part, the Ozarks. In many ways, like two different states all together, really. But it gave us something to talk about." Ray looked up, eyeing Lawrence evenly.

"And that's all we did. Talk about stuff. I'd like to see her again if I can." Lawrence nodded slowly, fishing for a cigarette pack in his jacket.

"Yeah, there was a couple of the ladies last night I wouldn't mind seeing again either, but I don't know how many more weekend passes we're going to get. I hear our amphib training schedule is going to get accelerated. At some point we get loaded up and ship out, probably right here from San Francisco. When that happens they'll black us out, quarantine the division, all leaves will be cancelled and one day we will be gone. South Pacific here we come, boy. Fuck." Lawrence lit his cigarette, taking a deep drag into his lungs.

The next time Ray came to San Francisco he came by himself and found a bunk at the YMCA before leaving a message at the house on Ashbury. It was Friday nearly midnight when he called and wasn't surprised when the girl who answered refused to wake Linda up. The YMCA's phones were constantly in use, so he told Linda's roommate, who would give out no information on Linda's schedule, he would call back first thing in the morning.   He had thought about calling ahead while still in Fort Ord, but for some reason didn't do it and just knew she would be home that weekend.   He changed into civvies before wandering out into the streets, which were predictably cold and foggy. He felt lonely and his jacket was too light for the weather.   Shivering, he looked left and right, deciding on the whim his direction.   *This place is colder than damned Alaska, I swear.*   He didn't recognize any of the bars on the street, so he caught an empty bus for Union Square, stepping off when he spotted the Gold Dust on Powell.   At least he knew the place.   The old bar was long and the drinks were cheap.

That first night back the dream came early, but he couldn't shake it when he recognized what was happening.   Water was everywhere this time, black, icy cold water, rising up over his legs, freezing them, numbing them so they wouldn't work.   They were leaden, useless.   His baby brother Orin was there too, close by, the cold water rising up over his legs.   *Orin!*   In his dream Ray called out to Orin, now recognizable in a uniform of some kind, but Orin couldn't hear him.   *Was Orin in the Navy?   Was Orin drowning somewhere?   Orin, little bro, where are you, bud?*

While it was still dark Ray took a long, hot shower after waking from the dream.   He woke bathed in sweat and surprised he had not made noise or disturbed the other sleeping soldiers and sailors in the iron bunks around him.   Dressed with nowhere to go, he sat on his bunk thinking about the dream and his brother.   Ray finally stepped outside with his small bag in hand when his watch hands lined up for six o'clock.   It was barely light and cold as hell.   He walked a half a block before finding an open, warm diner, flopping himself down at the counter to order coffee.   Unlike the other times he had the dream Ray felt thoroughly frightened, even after waking up.   Not for himself, but for his brother, Orin, who had never showed up in the dream before. What the hell does that mean?   He was probably in the Army, Ray thought.   He said that in his last letter.   You're just worried about him, is all.   Was he already overseas?

At eight o'clock Ray called the Ashbury house.   After a minute or so, Linda came to the phone.   She knew he had called the night before, she said.   She hesitated when he told her he was in San Francisco and wanted to see her; then acquiesced when he suggested another picnic in the park.   He even offered to pick up something for them to eat, but Linda insisted on preparing the lunch.   Its cheaper and healthier she said.   Ray spent the rest of the morning walking Golden Gate Park until their time to meet.   He didn't have anything else to do and never really spent anytime exploring the park.

"I really didn't think you would call again," she said as she neatly pressed down the corners of the blanket. "American boys prefer—well, European girls." This was spoken without malice, more of a matter of fact statement. She tucked her legs underneath her skirt and smiled sweetly. "I haven't had very many dates with American boys like you." Ray had to think about that for a moment before answering.

"You mean, soldiers like me, or white boys like me?"

"Either. In St. Louis our community is pretty tight. Chinese families mingle with other Chinese families socially. We really didn't interact all that much as a family with non-Chinese. I went to Christian schools that were mixed so I certainly knew non-Chinese children as students, but all girls. We didn't go to one another's home or mixed socially, at least not the non-Chinese. It just wasn't done. It was one of the reasons I came west to go to college. I knew San Francisco State College was coeducational, and after 12 years of girls only schools, I wanted something different."

"Is that why you stayed?"

"Yes, I wanted more. I wanted to widen my horizons a bit. Here in San Francisco people are more accepting of differences. There are many large, well-established and respected Chinese families here in San Francisco, in all walks of life, so the people accept we Chinese as part of the fabric of the city, of the culture here. There is a little more blending."

"What about the Japanese? Or some of the other Asian cultures who live here? Are they accepted too?" She peered at Ray with a sharp, quizzical glance before answering.

"Yes, they were accepted like the Chinese, or at least they were until December 7th of last year." She said this last sentence with a dry sadness, her eyes on the chicken salad she was spooning onto their paper plates. Ray realized he had hit on something very sensitive, very painful to her, something forcing a distance between them. He wanted to close the distance somehow, to put his arms around her but knew instinctively this was not what she wanted. She looked up, her eyes damp and he knew she wasn't going to say it.

"I—I suppose folks tend to blame all Asians for what the Japanese did—because your cultures are similar," he offered. "American folks—I mean, white folks…" Linda's eyes narrowed as he stumbled with this.

"Yes," she said flatly. "To Americans of European heritage who don't know the difference, we Asians all look alike. Yellow skin, slanted eyes, all the same, right?" She shook her head, looking blankly out over the expanse of green grass. "I had a Japanese boyfriend when I

47

was a student here, and when my Aunt in Richmond found out, she wouldn't talk to me for a month." Ray tried not to laugh at this, but he couldn't resist cracking a joke. "I had to break it off. It broke my heart."

"Your aunt doesn't like Japs, is that it?" Linda turned on him, her eyes blazing.

"You don't understand, do you? I love my aunt, she's a dear person, but she is *racist!*" Linda pointed over her shoulder in the general direction of the east, waving her slender finger accusingly. "In St. Louis, my grandmothers are constantly making fun of Europeans—the Italians are this, the French are that, the English are something else. They both agree the Germans created the best composers and the English the best silver, but they also say *they all look alike!*" Linda covered her mouth with embarrassment when she realized she had raised her voice to a shrill. After glancing left and right she cracked a thin, knowing smile.

"My Japanese boyfriend—who I liked very much—is an Assistant Professor of Chemistry at Princeton now. Or was, I don't know with the war. One of the smartest boys I knew. It didn't matter. He was Japanese. To my aunt, to my family, he was an old enemy. Our ancient, cultural wars with Japan from past centuries and now this—this war—has dug this old hate right to the surface again. My family, who hasn't set foot on Chinese soil except for some annual visits to ancient shrines, act as if we are somehow related to this China under attack from Japan. We're not. We're *Americans* now. I just don't understand why they insist on living as if it were true. It isn't. It perpetuates hate for no reason!"

Ray didn't know how to get Linda off this track. The conversation was so laced with emotion he simply did not know what to do. He ate his lunch as she talked of her family, of her other schoolteacher roommates at the Ashbury house, of her brother who enlisted in the Army after college and was an intelligence officer. It was all tied somehow to a world gone mad, a madness borne of ancient racism. All resulting in a renewed hatred of a new generation who had nothing to do with the ancient world, whose participation in this renewed hatred is linked solely on the basis of their genetic, racial outer covering—their skin and bone structure. *I feel cheated she said, cheated out of my life just as it is starting.*

In the late afternoon as the day grew chillier, she stopped talking, her lips open. Ray looked at her face and felt its fragile vulnerability, yet sensed the invitation to come closer. Ray took a corner of the blanket and brought it up to wrap around her shoulders, slipping in beside her.   She did not resist as he brought her body up against his. She shivered for a few minutes before settling down, then her hands responded, closing in around his waist.   She lifted her face when he looked down in her eyes and they kissed.

"You are beautiful," he said quietly.   "If anyone feels cheated, it's me.   I wished I had met you long ago when I was starting out.   I wished you had been a coed at my old school, Oklahoma."   She looked at him, puzzled.

"Ray," she murmured, a name he rarely heard anymore, "you sound like an old man near the end of his life.   You *have* just started."

Ray managed six more weekend passes over the following three months before the holidays.   He set aside every penny he had to ensure bus fare to San Francisco, coming up twice with Larry Lawrence but not spending five minutes with him between the time he got off the bus on Friday night and on the bus on Sunday afternoon.   It had got out somehow to the company Ray was seeing a "Chinee" girl, but not much was said about it after he nearly broke a man's jaw who didn't get the message and said the wrong thing.   He wasn't about to discuss it with anybody.   The word did get around that weekend passes would be a thing of the past right after the Christmas holidays.   *South Pacific, here we come.*   Most everybody was going to try to get a week's pass during Christmas.   It was time to see the folks before you head out for the big beyond, boys!   Ray had kept his nose clean and was a PFC and assistant squad leader now, so his pass was approved.   *Where you going, the first sergeant asked.   Home to Missouri, Top.   Home to Missouri.*

"I can stay, I really don't need to go home.   I would rather stay here with you."   Linda brought the toast to the small dinette table and sat down next to Ray.   She was wearing a long, sleek silk nightgown that clung revealingly to her curves, a garment she knew Ray loved to see her in.   She never wore it alone without a housecoat when her roommates where around, but both had already left for their respective hometowns for the holidays.   It seemed nobody in San Francisco was actually raised there.

"Your family is expecting you, Linda, and you're already two days late.   How would you explain not coming?   They don't know anything about me, do they?"   He said this with a smile, as he knew what her family would think of her seeing a white boy like him, a soldier.   The statement seemed to pain her, even embarrass her, so he

49

reached across the table to take her slim hand. He gripped it gently as she gripped back.

"I'll take you to the train station this morning so you won't be late. You need to leave now if you want to be in St Louis by Christmas Eve, this is really cutting it close." They had the conversations, several conversations on what was coming. Ray glanced at his wristwatch and pointlessly looked at the big electric clock over the refrigerator. It was huge, a foot in diameter, and he realized it was a classroom clock. It had a very visible second hand that seemed to be moving especially fast this morning. She knew he was not coming back, not because he didn't want to, but there would be no more weekend passes for the 7th ID. She didn't ask about where he thought he was going once he told her it would be the South Pacific.

"To kill Japanese," she said quietly. He nodded slowly. No more was said about it.

On the third or fourth weekend pass she had suggested he not go back to the YMCA after their picnics in the park. She brought him home and he met her roommates, two cute brunette school teachers from Nebraska from all places. He was introduced as Ray, but Linda noted he was a soldier *and* a former football player from the University of Oklahoma. The two brunettes from Nebraska were both cornhuskers but neither seem to know too much about football, so the conversations waned quickly. On future weekend passes, the two brunettes would be quick to say hi and quick to say bye on their way to some event someplace.   The third story of the house on Ashbury was pretty expansive when there was only the two of them around. Ray enjoyed trying out Linda's record collection, mostly swing and big band stuff, but it was okay, because he found Linda liked to dance.

The only time he felt out of place was when he opened, by accident, her large storage dresser. The two large doors revealed a top shelf covered with photographs. Obviously family, all Chinese, some in ancient garb and knotted hair and others in modern dresses and suits. They looked completely foreign to Ray, as strange as aliens from outer space. He could not relate in any way these people to the slim, beautiful girl in the kitchen cooking a roasted chicken. He sighed deeply, painfully, realizing the dilemma he was creating in his own heart. And hers, he thought reflectively. Jeez.

"Will you write me?" He asked the last night. He was on top of her, spent, his hands in her hair, his eyes close to hers, his lips kissing her on her nose, cheeks and lips. She watched him sadly, almost in pain. The tears that came were unexpected, because they had gone through this, and she was calm, understanding. She sobbed uncontrollably for

50

minutes, and all Ray could do was just hold her until her breathing settled down.   Ray held her this way most of the night, telling her he loved her.   She didn't say anything, but he felt the tears on her cheeks, which he kissed away as soon as they fell.   Just before he fell asleep he felt her hands reach up, stroking his chest over her breasts until she found his heart.   There she stopped and her hands stayed.

CHAPTER 5

0230 hours, May 11, 1943, D-Day Minus 1 Hour, off Austin Cove (Beach Scarlet)

"This way, Lieutenant," the sailor whispered, grasping Orin Craymer's arm.   The sailor guided him around stacked gear in the incredibly jam-packed forward torpedo room next to a vertical ladder leading to a lock-out escape trunk with an external hatch.   The torpedoes were removed to make room for the berthing of over half of the 7th Infantry Division Scouts on the sub.   The submarine was under night surface running conditions with all lighting reduced to red bulbs.   The escape hatch was open as was the lock-out trunk and Orin smelled the brine of the sea.   Looking up he saw nothing but darkness from the hole up to the deck forward of the submarine's conning tower.   As he climbed up the ladder and out on the bouncing, squirrelly deck, it took him a few seconds to get his bearings.   He could see but just barely. The air was saturated with cold moisture, a dim gray-darkness identifying the fog that enveloped them.

Dark shapes moved about on the forward deck in silence.   He remembered most of the LCRLs (landing craft, rubber) were on the aft deck, with only four of the rafts forward towards the bow.   The odd pneumatic hissing sound he picked up over the waves lapping over the submarine was the automatic air inflation of the big 10-man raider rafts, now slid over the foul weather safety railings onto to the surface of the sea.   Not a single light was visible anywhere.   It was only when he stared hard to his left where Attu was supposed to be did he determine the direction the noise of the breaking surf was coming from.   The briefing said they would surface about 500 yards from the shore, but it sounded closer.

Men were coming out of the escape trunk hatch turning Orin's attention back to the task at hand.   He began following the drill, organizing them as they stepped out on deck.   The first four men up should have been his platoon sergeant, squad leaders and boat captains. He lined them up next to him and told the one closest to the hatch to start sending up the rest of the men.   Twenty-seven more men came up the hatch, each silently snatched by their respective squad leader/boat captain to remain together as groups.   Orin glanced at the luminous dial of his wristwatch, already impatient for the last man assigned to his platoon—a last-minute extra man—to come up the hatch.   After this last man, the remaining two platoons of the Scout Company coming up would be directed aft to the seven rafts now stradding the sub off the longer, wider deck behind the conning tower.

The helmeted head of a large, heavy-set man appeared before he cautiously climbed out on the deck.   Captain Ed Ridgeway, looking frightened, confused and a bit ridiculous with the black greasepaint Orin had slathered on his face, spotted Orin and waved.   Captain Williamson, the CO of the Composite Scout Battalion, had seen Ridgeway and Orin together on a couple of occasions and when informed Ridgeway was coming along despite Williamson's protests, immediately assigned the responsibility of keeping Ridgeway out of the way to Orin.

"Can't kill him," Williamson had said in his clipped way of speaking, "though he might drown in the surf or get his ass shot. But beyond that, whatever you do, don't let him get captured!" Williamson had 400 men on four different ships landing on three different beaches that he had trained for weeks specifically for this assignment under his responsibility.   To have an untrained non-infantry, non-scout INTEL officer suddenly assigned to his lead scouting elements was totally unacceptable and made no sense whatsoever.   So he assigned the responsibility to his least experienced junior officer and forgot about it.

"Why *are you* coming along?"   Orin had asked, once he was informed Ridgeway was his responsibility.   Ridgeway had smiled and said quietly, *"Kikitai koto ga arimasu."*

Orin's jaw had dropped as Ridgeline added quickly,   "That means, I want to ask you some questions.   No one is to know this, you understand."

Ridgeway had appeared along the submarine wharf at Dutch Harbor where the USS Nautilus was tied up the night before they departed for Attu, May 1st.   Orin and 108 other 7th Infantry Division Scouts were loading their rafts and gear onboard in the semi-darkness after a full dress rehearsal on the deck.   Ridgeway had brought virtually nothing with him when he reported to Williamson, who stared at the overweight officer in a brand new field uniform in absolute astonishment.   Ridgeway was wearing a steel helmet and some kind of British Army long woolen overcoat.   On top of the coat was strapped a revolver in a shoulder holster.   He had no other equipment other than a small briefcase.

Williamson quickly called for Orin and introduced them unnecessarily.   "Lieutenant Craymer will set you all you up, Captain, get you some—gear, and all.   Now, if you'll excuse me I have a lot to do."   Williamson turned to Craymer with a piercing glance.   "Take

CARE of him, Lieutenant!" With that he turned on his heel and walked rapidly away. Orin looked at Ridgeway from head to toe, shaking his head woefully.

"Damn, Ed, do you have any idea what we're going to be doing?" His eyes locked on the shoulder holster as Ridgeway patted it proudly.

"Hey, I did get a weapon though! Nobody had a spare tommy gun or anything, but the XO on the transport had this .38 Smith and Wesson they got from a U.S. Navy pilot they picked up out of the drink down south a few months ago. I even got 12 extra rounds for it." He grinned broadly and Orin could only laugh.

"Let's get you below and find a corner to stuff you in, it's pretty tight down in there. The men are berthed in the forward and aft torpedo rooms, and they have us officers wherever they can roll out a mat. You're going to need some gear."

With his entire platoon now on deck, Orin got his hands on Ed Ridgeway's life jacket to secure him, motioning him to stay close to him. With Ridgeway in tow Orin lead the way, counting the inflating rubber rafts as they passed them. When they got to the first raft Orin pulled aside to let one of his squads move alongside the cargo net leading to the raft. They immediately started loading their gear into it. Then they went on to the second raft to repeat the procedure for the next squad. At the last raft, sitting practically on the bow of the pitching submarine, the last group of men gathered to get their equipment on board. Orin knew the Second and Third Platoons were right behind his men, loading gear and themselves into the seven rafts straddling the aft deck of the submarine. Their CO, Captain Williamson, would be in the first raft, number one, and Orin would be in the last raft, assigned as raft number 11.

Shadowing them somewhere out in the fog was their sister submarine, *USS Narwhal,* with 105 more Division Scouts. The fast-attack transport, *USS Kane,* a converted former World War I destroyer, was also out there with the 150 men of the Reconnaisance Troop. All would be arriving at the same beach Orin's platoon was headed for, staggered to ensure each group would land within minutes of one another. Another Scout Platoon would be landing 20 miles to the south of them on Massacre Bay with a completely different mission.

Orin and Ed Ridgeway squatted down in the center of the big raft, stepping around packs, weapons and oars. Technically they were overloaded but Orin was not about to let Ridgeway on another raft out of his sight. He also didn't want to break up a boat team of paddlers who knew their job and switch them around to other boats. The scouts had trained for this mission for weeks with the same crews in the rafts. This was not the time to mix them up. There were four to five paddlers to a side, so they were going to be okay. Orin glanced at his watch and adjusted his position. It was 0300 exactly.

CHAPTER 6

0930 Hours, March 7, 1943, D-Day Minus 65 Days, 600 Miles East of Paramushiro, Kurile Islands

It was close to three days since he had eaten any real meals. It was disheartening to Yoshi Nakagawa to find his stomach still convulsing up foul bile to burn his throat. *There is nothing there. Let me be.* The destroyer rolled and pitched as another ice cold wave of seawater sluiced down the narrow deck to pull at his soaked boots, drenching his clothes. He didn't care. He gripped the thin railings of the foul weather safety line, hanging on as the ship tobogganed down the back of another black, roaring roller and shuddered. The narrow ship, rolling port to starboard through 30 degrees every 10 seconds or so, shook its tail and stern airborne like a little terrier dog. *This is hell.*

Nakagawa was no sailor and didn't pretend to be. Although he was born and raised on Shikoku, smallest of the main Japanese islands and loved to visit and play in the sea as a boy, he never had any desire to be on the sea. Especially like this. His people were farmers, not fishermen. The ocean is for *fish*.

The destroyer was long and lean, built for speed, accelerating down the troughs like a cat with its hair on fire. Here in the open ocean with mountainous waves filling half of the sky, or so it seemed where he stood down on the aft deck, the destroyer felt very small, its narrow beam and speed making it too fast, racing away from following seas only to burrow its dagger brow into the next wave.

As an engineer he considered the forces pressing down on the ship as it accelerated, decelerated again and again, with long pauses as the bow of the destroyer slowly hauled itself free of the tons of water clutching at the structure. This is a steel ship, he thought fighting the nausea, *at what point will it turn into a submarine and keep on going straight to the bottom?*

He expanded his lungs with the wind even though it was so cold it hurt. The fresh air made him feel less nauseous. He heard the clank of a steel door, turning to see a petty officer in foul weather gear close the hatch. The sailor spotted him, staring at him in astonishment. The man carefully worked his way down the deck holding onto the safety line until he was within inches of Nakagawa's face. He looked angry, obviously about to scold Nakagawa until he noticed the Imperial Army cold weather coat and the officer's insignia on his collar. The petty officer stood up straighter, nodding abruptly, a gesture Yoshi assumed was some form of a salute since they both needed to hold the rail and safety line with both hands. Yoshi nodded back.

"Excuse me, sir," the petty officer spoke slowly, but loudly. "What are you doing here? We have no watches back here with the depth charge station because of the weather, and if you are swept out to sea no one would see it!" Yoshi nodded in understanding, motioning for the petty officer to lead the way back down below. It was good while it lasted, and he knew in his heart if he had to endure many more days of seasickness, being swept out to sea might be a relief.

The nausea returned immediately once he was inside staring down the passageway. It was so narrow he could hold himself up by pressing against the bulkheads on either side. The smell of diesel fuel, paint, wet canvas, human sweat, and cooking grease weakened his knees to the point he almost collapsed. Alarmed, the petty officer hooked his arm under Yoshi and half carried him into the tiny compartment of a radio operator. Yoshi slid into an empty seat, waving the petty officer away, who gratefully disappeared. Yoshi twisted around to stare at the radio operator, a very slim and young sailor with a headset on who nodded respectfully but continued to type whatever he was hearing on his headset. The operator was eating a rice ball as he typed, a sight forcing Yoshi to turn away as his stomach churned. He closed his eyes, sliding down in the chair as far as he dared. He opened them briefly when he spied a small calendar tacked to a corkboard above the radio set. The calendar picture was of a spring/winter mountain range in Hokkaido, the northern island in the Japanese island chain.

Three weeks ago Nakagawa was in a replacement company in Ominato on Northern Hokkaido, waiting for an assignment to the Northern Imperial Army. As a top student out of the Osaka University engineering school he had his sights on joining a first rate civil engineering firm building bridges and dams when he graduated. However, the army mobilized him almost as soon as the ink was dry on his diploma. Still, he was encouraged at first, for even in officer candidate school he noticed the instructors were impressed with his college credentials, suggesting he would get "fine opportunities" to build bridges and dams overseas for the Emperor. In 1942 the Japanese Army was growing by leaps and bounds, acquiring territories as fast as the Army could conquer them. Many of these territories were in uncharted, virgin places that needed all kinds of infrastructure. Yoshi started considering the South Seas, with warm waters, or undeveloped locations in the Philippine Islands or Indonesia. Many opportunities there, and the climate and cultures were interesting, he was told.

He knew this was not going to happen as soon as he received his orders to Hokkaido, to the Northern Imperial Army. At Ominato he was informed he would be replacing a young engineering officer who developed an acute infection in the Aleutian Islands. As soon as transport could be arranged he would be shipped to Paramushiro, in the Kurile Islands to catch yet another ship to the Aleutians. He had to find these places on a map. Yoshi was crestfallen and disappointed, but never showed it to the aging captain who handed him his formal orders. He saluted smartly, standing at attention as the captain briefly summarized his new assignment. It seemed in the army you were forever standing in front of people who felt they had complete control of your life and destiny, men who acted as if they knew all about you, yet they were complete strangers.

"You won't be building any bridges or dams, I'm afraid," commented the captain, apparently reading Yoshi's mind, clucking his tongue almost wistfully. "But, Lieutenant, the Aleutians are *strategic* to the Imperial Army's plan to keep the West from invading Japan." As the captain came around his desk, Yoshi noticed for the first time he also had the insignia of the engineer corps on his collar.

"I read your record, Lieutenant Nakagawa, and not everyone can say they got their engineering degree from Osaka University. You worked very hard to get into the university, and you worked very hard when you got there, or you wouldn't have the degree," The captain offered Yoshi a cigarette, which he politely refused. The captain lit his cigarette with an American Zippo lighter with an obvious flourish, holding the Zippo up where Yoshi could see the small emblem in what appeared to be English letters.

"Georgia Tech," the captain beamed. "Class of '33. A fine school in an interesting city. Ever been to America? Atlanta?" Yoshi shook his head.

"No sir." Yoshi had never left the beautiful mountainous region of his Kochi-ken prefecture until he was 15 years old, and then it was only to be tested and evaluated for possible advance study. It was a great time for his family, a great opportunity for the son of a successful farmer, a great honor. He received a special course for two years under the guidance and funding of a rich relative now living in Osaka. Although no one was more surprised than Yoshi when he turned 17 and was accepted and matriculated at Osaka University. The rich relative selected Yoshi for his continued financial support, and Yoshi vowed to not let him down or embarrass his family. Osaka is a big city on the main island of Honshu, necessitating Yoshi to live apart from his family for four more years, with only occasional visits back to his family's land on Shikoku.   He studied hard, but things did not work out as he had expected.   The military courses were mandatory at Osaka University, but the necessity to actually be mobilized and in uniform seemed remote.   Now, it just seemed naïve.   You do your part when your country asked for you.   Yoshi knew he was not worldly or particularly sophisticated, but he was not sure exactly what the captain was driving at.   The captain put the Zippo away and took a long drag on his cigarette.

"You will get your chance, Lieutenant, to use that degree.   But first you get a unique *opportunity*."   The captain noticed how Yoshi's eyes narrowed when he said the word.   He smiled, nodding in understanding.

"It's a term a little over used in the Imperial Army, isn't it? Well, I apologize, but when you work for the Emperor—and we all do— we use the terminology *he would use.*"   The captain glanced at his watch before walking back behind his desk.

"I lived with the Americans for over six years as I also received a Master's Degree from Purdue in Indiana.   They are, despite some of the information you may have received, intelligent people with a stronger sense of pride than we give them credit.   They are not a pure race of course, like us, because they are European mongrels.   They have no real history except conquest of the west, no real culture to speak of, and no real common denominator except their land.   And that, Lieutenant, is their weakness.   Their pride, as paper thin as it is, is based on the fact no one has ever *taken and held* American soil before, that is, until the Imperial Japanese Army took it from them!   The Aleutians are part of America, and Japanese troops and *engineers* captured and are now on *American soil.*"   The captain slowly rose, signaling, Yoshi assumed, the interview was over.

"You are going to be part of history, Lieutenant," the captain said casually.   Then he stood up straight almost to attention before nodding respectfully to Yoshi, his lips grim.   "The Americans, Lieutenant, will want it back."

59

CHAPTER 7

1300 Hours, April 30, 1943, D-Day Minus 11, Fish Hook Ridge

Yoshi Nakagawa accepted the steaming mug of tea gratefully from his lead NCO, placing his binoculars carefully on the sandbagged corner of the bunker's rimmed entrance. It had rained steadily all morning soaking everything, but the corner of the bunker had a thick wooden beam that extended out leaving a tiny dry patch on the canvas sandbag. Yoshi took his gloves off and wrapped his fingers around the warm cup, witnessing a single beam of yellow sunlight tracing down from the leaden sky to illuminate a circle of sea in the middle of Holtz Bay. It was a remarkably cheering sight, catching the attention of several of the soldiers toiling nearby on the ridgeline, pausing in their work to stare and comment on its beauty. Within seconds the clouds enveloped the sunbeam, withering the golden color into grayness. The illuminated circle of water where the beam of sun had been now appeared darker than the sea around it, as if the beam was still there. Yoshi smiled, deciding his eyes were simply playing tricks on him. Attu did that to you after awhile. Beauty was hard to find here.

The view on the ridgeline, when the weather permitted it, was spectacular in any event. Certainly one of the primary reasons the decision was made to reinforce the bunkers and gun positions along the ridge. The mountaintop was nearly 2,500 feet above Holtz Bay, directly to the west from his view, curving southwesterly to the top of the Sarana Valley. By turning around and looking southeast he could see, at least right now, over Pendergast Ridge and the lower ridge across Sarana Valley to Massacre Bay, five miles away, where the Americans were expected to land. Machine gun bunkers, trenches, tunnels, and spider holes were carefully stepped from the valley floor right up to the ridgelines, channeling assaulting troops to carefully prepared fire lanes of overlapping heavy weapons.

It was an amazing introduction for an engineer to view the effort involved to prepare the defensive positions. There was no concrete available and only limited supplies of construction lumber, so most bunkers and gun pits were dug directly out of the frozen hillsides. The few horses available were used to assist the artillery units in transporting 75mm mountain guns up impossible slopes so the guns could cover the valley approaches from the mountains to the beaches. Those were dug into deep caves with connecting tunnels so the guns could be shifted in

60

direction in minutes.   They were also used to drag the dual-purpose 75mm anti-aircraft artillery into protected pits so they could be used for both AA and direct fire support.

Yoshi listened in amazement as the young crews proudly explained how the mountain guns broke into 11 modules, the heaviest component weighing 95 kilograms, all routinely carried by artillerymen with six horses or 20 men.   Once in position, the gun could be assembled and ready to fire in 10 minutes.   At the top of one of the ridgeline gun pits Yoshi had glanced down the rugged, nearly vertical path the cannoneers had followed to bring their gun up to the top of the mountain.   He could not believe it was possible.

Yoshi had been so glad to get off the destroyer it was several days before the implications of his arrival began to sink in.   It had taken nearly a week to make the journey from the Kuriles to Attu in constant rough weather.   When he climbed down the ladder to the shuttle boat, he was amazed at how calm and flat the protected harbor was on the day of his arrival.   The destroyer hovered in thick fog for hours before it crept its way into the harbor.   With constant alarms regarding American submarines and aircraft, the supplies and personnel were unloaded quickly before it slipped away into the fog.

There weren't any vehicles moving about Attu because of the slick soil, a surface only really firm enough to walk on in the coldest winter months, he was told.   There was about three inches of snow on the ground that day.   Yoshi was struck by the gray, treeless landscape offering no warmth, beauty or inspiration.   The valleys were full of the strange nasty lichen-like plant, transitioning rapidly into virtually vertical black volcanic mountain ranges on each side forming peaked, curving bowls like a reversed mold of a boat's prow.   Nothing seemed to thrive except the lichen.   It was a desolate, immensely cold and lonely place, one that he wondered aloud but under his breath, what made it so valuable.   Certainly not the land itself.   Who would want to stay and defend it?   He had to laugh at the irony of his own thoughts.

While getting his orientation and winter clothing issue he encountered numerous comments from fellow soldiers on "how lucky of a fellow he was" and "you are probably the last" to the point he was becoming annoyed by it.   His new commanding officer, a youthful engineer major, offered a more direct insight on their first meeting. The man's shoulders were so slumped with fatigue it was clear to Yoshi he was near total exhaustion.   The man could hardly keep his eyes open. Yoshi was ushered into the underground bunker for what he anticipated would be one more Army introductory interview.   The young major slid back in his chair as Yoshi offered his order package and came to

61

rigid attention.   Nodding briefly, the major closed his eyes for what seemed half a minute.   Yoshi didn't know what to do so he simply waited.   When the major again opened his eyes, red-rimmed but fully open, they bored right into Yoshi.   The man slowly rose far enough to reach out and grasp Yoshi's order package, then just as slowly sat back down.   He set the orders casually on the desk, unopened.

"Your destroyer was the last surface ship available to us for resupply, Lieutenant.   There are not going to be anymore.   The Americans are sinking everything afloat with submarines and aircraft, and the fleet can't risk it.   You're lucky you made it.   We're lucky you are here."   A slight smile traced on his lips as he said this.   Yoshi wondered if the man was being insulting or not.   He thought suddenly of the aging captain back on Hokkaido who gave him his orders to this forsaken place, choosing to speak earnestly without permission.

"I welcome this opportunity to serve the Emperor, sir!"   The major's head lifted slightly as did his eyebrows, but if he saw any irony in the comment he didn't reveal it.   He did place both of his hands one on top of the other on Yoshi's orders.

"Very well, Lieutenant, and so you will."   The major sat up straighter, again closing his eyes as if in meditation.   "The officer you are replacing worked himself almost to death because we have so much we must do in so little time.   I hope you've rested well on your journey, because you won't get much of that here.   We have orders to complete the runway so Attu will be a stepping stone for our conquest of North America, but the Americans are bombing the runway with Liberators out of Adak every day the sky is clear enough to fly, so we live with a net sum loss because we have run out of time.   It will never be completed."   The major opened his eyes again, locking them with Yoshi's.

"You will assist in the supervision of the lengthening and hardening of the runway because those are our orders, but you are also going to assist in the construction of the defensive structures we are building to resist the Americans when they arrive.   There is no concrete and only so much lumber now the supply ships are no longer coming.   We are digging underground everywhere.   We are only about 50 percent complete on the defensive structures, and we have about six weeks to get them complete, as we expect the Americans the first of May."

Yoshi did not know how to respond to this.   An uncomfortable silence fell between them, interrupted by a rapid series of distant explosions drawing closer with each detonation.   An air raid klaxon began warbling after the bombs began to fall.   The major looked skyward to the ceiling of the bunker, then again leveled his eyes on Yoshi.

As disciplined as he was, Yoshi could not help but cringe and dodge his head when there were sudden loud rat-tat-tat-tat concussions right outside the door of the bunker from the twin-barrelled anti-aircraft cannon positioned there. He had walked right past the gun coming in, wondering how noisy it would be to have the gun so close. He quickly recovered but the shooting continued. Now he could hear whistling, howling projectiles screaming all the way to the ground, followed by huge ground-jumping explosions, one after another, some of them very close. The bunker sighed then shifted, shaking dirt and debris from the ceiling. Heavy aircraft engines throbbed in the background, now receding. The raid continued for another minute or so, then the bombing stopped abruptly. The anti-aircraft guns continued to fire for several seconds after the bombs stopped. Shrapnel from the anti-aircraft shells rained down for a full minute with heavy *CLUMPS* as they fell, leaden to the ground nearby. Yoshi realized rather numbly neither of them had moved during the raid, with the major never taking his eyes off of him. *Was it some kind of a test? Are these people crazy?*

The major finally rose and reached for his heavy winter jacket and helmet as the all-clear klaxon sounded. He turned to Yoshi, still standing at attention, with the slightest hint of a smile on his exhausted face. "Well, welcome to Attu. Get your equipment, Lieutenant Nakagawa, we have a runway to repair."

Yoshi considered that day as he sipped his tea. He wished he had some of his mother's rice cookies to go with the tea, but they were getting less and less mail with the limited shipments from the submarines. The six weeks since his arrival had passed very quickly. As his commanding officer had predicted he had received little rest and the runway was not completed. It was an impossible task with the stepped-up bombing raids, and he was relieved when he and the other engineers were pulled off the assignment after two weeks. The explanation for the withdrawal was the equipment necessary for the runway construction was destroyed by the incessant bombing.

Colonel Yamasaki, the commander of the garrison on Attu, redirected the engineers to the incomplete defense structures and to the back-breaking duty of hauling artillery shells up to the gun positions on the mountains. The days ran together for the engineers, the defensive projects refocused again and again, with the operative words being "made serviceable." Corners were being cut but the engineer's concerns were ignored for expediency.

The Imperial Army, all through the horrific winds and snow of the winter months, moved much of the heavy artillery and mortars up into the ridgelines with horses and sheer muscled manpower. Yoshi could

63

only imagine how difficult that must have been.   Once he arrived on Attu to began his orientation, he was incredulous at how extensive the defensive tunneling and trenching was envisioned.   They had done impossible work as it was.   When he started working on the defenses there was only four weeks remaining to meet the expected invasion on May 1.   The submarines were having difficulty getting through now, so the ration for troops was cut weekly due to the loss of regular food replenishment. Yoshi noticed with pride and astonishment how easily the men accepted and adjusted to this hardship when they were working so hard.   There seemed no shortage of spirit among these men, he thought, and I must prove I am of the same mettle.

He was inwardly ashamed of his reservations regarding the expressed purpose of all the defensive structures, or the intent of the Imperial Army.   Yoshi was not an infantry officer or a professional soldier, nor were most of the other junior engineering officers.   They did what they were told, did it to the best of their ability, he was sure. But the other officers, after gaining one another's confidence in knowing who could be trusted, passed on rumors.   As junior officers they were not privy to Colonel Yamasaki's planning meetings or strategy, but NCOs and friends of aides passed on tidbits of information that, to Yoshi's mind, didn't make a lot of sense.   Colonel Yamasaki purportedly revealed plans, originating from Admiral Hosogaya, the commander of the Aleutian command including Attu and Kiska, ordering the evacuation of all troops from Attu before the Americans invasion.   Then there was the rumor, again supposedly originating from Admiral Hosogaya, confirming reinforcements coming by submarine to assist the garrison in repelling the American invaders.

There had been no reinforcements since Yoshi arrived, he knew that.   The shortages of food and supplies negated the possibility of submarines bringing any sizable force to Attu, they simply did not have the shipping to support what they had on the island as it was.   As the weeks passed, he began to wonder how the weekly submarine was supposed to handle or withdraw the over 2,700 men still on Attu, if that really was the plan.   The logistical improbability didn't slow down the rumors though, with bright young officers who could calculate as well as anyone still insisted on whispering hopeful comments during the infrequent rests.   Yoshi politely listened and nodded with interest when such discussions came up, but he didn't believe much anymore.

This morning, the last day of April, revealed no landing craft but American bombers and navy fighter planes were reported strafing especially heavily near the beaches and the slopes covering the beaches whenever the weather permitted.   The reports from last night included

64

naval gunfire all along the western approaches to the beaches from Holtz Bay to Massacre Bay.   The naval bombardment only lasted a few hours, and unlike today, the night was foggy and wet and it was reasoned the gunfire was radar directed with significant caliber, suggesting battleships.   The latest rumor, which Yoshi accepted as probably true, was the American invasion fleet was over the horizon and if the Japanese fleet or air arm could not sink it within a few days, the Americans would land assault troops by the end of the week.   Colonel Yamasaki expected the Americans to be drawn into the Massacre Valley and destroyed there by the overwhelming firepower of Japanese artillery.   Yoshi looked out over the dark waters of Holtz Bay, mostly disappearing now with rolling fog and snow clouds.   He shivered, considering, for the first time, the prospect he would never see Shikoku or his family again.   The dark doubt would come now and again, with some rumor to either dispel it or confirm what he felt would come to pass.

He felt a deep sadness for a moment but no despair, as he was not alone.   He sipped his tea, turning his attention to observe the energetic yet careful work his men were doing on the foundation supports for a anti-aircraft gun mount.   *They have their work to occupy them, as I have mine.*   Yoshi set his cup down and unfolded his blueprints on the sandbags.

CHAPTER 8

0305 hours, May 11, 1943, D-Day, Zero Hour, off Austin Cove (Beach Scarlet)

Orin Cramer, his head down as his thoughts drifted for a few seconds, was confused by the sensation of vertigo as the LCRL lifted free from the deck of the submarine, bobbing with the swell. They could hear the hissing of escaping ballast air rising and bubbling to the surface as the *Nautilas* effortlessly slipped below them. In a minute the 11 rafts were alone in the sea surrounded by fog, the highly disciplined scouts paddling in silence towards the sound of the surf on a general compass heading. No signal lights were shown on the approach. As the scouts had learned in the surf of San Clemente Island in Southern California, twilight and the curling white foam of the sea help outline the other black rafts if you stay close together. The rafts approached the beach in three groups, each group representing a scout platoon.

Austin Cove was over five miles north of where intel believed there were any Japanese troops. The cove represented the back door, the back country. *That is what is believed*, Orin thought over and over. He could hear Ed Ridgeway's heavy breathing right behind him, anticipating Ridgeway would know in a few minutes how good the intelligence was. Orin had not really thought about the coming prospect of combat in any serious way all through the training, pressing it aside even on the submarine coming over from Dutch Harbor. Like many athletes, he never considered practice a true substitute or serious preparation for a real game. The only thing that prepares you for a real game is another real game. You know the capabilities of your teammates and you know the playbook for practice. Crappy, amateur game films and stat cards on opposing players cannot tell you the motivations or true capabilities of another person on any given day until you meet them on the scrimmage line. Not a single soldier he knew in the Composite Scout Battalion had any combat experience, so Orin could only hope his training and the basic skills and discipline of his soldiers would get them through the first few days.

He gripped the stock of his Thompson submachine gun and tried to concentrate his thoughts on getting his rafts to the right beach. The swell was heavy and there was no real telling how rough the beach surf would be. Aerial recon revealed a small, narrow cove pointing towards a steep inlet. Orin has stared at the photos for as long as they would let him, and even Ed could only shrug his shoulders. "Should be okay," he said, unconvincingly. "It's very remote and difficult to get to, so we figure the Japs will have no presence there because it would be hard to support."

Orin squelched the first tendrils of fear he found rising the longer he sat still. He had trained with these troops for months. He had complete confidence in their ability to do their jobs in *practice*, because they sure had enough of it in a very short time. They were all volunteers once they came to the 7th Infantry Division, volunteers who knew the Scout Company would be tasked for difficult assignments. Most were hand picked from the volunteers as he had been, based on youth, physical fitness, intelligence and motivation. They were good troops, as good as any in the 7th ID. He felt embarassingly proud of them, silently paddling in these frigid waters towards an unknown land and a fierce enemy, for he could see the rafts were online heading straight towards a barely visible white thread of rolling surf marking the entrance to the inlet. Somewhere to the east of them were the other rafts of the sister Scout Company off the *Nautilas* with the rafts from the *Narwhal* and the *Kane* right behind them.

The cove's narrow sides and flat approaches created a fast and powerful surf line that rushed up the inlet to thunder and break on a steep, pebbly beach. Paddlers worked hard to keep the rafts right behind the curling waves until they crashed into the rough surf and grounded temporarily. The soldiers in the front of the rafts bounded out immediately and attempted to drag the rafts up the beach before the next line of waves arrived to swamp them. In three minutes time most of the scouts were soaked through with the effort, dragging the LCRLs off the beach allowing room for the next company of rafts. Captain Williamson ordered a defensive perimeter established, directing Orin to send a squad up from the beach to confirm there were no Japanese waiting for them up on the bluffs.

Securing Ed Ridgeway with a trusted NCO on the firm orders not to let Ridgeway out of his sight, Orin took his First Squad and led the reconnoiter patrol himself. The inlet was steep and rocky, but within 150 yards of the beach the patrol encountered muskeg and forward progress dropped to a crawl. There was very little vegetation except the muskeg and the steep walls of the dark inlet eventually giving way to windswept bluffs. It was so cold and remote Orin was more struck by a sense of extreme loneliness than any presence of potential enemies. He realized the shimmering cream-like aura he could see on the bluffs was snow, as occasional drifts fell on his face. *This is like the far side of the moon*, he thought. *There's nobody here.* Nonetheless, the patrol backed off the bluff so as not to present any silhouettes, shivering for 10 minutes simply watching for any sign of light or movement.

Once his eyes got used to the scale of things, he noted a significant ridgeline to the east of them and the inlet from the beach turned into a draw. Orin led the patrol into the draw, dark and dangerous looking, soon discovering the creek they had been briefed about as the possible route up to Brannon Ridge. Once back on the beach, Orin reported to Williamson who now had both companies from the two submarines on the beach ready to move out. The fog had closed in behind them out to sea and the men on the *Kane* had not landed yet, so Williamson left a pre-established message on the beach for the Recon Troop from the *Kane* to follow as soon as possible. With strict orders for route march noise discipline, the scouts silenced their gear as best they could, preparing to leave the beach. Williamson, with Orin's platoon in the lead, set a very aggressive pace.

At times Orin thought his heart would burst out of his chest it was pounding so hard. Although young and in excellent general health, he was, like the rest of the Scout Battalion, out of condition after weeks of confinement on ships and the tiny, cramped berthing spaces allowed them on the submarines. Prior to boarding the transports in San Francisco, Captain Williamson had established a tough and rigorous physical training regimen above and beyond their exhausting beach assault training. Most of the scouts, almost all of them under 23 years of age and athletic, tolerated the constant training and enjoyed the elite status the Scout Battalion held in the division. They were the "eyes and ears" of the 7th—RECON--and could be found on maneuvers day and night and often on weekends. Williamson drove them hard, almost always to the point of complete physical exhaustion on every exercise, and Orin again recognized the familiar pattern of his growing muscular failure as he tried to negotiate the slick ground in front of him.

The muskeg was infuriating and overwhelming, especially close to the creek bed as lost footing invariably resulted in falls on sharp, jagged rocks or unwelcome dunks into the ice-cold creek. Williamson, showing no sign of personal fatigue, pressed Orin's platoon to move faster, doing so with hand signals only to maintain noise discipline. After several hours working up the creek bed the sky brightened as a gray, freezing day exposing an endless curving trail as it shadowed the easterly ridge. It snowed off and on, the cold and exhaustion revealed starkly on the young soldiers as their faces formed clear in the light.

Williamson rotated Orin's First Platoon with the Third, allowing the Third to take over the lead. This delay as the Third Platoon moved up through their ranks to replace them was the first real rest they had received.   They took over the rear guard of their Scout Company, with their sister Scout Company from the *Narwhal* coming up close behind. Somewhere behind the *Narwhal* scouts, most likely with the remainder of the Scout Battalion, the Reconnaissance Troop, coming off the *Kane* if they had found a hole in the fog, was the heavy weapons section carrying the 81mm mortars and a few .30 caliber machine guns.   Orin could only imagine how difficult it would be to traverse this terrain with those back-breaking loads, but Williamson insisted the Scout Battalion, being far behind the enemy positions and most likely out of range of friendly artillery on the beaches, carry its own supporting firepower. Orin questioned the wisdom of slowing down the battalion with such weight but kept it to himself.

Despite his own suffering, Orin felt especially bad for Ed Ridgeway.   Ridgeway gasped and wheezed for breath with every labored, stumbling step on the trail.   Orin knew Ridgeway had not trained in the least for this mission, probably couldn't remember the last time he had to run or even walked any distance.   This was not even considering the freezing cold or the pack on Ridgeway's back Orin had intentionally reduced by items he carried himself, and the energy-draining, at-the-double climb pace through the muskeg maintained by Williamson.   Whatever purpose was purported to have brought the intelligence officer here with them, now deep in enemy territory on the side of a cold black mountain, Orin could only guess at.   Ridgeway sucked in air noisily with each step, occasionally retching whatever remained in his stomach from breakfast on the submarine.   Orin had to give him credit, though, for on one brief pause after Ridgeway had dropped on his knees and dry heaved, Orin watched the big man slowly pull himself back onto his feet and wipe his mouth before reaching over and helping another soldier get up.   Ridgeway sensed Orin watching him and turned to reveal a lopsided, not particularly convincing grin combined with an exaggerated thumbs up sign.   Captain Williamson still insisted on trail noise discipline even after hours of no sign of any Japanese, so Orin only nodded wearily to his friend and returned the thumbs up.   Ridgeway somehow managed to keep up with the younger men despite his stumbling progress this far, but Orin knew the climb was going to get steeper and at some point they would encounter the back of the Japanese defensive line.

Pushing on relentlessly with the ridge as his objective, Williamson tirelessly guided the battalion up the Ballentine Creek bed until it ran out.   By late afternoon the battalion, thoroughly exhausted, was halted after turning due east and scaling the backside of Brannon

Ridge.   It was snowing hard but the fog lifted briefly with the upslope wind so Williamson spotted Holtz Bay through his binoculars. What he could see in between their ridge and the bay made his heart skip a beat. A long, steep pass stretched out in front of him to end in some dark canyons before it emptied into the valley floor.   He knew Japanese defensive positions had to be somewhere on the other side of the ridge dug in all the way down to the Sarana Valley, most likely in those canyons, waiting to engage the 17th and 32nd Infantry coming up from Red Beach.   Williamson did not bring field telephones and cable reels, relying instead on short range line of sight portable walkie-talkie radios and radio relays with specially equipped B-24 Liberators flying over Attu at established intervals.   While the battalion was still down below the ridge on their way up from the beach, the communication B-24 made a re-supply airdrop of extra blankets, shelter halves and dry clothing. Once on the ridgeline he contacted the B-24 to give his coded report, relaying the Scout Battalion's status and the difficulty encountered in their climb up the creek bed. It was a tedious process in code but they had to assume the Japanese were listening.

Williamson did not know it at the time until it was decoded, but the message he received in return confirmed the northern assault troops were on Attu at Red Beach, five miles north of their position approaching southward along Holtz Bay, with the main southern force now struggling off the beach 10 miles due west of them at Massacre Bay.   He would be especially glad to hear Recon Troop on the *Kane*, with radar guidance through the thick fog from one of the off shore battlewagons, finally landed their 150 men at noon and were coming up Ballentine Creek to join the Scout Battalion.   Williamson relayed to the circling B-24 the Scout Battalion would rest until first light. With the arrival of the Recon Troop they would find a way down the pass to join up with the 17th and 32nd Infantry Battalions coming south from Red Beach.

Ed Ridgeway joined Williamson, requesting permission to send his own coded report.   Williamson's irritation was apparent as he handed the radio over without comment. Once Ridgeway was finished and said nothing to Williamson except thank you, Williamson ignored him and sent out a request for all battalion officers for Officer's Call. Ridgeway stood aside for a few minutes before asking Williamson directly if he minded if Ridgeway attended the meeting.   Williamson did not hesitate after looking directly at Ed Ridgeway.

"I am in command of this little battalion, and if you want to be part of my battalion meetings we need to establish a couple of things." He stood up straight to his full, considerable height.

70

"I know you're regimental intelligence, and you work for HQ. I don't know your mission, and somebody decided it was in the best interest of the division not to clue me in. Fine. But I have a job to do, and this battalion will perform the mission assigned with whatever information we have." Williamson stepped right up to Ridgeway who instinctively stepped back before stopping his retreat.

"If you have something of value that might save the lives of my men, information *discovered* since you've been here with us, let's have it. You are communicating with HQ outside of my knowledge in that I have no idea what you're telling them, and therefore you apparently consider yourself outside of my command. Explain to me, Captain Ridgeway, why I should have you sitting in *my* battalion meeting?"

Ridgeway nodded slowly in understanding while unbuttoning his field jacket. With great interest Williamson watched Ridgeway bring out a metallic, silvery object sheathed in a thin leather sack. His curiosity turned to irritation when he realized Ridgeway had pulled out a silver flask and after unscrewing the cap, was offering Williamson a drink.

"You have someplace we can talk?" asked Ridgeway.

Now that the battalion—with the exception of the Recon Troop somewhere behind them—was off the trail, the men were visibly suffering from exposure even after the airdrop of extra supplies. Orin, like the rest of the scouts, had not noticed the cold quite so much because they had been moving as fast as they could and they had sweated freely. To keep their combat packs light the battalion carried neither sleeping bags nor shelter halves. They received a couple of hundred shelter halves from the airdrop plus blankets, but not enough for every man. Most of the soldiers were soaked through getting out of the rafts in the surf, and now, 15 hours later after constant climbing through snow and muskeg, their cotton uniforms were simply semi-frozen cardboard. There was no way to get dry. The ridgeline offered scant shelter from the wind and blowing snow, with the temperature continuing to plummet. The men were exhausted but too cold to sleep, shivering close together, seeking shelter from the wind and snow as best they could.

In Officer's Call Williamson sequestered the half a dozen officers in a tiny, protected draw. They were close enough to rub shoulders with one another, each looking drawn and worn out. Williamson quickly outlined the invasion situation as he understood it. It appeared the insertion and climb to the backside of the Japanese defensive positions

71

were completely undetected, mostly because the Japanese did not apparently have any observation posts on the western side of the island near the beach, as predicted by army intelligence. He quickly briefed the invasion situation as reported from his decoded message, confirming his understanding the *Kane* had found a way down to the beach in the fog and the 150 men of the Recon Troop were nine hours behind them. He anticipated their arrival around 0300. The Recon Troop would be allowed about three hours rest and then the entire battalion, all 400 of them, would assault down the pass towards the east and the Sarana Valley at first light, disrupting and destroying as many Japanese positions as possible. At some point in the next 24 hours or so, they hoped to join up with the men of the 17th and 32nd Infantry who had landed on Red Beach and were moving due south along Holtz Bay. As Williamson noted, Holtz Bay, if the fog would lift, was visible from the ridgeline they were on.

Orin, with great effort, kept his eyes open. He needed to move or sleep, the group of officers clustered together generated some warmth and then drowsiness. He was also famished. The rations had to wait. He did notice Ed Ridgeway was standing slightly to the left of Captain Williamson, close enough for Orin to suspect Ridgeway was part of the briefing.

"This will be just about the last rest we are going to get, gentlemen," Williamson noted with a slight grin, "although I don't think anybody is going to get much sleep with this cold." He turned slightly to Ridgeway, shoving his exposed hands into the pockets of his field jacket. "Anything to add, Captain?" Williamson asked without introducing Ridgeway to anyone. It was clear the question was a briefing prompt. Ridgeway nodded, mimicking Williamson by moving his hands into his field jacket.

"I've suggested to Captain Williamson we run a patrol to Buchanan Ridge—the ridge directly to the south of us running east to west—to determine if we can find any Japanese positions there. They should be observation posts only, with few heavy weapons, versus the defensive positions we will probably encounter once we go over this ridge. We're..." he hesitated and looked at Williamson, "trying to determine the strength of the enemy forces in front of us. We don't want to be detected if at all possible, obviously as we have managed so far complete surprise, but we need—information." Williamson kept a stone face and gave Ridgeway no support at all. Ed sighed and shifted his weight and looked at Orin, the only familiar and friendly face.

"We need documents, maps, letters, notes, orders—that sort of thing. And..." he hesitated again, "it would be very advantageous to

72

capture a prisoner, an officer or an NCO, preferably.   But any *live* Japanese will do."

Exhausted and frozen, the Scout Battalion dug in for the night. Some of the troops hooked their air-dropped shelter halves together to make tents if they could find some level ground.   Most simply dug holes in the snow to share body heat with another soldier, creating a small covered shelter using every layer they had to keep out the cold.   The wind rushed up the canyon from the Sarana Valley and Holtz Bay to whip over the ridgeline right into their positions.   It whistled and howled in piercing octaves as it carved around the sharp, peaked rocks. Orin had never heard anything like it in his life.   The wind, unlike the black and cold rocks of the ridgeline, seemed alive and infinitely more menacing.   He ate a cold ration and stared up hard to the south at Buchanan Ridge.   He could barely see it in the twilight of what constituted darkness on Attu.   It rose only several hundred feet above their own ridgeline, but its shadowy presence was the most prominent and highest peak around them and if anyone was up there, they should have detected the Scout Battalion by now.   The scouts had to be visible against the snow.   But after talking to Ed, who confirmed aerial recon had discovered the construction of numerous positions on practically every ridgeline in the eastern part of Attu, he viewed the ridge nervously and with trepidation.   *How do I get up there and not be spotted?*

Williamson had asked for volunteers and half of his officers offered to do the patrol.   Orin had raised his hand and without hesitation Williamson pointed while nodding his approval.   "Excellent, Lieutenant," Williamson said.   He dismissed the others and with Ridgeway at his side, outlined his requirements to Orin for a three-man reconnaissance patrol up to Buchanan Ridge.

In the dark? Orin asked rather unnecessarily.

In the dark.

Using what remaining light was available, Ed revealed a very detailed, close-up aerial photograph of Buchanan Ridge to Orin and Williamson.   They huddled their heads together under a borrowed field jacket as a small penlight was switched on.   With the tip of his light, Ed carefully traced a potential path for the patrol, tapping on tiny, circled areas on the ridgeline.   The targeted areas were indistinguishable from the rest of the terrain to Orin.

"Those," Ed whispered emphatically, "are fixed positions.   Any one of those may be manned."

73

CHAPTER 9

0100 Hours, May 12, 1943, D-Day Plus 1, Buchanan Ridge

The trenching and defensive emplacements on Buchanan Ridge were very primitive, certainly in comparison to the more elaborate interconnecting and overlapping bunker systems of the eastern facing ridges flanking Holtz Bay and the top of the valley overlooking Massacre Bay. Buchanan Ridge still had strategic value as it overlooked the entire western side of Attu Island, desolate and abandoned, and specifically the northern approaches of Holtz Bay. Colonel Yamasaki had reasoned, rightfully so, the most probable invasion beaches would be Massacre Bay because of the large protected harbor on the eastern side of the island and then Holtz Bay, with a deep inlet on the northeastern side of the island.

The unfinished runway was at the southeast corner of Holtz Bay, with most of the defending troops on the island on the ridges paralleling the approaches from Massacre Bay. The remaining part of the island to the west of Buchanan Ridge had no natural harbors or protected beaches to accommodate assault landing craft or the Landing Ship Tanks (LSTs) that would resupply the American landing force from cargo ships kept further out at sea. The Americans would also know most of the Japanese defenders were concentrated in the eastern part of the island from their constant aerial surveillance. Nonetheless, two thirds of the island was west of Buchanan Ridge which made it the backdoor, so Yamasaki wanted observation posts established and manned there.

It had taken Yoshi Nakagawa nearly a day to traverse the valley across the top of the mouth of Holtz Bay and pick up the hidden communication trenches and short tunnels at the base of the ridge. The building work for the defensive structures for Attu was complete, or deemed complete the minute the pre-invasion bombardment was anticipated.

It came a week late, but it came. Yoshi and the other engineers were essentially out of a job, as the intensity of the bombardment coming from ships offshore and from both U.S. Army bomber and fighter aircraft had been so relentless there was no opportunity to rebuild structures once destroyed. The many months of careful construction and camouflage paid off for the most part, as much of the bombardment seemed directed at potential target areas, clearly concentrating on the beaches where there were few actual troops except those in hidden gun

74

positions.　The weather was brutal and unpredictable, heavy fog and snow with ensuing low clouds and visibility for the first week of May. Each day of dark, low skies and fog was another day without assault boats on the horizon.　Yoshi and the other engineers took full advantage of the invasion delay to reinforce every portion of the main line of defense they could, including all of the eastern-facing ridges.

Yoshi volunteered to make a final inspection of Buchanan Ridge observation positions before the pre-invasion bombardment was expected to begin.　This was the most westerly and most remote of the ridges overlooking the western part of the island, and the most primitive of the OPs.　It was, in a word, an afterthought but no one protested his request to take on the assignment.　He volunteered mostly for something to occupy himself since the construction projects were halted. Engineering officers were becoming effectively infantry officers for the defensive lines, or even finding themselves assigned to lead groups of engineering troops on artillery resupply missions up the mountains.

The bombardment moved to Holtz Bay the day he started his crossing because of an unexpected break in the weather.　He was caught in it when he was halfway across the valley in front of the bay.　Twice he faltered, witnessing the violence of the bombardment and considered turning back.　Buchanan Ridge was not that important as an outpost, surely they wouldn't expect him to go on.　But then again he had his orders and as a junior officer he had no choice but to carry them out. There was no one to tell him otherwise.

The bombardment was horrific.　It was like nothing he had ever been exposed to, and was certain on several occasions he was living the last few seconds of his life.　Most of the shellfire was coming from American battleships and cruisers almost at the horizon, concentrating destruction on the beach approaches. It included inbound 14 inch projectiles erupting the earth like bolts of lightning, obliterating and vaporizing everything in their path.

He was crossing a two kilometer strand of rolling small hills, many with interlocking semi-underground gun emplacements and sniper spider holes designed to engage the assault troops two kilometers back from the beach, when the salvos from the ships exploded a quarter of a kilometer away.　It was the sudden fury of thunderous flashes erupting black earthern geysers that shocked him into frozen awe.　Even at these distances, the impact and shockwaves of the dozens of almost simultaneous detonations were so powerful they knocked him off his feet.　The salvos continued with short intervals, the impacting explosions moving up the beach with each series of salvos, walking their way slowly towards the hills and closer to him.

75

Caught in the open, Yoshi ran as hard and as fast as he could before the next salvos arrived, slipping and sliding on the snow and muskeg trying desperately to reach a semi-underground, heavily reinforced gun emplacement built into a hillside. The crew spotted him, encouraging him to keep coming as he ran, when suddenly a camouflaged door flung open on the side of the hill. He was dragged bodily inside as the shells screamed towards them. The crew pulled him down a short tunnel into another smaller room, deeper in the hillside just as the ground shook and bounced with bone-jarring energy.

"Away from the walls!" screamed one of the crewmen, and with the aid of the dim beam of an electric lamp, he noticed how the crewmen crouched down on the balls of their feet so that no part of their body except their feet touched the earth. He copied their motions just as the ground flung up and slammed into his face and the electric lamp hurled past him.   Disoriented and stunned, he tried to get up but the earth jumped again as the tiny room filled with dust. He could vaguely hear someone screaming very close a moment before a blinding white flash and then nothing.

When Yoshi regained consciousness the little room was quiet and still. His ears were buzzing with a high-pitched whine. As he lifted his head, he felt dizzy.   After a moment or two he realized where he was, but it was very dark and he fearfully knew something was wrong. Confused to his location in the bunker, he felt around him, hesitating when he found a man's face under his fingers.   He carefully touched the man's nose and mouth, sensing moving air.   He appeared to be still breathing. As he felt above him with his other hand he ran immediately into some obstruction. With a touch of panic, he wondered if they were buried alive. *I can breathe, there is air.   That is something*.   Other than his dizziness and hearing loss, he felt no pain and his limbs could move, although he couldn't see much of anything. He stopped feeling about to listen as best as his deafness would allow, and decided the bombardment was continuing, but the shelling had moved farther up the hillside.

Twenty minutes later Yoshi was sitting in a covered entry ramp on the other side of the bunker. He was still very dizzy and partially deaf, suspecting he had a concussion, but he was more aware of his surroundings.   A smaller shell, probably from one of the American cruisers, had landed about five meters from the bunker, digging itself deeply into the hillside at the perfect angle before exploding and literally cracking the two meter thick earthern bunker open like an oyster.   The gun crew had pointed out the impact to him with amazement, so he stopped to stare in wonder. The bunker collapsed on one side. On an engineering level, Yoshi was mildly surprised and disappointed at the level of damage to what was designed to be a naval gunfire-resistant bunker. But the reverse slope placement was vulnerable to high angle indirect fire. More importantly, he knew, to Japanese construction credit was the fact many of the crewmen had survived the almost direct hit. He and the others had been pulled out of the rubble by crewmen from a sister bunker 200 meters away, men who left the safety of their own bunker while the bombardment was still going on to assist in their rescue.

Yoshi was propped up besides two other men buried with him without visible injuries. Like him, they remained still and quiet. *Am I in shock*, he wondered. Turning painfully to his left, he could see the bodies of two men laid out neatly with their arms folded on their stomachs. He stared at them not quite registering what he was looking at. They looked asleep and uninjured too, but they were not sitting up.

Yoshi looked away, becoming conscious of how bruised his body was starting to feel, and the incredibly soiled condition of his uniform. He was covered with dirt from head to toe, tasting the grit of sand or rock in his mouth. The naval bombardment was still going on. With growing alarm as his mind slowly cleared, he noticed the screaming salvos appeared to be walking towards them again. He did not want to get caught out in the open like this. Before he could call out to someone three or four soldiers jumped into the entry trench to carefully hoist Yoshi and the others to their feet. *This way*, they directed urgently. With a soldier on each side of him propping him up, he was guided over the side of the trench to begin a journey away from the broken bunker over open ground. The sky was filled with smoke and noise and absolutely every single gun on the island seemed to be shooting at something. Tracers, pink and white, large and small, bobbed, hesitated and darted in all directions as the earth erupted with red and orange starburst explosions. *How was it possible to be in the middle of this and not be hurt*, he thought. It was just starting to dawn on him what was in store for them.

Yoshi spent the next two hours in the other bunker. The bunker was very crowded and stuffy. To his mind he no longer felt safe there. He didn't want to go back out into the explosive storm, but he didn't want to stay to be buried alive again either. He soberly remembered his mission, as insignificant as it was. The ground shook and bounced continuously now, and after awhile, the explosions and gunfire simply blended into one uninterrupted roar, like the open door of a blast furnace.

The crewmen relayed the news they received by radio the naval gunfire had lifted from the beach and American assault troops were reported both in Holtz Bay and Massacre Bay, but they were already being stopped a quarter of a kilometer from the beaches.   This news was met with some enthusiastic cheering from the crewmen.   Perhaps all that gunfire going out was actually landing somewhere, Japanese firepower repelling the invaders.

As the gunfire noise appeared to be more outgoing than incoming, Yoshi prepared to leave.   He crept around and personally thanked the crewmen who pulled him from the rubble, and thanked again the surviving crew of the first bunker for saving his life when the bombardment had begun.   He especially thanked them for their kindness in accepting him, a stranger, and treating him like brother. *You are a Japanese Officer,* they explained, we are Japanese soldiers. Their eyes shined brightly as they said this, inspiring Yoshi to bow his head towards them, as it seemed the right thing to do.   The thought of American assault troops on the beaches of Holtz Bay, right here in front of him didn't quite seem possible, but there it was.   He considered what that really meant to these men in these bunkers, and it humbled him to realize how remarkable they were.   *They will face the enemy right here, and they will either defeat them or die in this place.   They have no secondary line of retreat.*

He stood up outside the bunker cautiously, dodging his head instinctively from the ear-numbing noise and destruction going on all around him. He decided he had recovered well enough to remain on his feet, so he returned briefly to the bunker to shake the hands of the crewmen and bid them goodbye.   They implored him to stay in the bunker where it was safe but Yoshi briefly explained his mission, reminding them the importance of every soldier doing their duty as long as they could.   It felt strange having these words come out of his mouth and it made him feel, more than a little bit, a phony and a fraud. It was expected of him and these men—these brave men—expected their leaders to be strong. He knew because he had been working around the defensive line crews for weeks now, their spirit and acceptance of their role in what was to come struck him just short of incredible.

Yoshi felt uneasy inside but also noticed the respect the crewmen gave him as he left.   He also realized he may be the last contact these men would have of any Japanese leadership.   He doubted their own officers were anywhere near these defensive bunkers facing the coming assault troops.   Now that the invasion had begun, they wouldn't be coming back.   It would not make sense as nobody expects the Americans to be stopped this early in the terrain, that's why the tiered

78

defenses to draw the troops into an artillery trap up in the open slope above them.   These men are expendable and they know it, he thought. They are not the mainline of defense but the first line of defense.   They are the first stage of many tiers before the Imperial Army stopped regrouping and held the ground forever.   But by then all of these men will be dead.

The junior NCO from the first bunker came out with him, standing at attention, his hands quivering before bowing deeply towards Yoshi.   He wanted to say something, but he hesitated for a moment. Yoshi paused before turning towards him.

"Gyokusai!"   The junior NCO said firmly.   "Gyokusai!"   *The spirit of "glorious death".*   Yoshi knew the term, having heard infantry officers refer to the word with reverence as though it was some ancient mantra from the Samurai Bushido code, which it no doubt was, but it seemed overly dramatic and distant to him, an engineer,   a farmer's son, at the time.   But now the dark, deadly serious eyes of this young man bore into his and Yoshi knew what was expected of him. Yoshi stood straighter, slapping his hand onto the holster of his Nambu pistol with a crisp nod.   *I am not important enough for you men, you deserve better!*

"Gyokusai!"   He returned formally and emphatically.   *Glorious death?*   The young man held his gaze before again bowing deeply. He held the bow and Yoshi knew it was his cue to leave.   He climbed up and out of the bunker, glancing down at the young NCO, who kept his head down.

You deserve better.

Yoshi traversed the remaining terrain across the top of Holtz Bay as quickly as he could.   The naval bombardment seemed to be moving up towards the higher peaks, including the one he was headed for.   The naval gunfire attack was being joined, as the fog, rain showers and snow permitted, by bombardment or strafing by American aircraft of numerous types.   P-40s, P-38s, B-25 Mitchell medium bombers and other airplanes he was only familiar through flashcards and silhouette charts. The machines dodged in and out of cloud banks in ones and twos, even flew below the low clouds where they could, their wing guns winking and sparkling, the tracers hitting the ground seconds before the hammering of the guns could be heard.

He glanced up from a shell hole he had dived into to see a mud brown twin-tailed, twin-engine American fighter, a P-38, swooping up *below him* after a ground level strafing run on beach positions.   He could hear the throbbing drone of multi-engine heavy bombers above, unseen, and occasionally would catch glimpses of tight, dark strings of bombs falling from the clouds to detonate along the pass approaches, or even on open fields. He had no idea how they could see what they were bombing but the sky cover was constantly changing. Sometimes the fog would drop to the deck, other times the sky would part partially and blue sky could be seen. All that was really constant was the noise, the cacophony of tactile, eardrum pounding explosions one after the other.

It occurred to Yoshi as he scurried forward, he would be cut off from the main Japanese force if the Americans came straight up Holtz Bay, attempting a pincer-move to the east to join up with the forces landing on Massacre Bay. *What was I thinking volunteering for this?* He thought in a sudden panic. *Perhaps I should turn around and head back.* The indecision he felt stopped him dead in his tracks for five minutes. He hid behind the cover of a cluster of boulders, trying to think.

As he ducked his head to peer around, he did begin to notice the lack of precision of the bombardment and aerial attack. The naval and aerial bombardment was missing most of the gun positions as far as he could tell because they were so well hidden. *With so many intact, could they possibly repulse the Americans? If they destroyed the first waves, would the Americans keep coming? Would they come back?* He looked up with surprise realizing he was almost at his destination. The mountain was right in front of him. It was safer now to continue on, he reasoned, and left the safety of the rocks.

Before entering the underground communication tunnels at the base of the ridge, he peered down the slope towards Holtz Bay now that he had some height. The fog was lifting at that moment, revealing most of Holtz Bay and the open sea beyond. To his astonishment, there were no American ships or assault landing craft anywhere to be seen on the bay, not one. *What is all the shooting about, then? When are they coming?* The only option available to the Americans would be the huge inlet harbor of Massacre Bay, eight kilometers to the east. Massacre Bay was out of sight and on the other side of the ridgeline to his east, but didn't the gun crew get information over the radio Americans had landed at Massacre Bay and Holtz Bay? *Why all the shelling?*

A thunderous explosion 200 meters away dropped him to the ground. Twenty seconds later debris and metal shards started to shower Yoshi so he scrambled to his feet, dodging into a tunnel entrance. The tunnels at the base of the ridge were short but effectively guided troops into well-camouflaged connecting trenches up the ridgeline out of sight from aerial reconnaissance. Yoshi, who had only been to the observation posts on Buchanan Ridge once before, knew the rudimentary OPs was manned by a small group of soldiers and didn't even have an anti-aircraft gun position on the ridge.

With great relief to be under cover, Yoshi started up into the safety of the tunnels and was surprised when he almost immediately ran into what appeared to be dozens of soldiers, squatting quietly in the gloom. *Was this a bomb shelter? Are these men waiting for the bombing to stop?* He felt confused because he didn't expect to find soldiers here this high up in the ridge, but this was the entrance to the tunnel and trench complex. No one spoke when he stepped into the space, but he did notice there was no sense of panic or concern with his appearance. A light suddenly appeared and Yoshi blinked as the beam flashed into his face, blinding him. Before he could respond angrily, the light turned away abruptly.

"Sorry sir, I did not mean to blind you," said an authoritive voice, someone who apparently saw his insignia. With the light turned down to the ground, Yoshi could not really see anyone's face, but he turned towards the voice.

"What are you men doing here?" He asked quietly. Maybe they were infantry, but the fixed gun emplacements down the valley hillsides were not normally supported by infantry. A figure came forward and the same strong, oddly familiar voice spoke again, but more respectively.

"I am Sergeant Kobayashi of Engineers. We are prepared to engage the enemy if they land in this bay. This is our assigned staging area."

"Kobayashi?" Yoshi stepped up and peered into the man's face. No wonder his voice sounded familiar. It *was* Kobayashi, one of the NCOs from the original engineering company attached to the 301st Independent Battalion, the first troops who had landed on Attu the previous year. Kobayashi had been one of the lead NCOs on the runway project. When Colonel Yamasaki stopped the runway work, Kobayashi and the other engineers were reassigned to the main line of defense construction of trenches.

"It's me, Sergeant, Lieutenant Nakagawa!" Although a virtual newcomer having only been on Attu for six weeks, the two had worked together closely the first two weeks Yoshi was working on the runway, seeing each other frequently the last month on defensive construction. They had worked well together and Kobayashi respected Yoshi's quick grasp of the project. With his face covered with dirt, Yoshi realized he was unrecognizable. He quickly wiped his face with a handkerchief and grinned. Kobayashi seemed genuinely glad to see him. A few of the men, as Kobayashi swung his light around so Yoshi could see them, stood up to stoop in the low ceilings, nodding or bowing towards him. They were all engineers, after all. Sadly, Yoshi recognized like himself, these men were being placed wherever there was a shortage of manpower since there would be no more construction projects on Attu.

"Who is your commanding officer now?" Yoshi asked. "How many of you are there?"

"There are 27 of us, sir. They split up the engineer companies, as you know. We are assigned to the headquarters company of an infantry battalion. Our company commander is Captain Nakamura, and he has assigned us to the defensive line of the most western side of Holtz Bay." Kobayashi seemed to anticipate Yoshi's next question, answering it quietly.

"Once the bombing stops, we are to move out and get into our prepared positions on the northside of this ridge facing Holtz Bay. They're not much, just open trenches, but we have an excellent field of fire. The last two days we carried mortar and artillery ammunition to the guns on the western slopes. It was difficult work." Yoshi was appalled engineers were being used as pack mules and line infantry, but he did not reveal his feelings.

"Where is the rest of your *new* company, Sergeant?" He asked gently.

"Captain Nakamura has his men spread out in a number of these tunnels, so they will appear once the bombing has stopped. We are waiting for his instructions."

"I see." Yoshi reached out to clap Kobayashi's shoulder, hoping the gesture would not offend him. "He left you in charge of the section?" Kobayashi nodded slowly as Yoshi sighed.

Well," he said, "the men are in good hands with you, and I'm glad they are keeping you together. Perhaps," he added thoughtfully, "it will work out for the best. Maybe the Americans will be defeated in Massacre Bay, and the bombing and bombardment over here was just a way to get us to think they were going to land here. We may have the safest jobs on the island!"

"Do you really think so, sir?" Kobayashi asked skeptically yet hopefully. Then he added, "what about you, sir, what do they have you doing?"

"I'm just an errand boy, Sergeant. Make work, really. I'm checking on the readiness of our defensive positions, and somebody thought it was a good idea for me to go back up to the top of this ridge and make sure the outposts up there are ready."

82

"We have outposts on the top of this—mountain?"   Yoshi nodded as he turned to go.   He stuck out both of his hands and Kabayashi, after hesitating, reached out with both of his. Yoshi grasped them firmly.

"Best of luck to you, Sergeant," he said, his eyes getting damp. He blinked hard and hoped Kabayashi wouldn't see it.   He held Kayayashi's grasp for a moment longer, peering around the small space and dark faces of the quiet men waiting there.

"Best of luck to all of you, I hope to see you all in a few days after we have defeated the Americans!"

The engineers led out a small chorus of best wishes as Yoshi turned to go up into the tunnel.   He walked slower once he was out of their sight, knowing in his heart he was now officially in the goodbye business. There was no deceiving himself to what was coming. There are no reinforcements, no withdrawal.   There were no other options for any of them.   First line of defense or ultimately, main line of defense. In the end, what is the difference?   There was no escape possible now. There would be no luck to distribute like rations to save any of these men once the Americans enter Holtz Bay, or, as he considered it finally, for himself. No luck at all. He would never see any of them again.

83

CHAPTER 10

2405 hours, May 12, 1943, D-Day Plus 1, Buchanan Ridge

Orin had asked for volunteers for the mission and chose two of his young NCOs, both squad leaders. They all reapplied black greasepaint to their faces, necks and hands, stripping to the bare necessities for what they had to do. They each carried a .45 caliber pistol and either a bayonet or a KABAR combat knife. Because of the cold and snow, Orin decided to keep their field jackets on, leaving their rifles, packs and helmets behind.

The wind died down for a few seconds allowing Orin to hear the muted rumble of artillery fire miles away on the other side of the ridge. He wasn't sure if he had heard the battle on the eastern side of the island before, but it was a small comfort to know American forces were out there somewhere fighting their way towards them. The entire mission was stark in its absolute isolation so far, as if they were on a separate island completely with out any other trace of the human race. It was strange to feel good about distant artillery fire.

The three volunteers huddled with Captain Williamson and Ed Ridgeway, peering up at Buchanan Ridge to consider what they were facing. The dim twilight was about as dark as it was going to get. It was obvious with the pale luminescence of the snow in front of them, the patrol would be visible if someone was looking up and back from the western facing pass, or was looking directly down from Buchanan Ridge. They needed to stay on the reverse slope if at all possible.

"It's pretty late and damned cold and windy, so they certainly won't hear you unless you cause a avalanche or a rock slide," offered Williamson. "Don't do that. We have not been discovered yet, and I'm counting on you to keep things that way." He looked at them expectantly with half-closed eyes before rubbing his face vigorously, the first time he showed any sign of fatigue.

"But, we need to try. We need the information. If you get into a firefight up there, just get outta there the best way you can, no shooting unless you absolutely have to. We won't be able to give you any support because it will alert the Jap positions over the ridge of our presence. If they hear shooting above them on the ridge and no return fire, maybe they will think it's a nervous sentry, or an echo, nothing more. They can hear the artillery out there as well as we can, and these

84

mountains play tricks on your ears. The Japs expect us from the east, that's pretty obvious. So no shooting."

From their position on the reverse slope of Brannon Ridge, Buchanan Ridge rose above them to extend a couple of miles east and west.   Ed Ridgeway's recon photo revealed the suspected OPs were to their west, giving any observers a clear view of the western side of the island.   Orin proposed to continue on the western side of Brannon Ridge for a half of a mile, attempting to climb the several hundred feet to Buchanan Ridge with what appeared to be a connecting series of rock shelves leading up to the ridge.   It was essentially Ed Ridgeway's suggested path.   The path would keep the patrol out of sight of the defensive positions facing west on Brannon Ridge.   Once they reached the ridge they could work their way west until they found trenches or an outpost. Williamson approved the route and wished them luck.

"You need to be back before first light, as we will be assaulting over the ridge." Williamson warned.   "It would be nice to go over any intel you come up with before then."

Orin shook hands with Ed Ridgeway and Williamson.   The patrol carefully started picking their way across the shale rock of Brannon Ridge towards the west.   The snow covered everything at first appearance.   By looking carefully at the shadows and staying near the peak of the ridge, they found windswept rocks free of snow to traverse. The wind was brutal with Orin nearly losing his footing from the heavy gusts until they found a path farther off the leeward side of the peak. Orin kept looking up at Buchanan Ridge directly in front of him, wondering if it was actually possible somebody was up there.

The two young NCOs with Orin were strong, reliable men who seemed to trust him implicitly.   He hoped he was worthy of their trust. They followed his footsteps up the ridge silently. He realized nervously he was perhaps an hour or so away from his first face to face engagement with the Japanese.   The two NCOs had not questioned the mission and like many of the scouts in the battalion, volunteered for the unit to get the opportunity to experience these types of commando operations.   Williamson had embraced the tactical reconnaissance mission for the Scout Company wholeheartedly, selecting and training men accordingly, placing prime emphasis on long range silent patrolling, scouting and observation, and silent killing skills.   The Scout Company was always in the field, but the troops spent innumerable hours grappling with one another on the parade field learning ju-jitsu techniques or attacking one another with rubber knives.

They were well trained, no doubt about it.   But there was a big difference between wresting with another American soldier under the watchful eyes of the close combat instructors, jabbing each other with a rubber knife, and the intentional killing of another man with a seven inch unsheathed steel blade for real.

Unconsciously, Orin reached down and gripped the handle of his KABAR. *When the time comes, can I do this?* He had to believe he could and would, as would the two young NCOs following his footsteps as he led them along on this—*adventure.*

They slowed down once they reached the connecting rock bridges linking Brannon Ridge with Buchanan Ridge. It had taken nearly an hour but an OP directly above might be able to see them if they spotted fast movement. He stopped the team behind boulders while carefully examining the ridge with a small set of wide-angle binoculars. The lens drew little light from the night sky so the image was darker than the naked eye. Orin could see the snow on the ridge clearly as he watched for contrasting movement or shadows. After five minutes his eyes grew tired and he signaled the others to join him.

They began the hard climb up the rock shelves. It was cold, exhausting work. Some of the shelves were nearly six feet apart, forcing one man to hoist the other two up before being pulled up by the others. They stopped frequently to listen, hearing only the wind and murmuring rumble of artillery fire. After another hour they were within 20 feet of the curving top of the ridgeline. Using a hand signal to hold the others back, Orin crawled up the remaining distance alone, stopping at what appeared to be the edge of the horizon. After a moment he carefully lifted his head to be rewarded with the sight of yet another shelf of rocks. He peered around the rocks but there was no sign of a view port, periscope, radio antennae, or any other clue of a man-made structure. There certainly were no Japanese soldiers standing around. He didn't expect to see one right on the top like this, but then again he didn't know what to expect in such a remote, desolate place. Satisfied, Orin signaled the others up before crawling forward, scuttling sideways crab-like on his stomach to keep his profile low.

For the next half an hour they low-crawled on the ridge towards the west. They found nothing but rock and blowing snow, their elbows, knees and hands scraped raw and bloody. There was no evidence of a trench or trail leading them toward the western part of the ridge. The farther they went west the narrower the top shelf of the ridge became. Orin became convinced there was no OP to the west, deciding to back track to the point on the ridge where they started. The team hunkered down in a small crevice as Orin glanced at the luminous dial of his watch. It was almost 0300 in the morning. They had climbed around the frozen rocks for three hours finding nothing.

He tried to visualize the aerial reconnaissance photo of the ridge Ed has shown them, orienting in his head the circled dots on the ridge in relation to where they were now. The aerial photograph was taken on a day with light snow. Now nothing looked the same. Ed Ridgeway thought the OPs were to the west of the Brannon Ridge juncture, but the team came across zero going in that direction. *Did they miss something?*

Orin knew it would take a couple of hours for the team to return to the Scout Battalion positions, maybe faster since they would be going downhill. The planned assault over the ridge and down the pass would start at first light, which Williamson estimated to be about 0600. This meant they had less than one hour to search before turning back. Orin made his decision, signaling the team to lean in close.

"Okay, we're just about out of time, but let's take a look see to the east for about 20 minutes or so. If we haven't come across anything by then, we'll turn around and get the hell out of here. Stay in close." With that Orin climbed out of the crevice, walking slowly in a crouch towards the east. The ridgeline did start to widen out, but the rocks were covered with snow and footing was treacherous. They moved on an upslope for about 10 minutes in blinding, wind-driven snow when suddenly Orin, in the lead, spotted an exposed stack of filled sandbags and then another adjoining it. His heart lept in his chest and he froze. A simple wooden frame stuck out at right angles beneath the sandbags. Whatever it was it was man-made. He signaled the team to the ground as he flattened on his stomach, staring hard at the sandbags and wooden frame until he recognized he was looking at the corner of a structure with the sandbags *on* the roof. Whatever it was, most of it was underground or utilized a rock crevice as a natural depression. With the snow on the roof and the frame angles blending with the surrounding rocks, they had almost walked into it. It was virtually invisible. *An observation post. I'll be damned.*

Here on some of the highest terrain on Attu Orin could see the slightest hint of a lightening sky to the east. He moved his head slowly to look behind him towards the west and traversed back to the north. In the easing twilight, the best view of the island below was to the north, where he imagined when the clouds cleared the OP could see all of Holtz Bay to the north, and about 180 degrees of the island to the west. They apparently stumbled into the west side of the OP, with the view ports or periscope for the OP probably on the north side. That would place a probable entrance on the eastern side pointed up the ridgeline, with connecting tunnels or trenches. *Probable.*

Orin slid back next to the other scouts, signaling silently to stay put. He got up very slowly maintaining his crouch, stepping quietly behind the OP on the south side, gambling there were no view ports on what he believed to be the back of the OP because the roof was flush to the surface of the ground on that side. He examined the structure as he walked around it, especially alert for hidden entrance holes or periscopes. He saw nothing but sand bags and snow. It was a simple dugout with a wooden support frame and sandbags on the roof. The OP appeared to be about 20 feet wide. Dropping down to his stomach when he spotted another wooden frame corner, Orin slid his knife from the sheath and listened. The wind and artillery were ever present as he cocked his ear for human voices or even the static of a radio. After a minute, he crawled forward to peer around the corner of the frame, finding, as he suspected, the darkness and depression of either an entrance or a trench.

Orin stared to the left and the right of the dark hole, trying to let his peripheral vision to lock on and recognize something in the darkness below him. There was not a flicker of artificial light anywhere in his limited field of view, so he inched forward another foot to clear the corner frame. He turned his head ever so slowly fully to the left, revealing a closed door or entrance. There was a lightness on the bottom of the trench suggesting snow. He studied the entrance for a few seconds, then just as slowly, turned his head fully to the right, looking to the east to what he expected to be either a open communication trench or a tunnel. There was only darkness. The only way to determine what was in that direction would be to drop down into the trench. Backing up noiselessly, he returned to the waiting scouts.

Orin brought them together so their heads were touching. Whispering in their ears he explained what he had seen and his plan of action. He confirmed with Johnson, the most experienced of the two NCOs, the cloth bag and rope for the prisoner was readily at hand.

"Don't know if the OP is occupied or not, but we know what we're looking for." He pointed at Johnson. "I'm going down in the trench and try the door of the OP. If it's secured, I'll turn around and head east on what I think is a communication trench or tunnel. If I get the OP door open, you stay put and cover me. If I get a prisoner," Orin said carefully, "I'll try to silence him and then signal to you to give me a hand. We'll gag and bag him, and tie his hands. He has to be able to walk, we can't carry anybody down this mountain. Travis, you stay here and cover us. If all hell breaks loose and you don't see us coming out after about three minutes or you see Japs, get the hell out of here and off this mountain. We'll join you later if we're able. Clear?"

Travis was visibly disappointed to his role, but he nodded his understanding without a word. Orin reminded them again not to fire their weapons unless they absolutely had to, and wished them luck.

Orin stared down into the trench remaining motionless, listening again. After a minute, he tapped Johnson on the hand before carefully turning his body around, letting his legs slip over the edge of the hole. He suspended himself as far as he could then simply let go. He free fell only about a foot and cushioned the fall with bent knees, pleased that he landed on a flat surface covered with noise-dampening snow. In a low crouch with his knife in his hand, he remained frozen for a few seconds. He looked up finally to be surprised at how well he could see Johnson's outline five feet above him. Orin stepped forward carefully as he examined the entrance door. There was no doorknob but a short, handmade horizontal wooden handle. It was fixed on one side, so as slowly as he could, he leaned down on the handle until it stopped before placing pressure on the door. It gave easily but creaked at the rudimentary hinges, grating on the ground as it dragged along the surface for an inch.

At the first scratching sound Orin stopped, frozen to the right of the open door. There was a dark-colored heavy canvas curtain visible on the other side, a dim yellow light behind it. The curtain was a blackout, and probably helped control the cold draft from the door opening and closing. Orin listened before gripping the handle again to lift the door bottom from the ground. The door was heavy but the lifting assistance worked and the door swung free soundlessly.

Orin stepping into the room and pressed the blackout curtain aside with one motion. His knife out at his side, his eyes swept the room. Other than a simple wooden table and bench in the center of the room with a hooded but lit kerosene or alcohol lamp, the room was bare and empty. No bunks or extra furniture. As his eyes absorbed what they were seeing, he noticed the observation ports facing north and a shelf underneath. The view ports were wooden panels appearing to slide or hinge open somehow. They were closed now. The shelf contained large tube binoculars, navigation tools to measure distance, tea cups and numerous volumes of small books. In the shadows of the far corner, there was a large leather container for a portable radio telephone receiver/transmitter. He quickly examined the radio and the attached cables running from it and down to the side of the wall. Orin traced the cable along the floor all the way to the door and sliced it in half with his knife. Easily repaired he knew, but not without some time and effort. Getting familiar with the room, he noticed the food plate on the table and the small, unfolded map tacked on the wall near the view ports.

Orin pulled the map off the wall and folded it up, searching the room and shelf for any other document that might be useful. There wasn't much. He glanced at his watch, knowing they needed to find the quarters of the observation crews who apparently were either sleeping or taking a break, but they were out of time.

Carefully opening the door to keep the blackout curtain in place, Orin stepped out into the trench and as quietly as possible, lifted and closed the door behind him. He regretted not bringing a flashlight along because he was certain the observation crew was asleep somewhere ahead, and a shielded flashlight would come in handy ensuring they did not trip over something in the trench. Turning around so he could see Johnson's outline near the corner of the OP, Orin signaled with his hands to attract Johnson's attention. Johnson could not see his movement even against the background of the snow on the floor and gave no sign of acknowledgement. Orin crept to the side of the trench and whispered Johnson's name until Johnson eased forward and leaned over the trench. Reaching up and touching Johnson's hand, Orin whispered to him to slide into the trench.

Orin guided Johnson's body into the trench to muffle any noise. On the floor in a crouch, he turned Johnson's head so he had his ear.

"Nobody in the OP, maybe everybody is asleep," he said slowly. "Going to move along this trench and see if we can come across sleeping quarters or another OP. Didn't see any weapons in the OP. Stay right behind me, cover me when I open the next door. Going to try for a prisoner. If not, get as much information as we can. We just have a couple of minutes. If things go bad, take off and don't look back. Any questions?"

Orin couldn't see Johnson's face clearly, only a glimmer of his eyes.

"Let's do it, boss," Johnson answered quietly. Orin tapped the top of Johnson's wool cap and turned around, walking very deliberately heel first than toe, feeling for the surface of the snow covering the ground. As his eyes got used to the gloom in the trench, he noticed the light aura of the snow guided his path with the dark walls of the trench giving a strange sense of containment, like a tunnel. The path seemed to abruptly turn to blackness 10-20 feet ahead, but Orin continued forward until he picked up the white path again, curving to the right where it disappeared. The trench was apparently following the bend of the ridgeline, and as he crept carefully around the turn, he sensed at once they had gone underground. He looked up and sure enough, the hazy twilight of the dark sky was gone. Only complete blackness overhead and on the ground, with a hollow whistling of the wind behind him. A

90

tunnel. The space smelled damp from wet earth, with an odor of fish. They were close to a living area.

Orin stopped moving and slid to the side until he touched one of the walls of the tunnel. It was wet and cold. He felt Johnson's presence as he slid up behind him. There wasn't a speck of light to orient from, the tunnel in front of them carbon black. This did not look good. Orin made the decision, turning to Johnson to call it off when a door opened 20 feet in front of them. They both instinctively pressed their bodies against the wall, trying to blend in. Orin got a quick glimpse of a dimly lit space protected by another blackout curtain, more earth and some wooden structures—bunk beds? A man was silhouetted against the light for a brief second as the door opened and closed. He had stepped outside into the tunnel. The man was wearing a heavy light-colored winter coat with a fur-lined collar, open at the waist. Orin couldn't tell if he had a weapon or not.

Breathlessly, Orin and Johnson gripped their knives in the darkness, waiting to be discovered if the man turned on a flashlight or walked up the tunnel. He wouldn't be able to miss them. Instead, the man stood in the dark, grumbling to himself, making the rustling, snapping sounds of someone apparently buttoning up clothing. The man started shuffling his way up the tunnel until he was literally two feet past Orin before he suddenly stopped. They listened incredulously as the man poked around in his clothing until he brought something out. When Orin heard the scratch of the wooden match against the striker on the box he silently stood up and stepped behind the man.

As the match flared the man turned abruptly to his left when he noticed Johnson crouched down at arm's length. He froze holding the match and cigarette in midair, not apparently believing what he was seeing. Before he could react Orin had swung his left hand over the man's mouth, pulling the man backyards off balance into the downward falling tip of his combat knife in his right hand. His target was the joint of the man's neck and shoulder, only the blade thrust was not powerful enough to fully penetrate the thickness of the coat. The match was extinguished and the fight was on in the dark. The knife slipped from Orin's grasp as the man struggled to wriggle free. Orin grabbed the man's face with his stronger right hand but then the man bit Orin's index finger knuckle nearly to the bone. Orin could not scream or let go of the man's mouth. Johnson sprung up in the blackness, lifted the front of the man's coat by feel and drove his bayonet up under the ribcage straight into the man's heart.

The man gasped with sucking air under Orin's grip, then quivered once before slumping into dead heavy weight in Orin's arms. They

91

laid him down, and Orin, grimacing in his own agony, rubbed his hand carefully.

"Are you hurt, sir?" whispered Johnson, struggling to extricate his knife. Orin placed his hand over Johnson's mouth gently and nodded. Orin leaned his body weight down on the dead man's chest as Johnson wrestled until he successfully removed his knife. Orin recovered his own knife. There was no point in trying to search the body in the dark, so Orin, with Johnson's assistance, pulled the body up and out of the tunnel and over to one side of the trench. Again using the wall for concealment, they stared into the blackness where the door had opened for any sign someone had heard the commotion. *They needed to get inside where there was light.*

"Okay," Orin whispered, "we're going to go in the hut. If somebody is awake they might expect the door to open from the guy we just killed. We need to work together and fast, we don't know how many there are. I don't think more than a couple. I'll go in with my knife, but you cover me with your .45, okay? Don't shoot unless you have to!"

It occurred to Orin he was going to be killed in the next few minutes if he followed through with his plan as they crept forward again into the tunnel. He attacked and failed in his attempt to kill his first Jap because he didn't think about something as elementary as the thickness of an outer garment. If it wasn't for Johnson the man might have overpowered him and killed him with his own knife. Inside, his confidence faltered, especially with the knowledge his swollen and nearly numb right hand was practically useless. He stopped instinctively and Johnson bumped right into him, grunting with pain before checking himself.

"Sir?" Johnson whispered, confused.

"Sssh." Orin hissed, furious with himself. He sighed and took a deep breath, gripping his combat knife with his left hand as he crept forward again. *Kill or be killed, you dumb son of a bitch.*

The door handle was similar to the one attached to the door of the OP, he could feel it in the dark. Orin was counting on it working the same. With Johnson right at his back with a cocked Colt pistol at the ready, Orin pressed down the handle with his left hand and pressed the door with his shoulder, lifting the door as he did so. The second he recognized it was not locked he swung the door open smoothly, sweeping the black curtain out of the way. Slipping inside, they found roughhewn build-in bunk beds, two on each side of the room, with a small wooden table and benches in the center. The uneven walls were

nothing but packed dirt and solid rock.   What light there was came from
two low-yield kerosene lanterns hanging from ceiling hooks.   On the
other side of the room, opposite the door were two stacks of large
wooden boxes, perhaps storage boxes or personal trunks, separated in
the middle by another low doorway to another space.

A quick glance to the bunks revealed two of them on one side to
be occupied by sleeping men.   No weapons could be seen near the
bunks, although one Arisaka Type 38 rifle was visible leaning in a
corner.   Orin silently signaled Johnson to cover the sleeping men while
he checked out the doorway.   The next space appeared to be the cooking
and eating area, unoccupied and currently unlit.   A closed door with
light underneath caught his eye and he quickly pressed his ear against it.
Hearing only a single man's voice, Orin put his knife back in it's sheath
before drawing his .45 pistol from his holster, holding it awkwardly with
his left hand.   Somebody talking meant there were at least two of them
in the other room.   Thumbing the safety off slowly and confirming the
hammer was cocked on a live round in the chamber, he tested the door
handle.   Like the outer doors, the handle was a single swivel-style, but
the hinges suggested it opened outward, towards him.   Taking a deep
breath, he pushed the door handle down before pulling the door back
towards himself, shielding himself until the door was nearly half way
open.

93

CHAPTER 11

1800 hours, May 11, 1943, D-Day, Buchanan Ridge

Yoshi Nakagawa tried to press the last image of the engineers in the tunnel entrance out of his mind. He understood his thoughts were probably grounds for treason if they were actually voiced, so he let the confusion and frustration he felt lay dormant in his subconscious. *Stay there.* Engineers or not, we are all Japanese soldiers. We do our part. We do our duty. We do as we are told. *Stop this. You have already buried them.*

He hesitated where the tunnels dug at the base of the mountain ended and the first series of open trenches began. The tunnels were used only as connectors through the mountain from one side to the other, relying on the open but heavily camouflaged communication trenches to move troops up and down.

It was not yet dark, the twilight blending the sky and the valley floor below into an indeterminate grayness. The bombardment had been off and on for over 12 hours. If one counted the pre-invasion bombardment, Attu had been hammered intermittently by bombs and naval gunfire for over four days. Yoshi had no idea what the situation regarding the American assault troops might be other than what he had seen with his own eyes, the open waters of Holtz Bay without an American ship in sight. They must be somewhere, he reasoned, to explain all of this shooting.

Leaning against the wall of the damp tunnel, his senses were pummeled by the constant din of the incoming naval shells and the outgoing fire of the batteries down the hillside. The artillery was not shooting at the unseen ships way out over the horizon, so they must be shooting at American troops somewhere. *Did they land behind us?*

Yoshi was still dizzy from his concussion hours earlier. He had a throbbing headache with stomach cramps from not eating since breakfast. His mouth was parched but he did not think to ask for some water from the engineers down in the tunnel. He wanted more than anything to lie down and go to sleep. His body still ached painfully from the explosion, especially his ribs, where he was certain he had broken one or two because of his difficulty in taking deep breaths. He thought of the men in the coffin gun positions back down on the lower valley. He sighed, recognizing his personal plight was nothing in comparison.

Yoshi stepped out into the open communication trench to begin his trek up the mountain. Miraculously, he found few naval shells had landed on the trench complex, by accident or by direct targeting, the latter probably attributable to the excellent visual camouflage of the overhead frames. He stopped at a slit port to look only to be disappointed to find heavy fog forming up the valley, obscuring his view of Holtz Bay. At least the fog and low clouds kept the American airplanes from flying and bombing them. He climbed for what seemed hours, stopping some troops once to ask for some water.

Where the mountain leveled off at the summit, there was a small plateau narrowed at the peak to a rocky 50 meters width stretching the full length of the ridgeline. Observation posts were dug at the two highest points, approximately a half of a kilometer apart. These OPs utilized natural depressions in the rocks for depth, enclosing the OPs with simple wooden frames, packed earth and sandbags. The OPs were linked together by a single communication trench with short tunnels. They were supported by a 22-man communications platoon. The platoon alternated the OP duty with regular communications center duty at a tunnel facility established at the base of the mountain. Every 24 hours, two fresh four-man crews would climb up the mountain to relieve the crews on duty. Each OP had two hand power-driven, cable-linked radio telephone transmitters, so Yoshi knew Colonel Yamasaki was very aware of what was going on at the mountaintop OPs. Yamasaki certainly didn't need a junior engineering officer to give him any status reports. Yoshi understood he was sent to report the status of the *engineering situation,* which is to say, engineers built the facility structures and engineers wanted to ensure it was functioning as designed. About as pointless an assignment as possible considering the simplicity of the construction, he considered ruefully, but it was something to do.

Under normal circumstances of course, military custom and courtesy required Yoshi to check in with the local defensive commander—what was his name, Captain Nakamura—but there was no telling where he would be with the invasion. Nakamura would have no patience to either listen to or even create an audience to meet Yoshi. Yoshi was not in Nakamura's chain of command, wasn't even an infantry officer. As far as the officers who used the defensive structures were concerned, *the engineers needed to get out of the way once they were built.* So Yoshi would visit the OPs unannounced. A courtesy visit, then. He should be bringing them some sweets or food or something, he knew, but he had nothing. The more he thought about it, the more foolish the entire mission seemed to him now, but it was the only mission he had. He had his duty and his orders.

The eastern side observation post crew kindly shared their sparse evening meal with him, for which Yoshi was most grateful. Everyone was on reduced rations. The OP only had a single alcohol stove for cooking, yet there were rice balls with a little fish in them, and tea. Yoshi ate sparingly. Each OP crew was manned with three enlisted communications technicians and a communications non-commissioned officer. Yoshi felt very much at home with the communications troops because they tended to be, like the engineering companies, filled with well-educated young men most recently warming seats at universities all over Japan. They all had somewhat similar backgrounds and interests, and Yoshi, although an officer, was not in their chain of command and therefore safe. They were respectful of his position and rank, but comfortable in his presence.

During the meal the communication NCO marveled the point the American aircraft had not once bombed the two OPs during the pre-invasion bombardments, a fact he offered to Yoshi as testament to the quality of the camouflage the engineers designed. Yoshi laughed, denying any personal credit, admitting he was surprised the communication trenches were virtually unscathed. He noted the camouflage he had seen was excellent, with all visible areas either whitewashed to match the snow or were covered with white cloth. Like the troops manning the ridgeline gun positions, the communication troops wore white outer garments to blend into the mountain landscape when outside.

"The Americans are bombing empty spaces and rocks most of the time," he added proudly, "it's obvious their gunners and bombardiers are only dropping bombs where they *think* we should be. They don't know because they can't find us!" This made the OP crew jovial. He also mentioned his observation in the afternoon of Holtz Bay without American ships, which the OP crew confirmed. The Americans, they told Yoshi soberly, are on the peninsula to the west of Holtz Bay. They landed on a small beach there but were seen arriving in larger numbers, with more ships approaching Holtz Bay in the late afternoon until the fog rolled in and obscured their view. *They are here.*

After dinner Yoshi asked the NCO to contact the other OP to inform them he was coming over, asking if they had space for him to spend the night. He thanked the eastern OP crew for their hospitality, especially for sharing their meager rations. He observed once it grew dark the crew was very careful with their blackout discipline, helping him understand why the OPs had managed to survive the pre-invasion bombardment. They apologized profusely for their inability to give him a lantern or a flashlight to guide him on his journey through the short tunnels and semi-covered communication trench. Any visible light was forbidden. They did explain how the snow on the open sections contrasted sharply with the dark walls offering a natural path. Besides, they laughed, the walls of the trench and the tunnel would guide him the entire route, about a half a kilometer. Just lift your feet and walk slowly! No ghosts or bears, as far as they knew!

Yoshi did not want to reveal to these men his fear of the dark, waving confidently back at them before disappearing behind the blackout curtain and out the door. The first few steps from the sleeping quarters were the worst, as the facility was built mostly underground with the exit door opening into a tunnel black as coal dust. The NCO assured him the tunnel narrowed almost immediately directly ahead before turning slightly to the right into a semi-covered trench. You'll be able to see once you're in the trench, he reassured Yoshi.

The walk only took about a quarter of an hour but Yoshi was nearly frozen by the time he entered the tunnel entrance to the western side OP. It was very cold. The wind howled incessantly over the ridge and whistled through the openings of the trench. He could hear the murmuring *CRUMP CRUMP CRUMP* of artillery to the north, somewhere to the west of Holtz Bay. Not being an infantry officer he couldn't distinguish between the 75 mm guns of the Imperial Army and the 105s of the Americans. He was sure there was a difference, but today he had only heard the reports of the 75s as they left outbound from their numerous gun positions in the hills around Holtz Bay, mixing with the arriving detonations of American naval shells or the bombs from their aircraft. He had to assume at some point the Americans would get their artillery closer and he would soon know the difference.

The western side OP crew, although normally settling in at this time of night, were all sitting stiffly around the wooden bench in the virtual cave constituting the duty office. They were obviously waiting for him. A smokeless oil heater warmed the room almost to a comfortable temperature. Unlike the eastern side crew the enlisted men had their complete uniforms on, including their caps, as they sprang to attention when he entered the room. Their NCO, a young man with a barely discernible narrow moustache, saluted very smartly. Yoshi returned the salute self-consciously, waving them down.

"Please," he entreated, "I'm just a visitor, please go about your normal routines, which I suspect is some of you getting some sleep before duty tonight."

97

The experience of the western crew was similar to the eastern crew in that they had received no direct attacks from American bombers or naval shelling. Yoshi, who wanted nothing more than to crawl into one of the spare bunks, tried to keep the small talk to a minimum. What threw a wrench into his plans for sleep was finding out the young NCO had attended Osaka University when Yoshi had in the engineering college. The NCO was a second year student when he was ordered to report to the Imperial Army for indoctrination, and was not, for some inexplicable reason, pressed into the engineering branch when it came time for assignments. He too was a replacement and not from the Northern Islands. What really ensured a sleepless night for Yoshi was the NCO's admission he had relatives who lived on Shikoku.

The two of them spent the next six hours reminiscing over common locations and experiences. They were both so clearly homesick and desperate to connect to a place and time both familiar and *pre-Army,* the enlisted men who attempted to politely join in the conversation drifted away. Not that they were not welcome, but the two young men, their eyes bright with wonder and excitement as they talked, locked on each other like lovers and kept peeling the onion, recycling events, people, places and *ways of doing things* that quickly excluded the others from the conversation. The two former students simply never looked their way. The others made the required radio reports, cleaned equipment or simply prepared for sleep in the other space in the bunker. The last one out quietly closed the adjoining door between the cooking area and the duty room, rolling his eyes at the animated gestures and breathless conversation between their team leader and the visiting officer.

It was just before four in the morning when one of the soldiers opened the door, excused himself for interrupting but advised the NCO he was going over to the OP to begin his four-hour shift. The NCO, who was sitting at the small table in the duty room with his back to the door, turned to the soldier in surprise, asking him what time is was. *Four in the morning, Corporal!* The NCO stared at him for a moment, then turned back to Yoshi with a dismayed look on his face as both of them broke out in laughter, almost immediately resuming their discussion as loud as ever. The soldier shook his head, closing the adjoining door on his way back into the sleeping quarters. He slipped a white winter overcoat out of his locker as quietly as he could so as not to disturb the two who were sleeping. He considered taking his rifle along, the new orders with the invasion, but dismissed it. *There are no Americans up here on the mountain, they don't even know we're here!* He stepped around the blackout curtain before carefully slipping out the door.

Yoshi glanced at his wristwatch realizing the two of them had talked practically throughout the night. He was completely exhausted now, especially after the adrenaline of the shelling, his near brush with death and concussion, and the stimulation of talking to someone from home. So much has happened in such a short time, and here we are, two young fellows who had prepared our entire lives to do—what? He thought morosely, certainly not to be here on Attu, waiting for the Americans to kill us! *It is all so unfair.*

With loathing he knew he needed to get off the mountain this morning and find his way back to his command. He didn't have much faith in his future prospects, knowing he would probably be assigned the command of out-of-work engineers to hold another defensive line like Sergeant Kobayashi.

His new friend sensed Yoshi's exhaustion and change of mood, realizing in his own way the wonderful respite they had both found for a few hours had come to an end.

"Yoshi—I mean, Lieutenant, why don't you get at least a couple of hours sleep before the next shift change? Stay until at least six o'clock, then you can have breakfast with us before heading back." Yoshi, drifting back to the present, nodded and slowly stood up.

"I think I'll take you up on that." He unbuckled his leather harness with attached pistol holster, and placed it on the table just as the connecting door swept open halfway. Yoshi had to blink for a second, not believing what he was looking at. In the doorway stood a large man, over six feet tall, in a dirty, olive drab American uniform with a black-covered face and a woolen cap. The eyes, highlighted white against the black greasepaint, darted to Yoshi's pistol holster on the table as a large automatic pistol swung up towards Yoshi.

"*Ugoku, na!*" The American said clearly, *don't move.*

The young communications NCO, who was just getting to his feet when the door opened, had seen the shock and fear in Yoshi's face. He spun immediately around as he stood up, only to be clubbed severely across the face by the heavy American automatic pistol. The American, who seemed to be favoring an injured hand, glanced down at the NCO before stepping over him. The pistol was pointed squarely at Yoshi's head, the large black hole of the bore like the eye of a snake.

"*Ugoku na, goddammit!*" screamed the American. *Don't move!*

Yoshi had already drawn his Nambu pistol from the holster on the table when *BOOM* the American fired his weapon at less than three meters range, blowing the epaulet off Yoshi's uniform on the right side

99

with a tug.   The muzzle blast and noise was deafening, but Yoshi managed to point and squeeze the trigger of his pistol as he instinctively stepped back to the earthern wall.   The loud *click* was unmistakable, *empty chamber*.   He had not loaded the chamber.

Yoshi saw the flame arc and sparks as the American fired again, this time missing him completely.   *He is going to kill me*.   Yoshi cowered instinctively, sliding sideways along the wall, trying to control his shaking knees and hands.   He pulled the knurled charging handle back all the way as hard as he could and let it go, bringing the pistol up to squeeze the trigger as fast as he could.   This time it worked.   There seemed to be two Americans in the room now as his pistol bucked in his hand repeatedly.   One of the Americans appeared to fall but the other one kept shooting, the sparks, smoke and yellow flame from his pistol reaching out to Yoshi's face yet strangely not hurting him, like the blanks from the American cowboy films.   Something was wrong though, his right shoulder stopped working as he numbly watched his arm fall, slowly out of control letting the Nambu clatter to the floor. Something heavy was somehow attached to the side of his head, the weight pulling his head to the right when the ground came up so suddenly then blackness.

CHAPTER 12

0405 hours, May 12, 1943, D-Day Plus 1, Buchanan Ridge

Orin stepped right into the room, nearly walking into a seated Japanese soldier who was just rising, his back towards him.   What caught Orin's attention though were the saucer eyes of a young man, apparently an officer, slight and beardless who was standing directly across from him placing a pistol holster on a table.   The shock, confusion and fear registering in the young man's face evolved instantly from one emotion to the other all in the span of a heartbeat.

"*Ugoku, na!*" barked Orin, one of the few Japanese terms he knew. *Freeze, don't move!*

The words were barely out of his mouth when the Japanese soldier closest to him turned suddenly around, almost in arm's reach. Orin, holding the pistol in his left hand, whipped the heavy barrel of the .45 across the soldier's face hard with a solid *thwack* before the soldier was fully on his feet.   The soldier, another beardless youth, crossed his eyes as his nose splattered blood, his head jerking back.   He dropped straight down like a sack of cement, rolling instantly motionless.   Orin glanced down at the soldier before noticing the motion of the officer's hands on the pistol holster on the table.

"*Ugoku na, goddammit!*" Orin screamed as the frightened youth officer fumbled with the Nambu pistol, pointing it at Orin's head.   Orin fired instantly, shooting with his left hand. He shot high and left, hitting something on the boy's uniform.   The boy gasped, jerking back towards the wall while pulled the trigger of his pistol, a very audible *click*. Misfired!   Orin fired again at almost the same instant, missing the boy as he crabbed sideways on the wall.   Orin could hear voices, Japanese voices behind him just before the *BOOM BOOM BOOM* from Johnson's .45 silenced them.

During this frantic interval, Orin knew in his mind this boy was the *prisoner they needed,* but watched helplessly as the boy charged his Nambu, whipping it's barrel up again while squeezing the trigger at the same time.   Johnson shouldered his way into the room next to Orin, firing as he walked.   Everyone kept shooting until suddenly it was still, Orin realizing his .45's slide was locked to the rear, his magazine empty, both the officer youth and Johnson down.   Orin ejected his empty magazine to reload his .45 with a full one, glancing as he did so to his left at Johnson, who was lying down, but moving as he clutched his face.

101

Orin stepped around the table, his eyes and his .45 on the Japanese officer youth splayed in the corner.

A great deal of blood had come out of a temple wound on the youth but he was still alive, though unconscious. It appeared either Orin or Johnson had also hit him up high near his collarbone and apparently blown off two fingers from his left hand. *So much for my prisoner.* Orin found the Nambu pistol under the boy, tossing it to the other side of the room.

He peered around the room to assess what they had. *A goddamn SNAFU of royal proportions, that's what. THINK!* He scrambled over to Johnson who was trying to sit up still holding his face. There was a lot of blood and he seemed confused, even a little panicky. Orin examined the other Japanese soldier as he kneeled down next to Johnson, noting the drool and blood coming from the Japanese youth's open mouth. He didn't realize he had hit him so hard. The boy's eyes were partially open, as if he was dead, but Orin noted he was still breathing. He was in bad shape. *He's not coming along either, brother. Shit!*

"Where you hit, Johnson?" Johnson moaned before slowly taking his hands away from his face. It was a mess. Orin took a deep breath, almost averting his eyes. Johnson had a ghastly wound. A wooden splinter easily four inches long apparently caused by a bullet hitting the table, flew up to embed itself in Johnson's cheekbone right underneath his right eye. The splinter did not appear to have entered his eye, but the eye was significantly bulged out and sealing closed quickly, the skin of his cheek stretched tight and practically deep purple where the splinter was lodged. It looked frightfully painful. Johnson glanced up at him in agony with his good eye, before groaning again and touching his cheek. There wasn't much Orin could do about it, but he needed to get Johnson off the mountain. *Information first, mission first.*

Orin dashed into the other room to confirm what he already knew, the two Japanese soldiers in the bunks were dead. Johnson had shot them both before they could get out of their sleeping bags. He had to hope the shooting, being inside, contained the noise enough to not be a concern, but then he wondered, *what if there is another OP close by? Could they have heard the shooting? Is there a platoon of Japs heading for them right this instance?*

He had to believe no. This place is too isolated. *It's manned by kids, for pete's sake.* He decided the best place for information would be the duty room, exactly where they were. Peering at his watch, he could not believe his eyes. They'd only been in the OP five minutes. *0405.* Checking on Johnson and the two Japanese soldiers, Orin started looking around the room for what he came for. This was obviously the operations or duty room as a number of clipboards with information were hanging from hooks on one wall, another radio/telephone linked to cables was set up in another corner, and a number of area maps were displayed on another wall. *Bingo.*

There would be some kind of regularly scheduled reporting going on to headquarters with all these phones, but no one would expect them to report anything until first light. Nothing to see. Orin went over to cut the cable on the transmitter, quickly checked the other rooms for any other radios, just in case. He found a large flip top legal document holder and started stuffing everything of interest he could find into it. After five full minutes of searching, he had easily three pounds of documents in his folder. *Damn, not bad!* He guided Johnson back into the sleeping quarter area of the OP, preparing to leave.

As an afterthought Orin went back over to the officer youth to examine his pockets. The boy's breathing was very swallow with a weak pulse. He didn't have a lot of documents in his regular uniform pockets, but Orin did manage to pull out an identity card, a letter neatly folded in an envelope, a pay book and something he had only heard about, a new copy of the Emperor's Meiji Imperial Rescript of 1882. The intelligence officers called it a kind of a spiritual "company creed". It had a large cherry blossom embossed on the cover. He also noticed an officer's winter overcoat on a hook. He suspected it belonged to this officer, so he pulled it off the rack to examine the pockets. Inside one of the them he found a detailed map of Attu, an engineering map of construction sites full of symbols and scribbled notes on the margins. *Maybe Ed can figure some of this stuff out.* On the corner of the map was a neatly printed row of hand painted Japanese symbols, which Orin assumed was the officer's name. *Maybe an engineer, but awfully young.*

As Orin unfolded the map to examine it in more detail, he realized the scale of the construction with the reference to troop quarters on numerous locations throughout the eastern part of the island. He also noted the map outlined every major gun bunker on the island by caliber, with a small painted image of either a cannon or machine gun at each location with a number. The map also included the gun positions on the other side of Brannon Ridge down in the pass facing the Sarana Valley. *There are not just five hundred japs on Attu, that is for sure!*

Orin collected his document package, shoving it down his back under his field jacket. Time to go. He glanced at the two Japanese youths and decided they were not much of a threat. There was no point in killing them now. He gently got Johnson to his feet, guiding him through the bunker.   He had Johnson sit down for a moment while he checked the door.   Once he was sure it was clear, he grabbed Johnson by the arm before stepping outside into the cold and dark.

Within two minutes they approached the OP.   Orin could clearly see Travis outlined on the back corner of the roof frame.

"Don't Shoot!"   He whispered.   "Don't shoot us, Travis, we're coming up!"   Orin could see Travis lower his .45, breathing a sigh of relief.   "Give me a hand with Johnson, he's hit bad."

Orin lifted with all of his might as Travis pulled from above until Johnson's heavy body was finally up and out of the trench.   Travis reached down with his arm to assist Orin.   The sky was a little brighter in the west now, a dull shimmering to the north suggesting Holtz Bay, but he knew he was not looking at reflecting water, but probably snow or fog.   It was certainly still snowing up here on the ridge.   He gave the trench a final glance as he helped Travis with Johnson back to the path down to the battalion.

CHAPTER 13

0830 Hours, May 13, 1943, D-Day plus 2, Massacre Bay (Beaches Yellow and Blue)

First Sergeant Jonathan Bettencourt, Easy Company, 50th Engineer Battalion (Combat) realized Wheeler had left the clipboard on the far corner of the wooden crates fully exposed to the rain. Bettencourt could see it clearly, teetering on the edge of the highest box marked " OIL, LUBRICATING", the soggy, water-soaked top sheet of the division requisition form already curling.   There were at least 100 items listed on each page of that form, in alphabetical order, which Bettencourt and his two assistants had dutifully counted, checking them off as the material piled up on the beach.   Hand printed in ink per Army regulations, they would be unreadable now.   First Lieutenant Wheeler, the company exec, was responsible for signing off each form as Bettencourt confirmed their safe delivery.   *You dumb son of a bitch.*

Bettencourt closed his eyes and leaned against the crates.   If he was less tired he would be more angry, he knew, but 11 years in the Army had rubbed and scrapped his hide raw one time too many.   He simply accepted the stupidity and indignities thrown at him at times, not forgetting his transgressors, choosing instead to carefully deflect the events to personal internal shelves for later reflection and action.

Wheeler didn't care for Bettencourt.   An Army engineer, he resented the unique status given to Bettencourt by the Easy Company CO, Captain Greenley.   Wheeler had never been overseas in his three years of service, something apparently accounting for a lot in the eyes of Captain Greenley.   Bettencourt, on the other hand, served nearly six of his 11 years overseas.   Three in Panama, three in the Philippines.   In the Philippines his outpost, as there was no other way to characterize the incredibly remote, nasty jungle locations they lived in as they built the roads, was considered a true hardship assignment in the Army.   It was also a difficult assignment technically, besides the weather and environmental factors.   What he got out of it, other than his first exposure to malaria, was the reputation for being one of the best heavy equipment operators in the U.S. Army.   It also earned him the first rocker to his chevrons, *Staff Sergeant*.

In 1940 the Army activated the 7th Infantry Division in the preparation for the coming war.   Most of the troops would be drawn from draftees not yet even in the Army.   The cadre billets went to prewar professionals like Bettencourt, quickly promoted to be spread thin among the 17th and 32nd Infantry Regiments. Bettencourt returned from his hometown leave in Roseburg, Oregon to find new orders to the 7th ID at Camp San Luis Obispo in California. He stepped off the train to discover his record of achievement and experience in the Pacific of sudden great interest to the Army, who promptly offered him an opportunity for a commission through officer candidate school. Dozens of his fellow colleagues, non-commissioned officers with high school educations, were being commissioned to fill billets of a hugely expanding army. There was one catch, however, for Bettencourt. Not being a professionally trained engineer he would be eventually reassigned as a new second lieutenant to a non-engineer outfit. Administration. Supply. *Infantry*. The 7th ID needed all of them.

Bettencourt turned the commission opportunity down to stay with the engineers. He was assigned as a platoon sergeant for an empty company roster for Easy Company, 50th Engineers. Reporting to the new Easy Company CO, Bettencourt found Captain Greenley or rather, Greenley found Bettencourt. Greenley couldn't have been more pleased, it seemed. A re-volunteer, Greeley was an Army civil engineering officer who served his four years in the thirties before setting out to pursue a civilian career. He too served in the Philippines but not at the same time as Bettencourt. In any case, it was obvious he was very familiar with Bettencourt's file before he even set eyes on him. When Bettencourt reported in the captain took in Bettencourt's stocky and muscular frame before coming around his desk to offer his hand. His smile was friendly, appearing to be genuinely glad to meet Bettencourt. As an old Army hand, such overt familiarity from officers made Bettencourt suspicious and nervous. He hesitated only for a second before shaking the captain's hand, a little more confused when Greenley held onto his hand after shaking it.

Greenley looked down at Bettencourt's right hand, noting, Bettencourt assumed, the first half of his ring finger was missing, right above the joint. Greenley, prematurely graying even though he was only a year or two older than Bettencourt, nodded his tightly-cropped head sagely in understanding, adding to the fatherly persona.

"We didn't do that, did we?" He asked gently, turning Bettencourt's hand. Bettencourt knew instinctively Greenley already had the answer to that one.

"No sir, happened before I joined the Army. Use to work in a sawmill."

Greenley released Bettencourt's hand to lean back on the corner of his desk, still uncomfortably close to Bettencourt. Greenley seemed to be sizing him up somehow or making his mind up.

"You turned down a commission to stay in the engineers." Bettencourt bit his lip. *I knew it.*

"Yes sir."

"Don't want to be an officer?" Bettencourt had gone through this drill with two sets of officers at division. He was not in the mood to go through it again. He sighed, straightening up to a rigid position of attention.

"I wanted to stay in the engineers, Captain. I don't have an engineering degree, and it would have meant finding a new job in the Army. This is what I'm good at." Greenley didn't say anything for a few moments as they stared at one another. Greenley finally crossed his arms, nodding his head slowly. He frowned as if deep in thought. Bettencourt didn't want to upset Greenley on their first meeting, so he bit his inner lip to keep his mouth shut. His eyes gave him away, though. Greenley lifted his hands in a "hold on" gesture.

"Relax, Sergeant, at ease. No OCS spiel, okay? I have an immediate problem and I think you're the man to solve it."

That was it. Greenley came up with a pretty good offer and Bettencourt accepted it. The captain made the recommendation to the new battalion commander of the 50th Engineers who signed it to make it official. Bettencourt's new orders were cut within a week. The empty orderly room of Easy Company, 50th Engineers (Combat) gained a new first sergeant. Bettencourt added another rocker for the stripes on his uniform only six months after gaining his first, finding out in the ensuing months and years what Captain Greenley apparently already knew. Bettencourt was a solid administrator of the bullshit necessary to run an engineer company as well as being *one of the best heavy equipment operators in the U.S. Army*. He just didn't get too many opportunities to prove the latter these days.

As the battalion filled out the barracks with new replacements, including new company platoon officers, Greenley relied heavily on the recommendations of his first sergeant for personnel assignments. It was very obvious to any observer, including First Lieutenant Wheeler when he first reported to Easy Company in the spring of 1942, Captain Greenley trusted the counsel of First Sergeant Bettencourt more than any man in the company, including any of the new officers. In the intervening months not much changed. There was, for the most part, a professional truce between the two men as long as Bettencourt fulfilled

107

his normal duties as a company first sergeant. Wheeler acknowledged Bettencourt's skill as an administrator for company headquarters within the narrow confines of the orderly room. To Wheeler, Bettencourt was a good but un-educated heavy equipment operator with a knack for paperwork, nothing more. Bettencourt knew better than most how quickly things could turn around for him. It would only take a promotion for Greenley or worse, a bullet in a campaign like this one to move Wheeler to CO. He had to watch his step.

Bettencourt grabbed the clipboard, turning it sideways to let the standing water roll off the board. It was too late. Glancing at the blurred images in the wrinkled boxes, he carefully unclipped the forms to remove the top pages with their waterlogged carbons. Where he stood he was no more than 50 yards from the top edge of the high water mark on the wide beach, right on the fringe of the first appearance of the muskeg. Tides in the Aleutians were enormous, with the low water surf a quarter of a mile away. The Beach Master insisted this very location was above the high water line, so all the vehicles available unloaded the landing craft as they shuttled back and forth from the transports and the LSTs in the harbor, then drove the quarter of a mile up the semi-firm beach sand flats to the edge of the muskeg. That was as far as they could go without bogging down. The supplies necessary to support the assault troops, still struggling only a few thousand yards inland, were sitting right here on the beach. Stacked, with dozens upon dozens of vehicles among them, as far as the eye could see at the moment. If the infantry needed anything right now, it had to be hand delivered on foot. Getting this stuff off the beach was now an *engineering* problem.

Two days before on D-Day Bettencourt came up on deck of their transport with Greenley and Wheeler. The ship was completely enshrouded by thick, cold, oddly sticky fog. It was difficult to breathe. D-Day had been rolled back twice already, with every indication they would never leave the ship because the Aleutian weather, poor charts and lack of surface radar stopped the invasion in its tracks. Greenley had asked Bettencourt if he wanted to come up out of the holds for a breath of fresh air, so Bettencourt jumped at the chance. It was obvious to him the ships would not be launching any assault troops in the fog, new official H-Hour or no. Rumor circulated among the officers on deck the harbor was mined and there were rocks everywhere not listed on the charts. *What charts?* Added some Navy ensign when he overhead the comment. This caused some consternation for awhile, but

Bettencourt was more concerned he was not hearing any pre-bombardment naval gunfire. *We're assaulting this beach today (maybe) and the battlewagons are not pounding the shit out the island? What the hell?*

As if to answer his question, an Army major was casually but loudly commenting the battleships had *some* radar capability to shoot in the fog, yet would only fire on targets well inland to ensure they wouldn't hit any of our troops on the beach or the ships close to the beach. *Look at it this way*, the major stated emphatically to his growing audience, *we're not shooting at the Japs and the Japs are not shooting at us.* They can't see us either, and may not even be aware we're here! The audience murmured mostly in agreement. All Bettencourt felt was a sense of great vulnerability, realizing irritably the ship he was on was anchored because it could not see to go forward. *Didn't somebody say the Japs have subs in these waters, and an air force? What if the fog clears suddenly and we're sitting out here rolling around on our anchors? Shit!*

Bettencourt put a new form on the clipboard with carbon, just as an artillery shell exploded 200 yards away, dead center in the middle of a tightly packed group of parked trucks. *Jap 75mm!* He cursed, realizing he was so focused on his paperwork problem he stopped listening to the occasional incoming shell towards the beach. Some of the parked trucks hit were carrying ammunition. The first incoming explosion was followed almost instantly by a quick series of huge blasts with reverberating concussions. Bettencourt cringed as the shockwaves thumped his face, watching in fascination as the the trucks were flung up onto their backs, axles and wheels hurling off in all directions, before a sudden detonation and fiery obliteration blew them all to pieces. *WOW!* Small arms ammunition cooked off in all directions as men ran for their lives. Bettencourt held onto his helmet, sinking lower behind the crates. *We have to get off this damned beach.*

Arriving with some of the infantry battalions of the 17th, 32nd and finally the 4th Infantry Regiments on Massacre Bay beach were the 50th and 13th Engineer Battalions (Combat). Six full companies of engineers all milling around a beach in the fog, rain and snow showers surrounded by about a million dollars worth of equipment unable to move. After two days since D-Day, the infantry units were slogging their way through the muskeg up to the top of the Massacre Valley only to be blasted by Japanese artillery, mortars and machine guns dug in on all three sides of the pass. U.S. Army 105s were returning fire only from the beach since the earlier incident of 105s attempting to fire in pits too close to the muskeg. After the first fired rounds, an entire battery sunk their 105s up over the hubs of their wheels, aborting all future fire missions until they were pulled out of the muck with bulldozers. The ingenious sleds somebody dreamed up in pre-invasion planning didn't work because the tow vehicles couldn't get 100 yards into the muskeg. Nothing could tow them that didn't get stuck themselves. The wounded were being carried out by litter teams, again all the way to the beach. Other than an occasional airdrop when the sky cleared, resupply of chow or ammunition was all done by foot soldiers. *Might as well be Roman Legions*, some officer had quipped. *But then the Romans wouldn't be stupid enough to attempt to fight in the Aleutians!* Retorted back another. *Yep. Only the good old US of A Army would come up with such a thing...*

"Bettencourt! Wheeler!" Bettencourt turned before carefully standing up, peering warily in the direction of the burning trucks. There was just the one round, odd. From up the beach he could see Captain Greenley waving his arms. He was with a group of several officers, so Bettencourt brushed himself off before heading in that direction. He spotted Wheeler tramping head first from the other side of the beach. They joined up silently, neither acknowledging the other's presence. As the two of them approached Greenley, Greenley simply pointed towards a large administrative tent set up in the middle of another packed truck park a 100 yards away. Bettencourt hesitated when he realized where they were going, wondering, as he gazed up the slopes on the northern side of the pass, if an artillery observer was at that instant calling in the coordinates for another 75mm HE round from a hidden mountain gun?

The only saving grace was the constantly changing fog layers, sometimes coming down to only a couple of hundred feet, obscuring the passes from the ridgeline observers. Bettencourt witnessed in the last two days the flurry of incoming and outgoing artillery when the fog, rain and snow cleared or stopped. The sky would became visible and the 105s would pound the ridges as would the U.S. Navy destroyers with their five-inch guns. If it cleared for more than five minutes, a B-24 that seems to circle endlessly would occasionally lower its nose to drop a bomb or two, or there would appear a flight of P-38s or even Navy Wildcats from the small carrier. The planes would have only a few minutes before the sky closed up again. The ground troops could hear them above them but not see them. How the hell do they get back to their bases, Bettencourt wondered.

Once inside the tent he bristled when he saw all the brass. The only other enlisted men included a clerk assistant and a radio operator at

110

the far side of the tent. This was the battalion commander's tent for the 50th Engineers, but Bettencourt recognized the colonel in charge of all Alaska construction projects, plus numerous lieutenant colonels, all engineers. A group of six or seven hovered around the colonel as he traced the valley floor of Massacre Valley on a map with his finger. Colonel Wharton, CO of the 50th Engineers, listened attentively. Captain Greenley, with all the other company level officers held back to the walls of the tent were waiting, Bettencourt assumed, for some sign they should step into the inner circle.

"We need roads from the beach to the top of the valley, right here at the Sarana Pass," the colonel declared. "What are your plans?" He spoke directly to Colonel Wharton, but the force engineer, a lieutenant colonel, responded they had no road construction equipment. The colonel blinked as the tent grew very quiet.

"You mean you have no graders, that sort of thing?" he asked almost in astonishment.

"Well, yessir," said the force engineer quickly, "I mean—no, we don't. All we have are bulldozers." The lieutenant colonel turned to Colonel Wharton, who, looking embarrassed, said almost as a whisper, "He is correct, we really didn't anticipate the level of difficulty the muskeg is posing. The sleds were supposed to—um…"

The colonel shook his head while holding up his hands, effectively cutting Colonel Wharton off.

"Okay, Colonel Wharton, we are aware of what is *not* working." Wharton looked very frustrated, leaning forward over the map, trying to formulate an answer or a retort when the force engineer raised his hand over his head like a school child. The colonel in charge seemed to accept this role as head master, holding his hand towards Colonel Wharton to silence him, before tipping his head towards the force engineer.

"Yes, Colonel?" The colonel in charge asked testily. The lieutenant colonel leaned far forward over the map and placed his finger on the middle of the Sarana Pass.

"You want a road built right up that pass, correct, sir?"

The colonel in charge opened his eyes a bit wider, saying nothing at all. The tent grew silent again. Six lieutenant colonels and two full colonels within eight feet of him turned their attention to the force engineer leaning over the map, most with the barely concealed horror they might show for a man holding a gun to his head. The force engineer clearly sensed his peril, his eyes darted left and right as his protruding adam's apple bobbed up and down. He looked up at the colonel in charge to make his plea.

111

"I've studied this valley, sir, right up to the Sarana Valley, and although its covered with muskeg like the rest of the ground on this island that is not vertical rock, the Massacre Valley does offer a possible solution, I think. On the eastside, this streambed may provide it." He moved his finger slowly on the map and stopped. "If you follow the path of the valley around the Sarana Valley to Holtz Bay, you realize this little stream flows down the valley all the way to Massacre Bay."

The force engineer slowly pulled back from the map. The colonel in charge stared at him for a long moment before glancing down at the map again. He looked at Colonel Wharton, now chastened, who said nothing, then returned his attention to the force engineer.

"What are you saying, Colonel?" The force engineer hesitated as he organized his thoughts. He needed help from the other officers but none was coming, apparently.

"If you go down the center of the valley you encounter muskeg, some of it probably five or six feet deep. Impassable. We know that. This stream, carving itself along for as long as it's been there is all rock, full of boulders with a pebbly sand bottom. Not too deep where I saw it. I think we can level the streambed with dozers, widen it to make it shallower, or straighten it out when necessary to make a path for other dozers to tow supplies up the valley."

"This is true," added Colonel Wharton warily, after a hesitation, "with bulldozers, small ones as tow vehicles, we could possibly make that work. We will have a problem once we get up the Massacre Valley when the slope climbs steeply up through the Sarana Valley to connect with the combat units in the mountains."

The colonel in charge looked intensely puzzled, frustrated and angry. He glanced at Colonel Wharton then back to the force engineer.

"Goddamn it, man, *what are you saying?* Are you suggesting we can build a road up the streambed? How would that work? How deep was the water again?" His anger was palpable now, as was his growing astonishment. The force engineer coolly stood his ground, then stepped forward again to point at the map.

"Sir, I was thinking of *a way* to move equipment and material up this—this streambed—and thought maybe a ferrying system using bulldozers could do it. Regular trucks or jeeps can't, we know that. The water will still be there, but if the bed is prepared correctly, our dozers should be able to negotiate it if we can control the depth." The colonel in charge lowered his head, clearly trying to decide if he was dealing with a mad man. He placed both of his hands on the map as he lowered his head further. When the colonel didn't say anything, the force engineer looked around at his wide-eyed peers, addressing them

112

almost apologetically.   He was fully committed now so he had no choice but to spill his entire idea.

"I know it sounds a bit far fetched but when we encounter the higher ground up near the Sarana, I was thinking of a long-distance pulley system using bulldozers to winch the cargo sleds across the gulleys between the hills.   A skyway.   It's about four miles from the Bay to the head of the pass.   We start with dozers towing wagons or sleds of gear from the streambed at the base of the valley from the beach to the tip of the Sarana Valley where the finger of the ridge ends. Then we anchor a dozer down on one end—the streambed.   Run a cable and pulley from the dozer up the mountainside where it's steep and rig another pulley up on the ridgeline, keeping it all tight.   Then we use another dozer to winch the pulley cable with *attached sleds* across the gulley up to the ridgeline.   All we really need to do is to doze off the top layer of the muskeg on the rocks of the first level plateau on the ridgeline, because it's only a foot or two thick up there, and establish the—uh, cable anchor points for the high pulley, so to speak."

The colonel in charge looked up from the map and stared at the force engineer as if he'd never seen him before.   *Hell, this was starting to make sense.*   He turned to Colonel Wharton immediately.

"Colonel, you have bulldozers available for this—project?" Without waiting for an answer, the colonel in charge glanced around the officers huddled by the map table before turned back to Wharton.

"Do *we know if* a bulldozer can actually traverse this streambed all the way up?"

Colonel Wharton looked over his shoulders behind him, peering at the faces of the battalion officers present.   He spotted Captain Greenley and waved him over.

"This is Captain Greenley, Easy Company CO and one of my best engineers."   Wharton stepped back to let Greeley get closer to the map.

"Captain, did you hear what was proposed?"   Greenley nervously looked at the map before turning to Colonel Wharton and the colonel in charge.   "Yessir, using dozers to tow supplies up the streambed.   Not having seen the streambed I couldn't really tell how deep it is or if it can be done..." He caught the imperious glare from Colonel Wharton, hesitating to think quickly.

"However, I have one of the best bulldozer operators in the U.S. Army with me right here in this tent in my first sergeant, if any man can confirm it could be done, it would be him."   Greenley turned around, locking his eyes on Bettencourt.   Bettencourt, who had practically been dozing on his feet, jumped when Lieutenant Wheeler jabbed him especially hard in the ribs with his elbow.   Bettencourt looked up to see

113

what appeared to be all eyes in the entire tent staring at him. *Oh shit,* he thought.

CHAPTER 14

0930 Hours, May 13, 1943, D-Day plus 2, Massacre Bay (Beaches Yellow and Blue)

The Army, Bettencourt considered grimly, is an amazingly efficient machine when a man wearing eagles representing the task force ground commanding general wanted something done. Within a half an hour of the close of the meeting with the colonel in charge, Bettencourt found himself deposited by jeep at the beach spillway of the streambed. He had been asked what he needed so he walked the 50 yards to the nearest collection of parked bulldozers and made his selections. He chose a Caterpillar D4 tractor without a blade, a light, highly maneuverable tracked machine as his primary, asking for and receiving two of the battalion's *other* best operators to follow him with heavier tractors, an Allis-Chalmers HD10 and an International Harvester TD-18, both with bulldozer blades to move boulders. Colonel Wharton requested infantry support for Bettencourt and the other two operators in case the Japanese had snipers or spider holes near the streambed, and Captain Greenley immediately offered every available man in Easy Company.

Bettencourt fired up the diesel engine of the D4 and clattered up the beach to the spillway. The force engineer joined him and climbed aboard to hang on as Captain Greenley climbed on the TD-18. Greenley, with walkie-talkie in hand, guided two platoons of Easy Company engineers carrying carbines to split up one on each side of the stream, spreading out as far as they could from the streambed before they encountered serious muskeg. Bettencourt studied the streambed for a few minutes, noting the relatively flat bottom sections in the center of the bed where it was deepest. He knew he could easily negotiate three feet or so of moving water if the streambed was firm, but he did notice some parts of the shallower banks were relatively flat with few large boulders. The force engineer tapped him on the shoulder, pointing at the exact same place.

"Don't worry, Sergeant," he grinned, holding a large note pad, "you just follow the path you think will work and we'll map it."

Bettencourt answered by engaging the transmission, lurching the tractor forward across the sand and over the spillway into the stream. As if some lone Japanese gunner and observer knew their intentions, a single 75mm artillery shell screamed over to explode 100 yards up the

115

streambed, shooting a huge geyser of muddy water 75 feet in the air. The men on the tractors had no time to react or seek cover. All they could do was crouch lower in their exposed cockpits as shrapnel zipped, zinged and whined around them. Bettencourt heard a man cry out in pain on the left bank, one of the engineers providing infantry cover. A moment later he heard the call for litters and a medic. Another artillery round howled in, slamming into the muskeg on the right side of the stream farther up, with another muddy geyser erupting high into the sky. Bettencourt had stopped the tractor in mid-stream, leaning far forward from the single seat to use the engine as cover. The force engineer, fully exposed on the tiny rail over the metal tracks next to Bettencourt's seat, simply slapped Bettencourt's backside like he was a horse.

"Let's get up this stream, Sergeant!" Bettencourt lifted up, clearly furious, to glare murderously at the force engineer. The message was sent. The force engineer lifted his hands in surrender, acknowledging immediately his error.

"Sorry, Sergeant, I didn't mean to, uh..." Bettencourt, turned abruptly away to release the clutch. He kept both hands firmly on the control handles, but he knew he wasn't going to do anything foolish. He was however, not going to move one inch forward if he didn't feel it was the right thing to do. Both of them glanced around at the lowering cloud cover, knowing it would spell the end of the harassment artillery fire for awhile.

Within the first hour Bettencourt had mired the D4 in soft mud in the stream banks twice, both times almost to the top of the track. The TD-18, following behind but staying more in the center of the stream where it was deeper but flatter, towed the D-4 out. In two other occasions high boulders stopped all forward progress as the D-4 could not climb over the rocks and steep waterfalls. The TD-18 was used to simply push the boulders over to one side or the other with its huge curved blade, leveling or completely destroying the waterfalls leaving a suddenly fast but shallow water course the D-4 could plow through.

After two hours the streambed flattened out considerably but meandered about, winding around carved courses now turned into tiny hills. The TD-18 and the Allis Chalmers HD-10 tested the muskeg around these small flat hills finding them only a couple of feet thick. The bulldozers plowed and scraped the muskeg off the hills down to the firm ground, then literally straightened out the streambed by traversing from the flat stream across their newly made cut off. By the end of four hours the bulldozers were right up to the base of the Sarana Pass, with the stream around the finger ridgeline that extended from Sarana Pass all the way down to Massacre Bay. There was no far off echo of gunfire here. Bettencourt could hear furious rifle and machine gun fire right up the ridgeline, seemingly a few hundred yards away. Nervously he realized they had reached their goal. The force engineer slapped (comradely this time) him again on the shoulders, informing Colonel Wharton on his walkie-talkie the streambed was viable.

Bettencourt was ordered to return immediately back down the streambed to guide the first D-4s towing supplies. The force engineer stayed behind with the Allis Chalmers HD-10 to begin considering how he was going to establish his cable system to tow supplies from the streambed on the floor of the valley up to the finger point of the ridge facing the Sarana Valley. No tractor or bulldozer could climb the slope angle. The TD-18 went back down the streambed with Bettencourt, with orders from the force engineer to level specific areas of the streambed they had bypassed prior to the first D-4s supply tractors arriving. The path now proven, Bettencourt noticed he and the TD-18 went back down the stream without the benefit of an infantry escort. The force engineer and Captain Greenley were using the two Easy Company engineer platoons to reconnoiter and secure the area selected for the cable crossing.

With only his .45 pistol Bettencourt felt pretty naked and exposed. The D-4 tractor had no cage or armor plate of any kind. His only cover from direct, head on fire was the small space behind the diesel engine. He had no protection from fire from the sides or the rear. The TD-18 was not much better, so Bettencourt and its operator watched out for one another as best they could, although the TD-18 operator had the sense enough to bring along his M1 carbine. Bettencourt did not get stuck this time, arriving back down at the beach to the cheers of 13th Engineer troops standing by a dozen D-4s with attached wagons piled high with supplies. An engineering second lieutenant from the other battalion congratulated him before handing him a thick Spam sandwich with a thermos of coffee.

"We better get movin, Sergeant!" He said brightly. "The supply train is loaded with chow and ammunition for the 17th Infantry who are pinned down somewhere up in the Sarana Valley."

"Yessir, I understand. I do need diesel fuel for the tractor, and somebody needs to look it over to make sure I didn't drown it crossing the streams." The lieutenant turned to wave soldiers over before Bettencourt was even finished. Bettencourt unwrapped the sandwich and poured himself a cup of coffee as the maintenance guys arrived to start crawling over the D-4.

Twenty minutes later, freshly refueled and lubed, Bettencourt began the second of three trips he would make to the top of the valley this day.   For the most part the journeys were without incident, although on his last trip up the stream the 75mm gun that seemed to have the streambed zeroed landed a round virtually alongside a D-4 towing an ammunition wagon.   Bettencourt heard the howl and whoosh just before the artillery shell detonated about 50 yards behind him.   He turned in his seat to see the operator in the unlucky D-4 flung straight up out of his cockpit following the towering geyser, head over heels, to fall straight back down on the track on his D-4, which had hardly moved.   The attached supply wagon full of small arms ammunition looked unharmed.

The stream was wide and shallow here, so Bettencourt stepped off his tractor since someone had to check the damaged tractor, if in fact it was damaged. He could see the officer leading the re-supply team from the 13th Engineers, the same second lieutenant who had given him the sandwich and coffee, climbing on the D-4 to examine the body.   The lieutenant waved over some of the soldiers who came along as armed escorts.   They carefully lifted the broken body of the operator, obviously dead, over to the towed supply wagon of another D-4 and placed it the wagon.   Bettencourt watched the lieutenant climb up on the damaged D-4, sit down on the seat and attempt to restart it. Miraculously, the tough little tractor had not been seriously damaged even with a 75mm artillery shell landing right next to it. The streambed and the water somehow cushioned the impact or most of the shrapnel simply deflected off the steel sides and plates of the track. The unlucky operator—*the poor bastard.*   In any event, Bettencourt was impressed as the lieutenant fired up the engine, engaging the transmission before giving Bettencourt the signal to proceed.   *Well,* Bettencourt thought, *that college boy learned something besides operating a slide rule somewhere along the line!*   He climbed back onto his D-4 to lurch upstream.

CHAPTER 15

Manny Torre rolled back against the snow to retrieve his M1, staying below the lip of the rock shelf as the Nambu MG sent a burst less than a foot over his head.   He slid his rifle down his body so he could peer into the muzzle to ensure he hadn't clogged the barrel with snow from the tumble down the slope.   Twisting to his left he gave Ray Craymer a friendly pat on the back before lying back on the snow.   Ray ignored him other than to slowly turn his head in Manny's direction. Torre had shucked off his combat pack with attached entrenching tool to climb up the slope to throw the grenades—which he had not thrown. He realized he needed to get it back on.   If they got up over the ridge he'd need his pack and they might not be able to get back here.   Manny snorted to himself—*if they got over the ridge*.   There were what—two, maybe three MGs remaining up there just in the little section right above them.   Interlocking fire with Jap riflemen protecting the MGs and God knows how many infantry in the trench.   *Who am I kiddin?   In about two minutes he and Cray would be dead, just like Cooley.   Just like that.*

He stared at Craymer's back, shaking his head in disbelief. *What the fuck are we doing here?*   But Manny knew when Craymer turned his head again to send them up he would go.   The problem for Manny was the cold fact he really liked old Cray, with the pointless loyalty of a damned dog, he mused.   He figured Craymer was about his age, but he acted just like his Uncle Frank, the baby of Manny's father's brood and easily 12, maybe 13 years younger than Manny's father.   So in many ways Manny related to Uncle Frank more like a big brother because of the close age, but also because Uncle Frank acted like a big brother. He disciplined Manny when he was out of line like a big brother, that is, he yelled at Manny or kicked his ass.   Now of course, when he was out of line with his pop, his pop yelled at him and kicked his ass too, but somehow it was different.   Uncle Frank was smart, good looking, always had good stylish clothes on when he came around, with new shiny cars and really good-looking women hanging on his arm. Despite all the Hollywood stuff Uncle Frank seemed real serious about things, a seriousness Manny just knew would someday make Uncle Frank somebody special.   Just like Ray Craymer.

Uncle Frank never went to college, working at the docks off the Narragansett Bay making a good wage just like Manny's pop.

119

Providence, Rhode Island was a bleak place in the winter once the snow had been on the ground a few days and the factory silt and road grime dusted the white sheen to gray.   The difference between Manny's poppa and Uncle Frank was Manny's pop had Manny, plus Mary, his wife, and four other kids.   He always seemed tired, too tired to play with the kids, too tired to go bowling with friends (and drinking) when they occasionally stopped by the tired, paint-peeling old salt box the family lived in.

Manny always felt his pop acted wore out after 40.   Uncle Frank, despite his seriousness, was not melancholy like Manny's pop, choosing instead a more positive perspective of the life they were given.   He liked to read the papers out loud, liked politics, liked to argue sports and most importantly of all, would discuss all of those things with a little skinny shit like Manny, treating him like an equal and making Manny feel his opinion was important.   He'd throw a ball around with him, take him to the movies every now and then, and when Manny was in his early teen years even surreptiously bought him his first draft beer at the local pub and snuck him a cigarette or two.   It was a one of their little secrets Manny still kept warm and close to his heart.   You remember those little things.   Uncle Frank was all right.

Manny knocked around enough now to recognize his pop's situation had been tough, much tougher than Uncle Frank's ever was. He couldn't hold it against his pop, his tiredness, his lack of energy, but at the same time he *just knew* Uncle Frank was going to bust out to a better life.   You could feel it, his strength and manhood in the very way he carried his body.   He just looked strong.   He carried himself on the ready, well-balanced, coiled, like a boxer or a ball player, waiting, *ready*.

The only things Manny could really say that made Uncle Frank and Ray Craymer similar was this strong, fearless athletic presence, a steady, reliable quality you knew you could count on.   That had to be it. They sure the hell didn't look alike, as Uncle Frank was a medium-sized Italian with a tendency to put on the pounds, but like Ray Craymer, Uncle Frank had a strong, good looking face with a firm, dark jaw women were naturally drawn to.   Like Craymer, Uncle Frank also had steady, warm brown eyes that stayed with you during a conversation. Those were qualities Manny found few and far between during his general experiences with men in his short years away from home.   He found most men, co-workers or bosses, gave you just a part of their attention.   It was obvious in the way they would turn sideways to you when they spoke.   Like you weren't worth the effort, or there was some fear you would demand something of them.   It was like they were halfway out of the situation, of the conversation or even the commitment of whatever they were saying. They had no *stick* to them. Manny had no truck for people like that, they were like empty milk bottles drifting by in a river. Doomed to submerge at some point, to pass forever from his life. Uncle Frank and Ray Craymer are *rocks*, Manny considered with a wry smile, the good kind you can anchor to. So hard to find. *So I get killed because I'm as dumb as a dog.*

Ray Craymer took a deep lungful of air, sucking it in hungrily because he couldn't seem to get enough of it. It also helped to relieve his pain. His body ached everywhere, the dull throbbing from the shrapnel in his arm, thighs and legs somehow spreading to every part of his six-foot frame. He wiggled his toes in his boots again before stiffly pulling his knees up. They responded sluggishly, lead heavy with a cold numbness he found a little frightening. He needed to get that shit out of his body, it can't be doing him any good. But there wasn't much the medics could do for him here short of evacuating him, if any of them were still alive. He grimaced when he straightened out his legs. They were stiffening up. *We need to do this now before I can't move anymore.*

Manny Torre, a grenade in each hand again, peered over at Ray as he hugged the rock shelter. Manny had his combat pack on and his rifle slung over his shoulder. Drexel laid out three full magazines for his BAR and the other two soldiers from the squad, a tall skinny kid named Smit and a quiet boy named Wallace had extra clips beside their rifles. Ray stared at them hard, feeling like he was seeing them for the first time. They had their combat packs already on, ready to move up on Ray's command. Their helmets, dusted with snow, did little to keep the thick flakes swirling around their faces from sticking to their eyelashes and two and a half week old beards. Motionless, their faces up with the unique squint of infantrymen not quite believing what they were being asked to do, and who would trade places with anyone, almost anywhere rather than be where they were at this very instant. The snow removed the living quality of their eyes, reducing their unique colors to black dots surrounded by large ovals of whiteness. It was what stuck out, the oval whiteness of unblinking, peeled back human fear or of death.

To Ray the four men, lying so still looking up at him seemed frozen and already dead. He had to blink and look again. Like the men a few hundred yards below them who were killed earlier by the Nambu MG. The same gun that killed the big boy from Second Squad that saved Ray's life with his body after he was dead. What he seemed to see was the instant before the magic transformation from living person to one who has gone over, who has left. A shell of flesh and blood where the heart no longer pumped, the brain drained of thought, of *being*. Ray couldn't take his eyes off of them, confused, not knowing if he was looking at the past or the future in his own mind's eye. He forced himself to turn away, spinning to his right when he heard concentrated rifle and machine gun fire almost at their level on the slope. The snowstorm was furious, the snow dumping heavily with thick, sticky flakes, but the fog had lifted slightly to increase visibility enough for him to see dark figures moving up the ridge through the snow. It looked like Second Squad, and he heard the strong New England bark from Staff Sergeant O'Hearn for the first time on the mountain. The men were firing their rifles as a few others lept forward towards the ridge. *Damn, they were charging the slope.* Ray looked up to peek over the rock shelter when he heard the Nambu MG above them turn to fire towards the men climbing on the right. *This was the time.*

"NOW, MANNY, NOW!" Ray spun to his right to clear the rock shelter, climbing to his feet with a grenade in each hand. He no longer could feel his legs but his brain messages somehow got through as he found his knees pumping up and down as high and hard as he could, two blurs underneath his chin charging the steep slope at an angle. Ray was only partially aware of Dan Cooley's disemboweled body, the only registering images were of Cooley's beard, now white-crusted, and the snow blanketed entrails. The blood spoor was already covered and absorbed with white, sucked of color to a dark purple. A pounding roar came from within his skull, so loud he was barely aware of the BAR and rifle shots from Smit and Wallace providing covering fire. He charged the slope with all the speed he could muster, high stepping through deep crusted snow, looking up to see a foot long gray blur from the muzzle of the Nambu still shooting to his right at Second Squad.

With his index fingers he pulled one, then the other O-ring cotter pin from the grenades in his fists without missing a step. As soon as he was fifteen yards from the ridge he stopped and hurled two of his grenades virtually straight up, one to his left, one slightly to his right. He immediately pulled two more grenades from his pockets, yanking the O-rings before tossing them up and over the ridge. All four went out of sight as he threw himself forward against the snow, knowing it offered practically zero protection from rifle fire above him, but he did it anyway. Ray wasn't even aware of his breathing as he shucked his slung rifle off his shoulder to bring the muzzle around just as the grenades exploded. One, two, three and suddenly what sounded like three, maybe four more one right after the other, practically one explosion. *Manny's grenades!*

One distinct, human voice had cried out up there on the ridge in pain or fear, followed by sudden quiet right above Ray. No MGs, no BAR, no rifles, nothing, just the muffled shooting of the assault on the right, 50 yards away. Ray pushed himself up from the snow, climbing now on his hands and knees straight up the slope. The snow was deep, wet and sticky but Ray scrambled up so furiously it offered no resistance to him at all. Within seconds he was up to the top of the slope, rifle in his shoulder. With his trigger finger Ray flicked his safety forward as he spun right to where he could see the Nambu MG. The gunner's strangely deflated face stared at him with wide, surprised eyes, now sightless with out a brain to support them. Ray could see the back of his head was gone.

The ridgeline was wider than he thought it would be, but there was only a single deep communication trench carved through this winding section. The Japanese engineers had utilized a natural deep fracture in the rock along the ridge, exploiting it and widening it when necessary. The trench has some form of white cloth camouflage all over most of it supported by wooden frames. The most striking thing to Ray was every Japanese soldier he could see, and there were at least 15 laying prone in his small bend of the trench, was wearing white camouflage winter gear, including hoods and gloves, now all splotched indiscriminately with bright red.

Rifle fire directly to his left had Ray spinning around until he spotted Manny already in the trench about 30 feet away, shooting wounded Japanese. Movement among the bodies of the MG gun crews and riflemen down in the trench in front of him brought Ray back to the task at hand. He jumped carefully down next to the bodies, firing quickly into every Japanese soldier showing signs of life, pressing the bore of his M1 against their skulls before squeezing the trigger. The four grenades in his section had done a miraculous job of killing. It almost seemed to Ray the Japs had not tried to protect their bodies at all from the grenade shower, because that was what it was, as they continued to fire at Second Squad until the grenades exploded.

A grenade appeared suddenly about 10 feet to Ray's right. He threw himself down on the bodies in the bottom of the trench, cursing, but the grenade didn't go off, another dud. He quickly rolled over closer to the side of the trench when he spotted movement of two white camouflaged figures stepping noiselessly towards him from the right, both carrying rifles with bayonets attached. The first soldier turned the corner saw Ray just as Ray fired two rounds into the man's chest, dropping him. The metal clink of the empty eight-round clip as it was ejected out of his rifle startled Ray, as he thought he had just reloaded. He yanked out a new clip from his bandolier to drop in his breech as the other Japanese soldier stepped into view, clearly aware Ray was attempting to reload his rifle. The man raised his own rifle, aiming the Arisaka directly at Ray's head. Ray jerked his rifle up to fire, terrified, knowing he was too late when the chest of the white winter overcoat on the Japanese soldier blew apart. The man seemed to throw his rifle away from him as heavy slugs hammered him back and down. Ray was startled by the hot expended .30 caliber shell casings from a BAR ejecting down on his head and shoulders. He looked up to see Drexel standing up on the edge of the trench five feet above him, continuing to shoot at the dead man before moving his fire up the trench to some unseen targets around the bend of the trench. Ray crouched down hearing the noise of footsteps, his rifle in his shoulder as three more Japanese soldiers came up the trench.

None of them made it as Drexel, making the fastest BAR magazine change Ray had ever seen him do, stitched all three in one long burst. Reloading again, Drexel continued to fire at targets visible only to him up the trench to the right. Ray stood up cautiously, his rifle still pointed up the trench when he heard his name being called behind him. There was another muffled grenade explosion and what he assumed was Manny's rifle firing rapidly, then the distinct crack of several Arisakas.

"CRAY! CRAY! GODDAMN IT, I GOT A HUNNERD JAPS COMING THIS WAY!" Manny's cry turned Ray around to his left. He could just make out Manny around the bend, proned out on top of two dead Japanese, firing around a bend in the trench. Ray glanced up to watch in amazement as Drexel, as calm as Ray had ever seen the boy, dump another empty magazine and reload his BAR, firing from his shoulder standing straight up on the lip of the trench. Ray stepped around a body just as Private Smit jumped into the trench almost on top of him. Smit clumsily broke his fall with the stock and metal buttplate of his M1 on the chest of a dead Japanese, then stumbled instantly over another body, falling hard against Ray. The metal buttplate of Smit's rifle jabbed into Ray's injured shoulder causing stabbing blinding pain, forcing Ray to cry out himself. With his free hand, he roughly shoved Smit off of him, rolling onto his feet, cocking his right arm back in anger. He waited a split second until Smit's face appeared as he pushed himself up before thumping his balled fist into the side of Smit's head. Smit's head jerked to the left, then his entire body flopped back, his eyes rolling around.

"YOU DUMB SUMBITCH!"   Ray screamed, stepped right over Smit as he felt a presence right above him.   He glanced up just as Private Wallace scrambled up erect at the top of the trench, his eyes wide as saucers to the sight in front of him just as he was shot through the jaw.   Blood sprayed straight onto Ray's upturned face a half a second before Wallace's body hurled directly towards him.   Ray sidestepped before the body slammed into the bottom of the trench, but not far enough to avoid his rifle stock.   Wallace's M1, unattached, spun free to clout Ray's un-helmeted head a deflecting blow.   Ray heard a crack, saw stars and blackness, with a fraction instant of blinding pain before the bottom of the trench came up to pummel his face.

Ray regained consciousness a few seconds later, confused with his head pounding with pain.   He lifted his face, which was numb from his cheek landing so hard on the buckle of a chest harness on the dead Japanese underneath him.   He heard moaning next to him, forcing him to turn his head.   Wallace, apparently still alive, stared at Ray with dulled eyes, blinking slowly.   Ray could see the small puckered hole of the entrance wound on the side of the jaw visible to him.   The neat hole welled with blood before it pulsed out and ran down his neck.   Still stunned, Ray stared at Wallace for a long moment before his senses cleared enough for him to recognize rifle shots directly behind him.   He could not hear Drexel's BAR anymore, so he turned around to look up over his shoulder.   Drexel was gone.

Ray pushed himself up far enough to see Manny struggling hand to hand with a Japanese soldier with a bayoneted rifle, with another soldier coming right up behind him.   Ray sluggishly searched around for his rifle before discovering it tightly gripped in his left hand.   He watched in horror as the Japanese soldier parried Manny's rifle to one side and deftly sent a bayonet straight through Manny's shoulder.   Manny screamed in pain, a sound flipping a switch in Ray.   He shouldered his rifle and fired almost in the same motion, his front sight on the Japanese soldier's head as the soldier withdraw the bayonet and began the down stroke of a more accurate thrust into Manny's chest.   The man's head jerked back as his helmet, held under his chin by a strap, pitched forward as the skull was evacuated by the high velocity .30 caliber bullet.

Manny had the presence of mind to deflect the downward falling rifle and bayonet as the dead Japanese fell forward onto him.   Ray didn't see this though, his brain focusing entirely on the Japanese soldier directly behind the one who was bayoneting Manny, and the two others behind him.   He stood dead still and erect as he spun the muzzle from one Japanese helmeted head to another, barely conscious of anything

125

except a good sight picture on each round face before he squeezed the trigger, one after the other.   Private Smit, who had recovered miraculously from Ray's punch when he saw the Japanese soldiers attacking Manny with bayonets, would report later Ray had fired all four shots so fast they sounded almost as one.

What Smit did not report was the look on Ray's face when he finished killing the four Japanese soldiers.   Smit had moved or shifted his weight behind Ray, the sudden noise spinning Ray around 180 degrees in a perfect bayonet course pivot with the muzzle of his rifle pointed directly at Smit's head.   Smit would never forget the dark, piercing, murderous eyes of Ray Craymer behind the sights of the rifle for as long as he would live.   For about a full second, the longest in his life, he thought he was a dead man.   In his dreams Ray Craymer's trigger finger was pressing, continuing to press the trigger until the muzzle flared.   Smit had watched as the perfect witness the heads of four Japanese soldiers enlarge visibly before shrinking as their skulls were punctured, blown out and physically evacuated of much of their brain matter.   *How could that be, how could I see that, something taking only a millisecond to occur?*   Smit would close his eyes yet still see the heads flaring, deflated with the "poc poc poc poc" sound as the skulls cracked and were sucked out.   Then the vision of the big black bore of Craymer's M1, locked up following Smit's face, with Ray Craymer's eyes reaching out to him as the trigger finger began its squeeze.

Ray lowered his M1, glaring at Smit before glancing over at Wallace, who had not moved from where he landed.   His eyes were still open, blinking, a rapidly spreading blood pool over the white coat of the dead Japanese soldier he was lying on.

"Check him out!"   Ray commanded to Smit, "but keep your eye peeled for Japs coming from the right!"   Ray raised his rifle again at the ready, stepping quickly over bodies to get to Manny.   Watching warily around the corner of the trench, Ray pulled the dead Japanese off of Manny, relieved to see Manny had missed the bayonet as the dead man fell forward.   Manny was lying flat on his back looking very small, clutching a very bloody shoulder with an equally bloody hand.   He lifted his bloody hand to motion a pull up, so Ray gripped the wrist of the offered hand and stepped back, pulling Manny up to a semi-sitting position.   Manny groaned in obvious pain, but the smile that followed a second later was broad.

"What the fuck too you so long?"   He demanded, a little quieter than normal.   "I was fighting off the whole Jap Army while you were dicking off poking bodies!"   Ray ignored him, probing the deep wound

126

in Manny's left shoulder before realizing that two of the fingers of Manny's right hand were practically severed in half. He gripped the right arm and elevated it, examining the wound in amazement.

"I grabbed the bayonet with my fingers, pushing it away," gasped Manny, suddenly looking very pale. Ray gently eased him back down before dragged him over to the side of the trench.

"We need to get you out of here, Manny," Ray said gently, tearing open Manny's first aid compress to wrap around Manny's shoulder after dusting it with the sulfa packet. "You've lost a lot of blood, but you're going to be okay. Hold your hand up so we can control the bleeding, I'll find something to wrap your fingers with, maybe they can sew them back on or something."

Ray nervously looked up the trench to the left as he tended to Manny, knowing they were the farthest American advance on the ridge to the south end of the bowl, with no knowledge of how many other Japs were in the trench in that direction. If the Japs were sending reinforcements, no one was watching for them. To the right, he didn't know if Second Squad had gotten into their section of the ridge or not. If not, they could expect any number of Japs any second. Somebody must have seen them climb up into the trench, unless the mortar barrage got *everybody*. And where the hell is *Third* Squad? He turned around, spotting Smit still wrapping Wallace's jaw with a compress dressing.

"SMIT!" He barked as quietly as he could. "Did you see Drexel? Is he still alive? Do you know if Second Squad made it into the trench on the right?" Smit stared at him as if Ray was speaking a foreign language. He moved so slowly as he wrapped Wallace's face Ray suspected he was in shock himself. He continued to stare at Ray as his lips moved, but Ray could not hear his words.

Ray was beginning to realize what a bad situation they were in. He had two seriously wounded men—*hell, he was practically immobile himself,* and Smit, who was apparently useless now. Ray had lost the radio-telephone and cable reel when they were mortared down on the slope, so there was no way of knowing at this moment if anyone else from the platoon was in the trench to their right. If not, the first serious Jap probe will finish them. He stared at Smit for another moment, watching the noiseless lips continue to move. He turned his attention back to Manny, who was fading fast, but whose eyes were open and unwaveringly on Ray. The bandage was soaked red.

"So how fucked are we, Cray?" Asked Manny almost in a whisper. He turned his head as if to listen. Ray did the same, realizing how quiet it was, as there was only some far-off rifle and machine gun

127

fire, somewhere to their right.   Manny patted Ray on the arm with his injured hand as if to reassure him.

"Get me my rifle and prop me up so I can see down the trench. You go see if you can hook us up with Second Squad."   Ray nodded, knowing he had to find out if they were alone or not.   He retrieved Manny's rifle, frustrated when he could see Manny couldn't hold his rifle with either arm.   He shuffled over to Smit, grabbing him by the chin to get his attention.   Smit didn't resist, staring at Ray fearfully with his mouth open.

"Listen, Smit," Ray said with less force than he felt, releasing his grip on Smit, "I need you now, *right now!* You're not hurt, and I need you and your rifle to protect these wounded men, do you understand?" Smit stared at him before nodding slowly.   He started to look around then stopped when he saw his rifle a foot away.   Ray watched him retrieve it, slowly pulling back the bolt just enough to see if there was a round in the chamber.   This was a good sign.   Smit turned towards Ray in a half crouch, half standing position.   Ray waved him down until Smit eased onto his haunches.

"How is Wallace?"   Ray asked, glancing in the wounded man's direction.   Smit followed his eyes before answering.

"He's hurt bad, real bad.   He's lost a lot of blood."   Ray nodded, keeping his eyes on Smit.

"We've done all we can for now, but we need to protect them, Smit.   You're all I got right now.   I'm going to the right a piece to see if Second Squad made it in the trench.   If you hear shooting, be ready but try not to shoot me if I come flying back in here, okay?"

Smit nodded slowly, but not before glancing down at his rifle again and at Wallace, whose eyes were still partially open, the up and down movement of his chest the only sign he was still alive.

"I'm okay," Smit said, "I'm okay."   He crept back over to the side of the trench, stepping over bodies between Manny and Wallace. Ray nodded, not knowing what else to say.   He peered carefully down the trench to the left before looking for any sign of movement from the right.   He stepped over the bodies of the four Japanese soldiers Drexel had killed before cautiously peeking around the next bend to find six more, all stitched with heavy bullets in the chest.   Ray examined then cautiously, ready to shoot if necessary.   After darting from side to side for another 50 feet, he found four more Japanese corpses, then the first evidence of another American unit having got into the ridge trench before King Company.   Three American soldiers, dead at least a day, had been shot, cut up and bayoneted repeatedly next to the corpses of three Japanese.   Ray knew none of these men, most likely 17th Infantry guys.

He paused by the Americans, sickened by the savagery and butchery of the Japanese on these soldiers, who, Ray had to assume, were alive when they arrived in this section of the trench.   Most of the wounds appeared to have been caused by edged weapons, bayonets and sabers, hacking wounds leaving few limbs or appendages intact.   The blood loss was enormous, confirming his suspicion the men were alive when they were set upon.   Ray could feel his own body shutting down, failing him, so he moved on, but he could not help but look back at the dead Americans one more time.

CHAPTER 16

1300 Hours, May 27, 1943, D-Day Plus 16, Fish Hook Ridge

Ray Cramer stepped cautiously into a section of the trench that appeared to have taken the brunt of one of the Navy Wildcats' firing passes. The trench was wider here, possibly more visible from the air as the camouflaged cover was torn apart, ripped to shreds from concentrated .50 caliber machine gun slugs, dozens and dozens of them, rendering the blended carnage in front of Ray into a twisted mess of steel, wood, canvas, bones, muscle sinew and eviscerated, headless torsos. This section was apparently a strongpoint with revetments for a half dozen heavy and medium MGs, all flung apart, mixed with the blood and bone. He estimated maybe 20 soldiers had been in the trench here, maybe more.

Planting his boots carefully, Ray poked everything resembling a partial human body with the muzzle of his M1, but it was pretty apparent no one survived the strafing attack. Snow blanketed most of the remains, but the snow could not completely absorb the enormous amount of blood sprayed about in what had to have been only a one or two second concentration of bullets. It helped him understand the incredible power of the .50 caliber bullet, but mostly he remembered an Army P-40 pilot explaining the destructive power of the angle of convergence—the point in space where all six of the .50 caliber guns on the wings of the fighter converge on the target. The physical result of this momentary convergence on human beings was pretty evident here.

The trench turned sharply at the end of this wider section so Ray approached the blind curve warily. He could hear muffled rifle and machine gun fire farther up the trench but the swirling snow and strong, gusting wind made the direction of the shooting confusing. It was hard to think straight as it was. He was in bad shape, hallucinating maybe, not really remembering why he was in the trench or why he was heading in this direction. Leaning against the side of the trench just short of the blind bend, Ray slowly slid down onto his haunches and closed his eyes to make some of the dizziness go away. He tried to focus, away from the growing fear and confusion in his mind, away from the cold numbness starting to invade every muscle in his body. He opened his eyes slowly, watching huge snowflakes spin around inches in front of his face, damp, wet and sticky. For a long moment, he got the idea in his head he was already dead and didn't know it. *This must be*

what it feels like. Just like all these dead Japs in the trench next to me.
You didn't know when it happened, you were too busy doing something,
then—well, then you were dead.   Blown to bits to wake up and watch
the snow come down.

But then Ray thought of Dan Cooley and Dan's grenades,
realizing he had gone past Dan and thrown his own grenades.   Dan got
killed.   Somehow he, Ray Craymer, had managed to throw the grenades
and climbed up into this trench.   *I'm not dead.*   Ray shuffled around so
he could see down the trench from the direction he had come.   *How far
had he come?   Where is Manny?*   Ray squinted his eyes, shaking his
head trying hard to clear his muddled thoughts.   *Manny is hit bad, and
I'm going to find Second Squad.*   This came in crystal clear, loud as a
bullhorn in his skull.   *Second Squad.*   He slowly, painfully forced
himself to his feet, suddenly thirsty and hungry.

Reaching back for his canteen, he froze when he heard the
carefully placed boot steps crunching on snow somewhere right around
the blind corner.   Whoever it was stopped around their own blind
corner, the footsteps now silent.   Ray glanced down to confirm his rifle
was in both of his hands, his right hand moving into the trigger guard.
He was on the right side of the trench, his back to the trench wall with
his rifle muzzle pointed to the left—the wrong way.   As noiselessly as
he could, he pivoted his body to the right, bringing the muzzle up as he
turned to face his adversary.   To keep his body close to the trench side,
Ray shifted his rifle to his left shoulder, bringing the stock up to his
cheek and his eyes right over the peep sight, the muzzle aimed at the
apex of the corner, 10 feet away.   It was a clumsy, painful position with
his injured shoulder, but he had no choice.   He stood motionless for a
full minute, rewarded finally when the boot steps began to crunch again.

The muzzle of an M1 carbine slowly appeared, then the gloved
hand and dirty, olive drab sleeve of a field jacket gripping the forestock.
A second later a helmeted head with the swarthy, black-bearded face of
Staff Sergeant O'Hearn came into view behind the sights of the carbine.
Ray watched with great intensity as the gloved trigger figure on the
carbine eased its grip.   If the grip had tightened, Ray might have fired
his own rifle, he knew that.   It was only then that Ray looked into
O'Hearn's eyes, wide and white rimmed, no doubt just like his.   Ray
lowered his rifle a second after O'Hearn brought his down, the relief in
O'Hearn's face enormous, but the strain and fear reached through,
evident in his eyes.

"Who's that?" O'Hearn demanded.   "Who else you got with
you?"   He followed almost immediately, glancing first at Ray then

around him.   When O'Hearn saw the carnage in the trench behind Ray, his lips curled instinctively as his eyes widened.

"Craymer, First Squad, sarge.   I'm alone, trying to find out if you guys made it into the trench."

O'Hearn cautiously backed up to wave at somebody behind him out of sight to come up.   He came back in a second, viewing the destruction in the strongpoint more carefully with obvious distaste.

"So the Navy flyboys did some good after all," he said almost to himself.   Another soldier from Second Squad, a private named Carter toting a BAR crept around the corner to stop suddenly, awestruck by the sight of the former strongpoint.   He lowered the muzzle of his BAR when he realized the number of dead Japanese in the concentrated area, fanning it around as if looking for potential targets.

"They're all dead," Ray declared without enthusiasm, "I checked them out."   He turned to O'Hearn, who had only been the platoon sergeant for the First Platoon about six weeks to give him the situation in the trench to the south behind them.   O'Hearn's face fell when Ray reported he had only two effectives, including himself plus two seriously wounded holding the south end of the ridge.

"I kind of figured they're weren't too many of you up on that end, but that charge of your squad up that slope right after the mortars chewed the shit out of the platoon got them MGs off of us and onto you."   Ray could sense the respect in the words O'Hearn was saying, although most of it was conveyed in his eyes.   Ray explained quickly how the mortars missed most of the First Squad because it was inside the highest angle of the mortar beaten zone, and how Dan Cooley brought the squad up to the protected rock shelf.   O'Hearn nodded slowly, looking carefully at Ray's face.

"We were up online with you on the slope, so the mortars missed us too.   But I saw Cooley get killed and your men starting to slide down the hill.   You turned them around, I know you did."   He said this as a statement of fact.   "The gunners were on you guys like flies on shit because you were so close, so we took advantage of that and charged our piece of the ridge.   Third Squad was pretty tore up with the mortars and MGs down below us, but some of those guys survived and followed us up instead of you.   Six or seven of us got up in the trench after we used grenades, but there was a lot of Jap infantry between us and you.   They chewed us up good.   I thought we were goners, but then you charged the ridge with grenades and damned if that BAR gunner of yours got up there on top, where everybody could see him clear as you please, putting fire down the trench so damned effective the Japs were sending

132

everybody your way." O'Hearn grinned before glancing around the strongpoint, nodding to himself.

"Too bad he got it. Of course, if the Navy flyboys hadn't of shot the shit out of this fuckin place we'd all be dead, look at all the damned MGs. They would have cleaned our clocks for sure."

Between the two squads O'Hearn and Craymer determined they had five effectives and six wounded, most seriously and some critically, in the trench. O'Hearn didn't know for sure whether or not the Second Platoon managed to take their section of the ridgeline or not, but they could all hear continued rifle and machine gun fire to their right, to the north. Neither of them had a radio. They did not know if there were other Japanese troops south of them in the ridge as it curved to the extreme left. They also didn't know if the 17th Infantry had been successful in their bid to take on the northern section of the ridge.

"We don't know *shit*," declared O'Hearn in exasperation. "If Bowles ain't dead, he *must have* seen our squads take these positions. If he did, he's been talking to the skipper and hopefully Third Platoon is coming up to reinforce us. If he didn't..." O'Hearn smiled conspiratorially, "we're gonna have a hell of a fight on our hands!"

O'Hearn didn't want to risk any men climbing back down from the ridgeline to try to contact Lieutenant Bowles. He felt the best course of action was to stay put where they were because of their wounded, and let Bowles come to them. O'Hearn made Ray an acting sergeant on the spot and gave him Carter, the BAR man to shore up the south end of the ridge.

"I do need," O'Hearn said carefully, "you to recon as far as you can to the south to confirm there are no Japs holding up in that direction, clear? It looks to me we're in good shape between our two positions, and the most likely direction of any counterattack will be from the north, on my position. Although I don't even know where the Jap mortar positions are to our west, supposedly on the opposite slope and supposedly knocked out by the Navy flyboys. Haven't heard from them in an hour. So if Bowles or the Third Platoon or the goddamn 7th Calvalry ever fuckin gets up here and joins you first, send them fuckers on to me!"

As O'Hearn spoke Ray remembered the concerted attack from the south ridgeline that resulted in Manny getting bayoneted. *Were they it?* The snowstorm lifted slightly for the next half an hour, so Ray and Private Carter quickly went back down the trench to where Manny, Smit and Wallace were. Manny had passed out but still had a pulse. Wallace moaned feebly but seemed more alert than before. Smit was frightened but alert, not at all pleased when Ray announced Smit would be left alone with the wounded men again as Ray and Carter checked the trench to the south for any sign of other Japanese.

Before they started their reconnoiter Ray quickly checked their combat packs for blankets for the wounded men. Both Smit and Wallace had theirs, so Ray pulled them out to wrap around Manny and Wallace. He was sick at heart to look at Manny, as his face was pale white from loss of blood. Ray didn't expect him to survive more than an hour or two longer. Smit and Ray moved Manny closer to Wallace as Carter provided security, snuggling the two injured men as close together as possible before rigging a temporary wind and snow break over their faces. Wallace was breathing very shallowly and kept his eyes closed now, but Ray was encouraged with his decent pulse. Smit huddled close to the wounded men, saying nothing when Ray reported every Jap he had seen between their position and Second Squad was dead.

Ray was almost dead on his feet from fatigue, the shrapnel wounds in his shoulder and thighs throbbing dully again. He found he could not lift his left arm much higher than his waist now, making him question if he would be able to lift his rifle to shoot. So as not to alarm Carter, Ray stopped and made as if he were examining around the next corner, keeping his M1 low and supporting the fore stock with his left hand. He couldn't lift his rifle much beyond his waist, so he kept it there, pivoting the muzzle in the direction he was ready to shoot. His little charade didn't work as Carter picked up pretty quickly Ray was in bad shape. He stepped around and signaled to Ray he would take over point, which Ray gratefully let him do. They had not gone 50 feet when Ray heard a sharp whistle behind him to the north. Turning abruptly around, they were surprised to see Lieutenant Bowles up on the edge of the trench 20 feet away, waving them to his position with his .45 pistol. Bowles, suddenly realizing what a target he was, shrunk down onto his haunches before jumping into the trench, dropping out of sight.

Bowles was quickly joined by five other men crawling up over the edge of the trench, each looking in and hesitating before dropping down, wide-eyed and fearful. Ray recognized them as all from Third Squad, noting every single one of them was wounded, including Bowles, who had a nasty looking shrapnel wound, untreated and bleeding on his left hand, and a blood-soaked compress on his neck. Despite the obvious pain from his wounds, Bowles cracked a slight smile towards Ray and like the earlier meeting with Staff Sergeant O'Hearn, Ray sensed a new-found respect in Bowle's eyes.

"Where are the Japs?" Bowles demanded immediately. Ray told him as briefly as he could the tactical situation in the trench between

134

their current position and O'Hearn and the Second Squad.   Bowles seemed particularly distressed when he heard there were less than five combat effectives, including the two men in front of him, from the platoon stretched out over maybe 75 yards of trench.   As Ray finished his report he noticed one of the five men with Bowles had a radio-telephone and a cable reel.

"We don't have a radio, sir, I lost mine when we got mortared."

Bowles nodded towards the radio the man was carrying, "I know, we picked it up."   He grew silent for a moment, apparently digesting Ray's information.   He squatted down in the trench, glancing at his watch before turning his attention to Ray.

"The skipper sent Third Platoon up to provide litter bearers so we could get the wounded, both ours and the guys left by the 17th Infantry, down this fuckin slope.   But they got caught in the mortar barrage too, and Lieutenant Wiemar and his platoon sergeant got killed. Technically, I have command of both platoons right now, what's left of them.   Weapons Platoon hasn't been able to be much good for us on this slope, so the skipper's using them for litter bearers too, but both weapons and third are sending up a squad to reinforce us within the next hour.   So we got 11 men right now to hold this end of the ridge."   Ray was not used to having Lieutenant Bowles explain his strategy or tactical situation to him, so he shifted around uncomfortably.

"What about getting our wounded out, Lieutenant?"   He asked. Bowles shook his head slowly.

"I think between the three platoons we have two medics left, and they are pretty busy down there, the mortars and the MGs tore em up pretty good.   Once we get some reinforcements and we can secure this fuckin place, we can get our wounded out."   Ray thought of Manny, knowing it probably wouldn't matter anyway.   Wallace might make it another day.   Bowles still hadn't dismissed him, so Ray stood up on his own.   Bowles looked up at him, then signaled him to come back down, closer.

"I'm going to give you two men to back you up while you check out the trench line to the south," he said thoughtfully.   "I don't think it goes on much further, and I just don't see why the Japs would have anybody much beyond this point.   Look around, not even a revetment for an MG.   But we need to be sure."   Bowles pointed to two of the men with him, signaling with his hands for them to join Ray and Carter.

"By the way, Craymer," Bowles added, again with a slight smile, his eyes respectful.   "You're an acting sergeant now.   I saw the whole thing—Cooley getting it, you turning the Squad around and taking the ridge with the grenades.   It was pretty impressive.   O'Hearn made his assault because your squad was so aggressive the Japs were pouring it all down on you. Skipper wanted to know who made the ridgeline assault and I told him."

Ray didn't tell Bowles O'Hearn had already made him an acting sergeant, choosing instead at that moment to glance down at his feet. Bowles reached forward, patting Ray affectionately on the shoulder before standing up.

"I'm going to join up with O'Hearn and I want you to do the same as soon as you clear this ridge to the south, understood? You got enough men to carry the wounded."

"Yessir." Ray slowly, painfully got to his feet. Bowles watched him carefully, eyeing the way Ray was holding his rifle.

"You all right, Craymer? You look, well, pretty rough." That brought a round of snickers from everyone present, since every single one of them was wounded and hurting himself. But Ray, with his burnt fatigues from the close encounter with the Nambu, the blood-soaked field jacket from the dead boy from Second Squad and untold big and small shrapnel punctures from head to toe, did look *pretty rough*.

"I'm fine, sir," he stated flatly, clearly annoyed. Bowles smiled again nodding in dismissal, waving his small charge forward. He glanced back at Ray as his men moved out one after the other.

"Hey, Sergeant Craymer," he asked quietly, "who was that BAR man who stood up there on the top of the trench for like five minutes shootin the place up until some Jap killed him? You must have been right next to him."

"Drexel, sir, Private. My squad—er, Sergeant Cooley's squad."

"Your squad now, Sergeant Craymer. Drexel. Don't remember him very well, but I've never seen anything like it in my life. I'm going to write him up, everybody on the top of the slope could see him when the fog lifted. Just shooting mag after mag. I think he broke their back with that fire. Remarkable. And I'm going to write you up too, Sergeant!"

"Lieutenant?" Carter, emboldened by Lieutenant Bowles friendly chatter, leaned the butt of his heavy BAR on his boot. Bowles, who had turned around to start up the trench, carbine at the ready, stopped abruptly to look over his shoulder. He stared first at Ray then at Carter, who like a school kid, lifted his hand to acknowledge he had asked the question.

"Yes, soldier?"

"Sir," asked Carter, now feeling embarrassed, "what is the name of this place?"

"You mean, Attu Island?" Asked Bowles, irritably.

"Nossir, I mean right here, this place—this mountain." Bowles turned to look at all the men present.

"Fish Hook. Fish Hook Ridge." It sounded unimpressive to Ray, something to do with fishing or Eskimos or something like that. Carter looked puzzled with the name, saying nothing.

"This might be the last big fight for the Japs on this island, so if we all survive this, we can tell our grandkids about the battle for Fish Hook Ridge. It's already cost King Company plenty."

Ray watched Bowles and the three soldiers cautiously disappear around the bend in the trench. He turned to find Carter and the two other soldiers watching him. Like Carter, the two soldiers had the buttplates of their rifles on their boots, as if they were at home at Fort Ord waiting for some trucks to take them to some maneuver exercise.

"Get them weapons up!" He barked irritably, "there can be a hundred Japs around the next corner for all we know!" All three of them lifted their weapons to the ready, realizing this big guy who the lieutenant seemed to like so much really did look a little rough around the edges, a little on the crazy side, with a blood soaked uniform and all those puncture holes. Ray took the point this time, exploring the ridgeline to the south for another 150 yards until there was nowhere to go. The trench itself only extended about 50 yards in that direction before the natural crevice filled with fractured rock, the ridgeline curving around the edge of the bowl to peter out into steep drop offs.

An hour later Ray rejoined Lieutenant Bowles and Staff Sergeant O'Hearn about one quarter of the way around the ridgeline bowl in a small defensive perimeter. There was no sign of the reinforcements from Third and Weapons Platoons. Second Platoon had also assaulted and successfully overran a portion the trench farther north on the ridge according to Captain Stinson, their CO down at the base of the slope. Unfortunately, there had been no radio contact with them since the assault. Sporadic firefights were occurring about 100 yards up the trench, assumed to be Second Platoon.

Nothing could be seen. The snow limited visibility to about 50 feet if the wind wasn't gusting. Even farther around the bowl, north on the ridgeline, the 17th Infantry were noisily but distantly engaged. No one knew for certain if they held their end of the ridgeline or not, but it really wasn't a King Company concern—yet. Bowles believed there were pockets of Japanese infantry between their defensive perimeter and Second Platoon, unwilling to commit men for a probing patrol until they received the promised reinforcements from Third and Weapons Platoons. They had moved the six severely wounded men, including

137

Manny and Wallace up the trench to a covered Japanese bivouac area. O'Hearn's men had discovered this space earlier, strangely abandoned. The soldiers found bedding, extra blankets and even some Japanese rations. Nobody wanted to sample the rations fearing they were poisoned, but the blankets and bedding were used to make the wounded as comfortable as possible. Any spares were grabbed to wrap around the frozen shoulders of the few soldiers who could hold their rifles. It was very cold up here, with the snow a steady noise dampener.

The portion of the ridgeline Bowles decided to defend was a bit flatter and wider than normal, almost a bulge. The Japanese engineers utilized this naturally deep crevice to build the bivouac area. Then they channeled the defensive trench into a narrow slot to more easily protect the defenders with both cover and concealment. With his radio, Bowles requested 81mm mortars on the reverse slope facing west to probe by fire his one very exposed flank. The Japanese mortar crews were supposedly all in this direction but the unknown reverse slope could conceal just about anybody. So after a brief delay, the small band of defenders hunkered down as the 81s dropped two-dozen rounds following Bowles coordinates.

The 81 crews were deadly accurate so the men felt confident the rounds falling 50 to 100 yards away would stay out of the trench and their perimeter. Not a round of fire came back from the west after the barrage but Bowles had three of the men, including Ray Craymer and Carter with his BAR, dug in to watch in that direction. The sky grew dark again making Ray suspect it was drawing towards evening instead of morning. In his confused state he knew he was hallucinating some. He had lost track of time. His Elgin watch crystal was shattered by some of the action earlier in their assault up the slope, the dial fixed at 1130. He stared at it for a full minute before un-strapping it from his wrist. He didn't know what to do with it so he simply placed it in one of the large pockets of his field jacket. If the mortar barrage has occurred nearly at noon and it was now growing dark, did that mean they had been in the trench seven or eight hours? Ray shook his head slowly before adjusting the new helmet he was wearing, confiscated from one of the wounded men.

He simply could not say exactly when the company had started their way up the slope. He must have known at the time, but he was too beat and punched out to remember. It must have been morning, but the confusion now went all the way back to the time they had arrived on Red Beach. It all blurred together. The days were slightly brighter versions of the twilight evenings. The cold rain near the beach was replaced by the sleet and half snow across the muskeg. Then at some point they started up into the black, flinty straight-up mountains and snow was all there was.

They had two hot meals, both provided by 17th and 32nd Infantry cooks since the meal on the beach on their first day. By the end of the first week there were no rations for nearly two days because of the difficulty of getting supplies off the beach. Sleep, Ray could not remember when he had slept more than an hour or two in succession. Usually a few catnaps caught during a lull when the companies were held back. It happened day and night, once, twice, three times a day. Advance. Dig a fighting hole. Not that any of that mattered to the Army. As long as the 17th Infantry advanced, the 32nd Infantry coming across the top of Holtz Bay behind them moved up too.

When they stopped they dug in because the Japanese mortars and artillery shells would arrive the minute the sky parted enough for the observers on the slopes to radio in the coordinates. What amazed Ray, now two and half weeks since they had stepped out onto Attu, was his feet were still in remarkably good shape. They looked bad out of the boots, granted, with the puckered, flayed bleach-white aspect of skin too long immersed in water, but they didn't hurt too bad and he could still walk on them.

They were all issued the new leather boondockers, ill-fitting, stiff leather combat boots virtually useless as a cold weather boot either dry or wet, but especially when it was wet. They all got them wet on the very first day of the invasion to never be really dry again. King Company alone had lost 25 percent of the TO of manpower to "cold weather injuries"—frozen feet, frostbite, trench-foot, all men carried off to the beach as effectively gone as if they had arms and legs shot off. And there was no doubt in Ray's mind many of those men *would* have to have their limbs—usually hands, fingers, feet or toes—amputated. He saw them, the black, dead tissue, putrescent in full progress, the owners of the shriveled appendages writhing in agony.

In a certain small way Ray might even admit he wished he could join them, for no other reason other than the chance to get dry and warm. But there was no way he was willing to voluntarily give up a hand or a foot for the privilege, it was just too much of a price. It was not a Craymer trait to seek a way out of a situation, however challenging, if the situation was part of the job or the assignment. The irony of his willingness to risk having his *head* blown off running up the slope to silence the MGs in the trench was not lost to him either, although his muddled, confused state left him, he knew, with nothing more than *instincts*.

139

He tapped Carter on the shoulder to let him know he was going to slip back down the trench to check in on Manny and Wallace. Smit had chosen to huddle close to Lieutenant Bowles, ignoring Ray and Carter. The other man on guard to the west was a draftee named Kinderly or Kimberly, a man from the Third Squad Ray didn't know at all. Ray motioned to him to stay put, wiggling back from the edge of the trench like a man with wooden legs. What was clear to him was his body was shutting down. His legs seemed totally detached from his body. Cold, dead numb in places, yet with deep, pulsing pain up his thighs and all along his left shoulder. His only weapon at the moment was a .45 pistol in his right hand Lieutenant Bowles picked up from the dead platoon commander of Third Platoon. Earlier Bowles had simply shuffled over to Ray to ask for his rifle and bandoliers of ammunition. *It's a trade, man.* He gave Ray an M1 carbine, lighter than the Garand with a bandolier of 10 full 15-round magazines. A minute later Bowles returned with the holstered .45 and four extra magazines, laying them carefully beside Ray.

"I know you like that M1, but you can hardly lift the damn thing right now, so O'Hearn is switching with you, his choice." Ray gratefully took the carbine, buckling the .45 around his waist while shoving the extra magazines into his field jacket. His left arm hung limply down from his shoulder, although the injuries curled his forearm up so it rested unnaturally across his stomach. Staff Sergeant O'Hearn rigged a sling for the forearm after looping it over Ray's head, spending a few minutes to clean out the shoulder shrapnel wound as best he could. He noted, like Manny before him, there was a big piece of something in there but it wasn't going anywhere.

Ray kneeled down beside Manny, tucking the blankets around both him and Wallace, brushing the accumulated snow off their chests. Wallace seemed to be sleeping, with the other wounded lying so quietly Ray suspected a few of them were dead. Manny opened his eyes briefly to gaze blankly at Ray, then a slight hint of a grin crossed his lips with the recognition.

"Man, Cray, you don't look so good!"

"I know. I don't feel so hot, either. Anything I can get you?" Manny's eyes seem to clear, focusing suddenly on Ray. With his chalk white face drained of pink, Ray wondered for a second if Manny was going to die, right now, in front of him.

"Get me outta here," he gasped, turning his head slightly. "Hey, buddy, you took care of them Japs, man," Manny added, "you got em all, otherwise neither of us would still be here."

140

Ray snorted, too tired to respond.

"We'll get you out of here, Torre." Manny's eyes quickly lost their clarity, drifting off unfocused before closing as Ray spoke. Ray leaned in quickly, feeling for a pulse. It was still there, very weak. He felt helpless, strangely angry without being able to understand exactly why.

A bloodcurdling scream from behind spun him around and on his feet. Two grenades landed in the trench, one disappearing between two of the wounded men, the other literally three feet in front of Ray. Ray stepped forward, switching his pistol to his left hand as he swept the grenade up with his right, flinging it up and over the trench. It never went off.

The other one exploded with a *WHUMP* between Wallace and another wounded man, hurling both men up and over, the blossoming, protected blast punching Ray's back and head, knocking him over on his face. Otherwise unhurt, Ray struggled to his feet as a Japanese soldier, completely sheathed in white clothing, appeared at the top of the trench at a full sprint carrying a bayoneted rifle. He was a half of a second from launching airborne directly at Ray, as their eyes met. Ray, still clutching his .45 with his left hand, had the instinct to thumb the safety off and painfully raised the pistol just high enough, firing twice, to hit the soldier once in the stomach just as he leaped, the second shot hitting him in the groin area as he fell towards Ray.

Ray didn't have time to move out of the way, he could only shift to the left slightly, pivoting his body as the bayonet on the rifle flashed past his head. The momentum of the Japanese soldier kept his body hurtling right past Ray to crash directly into the cluster of wounded men. Their animal howls of pain and fear gripped Ray but he did not look back as two other Japanese soldiers bounded right up to the trench behind the first one. He saw the muzzle burst of one of the Arisakas and felt an instantaneous burning sensation at his throat. Ray switched his Colt to his right hand dropping both men before they reached the trench.

Carter was fumbling with a magazine to reload his BAR as another Japanese soldier jumped up on the parapet of the trench raising his short fighting sword. Ray heard furious fire from the right and before he could fire his pistol the sword wielder was cut down. Ray made it to the edge of the trench as three more Japanese soldiers appeared, heads coming up first as they ran up to the trench. Two were carrying rifles with attached bayonets with the third bumping his grenade on his helmet to prime it, before he threw it. Ray fired at the grenade thrower at the very instant the man's grenade exploded in his

141

hand in a flash of light, killing all three soldiers instantly. Ray felt the sting of shrapnel hitting his face and hand, hearing Carter scream with pain before slumping back. With only his single usable hand, Ray could not pick up Carter's BAR, so he shot three more Japanese soldiers with his pistol before the slide locked to the rear, the magazine empty.

He tucked the pistol under his left arm as he reached in his pocket for a new magazine with his right hand. A Japanese soldier appeared out of nowhere from the trench to Ray's left. This one was an NCO or an officer with an infantry fighting sword. He stopped, miraculously, a few feet from Ray recognizing Ray was wounded in one arm and had an empty pistol. Unlike the other Japanese, this officer was dressed in a light brown tunic, his dark eyes shining for just a moment. Ray spun to face him as the officer changed his grip on his sword, bringing it back and across in an elegant, sweeping motion as the brilliant blade was succinctly laid level. Caught with an empty gun, Ray froze.

CHAPTER 17

1700 Hours, May 27, 1943, D-Day Plus 16, Fish Hook Ridge

It was one of those moments of crystal clarity. Ray's brain seemed to see everything. His eyes were instantly drawn down to his right hand where he saw the wooden handle of the GI entrenching shovel for the first time. Propped straight up a foot in front of him when Carter had dropped it. He sensed the Japanese officer watching him as he took his hand out of his pocket to lean forward enough to grab the handle, swinging it up in one motion just as the Japanese officer stepped in himself, slashing the sword tip towards Ray's mid-section.

The sword collided with the shovel, deflecting the sword blade just enough. The spade shovel had a feature so the blade could be folded 90 degrees to turn it into a sort of pick axe, and the shovel Ray grabbed was folded, saving Ray's life momentarily. The angle of the folded blade had caught the leading edge of the Tanto sword blade in the elbow, pulling the blade up and away from Ray. The Japanese officer grunted heavily in surprise, deftly withdrawing the sword instantly as he stepped back, adjusting his fighting stance for a follow-up direct thrust. The man grinned at Ray as he pivoted his body to close the space between them. Ray was off balance, his right side open with the shovel now up over his head, and there was no way he was going to be able to deflect a direct thrust in time. Instinctively he knew his only option was to keep his momentum going in the opposite direction, *to run*.

With his right foot leading, Ray rolled forward to the left trying to hoof it down the trench as far from the sword as he could to build space. His leaden, numb-heavy legs betrayed him, turning his short escape into no more than a comical shuffle. He could hear the Japanese officer growling right behind him. In the split second he had facing to the north end of the defensive trench, he was imprinted with the image of other Japanese soldiers climbing up and into the trench, battling hand to hand with the remaining King Company defenders. There was nowhere to go. Ray spun around again, expecting to be instantly impaled by the sword. Instead he found the Japanese officer three feet behind him motionless, the sword gripped with both hands high over his head. *The man was waiting for him to turn around!*

For what seemed an eternity but only a fraction of a second, the two men stared at one another. Ray was so weak he could not say for certain how he felt. He had lost. He was about to die. The fear gripping his heart may have pumped an extra ounce of adrenaline in his veins, he couldn't say. All he knew was the Japanese officer swung the blade down, a finishing stroke designed to cleave a man's head in half. The noise of the blade passing as he side-stepped to the right, barely missing the blow, he would never forget, but he did side-step instinctively, saving himself.

His opponent recovered instantly as if expecting the maneuver, transitioning the downward stroke smoothly into a short, upward slash with a twist of his upper body and wrists. The blade flashed, the tip slicing deeply into Ray's left knee and thigh, carving down straight to the bone. Ray gasped in pain, suddenly very afraid, knowing the man was too quick and skilled to avoid again. As the Japanese officer leaned forward to make his upward slash he was slightly off balance, his upper body low and exposed. Ray stepped in with his right foot, clumsily swinging down the folded shovel with all of his remaining strength. The officer writhed his body like a cat, swinging the blade under his arm to thrust upward into Ray's exposed abdomen as the shovel swung down, deflecting off the officer's elbow.

The man grunted in shocked pain, hesitating for a moment as Ray followed the momentum of his deflected blow downward, then twisting his wrist to sweep the shovel tip back up with all the force he could muster with his right arm. The pointed, semi-sharp blade swept back to sink itself into the man's open jaw with a distinct *CHUCK*. Ray released the shovel instantly as it buried itself solidly, the body now pure dead weight falling straight down, the man gagging and groaning, his hands clutching at his face.

Ray dropped to his knees, gasping for air, totally drained of strength. He turned to watch the Japanese officer, his hands gripping the shovel as he fell back, gargle noisily in his own blood as he fought to pull the shovel out of his face. Ray, still on his knees, stumbled forward while drawing his bayonet from his sheath. With both hands he slammed the bayonet tip down into the breastbone of the Japanese. Seconds from passing out, Ray heard the heavy *THUMP THUMP THUMP THUMP* of a .30 caliber machine gun, now confused knowing Weapons Company hadn't come up the slope with machine guns because it was too steep. Yellow-red tracers were slowly arcing right above him, matching the sound of the machine gun, his dulled brain not quite making the connection. As he fell forward in unconsciousness, he had a short image of what looked like the profile of a Browning air-cooled on a tripod on the top of the trench, it's muzzle spewing a long flame up over his head. *Where did that come from?*

When Ray opened his eyes it seemed very, very dark. He felt cold and numb. When he moved his hand the world suddenly became light again as something was lifted from his face. A dark, furry object drifted into his vision, blocking the light again. As he focused his eyes he realized he was looking at Staff Sergeant's O'Hearn's thick, black beard. O'Hearn stared at him with curiousity.

"How you feeling, Craymer?" Ray tried to speak but something was wrapped tightly around his throat. It hurt. He grunted something, confused when O'Hearn moved away. Another bearded fellow, a youth Ray recognized as one of the company medics, leaned in close to place a couple of cold fingers on one side of his neck, next to a large bandage.

"I ain't *dead*," Ray tried to say, but it came out as a groan. The medic ignored him, talking quietly to someone out of Ray's line of sight. Whatever warmth he had was suddenly drawn away, cold air exposing his chest. The medic leaned in close again, pulling at Ray's clothing.

"He's lost a lot of blood. I can't do much about that, sir, I've bound up the big stuff, but he's full of shrap, with a couple of stab wounds and a bullet hole in the neck. I was going to give him another syrette of morphine, but his pulse is pretty low. I'll wait a bit. We need to get him and the rest of these fellas out of here as quickly as we can."

He could hear more low voices as his tunnel vision was blocked again, this time with Lieutenant Bowles and Staff Sergeant O'Hearn right behind him.

"You're going to have to spend another night with us, Sergeant Craymer," drawled Bowles, his neck now wrapped with two compress bandages, one on each side of his neck. His face was so dirty the sudden appearance of white teeth fracturing his face as he smiled was almost comical, except no one was laughing. His disjointed thoughts and body didn't seem to be in concert at all.

"As you might have guessed, third and weapons kind of saved our asses," Bowles continued drolly, "especially when they brought up the Browning. Broke the attack, and the Japs ran off." Bowles looked down at Ray sympathetically, glanced towards his arm.

"We kind of all had our hands full." He sniffed the air before returned his attention back to Ray. "I think I turned around just in time to watch you hack that fuckin Jap captain's head nearly clean off! I never would have thought you could win a fight against a Samurai sword with an E-tool, that's for sure. You proved that wrong!" Bowles grinned as others outside of Ray's vision snickered.

145

"Who's left, sir?" Ray finally croaked out. He had to think hard for a second to realize he had spoken. It didn't sound like him at all. It felt like he was lying next to somebody else. Bowles stared at him as if he misunderstood, the rubbed his face.

"Left? Well, hell, there's O'Hearn and me, Smit from your squad, a couple guys from Second Squad still standing. Our wounded took a beatin when a Jap grenade landed in with them."

Ray lifted his head slightly to stare at Bowles and then O'Hearn. He remembered the grenade landing behind him in the trench where the wounded were. He remembered the cries of pain from them just before he had to face the Jap with the bayonet. O'Hearn leaned in closer. "Torre is still alive from your Squad. Wallace got it, so did two others from Second Squad, Kimberly and Carter. A good platoon sergeant that always remembered names, O'Hearn recited a few more names but Ray wasn't listening. Manny is still with us. Manny, Smit and himself were pretty much all that was left of the old First Squad. I have to talk to Dan about that. Dan will know what to do.

He passed out again, the light turning off his vision as quickly and as distinctly as flipping a switch. He woke up once, or rather he thought he woke up, hearing the mournful horn of a distant freight train. It was a comforting sound, the comfort of home, the warmth and the surrounds of people who love and care for you. His brain wrapped around the sound for a moment or two, then released it to bring the dark blanket of peace and calm once again.

146

CHAPTER 18

0600 Hours, May 12, 1943, D-Day Plus 1, Buchanan Ridge

Captain Williamson had a small patrol waiting at the foot of the rock steps joining Brannon and Buchanan Ridges. Without their assistance, Orin Craymer was certain his recon patrol would not have been able to make it to the Scout Battalion bivouac before sunrise. Corporal Johnson was delirious with pain and difficult to guide or support. He was trying to help, but his wound had swollen part of his face to the point he was unrecognizable, his eyes swollen shut with his skin tight as a drum. Every jarring step created agony. They lowered him down as best they could on the big drop steps, his nearly dead weight taxing exhausted muscles to the limit. All three of them were large men, but the straight down drops and icy rock faces made Johnson's size a formidable burden. Once the waiting patrol took over Johnson's transport, Orin and Travis moved as quickly as they could to get back to the battalion to report.

Captain Williamson and Ed Ridgeway devoured the captured documents Orin picked up, especially the troop disposition maps and the Attu engineering map from Yoshi Nakagawa detailing every defensive construction site. The maps provided by U.S. Army intelligence for the invasion had no dope on the terrain of the front side of the slope and valley they were going to assault, the space shown as blank and noted with "unknown" in block letters. The Japanese maps in front of them had detailed gradient and height information. The Scout Battalion was ready to move, with all the tents made from shelter halves dismantled and discarded because of their weight. Williamson explained there would be no further opportunity for sleep in the next 24 to 36 hours. The scouts were spread out on the back slope, well concealed. Orin's patrol report was met with almost disbelief even from Ed Ridgeway, especially as Orin narrated their actions once he and Johnson got inside the sleeping quarters of the OP. It started to dawn on Orin how bold the patrol's mission really was, and how lucky they were to get the information they had and to all return.

Williamson ordered a medic to attend to Orin's bitten hand, now virtually useless with most of the fingers too swollen to bend, as Orin made his report. Corporal Johnson was carried in by the second patrol and made as comfortable as possible, but evacuation was out of the question. The battalion's only route out was down the pass to the east, right through a concentration of Japanese defensive positions waiting to ambush the 17th and 32nd Infantry coming from the north out of Red Beach. Williamson's command post had about the only large level space on the back slope so Johnson was brought there. They all had to suffer through Johnson's cries and whimpering until one of the other medics injected him with morphine before lancing and draining the huge swollen abscess under his eye.

All of them looked away as two other soldiers held Johnson down as the procedure was performed. It was a ghastly wound, but the draining had one enormous consequence for Johnson. It loosened the tissue around the four-inch chunk so much the wooden projectile became dislodged, a significant portion of it sticking out from Johnson's face. The medic grasped the wooden sliver with a hemostat and simply tugged firmly. The huge sliver, with only slight resistance, slowly slipped out of his face. Everyone was relieved, especially Johnson.

Orin sat down and gratefully accepted a blanket around his shoulders. The makeshift CP, a level shelf of approximately 10 by 15 feet, was protected from the wind and snow with several canvas shelter halves snapped together. The canvas whipped around noisily in the wind, but the shelter offered a respite of warmth and stillness. Williamson's exec handed Orin a ration tin, already opened, so Orin wolfed it down, cold. He had no idea what it was. He watched Williamson and Ridgeway shift their attention back and forth to various documents, referring to both the area map Orin had plucked from the OP and the engineering site map from the young Japanese officer Orin had shot. Williamson was noting the location and caliber of all of the defensive gun positions once Ridgeway translated the symbols and character descriptions.

"Remarkable—absolutely remarkable!" Williamson stated repeatedly. Both he and Ridgeway were preparing a coded report for the communication B-24 they hoped would be up and within range. Williamson's radioman stepped inside to report the B-24 was on station and had responded to his contact call, so Williamson immediately took the walkie-talkie and began transmitting his coded report. Ed Ridgeway put the documents down for a moment to peer over at Orin who had his eyes closed. Orin sensed someone staring at him, prompting his leaden eyelids to open.

"I can't tell you, Orin, how valuable these documents are to the people overseeing this invasion." Ridgeway held up the engineering site map and pointed to a location too far away for Orin to recognize. "This map alone confirms there are facilities and an infrastructure designed to support around *3,000* men—not even close to our latest outside estimate of say, 1,500 two days ago. The Japs have gone almost completely underground on Attu, and even though we had only so many so-so days for decent aerial recon photos, they fooled us completely on the size of the garrison. My photo specialists figured the Japs were camouflaging their facilities very well, and it was a pure guess on their part of there being any OPs on Buchanan Ridge. They spotted what they felt were signs of man-made structures and concluded they had operational OPs on some of the eastern ridges bordering Holtz Bay, but Buchanan was a stretch to me. You sir," Ridgeway smiled, "confirmed it in spades and came up with *all of this!*"

As Orin had suspected when he had examined the detailed site map, the young Japanese officer he had shot was an engineer. Ridgeway confirmed this and even noted the youth's name—*Nakagawa*, identified on the map. Ridgeway also asked him a lot of questions regarding the condition of the soldiers in the OP, their general health, weapons, communication tools, what their uniforms looked like, and the layout and construction of the OP. Ridgeway took no notes but listened very attentively, and Orin already knew Ed Ridgeway had an incredible memory. He asked Orin twice if he had taken anything *else* personal from the Japanese officer—other letters, pictures, talismans, watches or rings—anything. When Orin reported the boy had nothing in his pockets except the map, the one letter, the military pay and ID documents and the Emperor's Rescript, Ridgeway seemed genuinely disappointed.

Orin was annoyed at first because he sensed somehow Ed thought the mission was a failure, as if Orin should have figured out a way to bring the boy back down the ridge as a prisoner. *What the hell good was the boy going to be with a hole in his head like that?*

"We can draw an awful lot from what you pulled out of that officer's pockets," Ed added hurriedly, as if to placate Orin's feelings. "An awful lot. This uh—Lieutenant Nakagawa," he referred to both the letter and the identity card now, "is not from the Japanese prefecture most of the troops here are from. So he was a last-minute transfer, a replacement. He's from Kochi, a prefecture on the island of Shikoku, one of the smaller southern islands pretty much out of the way. His parents are farmers, probably prosperous since he has an excellent education as an engineer. He went to one of the best schools in Japan. His mother hopes he is doing something useful not only for the war effort, but for his continuing growth as an engineer. Only a mother would say something like that!" Ridgeway laughed as he folded the

149

letter neatly back into the whisper thin envelope. Orin thought briefly of the frail boy he had shot before he pushed it out of his head.

"He was a replacement for some guy who got sick and just got here a few weeks ago," Ed continued, looking carefully at Yoshi Nakawawa's identity card and paybook, "and just found himself at the luck of the draw. Poor bastard. His mother was hoping, based on the news the folks at home were getting from Mr. Tojo, her son would be coming home soon after the great victory. Home, and a good job near home. Most of the troops from the Imperial Northern Army are from prefectures on the Island of Hokkaido. That's how the Japs build unit cohesion, they recruit from prefectures and form combat units among young men who all know each other. It's a lot harder to run away when you are surrounded with guys who know you from back home. He must be complaining of being lonely and not knowing anybody. The way his mother goes on and on worrying about whether he was getting enough rest or enough to eat, you can figure he wasn't too far from the nest when he joined the Army." Ridgeway realized he was losing his audience to sleep, so he shut up and began carefully packing the documents away. He was surprised when Orin opened his eyes again and pointed at the Emperor's Rescript.

"What's the deal with the flower pamphlet?" Orin asked. Ridgeway grinned and held up the book, turning it around carefully.

"This is no "flower" pamphlet, Lieutenant," he said firmly, mostly for Captain Williamson's ear. "This is the code these guys live and die by. This *must be* in their possession at all times because the words in it are from the Emperor—god to them.   We are just beginning to understand this—spirit—this emphasis on individual strength that goes beyond, well, beyond what is visible."

"You mean, like religion?" Asked Orin. Ed Ridgeway puckered his lips thoughtfully, looking at the cover of the pamphlet.

"Well, Lieutenant, yes and no. Because they are governed by a living god, the Japanese can be led to believe they are different from other peoples—whether they be other orientals, Europeans, black or brown people or especially mutts like us Americans. This Imperial decree explains to the Jap soldier he is different, and difference is defined in his unique spirit. The spirit is embodied in the perfection of the cherry blossom, the very first flower to bud in the spring in Japan. It is a perfect flower just for a short while, then is withers and dies. They believe they can go farther, fight harder and do it with less because they have this unique spirit. If you seek perfection, you will find it."

"I guess, Captain Ridgeway," Orin said wearily,   "I'm not philosophical enough for this. I don't get it.   All I know is I had that

150

boy cold and he drew his weapon anyway and I had to shoot him. Don't make much sense to me." Ridgeway looked at Orin levelly before nodding.

"That's it exactly, Orin," he said, forgetting the formality, "we don't understand each other at all."

Williamson listened to this conversation with half an ear, watching Orin's in genuine respect and flat-out amazement. Once he received the confirmation of his report from the communication B-24 and a message in return, he ended the transmission. There was no separate report from Ed Ridgeway this time. Williamson had the message from command decoded and ordered a final Officer's Call, this time with the five additional officers from the Recon Troop.

The officers arrived in minutes. When Orin started to get to his feet, Williamson waved him down.

"Take the load off, Lieutenant, you earned it! It's about all the rest you're going to get!" Williamson silently handed out the two maps Orin had acquired, the other officers hovering around them hungrily. A few whistles were heard, but before they began to talk about it, Williamson caught their attention.

"Lieutenant Craymer and a small patrol spent most of the night getting up and down that ridge," he motioned towards Buchanan Ridge, "and confirmed a suspected hilltop OP for us. In the process we asked for either a prisoner or information. Unfortunately the Japs weren't interested in being prisoners." Some of the officers snickered as Williamson smiled and pointed towards Orin, "so they had to shoot a couple of em, but they did not come away empty handed!" Williamson retrieved the engineering site map from one of the young officers and with his usual dramatic flair, held the map up so all of them could see it, pointing his finger at a location.

"Gentlemen, we know the location of each defensive gun position and the probable location of every troop concentration on this island. Command has this information now. Not to mention we know the terrain we are facing on the front side of this ridge. Captain Ridgeway and I have determined there are at least *3,000* Japs on Attu, mostly on the eastern side of Holtz Bay, the ridgelines up there and Chichagof Bay. They are also all up and down the ridgelines on the approaches to the east towards Massacre Bay. The 17th and 32nd Infantry coming across *here*, at Red Beach, are heading south to the top of Holtz Bay and the Sarana Valley. My latest update is they are encountering heavy resistance from Red Beach but will attempt to coordinate an attack tomorrow the same time we arrive at the bottom of this pass in front of us. The other battalions of the 17th and 32nd Infantry Regiments, with

151

the 4th Infantry joining soon from Adak, are coming up from the southeast through Massacre Valley.

"We're going to come in from the backdoor, down through this long steep slope on the backside of Brannon Ridge to attack any Jap units getting ready to ambush our guys coming from Red Beach. It's a lot steeper than we anticipated, but there is a flip side to that to our advantage. As you can see from this site map, the Japs have defensive positions down lower in this chute in front of us, but not up high, thank God!"

Orin listened to Williamson with as much attention as he could muster, which was not a lot. Now that he was sitting down with a warm blanket around him, had a bite to eat and his injured hand attended to, his enormous fatigue weighed heavily on his ability to pay attention.

"Unfortunately," Williamson added soberly, "with this little foray up in the mountain to get this information the Japs *are* aware of our presence now. They don't expect us in force, they have no idea of our size. I don't know why this hilltop OP we raided didn't spot us coming in, but this weather might have something to do with it. It hampers their visibility as much as it does ours. We're going to be even more visible once we cross this open gorge. We have no time to lose, and we will not stop moving until we hook up with the 17th and 32nd coming from Red Beach. If nothing else, we will divert significant Jap resources from attacking the landing force once they are aware of our presence, and that, gentlemen, will be within the hour!"

Orin listened to the reports from the other officers, realizing the difficulty the battalion had during the night in keeping the troops from freezing to death, let alone keep them dry. With the frozen temperatures, wet clothing and biting wind, the tent shelters had offered some protection. The lone medical officer, a first lieutenant, confirmed to Williamson's consternation nearly 25 percent of the battalion was suffering from the initial stages of frostbite for their hands and feet. Here up on the ridge where the snow was three to four feet thick on top of solid ice and rock and the men had been unable to move more than a few feet all night, the percentage was probably higher, he said, as some of the men didn't realize what was happening to them.

"Then we need to get down off this goddamn ridge and into warmer terrain!" Williamson retorted. "Part of the problem is being stuck up here and not being able to move. That is going to change, because once we start down this front side the only thing we'll see that could stop us will be Japs. We are going to fight our way out of this, gentlemen!"

152

The Scout Battalion, now numbering over 400 with the addition of the Recon Troop from the *USS Kane*, shuffled around in position as the Scout Companies reorganized in the assault order Williamson requested. The snow had lifted slightly to be replaced by wet fog blown *upslope* from the front side of the ridgeline they were preparing to go down. Williamson and all of the battalion officers were met with the strange, alien sensation of damp, warm fog hurtling up the slope as they peeked their heads over the ridge. Binoculars were useless in minutes because the lenses became wet and misted over. It didn't really matter, you couldn't see more than 100 yards right now anyway. All of the officers wiped the water off their faces, looking at one another with dismay and growing concern when they actually examined the terrain directly below them. All they could see was what appeared to be the smooth sides of a bowl, nearly as steep as the walls of a concrete dam, totally white and featureless.

"According to the Jap map this is the steepest part, about 40 degrees for about a quarter of a mile, then it levels up some," Williamson offered. If it was supposed to comfort his officers, it didn't work. "Any of you snow ski?" He added. "It's been snowing non-stop the whole time we've been up here, so most of the slope is fairly new snow, maybe not so slick and hard as it looks."

There was no other route available to them, so Williamson decided to let a small group try out the slope while all of the battalion officers watched. Despite his request, Williamson would not let Orin lead his platoon down first, choosing instead a single squad from a platoon from the Recon Troop. The 10 man squad crawled over the top of ridge all at once, their squad leader acknowledging Williamson's admonishment to "stay close to the slope, use the butts of your rifles to slow down your descent, and use the heels of your boots at an angle to the slope like you were on a sand hill. Don't go straight down, zig zag across!" All 10 men got over the side and were standing together 20 feet below the observing officers. The squad hesitated as the leader started down, his boots sinking a foot into deep snow with each step. The men stayed close together, following the leader, moving slowly to the right for about 30 feet before the squad leader turned to the left, starting his next traverse. After nearly 10 minutes the men were only about 150 feet below them. From the ridge the slope appeared to be almost straight down.

The squad leader steepened his next traverse and almost immediately slipped. He fell sideways, his boots finding no traction. His cry, clear as a bell, was instantly lost as he dropped unrestrained, falling head over heels straight down the bowl until he disappeared from sight in the fog. The assistant squad leader turned his shoulder in alarm to stare, open-mouthed up the slope to Williamson and the other officers. Williamson simply lifted his arm high over his head, jabbing his fingers straight down the slope—the message was clear—get going, down the slope and catch up with your squad leader!

The assistant squad leader, his rifle butt now buried in the snow on the slope as a brake, started down, infinitely cautious. Despite their slow pace, a second man lost his footing, crying out, as the soldier below him instinctively reached out trying to stop his descent. Both men careened down the slope, one on his back feet first carrying his rifle away from his body, the second on his face, head down before something forced his body to tumble like a ball until he too disappeared from sight. Their screams could be heard only for a second or two before their presence was totally blotted out by the whiteness below.

The rest of the squad stopped, frozen. One by one, following the motion of the assistant squad leader, they squatted down in the snow. It was obvious they were not going anywhere at this moment, none of them looking up towards the observing officers for guidance, clearly afraid to move in any direction.

"SHIT!" Williamson barked in anger and frustration. "This is going to be harder than I thought." He wiped the water droplets off his face with the sleeve of his field jacket before turning to stare at the pensive faces of his officers. Orin, trying to get used to holding his Thompson submachine gun in his left hand and supporting the fore stock with his gauze-wrapped right, was too exhausted to be overly concerned. He did realize, after listening to the medical officer talk earlier about the cold injuries and the real risk of frostbite for all of them, that his feet were completely numb in his leather boots. He was concerned about that. His feet were wet all day yesterday; then freezing cold through the night, even as they climbed up the ridge. There was no feeling in them at all right now. He could hardly control their placement in level snow, let alone try to negotiate and use his heels to traverse the snow and ice on the steep slope in front of them. He wouldn't be able to walk down the slope very far before he joined those other men who had fallen. It was Ed Ridgeway who seemed to voice what maybe all of them were thinking.

"Well, I know my feet are frozen solid and I would love getting off this ridge any old way I can. I'll probably fall all the way down sliding on my ass. At least we know there are no Japs for a couple of miles or so down this raceway!" Williamson stared hard at Ridgeway for a few seconds, almost with open hostility, but Ridgeway didn't appear to notice. Maybe he meant to be humorous. Williamson was

dead serious.   Williamson's frown softened, his eyes not leaving
Ridgeway.

"You might have something there, Captain Ridgeway."   He
peered down the slope one more time before making his decision.   He
turned to his company commanders.

"I know we dumped the shelter halves and stuffed them
somewhere, but have two men from each squad go back and get one for
each man until there aren't anymore.   If this works, we'll try it with
three men since we don't have enough shelter halves to go around.
We'll rig them together, two at a time, to make kind of a sled.   What do
you think?   I think if the men slide down together on their backs, they'll
slide a little slower and the combined weight will keep them from
tumbling all over the place.   It's worth a try! Make sure the men hold
onto their weapons no matter what, and keep the snow out of the actions.
They might need them as soon as they get down to the bottom of this—
ski slope!   Same order of march, Recon Troop down first.   Then my
old Scout Company.   Then Weapons.   Establish a defensive perimeter
once all the men are down and stopped.   The first known Jap positions
are approximately two and a half miles down this gorge.   Don't slide
that far!"

Williamson cast a sidelong glance at Ridgeway, who was still
looking down at the slope.   "Might as well have some fun, eh,
Ridgeway?"

An observer of the Scout Battalion at some distance might decide
the men were having fun.   They weren't.   Williamson tried to make the
descent as systematic as possible, bringing the men up to the ridge two
and three at a time at first, having them walk down to the first staging
area about 20 feet below the rim of the ridge.   They laid down on their
shelter halves in the growing groove of the snow chute like a bride and
groom, side by side, their weapons tight against their chests.   A platoon
sergeant from the Recon Troop pushed them forward and down they
would go, some hollering like banshees despite strict threats from
Williamson and the Recon Troop officers and NCOs to maintain silence.
They were falling practically straight down an icy slope for at least a
quarter of a mile, descending into fog and an uncertain fate.   No one
could really blame them for screaming, it was frightening enough just to
watch.

After 30 men were dropped down with no sounds of gunfire,
Williamson sent an officer with a walkie-talkie.   The young platoon
leader was given orders to send one of two brief messages in the clear,
one confirming safe arrival and a safe established perimeter, or another

reporting danger, enemy in the area.   Williamson watched the young officer disappear down the hillside with one of his NCOs, waiting impatiently for over five minutes before he became concerned.   The short-range walkie-talkie worked only as a line of sight transceiver, but theoretically, they should have that on this slope.   After eight minutes Williamson stopped sending men down just before, to his considerable relief, he received the voice message: *SAFE ARRIVAL, SECURE PERIMETER.*

With this message Williamson decided to speed the descent process up, bringing troops to stage and releasing them about 20 seconds apart.   He had no idea the chaos he was causing by doing this.   At the unseen bottom end of the chute men were barely struggling to their feet before two more men, moving in excess of 25 miles an hour unrestrained would slam into them, weapons and gear flying in all directions.   Two compound fractures and numerous lesser injuries exposed the violence of the collisions.   Williamson was also not aware there were segments of the quickly worn down chute where the snow was rubbed away to exposed raw rock or ice.   More than a few men, unlucky one way or the other, had limbs or buttocks sliced open as neatly as if it was done with a razor.   These men, injured and moaning, could not get out of the way fast enough when the next shelter half "sled" came flying down from the top.   The young lieutenant with the walkie-talkie, seeing the extent of the injuries finally called Williamson in the clear with a brief message: *SPREAD THEM OUT MORE.   MEN GETTING HURT.*   Williamson double clicked his handset and set it down.

He stopped the next group of men, a double section of heavy weapons with 81mm mortar tubes, base plates and tripods in their hands, before releasing them 40 seconds apart.   As far as he could tell the shelter half sled idea was working, as the men seem to stay together as a pair or a trio until they disappeared into the fog, their feet still downhill, their weapons close to their bodies.   Orin jumped with his platoon sergeant.   The speed of the descent was terrifying, the heat building up to blistering pain as the shelter halves skidded with a loud ripping noise. Both men kept their combat packs on offering them excellent back protection, but their thighs and arms had to stay down to keep them stable.   All took a severe beating.   They had turned sideways just for a moment halfway down and Orin thought they were lost, but somehow their combined weight or gravity brought their feet back pointed down into the chute groove, stabilizing them.   They raced down until suddenly they skidded up and level at break-neck speed, slowing down finally across a small plateau where other soldiers suddenly appeared to snag them, pulling them quickly aside and out of the way.   Both of them were very aware of what was coming right behind them, gratefully accepting the help to get to their feet and away from the landing area.

Orin looked around, stunned at how fortunate the battalion had been. The steep chute they were using leveled out gently in a very narrow corridor, naturally cushioning their descents. Only 30 feet or so to the right of their arbitrarily chosen descent path was a large boulder field, the debris of some geological shifting from above, many of the boulders six feet in diameter. If the battalion had chosen to slide down the slope following this path, many men would have been killed or seriously injured. As it was, the entire plateau they were landing on was only about 80 or 90 feet wide and 100 feet deep. The truly safe area, where they landed by pure chance, was a narrow saddle 20 feet wide. The soldiers catching the others as they arrived were stopping the shelter half sleds only 10 or 20 feet from the edge before the mountain dropped off again. Orin was certain most of the soldiers had no idea how close they had come to complete disaster, most seemed content to be down and off the ridge, a few giggling nervously or stating loudly, *let's do that again!*

Orin noticed most of the soldiers were being kept over to the right on the other side of the boulder field, apparently for their own safety. *Someone* was paying attention, realizing the peril they were in from the men not yet arrived. It was here he discovered not everyone made the trip down with only bumps and bruises. The squad leader who had fallen first had tumbled hard, fracturing both arms and possibly his skull. A dozen men had deep cuts from hitting rocks and ice, and there were another dozen soldiers with broken bones. Miraculously only two had fractured their legs, the rest of the breaks, including the two compound fractures from collisions at the bottom of the chute, involved upper limbs or clavicles. This meant most of these men could walk out on their own, not requiring a stretcher team.

Orin guided his own platoon over to the side as they arrived, grateful none were injured seriously coming down. He watched in horror as the first of the heavy weapons crews arrived, hard, bouncing slightly left out of the saddle at high speed, hurling men and mortar equipment in all directions. Incredibly, the two men rolled up, got to their feet unsteadily, and began looking for their strewn apart gear as if it were an everyday occurrence. A few seconds later another mortar crew, this time one soldier with a 50 pound base plate on his chest and his partner clutching the folded up tripod, slammed into the saddle, careening over to the side past the chasing "grabbers" before nearly sliding right off the edge. Six soldiers ran hard and stopped them.

A few minutes later Captain Williamson and Ed Ridgeway flew out of the clouds and hurled right past the saddle to whip both men suddenly left and over, tumbling head over heels until they both landed flat on their backs. They continued to slide independently from centrifugal force until soldiers grabbed them by their arms and legs. With such large men, Orin had to admit it was a comical sight. Williamson got to his feet slowly, pushing men away offering assistance, looking around for Ed Ridgeway. Williamson brushed himself off, examining his carbine as he strode over to Ridgeway.

Orin joined them because Ridgeway was not getting to his feet. A quick examination revealed Ridgeway had somehow bloodied his nose, possibly breaking it, but as he pushed himself up, sputtering blood, he gasped in pain. His right wrist was visibly swelling as they manipulated it, but the most pain seemed to be coming from his right shoulder area. He was turning white and didn't want anyone to touch his shoulder, but under Williamson's direction a medic unzipped Ridgeway's field jacket and probed his upper back with his fingers.

"It may be broken, but definitely dislocated," the medic declared. Williamson looked at the medic before glancing knowingly at Orin.

"You've seen these before, right, Lieutenant?" Williamson said flatly, "I got one myself when I was playing tackle in high school." Orin nodded, he had one himself but not from football. He dislocated his shoulder jumping from rock to slippery rock next to the White River showing off to girls. Ed Ridgeway, who never played sports if he could help it, whimpered and moaned.

"Let me see," said Williamson, gently pushing the medic aside so he could feel for the bulge. "Stand up, Ridgeway, I need to try something." Before Ridgeway could say anything, Williamson had reaching under Ridgeway's left arm and pulled him to his feet. Ed gasped and rolled his eyes back from pain, and Orin thought for a second Ed was going to pass out. Williamson caught Orin's eyes and directed him, with a nod, to get behind Ridgeway.

"Put your weight against his back and hold him steady." Orin recognized what Williamson was about to do. He came up behind Ed Ridgeway and pressed firmly against his upper back with both hands, steadying him. Ed turned his head towards Orin with alarm but it was too late. Williamson reached in under the field jacket, gripped the upper part of Ed's right shoulder firmly and jerked it hard towards him. Ed gasped again sharply as his eyes bulged, but after a moment of shock, it was obvious his pain was subsiding.

"Oh, Jesus, *that hurt*!" He groaned. "What the hell did you just do?"

158

"Popped that out-of-shape shoulder of yours back in, that's what I did." Williamson grinned wickedly, winking at Orin before walking away. Orin guided Ridgeway over to a boulder so he could sit down. Ridgeway moaned loudly but Williamson never looked back. The last of the Scout Battalion was arriving down the chute. He glanced around noting the cluster of injured before stepping to the edge of the shelf to see what they had to face next.

The shelf offered a strange view of the middle of the gorge. Fog shrouded the long, steep slope behind them they had somehow managed to negotiate with only a few casualties. Orin noticed immediately it was warmer—not balmy warm by any means, but the quarter of a mile ride down the chute had brought them 700-800 hundred feet lower in elevation, maybe more. The wet uphill fog was still blowing, but now there was sticky snow again reminded him of when they climbed up off the beach. Snow was still all around on the ground, but it was wet, crunchy snow, dangerous snow, he knew. He stood five feet from the end of the plateau with all the other battalion officers, peering down at the next stage of their descent. From the plateau, the steep smooth bowl they had seen and experienced from the top of the ridgeline was replaced with the beginning of a wide pass in the shape of a large, flat "W". The partially visible sides of the pass were steep and white, with a dark, stubby ridge right in the middle like the back of a hog rising and disappearing into the mist below them. Depending on which route they chose, the slope gradient was between 25 to 30 percent.

"Well," Williamson sighed, "at least this part matches the terrain features noted on the Jap map. We won't need those damned shelter halves any further, we can hoof it from here. This uh—low hogback— in front of us descends down about two or three miles before disappearing into a whole bunch of little canyons and dead ends as the gorge empties out into the Sarana Valley." Although no one could see beyond about 200 yards in the drifting mist, Williamson pointed to the left and to the right of the so-called hogback with the muzzle of his carbine.

"Jap defenses—gun positions, bunkers, infantry trenches—are on both sides of the bowl down there, in those little canyons we can't see yet. We'll have to clean them all out. Appears the Japs have no idea we are here—even after all that screaming racket and carrying on as we fell down this damned hill!"

The other officers, some more seriously concerned about the situation, some maybe embarrassed, didn't respond much to the comment. A couple had screamed most of the way down the chute like some of the men—they couldn't help it. Fact is, Orin thought, they are all realizing like me we are an hour or two away from walking into a hornet's nest, and it ain't no laughing matter.

"We have complete tactical surprise, so we have a couple of options here. We can follow this hogback in front of us, fairly snow and ice free, and follow it as long as possible until we encounter Japs. Problem is I don't know, even after looking at the Jap map, exactly what the front end of the hogback looks like. We could find ourselves high above the Japs, so we can descend down on them, or we may get stuck and have to retrace our steps…"

With almost a year with Williamson in the Scout Company, Orin already knew where Williamson was going.

"The way I read this terrain the hogback will peter out and blend into the little canyons and passes that are right down there near the front of the Sarana Valley. The Japs knew that if we land in either Holtz Bay to the North or from Massacre Bay down south, we would have to come around the Sarana Valley to link up, so they put up some blocking forces to support the bunkers and gun positions. We just don't know how many for sure, but our captured map reveals where they *should* be. So," he turned around to face his officers, "we're going to cover all our bases.

"I'm going to send one platoon across the hogback to flush out any Japs that might be holding the higher ground up there, and we want to control the higher ground. If there aren't any Japs, they'll join us at the bottom of the pass down in those little canyons. But I also think it would be good place to establish our 81s. Should be above most of the Jap infantry positions, and we'll have clear line of sight so we can communicate with them with our walkie-talkies when we need them. So mortars are going with them. The rest of us are going to go down the right side of that snowy pass, staying as high as possible to hug the rocks on the side of the hogback so we don't stick out like matchsticks coming down the gorge." Williamson turned around again facing the gorge, dropped the muzzle of his carbine to the lower end of the gray mist.

"Somewhere down there at the bottom of this gorge we will encounter the Japs. They don't know we're coming, so we'll envelope them from south to north, towards our approaching landing force. We'll hit em with everything we got, staging our approach so we will always have the 81s and the gun teams ready to provide supporting fire as we move across the Jap positions. Believe me, we're going to need them!"

Orin casually glanced around at his fellow officers, noting a third of them were wearing white bandages of some sort on their hands or faces, with a couple swinging their arms in slings. Orin had turned down an arm sling since it hampered his ability to swing the muzzle of his Thompson. He caught Ed Ridgeway's eye and damned if the guy didn't make him laugh even in such serious circumstances like this. The medics affixed a huge splint and bandage device on Ed's suspected broken nose, looking all the world like a miniature pup tent and suspended his right arm in a sling to reduce injury to his dislocated shoulder. His suspected broken wrist was also splinted and wrapped with numerous bandages. Despite all of this, plus pain medications that left his eyes droopy and his mouth a little more slack-jawed than normal, Ridgeway stood straight and puffed out his chest for Orin's benefit, patting the butt of his .38 revolver still nestled snuggly in the shoulder holster. His mouth formed the silent words: *I'm ready for bear!*

CHAPTER 19

0900 Hours, May 12, 1943, D-Day Plus 1, Buchanan Ridge

Ready or not, this time Williamson would not allow Ed Ridgeway to join any of the assault companies. With nearly a third of his force of 400 suffering from frostbite or injuries incurred during the descent from the top serious enough to make them combat ineffective, Williamson had a sizeable rear echelon to contend with. With enemy contact now imminent he also had no wish to risk the capture of the intelligence officer.

Referring to the two Japanese maps that revealed themselves to be very accurate terrain-wise, he decided there was little risk of moving the entire force down the gorge about a mile and a half in the poor visual conditions. Most of the injured were ambulatory, with maybe two-dozen requiring extra assistance or litter teams. The low hogback they were going to traverse on the right side of the gorge appeared to blend partially into a protected draw a full mile above the Japanese positions established on the map. That was his next objective. It was perfect. Williamson's intention was to find a safe rear area where he could leave the injured. He couldn't afford to leave a security force with them, but the walking wounded could handle it if they were well concealed. The battalion would come back for them once they linked up with the assault battalions coming from Red Beach and the bottom of the pass was secure. It was also a good place to leave Ed Ridgeway.

Orin was secretly pleased Williamson assigned his platoon the job of clearing the hogback down the middle of the gorge. The rest of the assault force would be negotiating deep snow all the way down. The air was getting warmer as they descended, the snowflakes larger, wetter and stickier. It was almost like being in a white rainstorm, the large spinning flakes adhering to their cotton field jackets with a loud "smack" to instantly soak in. Williamson had led the battalion down the gorge at practically a trot, if you considered high stepping through snowfields sucking away at boots and legs trotting. To Orin, who could feel nothing in his feet below his ankles, the movement was totally exhausting and akin to trying to run with rubber farm boots half filled with water and completely caked with gray clay mud. He stumbled constantly, slowing down with every step, but he certainly was not alone.

162

The lead companies spread the men out to open-field spacing in case the Japanese had OPs on the sides of the gorge. It was a gut-knawing, back-of-the-neck hair-raiser to be in the middle of open terrain like that without any cover whatsoever. The only comfort, if the men chose to contemplate it, was the constant changing visual conditions around them. As the snow and fog blew up into their faces, soaking them before freezing, they blinked in the storm to look up at the sides of the pass as they descended. One minute they could almost see both sides, a mile and a half apart with a low dark fog layer 300 to 400 feet above them. The next minute both sides of the gorge would be gone, visibility down to 100 yards or less as the cloud ceiling descended almost to the ground. The stumbling trail prints in the wet snow of the soldiers in front of them the only path to safety. Forward to higher ground, closer to the hogback now a quarter of a mile in front them, somewhere where there was some cover.

It took 45 minutes to cross the snowfield before Orin's platoon stepped up on the "tail" of the hogback. The snow, as usual in the strange rock formations found on Attu, didn't seem to adhere well to the black rock. Orin led the platoon carefully up the rocky formation to hold them up on a protected shelf until the weapons section caught up.

Orin watched the small figures of the crews trudge across the snowfield with what appeared to be infinite slowness. He felt truly sorry for them, a real empathy borne from the heavily burdened towards the outrageously overburdened. What was amazing to him was the fact these men were still upright despite the incredible loads they were carrying. A regular infantry battalion had a Heavy Weapons Company, comprising of two major sections, heavy machine guns and heavy mortars. The heavy machine guns, water-cooled, .30 caliber Brownings—were throwbacks from the 1st World War. The heavy mortars, 81mm tubes designed to lob a 15-pound high explosive projectile as far as 3,200 yards, were the battalion commander's personal artillery battery.

The Composite Scout Battalion was a 7th Infantry Division hybrid unit put together for a specific purpose, this singular reconnaissance mission in support of the Attu invasion. With three Scout Companies whose mission was to operate independently behind enemy lines and to create as much disruption as possible, Captain Williamson knew if fire support was required they would have to bring it along themselves. Orin had to admit he questioned the need of having these weapons along for a reconnaissance mission, but understood now the battalion had no real ability, other than through the link of the communications B-24 somewhere overhead, to call for fire support. The closest 105 artillery battery would be over at Red Beach, if the cannoneers had found a suitable place to dig in. Of what Orin had seen of muskeg, he knew that was a problem. By the time the request for fire was relayed, confirmed and approved, well, he thought, we probably wouldn't need it anymore. Reliable close air support with the cloud cover was out of the question.

Williamson requested and received a mission-specific weapons section. A regular infantry battalion had six 81s with four man crews. Williamson didn't need the heavy machine guns but did want four 81s. Each of his three Scout Companies had their own machine gun sections, with air-cooled .30 cal Brownings with folding tripods. There was normally a small integral 60mm mortar section with each company, but Williamson left the 60mm tubes at home, using those mortarmen as extra ammo bearers for the 81s.

Each of Orin's men was given two of the 81mm mortar bombs before they set off across the snowfield, 15 pounds each, to strap onto their combat packs to give the 81 crews an additional 60 rounds. These mortar bombs had been carried by the Recon Troop all the way up from the beach. The Recon Troop gave up their loads without a murmur. The extra weight dragged Orin's platoon down in the wet snow, but their personal complaints, if they voiced them, were cut short when most of them saw the mortarmen were carrying three rounds per man on top of their regular gear and their primary mortar elements (tube, tripod and baseplate)—none of which weighed less than 30 pounds. As the mortar crews got closer, Orin waved the 22-man section to their rock shelf.

The Scout Battalion's assault companies were already past even though they were plodding through deep snow. Williamson pushed them hard, trying to get them as far down the gorge as possible to put the hogback on their left for both cover and concealment. The trailing element, the 120 odd men who were either injured or sick, were strung out over hundreds of yards on their way to the protected draw. Orin could not see the end of their procession. These men were suffering, but with the exception of a half a dozen who were being carried by four-man litter teams less injured than themselves, all were upright and struggling on their own two feet.

Crossing the hogback Orin set out a point squad 100 yards in advance of the platoon, with the weapons section another 100 yards behind the rest of the platoon. Williamson had insisted Orin bring along one machine gun team, so as the point squad leap-frogged across the hogback from one rock to the next, Orin had the gun team move forward and set up to cover the advance. As they cleared ground and the minutes and hours passed, the curvature of the hogback seem to curl to the left, to the north, the mist revealing craggy rock formations rising to the right. Orin had expected the hogback to continue to flow forward according to Williamson's interpretation of the Japanese map, rising itself above the terrain. Instead it seemed the hogback was descending to the left and the gorge sides were closing in, certainly on the right side, to the south. It was hard to tell if it was an optical illusion or not. He stared hard at the rock formations with his binoculars as long as he could before wiping them again. In the poor visibility he couldn't really judge how close they were. The point squad stopped moving, the squad leader crawling on his stomach to peer at something to the right from the side of a boulder.

The wind howled differently here, leading Orin to speculate the ridge had led them down the canyon farther than he had first thought with the walls much closer than before. He admitted the limited visibility had him focusing entirely on the hogback directly in front of his point squad. He had lost his sense of time, glancing at his watch— 1135—with a jolt. They had stepped off into the snowfield over two and half hours earlier. *How far had they gone?* They might have stumbled right off the end of the hogback without realizing it. *Right under the nose of the Jap positions!* It had been so long since he had slept he knew he was punchy, his reaction time slow or non-existent. *I've screwed up, advanced too far forward of the assault force on my flank.* Fear crept up around his shoulders, prickling his short black hair straight up against the wooly cap he wore under his helmet.

No one moved, the point squad clearly spooked. Orin turned slowly around, catching the eye of his platoon sergeant and every soldier he could see, signaling them to go to ground. He only hoped the weapons section, following 100 yards behind, would see the platoon going down and do the same.

Now that he was completely still, Orin heard the distant rumble of artillery over the wind somewhere to his left, to the north. If he turned his head and closed his eyes, he could just pick up the shadowy, in-and-out *poc-poc-poc* of an echoing machine gun, slow, distant and fading. U.S., .30 caliber. It warmed his heart, but the sense of danger nibbled back almost instantly. He watched the squad leader up ahead for a full minute but the man did not move a muscle. Orin followed what appeared to be the target of the man's attention with his binoculars, starting close then searching up as he was taught months before in scouting and patrolling classes. He moved his eyes from left to right, slowly traversing at one distance at a time, focusing and hesitating, letting his brain and peripheral vision capture something out of the ordinary. After a moment he lifted his focus up to what appeared to be a very misty 200 yards, up off the hogback across some gulf of space and the rock formation beyond.

Orin watched the rock formation, unblinking, for as long as he could. He closed and opened his eyes again to stare at the dark spots in the rocks when a small white flash popped from one of them. The wind barely concealed the small *BLOOP*. He stared at the black hole, not quite certain what he had seen, lifting the glasses from his face when he heard the *WHOOSH* and spotted a tiny black projectile zip across his vision, exploding with a loud bang about 30 feet behind the lead squad leader.

"MORTAR!" Screamed somebody to his left, following instantly with the *THUMP THUMP THUMP THUMP* of the .30 caliber Browning echoing from the same side. The .30 caliber tracers carved straight across the hogback directly into the hole Orin had been watching. Apparently this gunner had been too. Rock shrapnel zipped and whined all around them from the exploded mortar round. The gun team didn't miss a beat. Orin lifted his glasses again to look at the hole at the rock formation only to see another white flash, instantly followed by another *BLOOP*. He didn't wait to look for the little grenade flying out of the Jap knee mortar this time, diving down as a *WHOOSH* filled his ears.

The mortar exploded with another loud bang to Orin's left, the shrapnel whizzing much closer. He lifted his head to see his platoon sergeant pulling the body of the assistant machine gunner away from the Browning. He appeared to be unconscious or dead. The gunner seemed unhurt and continued to shoot at the mortar gunner who had very nearly killed him. He fired an extra long burst right into the same hole. As another soldier slid in next to the machine gun to feed the belt, Orin cautiously observed the cave with his binoculars. No other mortar flashes came from the cave, but all hell was breaking loose over to the right side of the hogback where Williamson's lead elements must be. There was furious machine gun and rifle fire. No other fire seemed to be directed at his platoon, so Orin signaled to the lead squad to keep moving forward.

Orin, carrying a line-of-sight walkie-talkie, checked in with the weapons section. He was surprised when the section leader responded, reporting five by five reception. Of course the mortar section was right behind the platoon. Orin told the section leader he expected contact any moment and to dig his section in as best he could, preparing at least one tube ready to fire in five minutes. Not having a good map to give accurate grid coordinates, Orin established his baseline target, a mid-point on the hogback in front of them, as approximately 150 yards on a

166

due East azimuth in front of the point squad elements, who were approximately 200 yards in front of the mortars, or out 350 yards.

"That the best you got, Rattlesnake One, due East, base target 350 yards?" Asked the exasperated section leader.

"We'll observe and adjust fire directly, Thunder," Orin fired back.

The point squad advanced cautiously another 150 yards, nearly stumbling across the backside approaches of two well-concealed machine gun and mortar emplacements. As Williamson had surmised, the hogback blended near the bottom of the gorge into a number of small canyons, but here, 100 feet up where the Japanese gun positions were established, there was a clear view of both sides of the gorge and nearly a mile down the pass if the weather permitted it. The gun fortifications, with two heavy Nambus each, were positioned to provide interlocking fields of fire covering about 150 degrees due north, south and east. A hundred feet behind the northernmost gun emplacement was a wide, four-foot deep trench for a four-tube heavy mortar section. The earlier firefight alerted the gun crews who moved a small reaction force up the hogback with a light Nambu and six riflemen. Luckily for Orin's point squad, the point man spotted the Japanese moving into a pre-prepared position pulling the squad back at the last moment.

Without a radio the squad leader came back to give Orin his report personally. He was not aware of the eastward-facing gun emplacements or the mortars, but his point man had seen something built up just before he spotted the reaction force. Since the Nambu was in a prepared position, Orin wasn't about to assault it head on across the open terrain of the hogback. He listened carefully as the squad leader described where the Nambu was placed, and how the reaction force seemed to be protecting something. Orin directed the man to get back to his squad and to standby to assist in the fire adjustment from the 81s with runners.

Orin then keyed the handset on the walkie-talkie to see if he could make contact with Captain Williamson, but all he got was static. He had no line of sight yet, as Williamson was apparently well below them on the south side of the hogback. The firefight down to the right, to the south below the rim of the hogback near the top of the canyon sounded very close. Orin knew Williamson was counting on him to get the 81s in action to support the battalion assault, so clearing the hogback was now a number one priority. He called the mortar section leader again, raising him immediately.

"Thunder, Rattlesnake. Add 200 to base target, fire marking round, wait for my adjustment!"

"Roger, Rattlesnake.   Add 200 to base target, marking round, Rattlesnake to adjust. Thunder, out!"

Thirty seconds later the heavy *WHOOP* behind him signaled the marking round was outbound.   Even in the wind and snow, the *WHOOSH* of the outgoing mortar arcing high up into its trajectory could be heard.   Orin watched carefully for several long seconds, then blinked when the low-yield, mostly smoke marking round landed just about 350 yards in front of him, bearing left to true North.   He was lucky to see it. It made a surprisingly sharp bang, but the wind was blowing in their direction.   From out of the rocks a soldier lept up to run a low-crouch, zig zag back down the hogback. The Nambu spotted the movement, the gunner firing instantly in two long searching bursts, tracking right across the path of the running soldier.

"COVERING FIRE!" Orin and his platoon sergeant yelled at almost the same instant.   Miraculously the runner was not hit as he flung himself down behind a low rock shoulder 30 feet from Orin. The man looked up, spotted Orin and slid forward, moving from rock cover to rock cover.   Orin could hear the gun but couldn't see the flash of the muzzle, mostly because there wasn't any.   The Japanese used an excellent smokeless powder, creating very little muzzle flame or smoke.

The Browning machine gun team and a couple of the BAR men continue to fire back in the general direction of the Nambu for a few more seconds, the MG tracers hosing left to right.

The runner, a new man Orin didn't know very well, was gasping for breath because he had run so hard.   He tried but was unable to speak.   Orin keyed his radio, waiting.

"Thunder, Rattlesnake, stand by."   The young soldier used his hands instead, giving a thumbs' up gesture that confused Orin for a second.   He repeated the gesture.

"Up?" Orin guessed, as the soldier nodded.   The soldier then used his fingers to hold up seven digits, then five.

"Up, 75 yards?" The soldier nodded, then turned to face towards the east, pointing to the right, holding five fingers on one hand and the universal symbol for "0" with this thumb and forefinger.

"Right--50?"   The soldier gasped and nodded, then spoke finally. "Yes, *right* 50."

"Thunder, up 75, right 50. One round, Rattlesnake will adjust."

"Roger, Rattlesnake, up 75, right 50.   One round, Rattlesnake will adjust, Thunder, out."

The young soldier who heard the exchange, was up and gone in a flash.

"COVERING FIRE!" Howled his platoon sergeant again, but when Orin lifted his head to see what had become of the runner, he saw no one moving on the hogback. He had to assume the soldier returned back across the hogback without attracting the Nambu this time. A few seconds later he heard the mortar leave the tube, the round outbound. The heavy fog was returning again, even with the snow, the mist up the hogback making it more difficult to see as far as before. After a short delay there was another *BANG*, much noiser which meant the mortar crew had fired an HE round this time. Orin saw no flash of the explosion, hoping the point squad could see where it landed better than he could.

He waited and sure enough, another soldier was running, bent over, flat-out across the low rock field for all it was worth. The platoon popped away with covering fire a little late, but the runner was halfway across before the Nambu opened up with another long burst right behind him. The visibility was just poor enough the gunner was only getting glimpses of his running target. As the squad leader dove behind the rock shoulder they both heard the heavy *THUMP THUMP* of a big bore mortar upwind from the east, then a few seconds later the high pitched screams as the rounds pitched down for the downside of their trajectory parabola. These weren't 81s.

"INCOMING!" Screamed Orin as two explosions erupted a second apart, *SPLANG SPLANG* 75 feet from where they were lying, bouncing both men off the cold ground. Shards of steel and rock whizzed around them. Orin lifted his head grimly staring at the squad leader.

The man pointed towards the east.

"THEY GOT MORTARS!" He yelled unnecessarily loud and breathless, mostly because he was partially deaf from the explosions. After gulping some air he added, "my point man realized he was looking at big pipes set at an angle, which confused his dumb ass. It's a *mortar* position up there."

It didn't take a genius to know the Nambu or the riflemen in the Jap reaction force had a clear view of their positions and probably had a radio to talk to their mortar crews. They had seen the runners coming to Orin's position in the big rocks and put two and two together. The observers could also track the MG position from its tracer fire. The Browning was silent and Orin hoped the crew was moving to another position or changed out the tracer belt. In about 30 seconds or less they would have mortar bombs rain down on the platoon, or even worse, figure out where the mortar section was and wipe them out with counter-

169

battery fire. He turned to ask the squad leader where he believed the mortar position was then changed his mind. The squad's point man had seen the position, not the squad leader. The squad leader could only give a guess. Orin needed to know for sure. He looked down at the walkie-talkie in his hand, realizing he was the only one with the ability to get the mortar crews on target. He temporarily forgot about the Nambu.

"Thunder, Rattlesnake. Standby, same target, Rattlesnake will adjust," he croaked, his mouth very dry.

"Roger, Rattlesnake. *Make it snappy*. Those were 90mms, and we're practically in their bore! Thunder, over." The fear and frustration in the voice said it all. If the section leader was smart he was scattering his men as he spoke so only one crew would face the obliteration soon to arrive inbound.

With his injured hand, Orin couldn't run and carry both his Thompson and his radio. He slipped his combat pack off and laid the Thompson on top of it.

"Get me where I can see the mortar position," he ordered. Turning he signaled his platoon sergeant, "COVERING FIRE!" He yelled hoarsely, already up and running without waiting. The Nambu fired almost immediately, missing Orin but hitting the squad leader, running 10 feet behind him. Orin heard the bullets zipping past him and the other man's grunt of pain and surprise. He did not turn around to look. The Browning MG was shooting back with a couple of the BARs. He hoped his platoon sergeant could figure out what he was doing and would keep the Nambu off of him.

His numb feet forced him to run wide-legged so he would stay upright. Maybe a funny thing to watch if there wasn't a .25 caliber light machine gun trying to kill him as he stumbled left, then right. He ran past the first men of the point squad, all splayed out flat behind low rocks, their heads down. None of them were firing back. He could hear the Nambu, with single shots of Arisaka infantry rifles accompanying, all of them much closer now. The *zip zip zip* of passing bullets matched the rushing, gasping noise of what sounded like a running, panting dog. When he finally fell behind a small shelf of black rock, he listened to the panting dog and looked for him before realizing he alone was making all the noise.

Orin distinctly heard the *THUMP THUMP* of the big mortar again, then the screeching howl just before the rounds exploded one in front and one in behind him. Instantly deafened by the sharp *SPLANG SPLANG* of the rounds detonating on contact on rocks, he was bounced up just as hurling shards of rock and metal whizzing and ricocheting in

170

all directions. He felt sharp, stinging pain in his face and neck, with an instant dullness along his right shoulder, back and thighs. He grunted and cowered instinctively as he was hit, fearful he had been hurt bad, but when he opened his eyes he could see the point squad's point man crawling straight to him. The man was wounded himself in the face and upper shoulder.

"Where are those mortars?" Orin asked huskily, his mouth dry, revealing the walkie-talkie in his hand.

"Follow me, sir," the point man said, "I'll get ya as close as I can."

Orin now had a nearly useless right arm. It felt cold, strangely numb and full of cement. His legs still worked okay. He just didn't have the time to determine the extent of his injuries. He pushed himself painfully up on his knees and elbows to dart forward a few feet before throwing himself down behind the rocks, following the pattern set by the point man. The Nambu searched for them but the terrain was elevated here, with a slight defilade. The bullets chipped and whirred away inches above their helmets, but the gunners couldn't actually see them. After about five minutes of turning this way and that, the point man, 10 feet in front of Orin, finally rolled over on his back and tucked his head down to stare back at Orin. He did it to keep his head as low as possible.

Orin stopped and stared as the soldier brought his bloody hand up to his face, directing his index finger straight up, then slightly to the left.

"You see where I'm pointed?" The soldier asked, his eyes very wide and white. Orin brought his eyes up without lifting his head, following the direction of the finger.

"Look between those two gray-white rocks just to your left." Orin felt very exposed where he was, thinking furiously his head was a great target for a Jap rifleman. He let his eyes drift up and found the two large rocks, focusing his attention on the "V" between the two rocks. He saw them instantly, however, the faint tops of two fat tubes propped by their tripods at about 70 degrees, two more farther away, the position not more than 100, maybe 120 yards from where they hid. As he watched he saw the shadow of the crews dropping mortar bombs in the tubes. *SHIT!*

Orin wasn't really sure how far they had traveled getting to this position, or how close they were to the reaction force and the Nambu. He could hear the machine gun, somewhere forward, but distinctively to his left and close. He heard the big mortars whoosh and scream past on their way down the hogback to land by his platoon, maybe even among the mortar section. He could also now hear a new set of Jap guns, fast-

171

firing machine guns somewhere forward on the hogback. He didn't know what to make of that.

"Where do you think the Nambu is from here?" He asked the point man. The man did not hesitate as he waved directly to their left, to the north.

"Maybe 50 yards," he stated flatly. "Maybe less. We're pretty close." Completely exhausted, Orin closed his eyes for a moment to try to concentrate on making the mental picture of the Nambu and the mortar position in relation to where the 81s had been shooting. He would not have too many chances to adjust before the Jap mortars took out the 81s, the Browning MG, and much of his platoon. The Jap reaction force might even find *them* first.

"How close were we getting with the 81s to the Nambu?"

The point man nodded and held his thumb and forefinger apart about an inch.

"Short maybe 20, pretty much in line with them though."

Orin keyed the walkie-talkie, praying the radio wasn't damaged. He needed to take out the mortars first.

"Thunder, Rattlesnake. Up 100, one round, HE, Rattlesnake will adjust." The section leader responded instantly.

"Roger, Rattlesnake. Up 100, one round, HE, Rattlesnake will adjust, Thunder, out."

Orin knew he wouldn't be able to see the impact from where he was, so he pushed himself up to crawl towards the two big white and gray rocks. He was almost there when he heard the whistling scream of the 81 coming in. He had no choice but to force himself up onto his knees so he could see, keeping the rocks between himself and the expected mortar impacts. His sudden movement and his big exposed head were immediately spotted by the reaction force. They fired several rifle shots in his direction, a couple whining away within a foot or two. Orin ducked instinctively, but not before he saw the flash and explosion funnel of the 81. The round was short about 15 yards and appeared to be too far left of the mortar position. The Nambu joined the fray, scything the rocks around him with bullets.

Hovering behind the rocks Orin began keying the handset of his walkie-talkie when he heard a faint incoming transmission.

"Rattlesnake One, King Snake, over." Orin recognized the voice of Captain Williamson's radioman, as the transmission faded in and out as the man repeated his call. By coming right a 100 yards or so they had established a line of sight signal. Orin heard the heavy Japanese mortars leave their tubes again. There was no time to lose.

"King Snake, Rattlesnake One, stand by." If the signal remained, Williamson's radioman would hear his next transmission.

"Thunder, Rattlesnake. Up 15, right 20. *Fire for effect!* 10 rounds!" The mortar section leader responded instantly.

"Rattlesnake, Thunder. Up 15, right 20! Ten big ones!" Before the section leader even finished his message, Orin could hear the first one leaving the tube with the heavy, but distant *WHOOP* downwind. Nine more followed. Orin slid down off the big, exposed rocks, falling into the small draw to join the point man, both pressing their helmets down on their heads as they hovered as low as they could. The mortars came down one after the other, having been fired out of the 81 about two seconds apart. About a third of the way through the barrage one of the HE rounds must have landed in a stack of Japanese mortars or some type of stored high explosive in the trench, because there was an enormous explosion, then another, drowning out the puny mortar impacts. Orin and the point man were bounced out painfully from their little rock draw, only to scramble, dazed and numb, back down as shrapnel and big chunks of rock debris began to rain down on them.

Orin crawled back up to the big "V" between the rocks to peer cautiously at where the mortar position was. The big tubes were no longer visible, none of them, but there was considerable smoke coming from the hill where the mortar emplacement had been. If he could get this point squad organized, they could rush the position. But then realized he had almost forgotten about the Nambu and the reaction force. If there was any hope in his heart the 81s had somehow taken care of them too, it was dispelled instantly by the long, searching burst racking the rocks above his head as he crept down the simple defilade formed by the shallow draw.

Orin calculated in his head, based on the sound of the gun, where he thought it was. He called the mortar section leader and was waited patiently for the first round to arrive when he heard the rustling sound over to his right. He was a few feet out of the draw as his eyes spotted the motion almost 25 feet away, a white and gray rock on the hill slowly, unnaturally lifting up off the snow. The motion stopped momentarily, the gap between the ground and the false cover of the phony rock only about eight inches. Motionless, Orin stared at the gap, knowing he had been spotted and was only a second or two from being shot. After a few seconds, the rock continued to rise as the white camouflaged coat sleeve of a Japanese soldier reached out, clearing the spider hole or tunnel he was in under the rock. What happened next must have all occurred in the scope of a few seconds, but later when Orin tried to

173

spread out the details, he was puzzled how so much could transpire so quickly.

In the grip of the Japanese soldier was a small hand grenade. The soldier struck the bottom of the grenade firmly against a rock with a quick rap, whipping it forward sidearm into the bottom end of the draw where the point man was. In Orin's good hand he was still holding the walkie-talkie, ready to adjust the fire from the 81s on the Nambu. The view from the spider hole was obviously limited, but the Japanese reaction force knew exactly where the draw was, and how to defeat it. For whatever reason the Japanese soldier in the hole did not see Orin, his focus on the draw.

Orin heard the grenade clatter down into the draw just as the 81 screamed in and exploded, seemingly right above him. The Nambu MG was somewhere, maybe 30-40 yards to his front, now that he was facing north. The mortar rounds exploded above him, slinging shrapnel in all directions to whir out of sight. In the brief barrage he heard a single human cry, surprised and abrupt. The mortar blasts forced him to the ground instinctively, but even the close concussions and whizzing shrapnel could not draw his attention off the Japanese hand grenade suddenly appearing four feet to his right. There had been something, some motion catching his eye that turned into the hand grenade. One second it was suddenly there. *It was the grenade the Jap sniper had thrown down into the draw. Orin's point man must have thrown it back!*

The sniper, seeing the grenade coming back and possibly seeing Orin, wanted to have nothing to do with either. The gray and white phony rock flopped down without ceremony just as Orin slid backwards towards the draw, dropping his radio as he scuttled away from the grenade. It exploded with a flat, ear-splitting *BANG* being so close and lying on a hard rock. His ears buzzing, Orin remembered his walkie-talkie. Cursing, he drew his .45, peering cautiously over the lip of the draw. The "rock" was down and more or less looked normal. He crawled forward only far enough to grab his radio and return to cover, grateful it appeared undamaged. The point man crept up to the ledge of the draw beside him, possibly aware of what he had done. Orin ignored the sheepish look on the man's face, pointing out the spider hole.

"Cover that gray and white rock thing, it's a spider hole," he ordered, "but stay down. There's a Jap in there. I'm going to get closer to the gun position, see if we knocked it out. There may be other spider holes around." The point man nervously shouldered his M1 and aimed it at the spider hole, but looked furtively at all the rocks on the hillside. They all looked the same.

Orin crawled forward, turning down the squelch on his walkie-talkie before he set it down behind a small ledge. He gripped his .45 with his good hand, continuing to crawl another 20 feet or so until the ledge ran out. Laying the .45 down, he removed his helmet and slowly peeked around the corner of the ledge. What he could see to his left, back up the hogback, was three of his soldiers from the lead squad, huddled together in a small rock depression about 200 feet away. He could barely see the tops of their helmets and the muzzles of their rifles. He knew they weren't dead because the rifles and helmets moved around every now and then. None of them ever raised their heads to look over the edge of their hole. The Nambu was silent, maybe because no one was moving around. That is, beside himself. There was one way to be sure. Orin slid back, hugging the ledge as much as possible before chucking a large rock up forward as far and as noisily as he could. It wasn't a huge rock, but it made a lot of noise. Nothing.

His ears were ringing incessantly now, but he could still distinguish machine gun and rifle fire back down to the south in the canyon, and the secondary heavy machine guns from somewhere up the hogback. He needed to move the platoon up, clean up this strongpoint and establish a mortar position so they could support Williamson's assault. The only way to determine if the gun was gone was to try to draw its fire. Orin withdrew, crawling back down the ledge to rejoin the point man. With the walkie-talkie in weak range, he contacted Captain Williamson and gave his report. He was surprised to find Williamson more sympathetic to his slow progress than he expected. The Scout Companies were also bogged down, stopped cold by a series of defensive positions requiring slow, coordinated efforts to defeat. He also informed Orin what he could expect on the front side of the hogback.

"You got a major stronghold up there. Actually does show up on the Jap map, but I misread it somehow. If you took out those 90mms you've removed half of their sting, Lieutenant. But from where I'm sitting, we can't move forward into the canyons with those heavy machine guns up there. They have to be taken out, pronto! They know you're up there now, but you might have destroyed their defensive force already. Knock em out! Keep the pressure up, get those mortars in battery so they can lay down some indirect fire down on these troop trenches we're running into!"

Orin pulled back, dodging around the rocks to join the point squad. One or two rifle shots rang out, the bullets not even close, the Nambu remaining silent. The lead squad leader was dead, so the assistant squad leader, a private first class, took over. Orin told them to

175

regroup and wait for the rest of the platoon to join them before the platoon assaulted the strongpoint.

He checked in with his platoon sergeant and medics to confirm casualties—three dead and four wounded, two seriously—before sitting down and letting a medic tend to his injuries. He had two-dozen small shards in his body, some near the surface, some well imbedded. The medics plucked out the ones protruding from his skin or within probe range, but a half dozen had to wait for a surgeon and, he knew, the end of the campaign.

Orin told the mortar section to stay put until he could find a more secure place for them. The section leader laughed at that before turning serious, offering at least seven of his men to assist Orin on the assault, to temporarily replace the men already fallen. Orin accepted the offer immediately, wondering how much longer any of them were going to last. According to his slow-moving mind calculations as the afternoon waned, most of them were operating well into their 40th hour without sleep. Williamson had trained the scouts on field problems exactly the way he anticipated to operate, non-stop until the mission was complete. Orin never remembered any field problems going much beyond 40 hours, however, for even Williamson admitted the human body could only take so much. Orin knew he was young, healthy and always considered himself as tough as anybody. But his fatigue was overwhelming. With the shrapnel wounds, his infected hand and his frozen feet, he was almost dead on his feet.

For the first time in two days Orin suddenly thought about his brother, Ray, who was supposedly safe and secure as a held reserve with an infantry company with the 3rd of the 32nd. He remembered how Williamson had updated them with the battalions coming up from Red Beach, battalions they would eventually join up with at the end of the Sarana Valley. It didn't register at the time, since he was just off Buchanan Ridge after that strange prisoner-hunting mission. The *3rd of the 32nd* was one of the two battalions now bogged down against the Japs south of Red Beach. *Are we supposed to rescue them or are they going to rescue us?*

Whatever the situation, Orin felt a wave of guilt and fear thinking about his brother again, a line Joe with a rifle, just another guy with frozen feet... he prayed to God he'd get a chance to see him again.

176

CHAPTER 20

0800 Hours, May 14, 1943, D-Day Plus 3, Sarana Valley

A soft murmuring voice, somehow familiar, swept away the fabric of the linen-like haze in front of his eyes. The haze, fading darker or lighter, was accompanied by warmth and strange distant sounds. Yoshi Nakagawa was conscious. His eyes were open, but when he tried to focus on anything he couldn't do it. When he moved his head he felt an instant throbbing pain on the right side, so he closed his eyes and remained still. He listened instead, hearing the soft voice, knowing he was hearing someone singing quietly to himself. It was a lullaby, a song his mother sung to him when he was little but he couldn't remember what it was. He only knew he recognized the tune, frustrated he couldn't remember its name. Keeping his eyes closed eased the pain, relaxed him. The haze returned and he drifted away.

Yoshi awoke abruptly, the haze gone. He was frightened. There was the strong scent of kerosene and alcohol in the air, mixed with the distinct smell of the earth, damp and musty. Someone was coughing very close to him, and then he coughed himself as a reflex from all the dust in the air. There was thunder right above him, a booming reverberation he recognized fearfully with the noise and blackness of his near-death experience being shelled in the bunker down by Holtz Bay. As he opened his eyes he was immediately overwhelmed with a sense of vertigo. Light and dark shapes were moving around in front of him. Where am I? Fearfully, he instinctively reached out to protect himself from falling with his hands, but only his left arm lifted on command while his right was somehow restrained.

A small pale face appeared in front of him, a young man in his late twenties with several days' growth of beard. He leaned forward to gently grip Yoshi's hand and arm, bringing them back down on the bed slowly.

"Relax, Lieutenant!" He said quietly in a soothing voice, "you mustn't move around, you'll open your wounds!" Yoshi calmed down, letting the man lay his arm across his body as he focused on the man's face. He studied it carefully, knowing he had never seen him before and the last man who touched him so gently was his father, especially when he had nightmares as a child. It was a kind face, he decided, a man of patience and humor. Still confused by the shifting light and dark images passing behind the man, he turned his head slightly, which hurt with the motion, to look beyond him. Another man, taller, lifted up his arm to steady a globe of light Yoshi instantly recognized as a kerosene lantern. Looking around, he understood now what had confused him. The ceiling was dark, as was the room. The shifting, blurring light and dark images overhead were lit kerosene lanterns swinging freely every time a bomb or a shell landed close, shaking the—shelter—and everything in it. Each lantern had a small cone of light above and below it, the light dancing in the dark with the shelling.

The taller man who had steadied the lantern leaned in next to the bed and peered at Yoshi with focused curiousity. The other man, who was apparently a medical orderly, stepped aside respectfully and said nothing. The taller man wore no insignia but Yoshi assumed he was a medical officer. He had a narrow, rather severe face that combined with his old acne scars and dark, piercing eyes made him look a bit dangerous, perhaps even mean. The man's fatigue was also very evident despite his fierce looks, as his eyes were sunken and droopy from lack of sleep. He seemed to sense Yoshi's apprehension, averting his eyes downward as he checked Yoshi's pulse.

"I am First Lieutenant Yamada, Lieutenant Nakagawa. I am glad to see you are awake. You've had quite an experience. Look at the light, please." Yamada had a small penlight in front of Yoshi's face, flashing it on and off across both of his eyes. Satisfied, Yamada put the light away to carefully probe around the large bandage on Yoshi's scalp.

"You do remember what happened, Lieutenant?" He asked casually, his hands already moving from Yoshi's head to his shoulder. Yoshi listened to Yamada and followed his hands, realizing with alarm he had no idea what happened, or the extent of his injuries or how he came to find himself here in this hospital. Yamada stopped his examination to look carefully at Yoshi's face.

"Do you know who you are, Lieutenant?" Yoshi nodded, hesitatingly, before answering.

"Yes sir, I know who I am. Lieutenant Yoshi Nakagawa. I'm an engineer." He opened his mouth to continue but he stopped, his mouth hanging open for a long moment, confusion crossing his face. Yamada waited for a few seconds, saying nothing, then reached over and patted Yoshi's hand.

"A bullet took a nice chunk of bone from your scalp, giving you a pretty good concussion. The bone will heal, as will your memory. A little amnesia is normal for awhile." He waited for Yoshi to look at him again.

178

"You are a very lucky fellow, Lieutenant. You lost a lot of blood and I wasn't sure if you were going to make it, frankly. But, you are young and healthy! I understand your actions were quite heroic up on the mountain." Yoshi stared at Yamada with a blank look on his face, so Yamada simply nodded as he began pointing with his hand. Yoshi followed the directions of his fingers.

"The Americans you fought with were bad shots, apparently. A Colt .45 pistol or a Thompson submachine gun, perhaps? A millimeter or two would have put the bullet in your brain and we wouldn't be talking. I did take a .45 bullet out of your shoulder under your right clavicle, and apparently another bullet severed your pinkie and ring finger from your left hand—I'm sorry."

Yoshi immediately glanced down to his left hand, fully wrapped in a very large gauze bandage. Two fingers? His right arm was in a sling, strapped to his chest. He scoured his memory to get some hint of this shooting battle Yamada was speaking of, but his mind came up with nothing. Now that he knew what was wrong with him he realized his shoulder and hand really did hurt. Dr. Yamada only had morphine to give him for pain. They had restricted the amount earlier because of his head injury.

After Yamada had gone away to continue his rounds, Yoshi found he was totally exhausted and fell almost instantly to sleep. When he awoke later in the afternoon, he started plying the medical orderlies for information of how he came to the hospital, only to be shocked when informed it was the 14th of May. No one could really tell him any details, but he also discovered the hospital he was in was not really a hospital at all, it was a converted troop barracks in a large tunnel at the base of a mountain on the east side of Holtz Bay, near the abandoned airstrip Yoshi and the other engineers had been working on. The facility was 20 feet underground but the shelling felt like the bombs were landing right outside.

He and Kenji were carried all the way down the mountain by litter to an aid station near the base of the Sarana Valley, but the American shelling forced the evacuation of the facility. He was lucky, he was told, some of the wounded were then sent to another aid station on the west side of Holtz Bay. The Americans, some coming from Red Beach and another group coming down from the western pass, the so-called parachute division, closed in on the forces holding the hills there from both sides. The aid station was destroyed by American shellfire with most of the wounded killed.

In the evening his new friend, Kenji the communications NCO from the mountaintop OP, came in to visit. Yoshi recognized him

179

immediately, his brain suddenly saturated with confused images as they shook hands. He could not fully believe all the events Kenji related, especially Yoshi's "gunfight" with the Americans. Kenji was subdued and spoke quietly, a sadness Yoshi finally understood as Kenji explained the American soldiers who clubbed him and shot Yoshi also killed all three of his men. Two were shot in their bunks and the third stabbed to death in the tunnel. Kenji, who still wore a large bandage on his nose, said they were discovered by the eastside OP crew when Kenji's OP didn't give a morning report, and then didn't respond to radio calls from either HQ or the eastside OP. Kenji became silent, staring down at his feet.

"There is going to be inquiry," he said quietly, "a disciplinary inquiry."

"For who, Kenji? I thought you said we were some kind of heroes!" Kenji, a very fair and youthful looking young man in the first place, raised his head slowly like a little boy, unable to look directly into Yoshi's eyes.

"You're a hero, Yoshi—I mean, Lieutenant. You were a visitor, and you fought them until you were shot down." He finally looked at Yoshi, misery in his eyes.

"You don't know because you've been unconscious. The Americans landed a parachute division behind the western ridges, then sneaked in behind our lines right down the pass to the Sarana Valley, it's a huge battle." He sighed heavily, his shoulders slumping. "We may lose the island because of it.

"They sneaked in on the day of the invasion, right under our noses. Right down the pass in front of the OP. None of us observers saw them, neither OP. So, we're being accused of sleeping or not watching even on the day of the invasion. Command decided to abandon the OPs on the ridge. No one is up there now. I was taken away with you because they thought I was shot too at first, and helped them identify you. The Americans took your identity papers." He looked up again, glancing furtively left and right to ensure no one could hear him.

"I don't know what to do," he whispered. "I can't get back to my unit, the Americans advanced to the top of Holtz Bay. I understand our forces there are pulling back over here, to the eastside of the Bay. I don't know what happened to my unit. I'm—I'm placed under house arrest!" Yoshi simply stared at Kenji, not believing what he just heard.

"The weather was terrible that day, now that it's coming back to me, and the day before! How could the Americans land a parachute division in that kind of weather?"

"Doesn't matter," Kenji said lightly, "none of the senior officers ever get up there to see what we can see—which is nothing most of the time. But right now I wish the Americans had killed me. This will disgrace my parents." His face fell, distraught, his eyes wide as yet another option raised its head. "Do you think they will shoot us?"

This time Yoshi couldn't meet the eyes of his friend for long. This was all confusing. The inquiry board, whenever it convened, would want his testimony too. Kenji asked him what the Americans had looked like and Yoshi could remember nothing of their facial features. He only vaguely recalled there were two of them in the room. What he did remember were the large black empty bores of the huge .45 pistols as the American soldiers shot at him. Kenji told him it was reported there were large pools of blood from the dead or wounded Americans, but the Americans took all the bodies away.

"All I did," he said miserably, "was get my nose broken and crap in my pants."

Yoshi did what he could to sooth the fears of his friend. Kenji, who was now fully ambulatory, no longer had a bed in the tunnel. For the present he was assigned a small mat in a cold, far corner packed in shoulder to shoulder besides two-dozen other soldiers with healing wounds. Most of the other soldiers, Kenji said, were engineers, communication specialists like himself, or crewmen of gun positions who had somehow survived the shellfire that killed all of their colleagues. They either had no idea how to get back to their respective units or if their units no longer existed.

As the evening closed in the shellfire seemed to taper down, although Yoshi was very aware there was a tremendous amount of activity here in the makeshift hospital. The medical orderlies kept moving the beds around to make room for more new wounded, many who had no beds and were lying on mats on the cold ground of the tunnel. The tunnel air got stuffier and stuffier, the smell of dirt, alcohol, kerosene and some undefined rancid, yet sweet odor permeating every inch of the atmosphere.

The morphine was making Yoshi sick to his stomach, especially since he had had very little to eat. But even with the morphine his shoulder throbbed dully every time he took a deep breath. Oddly enough, his head would occasionally feel no pain for a little awhile and he would almost forget about it. Other times, when he turned his head too far or when he first woke up, the pain stabbed deep into his brain, almost shuttering his vision, bringing tears to his eyes. The morphine, he suspected, also brought unwanted dreams—horrible, frightening dreams involving large, dark creatures lurking outside the threshold of his consciousness. He knew they were coming as he was waking from a dream so he would look for them, fearfully. Then, sure enough, one of the creatures would shoulder suddenly into his vision, pointing an ugly claw at his head, rocketing a bolt of light and pain straight into his brain to erupt as a numbing, blinding blast of white. This happened several times a day. It got to the point he didn't even want to close his eyes but he always lost that battle.

He dozed on and off all day, in some instances without realizing it, finding his consciousness a confused medley of tinkling metallic sounds, murmuring voices, then a transition to a dream or half dream. He dreamed of his mother and father, of soft forests with flowers with white petals—cherry blossoms, and spinning windmills. Without warning he would sense one of the creatures, the morphine creatures, stalking him as he walked in the forest or with his mother. If he could control it soon enough he willed himself awake. Sometimes it worked, abruptly, and he would arrive, alert, in his bed. He felt suspended in this place, time having little meaning since the light in the tunnel stayed the same. It remained constantly dim with isolated beacons of light from the kerosene lanterns.

The medical orderly with the kind face brought him soup one time. It was a watery miso but it smelled so good to him. He craved the salty taste. The orderly helped him bring his head up and held the bowl to his lips so he could slurp it. He finished the first bowl in two gulps. He asked for and received another, only to promptly throw it up within two minutes. Yoshi apologized profusely to the orderly, who cleaned up the mess without complaint.

"Very normal for head injuries," the orderly said patiently, as he changed Yoshi's blanket with a dry one. He motioned Yoshi back down on the bed. "You must rest. It is good your appetite is returning." The man smiled in his level, calm way. He began humming as he walked to another bed, this time Yoshi recognizing his mother's lullaby immediately. Sakura Sakura.

He began singing the words softly to himself, letting his head drop back on the pillow. He thought of his mother, of her peaceful voice as she sung the song, night after night until one night when he was about ten he had told her he was too old for his mother to sing him a bedtime song. She had laughed, sadly, and agreed. She never sang it to him at bedtime after that, but he would hear her from time to time, singing it to herself when she was folding clothes or cleaning after a meal. It always calmed him, wherever he was in the house. He fell asleep singing to himself, his mother's voice in his head. He slept deeply and there were no dreams.

Sakura sakura
Noyama mo sato mo
Mi-watasu kagiri
Kasumi ka kumo ka
Asahi ni niou
Sakura sakura
Hanazakari

Sakura sakura
Yayoi no sorawa
Mi-watasu kagiri
Kasumi ka kumo ka
Nioi zo izuru
Isaya izaya
Mini Yukan

Cherry blossoms, cherry blossoms
On meadow-hills and mountains
As far as you can see.
Is it a mist, or clouds?
Fragrant in the morning sun.
Cherry blossoms, cherry blossoms,
Flowers in full bloom.

Cherry blossoms, cherry blossoms,
Across the spring sky,
As far as you can see.
Is it a mist, or clouds?
Fragrant in the air.
Come now, come now,
Let's look, at last!

-18 century Japanese folk song

183

CHAPTER 21

0800 Hours, May 14, 1943, D-Day Plus 3, Sarana Valley

Orin would have never thought it possible for a man to fall asleep in the middle of a battle and certainly not in the middle of a firefight. To have claimed to do it during radio communications with your commanding officer in the middle of the firefight would be too much. He had heard these wartime tall tales from his father and other old men and he didn't really believe them. That is until he did it himself. Sometime during the afternoon on May 13 while a Japanese machine gunner tattooed the air two feet above the small depression he was lying in, Orin was talking to Captain Williamson when suddenly the light switch was thrown. His vision closed like a theater curtain to go completely black.

There were no dreams or visions of any kind. The blackness, sweet restful blackness had sponged every sparkle of light in his subconscious. He remembered nothing. When he woke up he was frozen stiff, lying on his back, his throat dry and painfully sore. His platoon sergeant was on the walkie-talkie, confirming some reference points down in the valley for the mortars to register on. Machine gun and rifle fire, with the dull *whumps* of mortars and grenades echoing down the valley seemed remote and distant. Orin coughed and his platoon sergeant glanced at him over his shoulder. Orin vaguely remembered doing something with the radio before he—*fell asleep? Oh, Christ, I was talking to the skipper!* Groggily pulling himself up, he tried to remember what the discussion was about but drew a blank.

"*Ho-ly shit…*" he groaned, trying to move his stiff joints. His platoon sergeant covered the mouthpiece on the walkie-talkie and leaned in closer.

"Welcome back," he said. "You look like you needed the rest." He pointed at his watch before sticking out three fingers.

"Three hours?" Orin whispered, incredulous as the man nodded.

Orin and his big brother Ray loved to go into town with their dad on Saturday afternoons after all the chores were done. Their dad would park the old Ford Model T behind the dry goods store and push out the wheelbarrow. When they were still little he toted them around in the wheelbarrow as he made his quick shopping rounds, but as they grew older he'd give each of them a nickel to spend on some candy and let them explore on their own a bit.   Ray would be in charge, and there would no Tomfoolery or there would be no more trips to town, by God. Main Street was only a half a block long, but in a half an hour or so an enterprising young lad could find something new and interesting to look at.

When the time was up the boys would head over to the dry goods store to wave at their dad, already deep in some discussion with a couple of the men who seemed to always be there.

"Okay boys," he would say, "be right with you, don't run off!"

Doing the prohibition there were no legal liquor sales but absolutely no shortage of liquor in Stone County.   Orin picked up pretty quickly the coffee pot on the back counter near the larger wooden barrels where the men sat was never hot.   Old Man Collier, the proprietor, would ask the men if they wanted a cup a coffee and they would always have some, putting a couple of nickels in the can for the "coffee grounds" as Old Man Collier poured.   He even added some dark caramel color to his white lightning to ensure it would look right to prying, outsider eyes, only there were never any of those around.   It was all for show, or maybe for certain womenfolk.   A stranger in a one-horse town in southwest Missouri would stick out like a farmer on his tractor wearing a seersucker suit.

Sometimes the discussion would include some experiences in the Great War, catching the boys' ears to draw them inside early.   Their dad was a World War veteran, serving his overseas time in France with the 2nd Infantry Division.   If their dad's friend, Art, happened to be around the discussion would center around the war or Army service. Art was born a French-Canadian and served three years overseas attached to British forces and was reputed to have been wounded *SIX* times, not counting a half a dozen gas attacks that left his lungs weak and breathless.   His experiences in the trenches seem to haunt him, but unlike their father who rarely spoke of the war at home, Art wanted to talk it out endlessly, especially with other veterans.

The only thing was Orin and Ray never could quite be sure where the truth ended and the tall tales began.   Orin suspected the rate of truth fell about as fast as Old Man Collier was pouring coffee, the veterans vying for honors of who had gone the most days without hot food, or who could replicate the exact sound of a German artillery round as it pitched down and was two to three seconds from impact, *real* close to where you were, and so on.   Art would usually win those minor honors, grudgingly, as their dad only had his nine months in the American trenches and single Purple Heart wound compared to Art's *thirty-four*

185

months of continuous service on the line. Some of it during the worst, most horrific blood-letting campaigns the world had ever seen.

The real nasty stuff, the true war stuff boys lived for so hungrily was only hinted at. The men would glance at each other knowingly and only nod to a referenced battle or what happened to men under a sustained artillery barrage. Those experiences remained unsaid. It was the experiences on the edges the boys weren't sure about. The experiences drawing laughter and the slow shaking of heads were the ones the boys could only glance at each other over. *Could that be true?* The two veterans seemed to stretch some incidents a bit too far, even for the sensibilities of a seven and a 10 year old.

"One day I was popping up and down in the trench trying to catch a Jerry sniper with the sun over my shoulder while he was trying to do the same to me," says Art, swilling his coffee as he looked down in the cup. "I figure he was about 450 to 500 yards away. I had damn good eyesight then and my Springfield was about the most accurate in the compny'. I'd seen his spot earlier and noticed the change in color and background when he came and went from his spot. I fired clip after clip at him, and he did the same to me with his Mauser. I personally think he was using a scoped sight, he was, because he was shooting into the sun, I wasn't. As the day went down it got worse for him. I'd hear the pop and snap of his bullets every now and then, but I was laid down 'bout as flat with the dirt as I could, so he was guessing, same as me. I was so damned tired I fell asleep up there on the step, my head on my rifle. Why that kraut didn't drill my brains I'll never know. Maybe he thought he got me since I stopped moving. I was awake one second, out the next! I didn't fall off the parapet, just laid there and knocked off as it got dark." Art drained the cup before he looked away at some distant spot beyond the store. "I wonder what ever happened to that old son of a bitch?" He said half to himself.

Orin had a hard time believing a man could be so tired he could fall asleep standing up, but while he was in the middle of a duel with another man trying to shoot him? To a kid it seemed impossible.

"Well," Ray had said reasonably to their dad as they rumbled down the road in the old Ford, "Art was a lucky man not to be shot by that sniper, huh, Dad?" Their dad had glanced over at the boys, their eyes on his in expectation. "Naw," he said after a moment, "Art was just plain tuckered out that day. His guy across the way probably did the same thing. Got tired and nodded off." His own eyes took a faraway look and he returned his attention to the road.

"Things are different in a war, nothing is normal. Things just start and stop, no sense to some of it." He shook his head and reached

186

across the gearshift lever to knock the caps off the boys' heads to rub their hair playfully. "You boys stop listening in to all that stuff. Art had a lot of bad experiences he can't seem to shake and put behind him, that's a fact. You keep listening you'll start to think us old soldiers are all crazy."

"What did the skipper say—when I—fell asleep?"

"He said let you sleep," his platoon sergeant said drolly. "We got that gun that was pecking away at us over across the pass there." Now it was coming back to Orin, the gunner about 300 yards away in some kind of a cave opening who killed four of his men. They had just destroyed the last of the heavy machine gun positions in the front of the hogback with grenades after a six-hour struggle. This Jap gunner was one of two across the pass protecting the stronghold at the front of the hogback they didn't know about until it was too late. Williamson's men destroyed one, but this one didn't reveal himself until the last minute. The gunner had waited until the four men were climbing out of the side hatch of the strongpoint before he killed them all with the same long burst. Then he pinned down the rest of the platoon, all out here in the open behind the gun position.

"How'd we get the sonofabitch?"

"Them 81 guys are pretty good. One of the gunners almost bore sighted his tube and dropped a HE in the cave entrance within three— four rounds. It was beautiful!"

The 81 mortars were now set up in the same gun pit the Japanese 90 mm had been. The crews dragged the Japanese bodies out, pushing the twisted tubes out of the way. It only took about 30 minutes to fully register most of the valley within sight, and the old forward-facing bunker top was just high enough to afford good cover from direct fire coming up from any part of the valley below. Williamson was adjusting fire on Japanese trench positions up and down the little canyons below them now, with the biggest problem being the mortar ammunition supply was running low. The weapons section carried about 70 rounds and Orin's platoon had carried over another 60 to pile in the trench.

Orin called Williamson to confirm the strongpoint was secure. Williamson sounded far away with the off and on reception, but as usual, he was optimistic.

"Good job up there, Craymer, those guns were stopping us from coming across and once you got the 81s working on the troop trenches up in the pass, we might actually hook up with the 17th Infantry before the end of this campaign!" This was a reference to the failed

187

coordinated attack on the evening of the 12th, since neither the 17th or 32nd Infantry could move forward fast enough nor could the Scout Battalion get past the stronghold positions in front of them to hook up. As it currently stood it appeared the 17th and 32nd Infantry Battalions coming up from Red Beach were stalled about two miles away. It might as well be 100. Then Orin remembered the 32nd Infantry Battalion was the 3rd of the 32nd, Ray's unit. King Company. *Might see you yet, big brother!*

"King Cobra, do you want Rattlesnake to join you, over?"

"Rattlesnake, King Cobra. What's your casualty situation, over?"

"King Cobra, Rattlesnake. Ten dead, eight wounded." There was a long pause, with static.

"Rattlesnake, King Cobra. Maintain security for weapons. If you can, move your wounded to Camp Ridgeway. Will advise. Out."

Camp Ridgeway was the draw about a mile back where the battalion wounded and frostbite cases were being kept. Orin came up with the name. With 11 effectives and the rest dead or wounded, he wondered how he would get them there. After thinking about it a couple of minutes, he sent his platoon sergeant and four men back to the draw. They were to pick up four litters and as many walking wounded as they could to be used as litter bearers. Orin set up his one machine gun team on one side of the strongpoint and his remaining men in two small trenches on the other side. The only Japanese he expected to see would be snipers on either side of the pass, but Williamson's men were enveloping the draws and canyons down below so fast those were being flushed out. The 81mm mortars had been very effective on troops out in the open in the prepared trenches, and Williamson had been rushing those positions essentially non-stop all day and all night. It was remarkable to Orin those men were still on their feet.

After about an hour Orin's platoon sergeant returned with six additional men. Two of Orin's wounded were ambulatory and could walk back to the draw, but the other six needed to be carried. His platoon sergeant organized the 10 men into two stretcher groups with four men on each stretcher, and three extra men, himself included, rotating with the others. It would take them awhile but they would move all six casualties down to the draw by evening. Orin had the dead stacked by the mortar pit to be dealt with by Graves Registration later.

On the last trip back from the draw Orin noticed the large man stumbling up the hogback with the litter teams. Ed Ridgeway trudged along, his arm still in a sling and his .38 revolver in his free hand. Orin slowly pulled himself up to greet his friend, who actually looked pretty good considering, if you didn't look at his comical nose splint. Color had returned to his face and other than his deep-set, shadowed eyes from exhaustion, his nonplussed humor had returned. Ridgeway, on the other hand, lost his grin when he drew close to Orin and had a chance to look him over.

"Man—Orin—you look pretty rugged!" His eyes dropped to the numerous torn and bloody rents in Orin's field jacket and trousers, from his shoulder to his calf.

"Should you be here? You look like you got wounded again!" Orin nodded and looked around for a place to sit down. He plopped by a wide rock and Ridgeway joined him. Orin grinned at Ridgeway, who just shook his head in wonder.

"I wanted to see this stronghold for myself, your platoon sergeant said it was quite a battle to take it." Orin knew Ridgeway wanted to look inside the bunker and examine the dead Japs inside. It was his job, he was an intelligence officer and he was fascinated with understanding the enemy. But it seemed almost macabre to Orin, this fascination with the dead.

"It was. They had a 90mm mortar position and four big Nambu's to cover the pass down below. They also had a small reaction security force to protect both positions. It was a solid strongpoint and it took us damn near a full day to take it. Cost me most of my platoon." Ridgeway, who watched Orin carefully, opened his field jacket to produce his small silver flask, offering it to Orin. Orin, who could not remember when he had eaten last, looked at the fine scratched English silver as if he had never seen it before, upending it. The raw scotch liquor burned his throat but the warmth was immediate.

Half an hour later Ed Ridgeway, after entering both machine gun bunkers and examining the damage six or seven hand grenades can do to the human body in a confined space, stumbled out of the escape hatch and vomited. He wiped his face after rinsing out his mouth with his canteen, then stood in the cold, damp air for several minutes. After awhile he examined the bodies of the Japanese soldiers killed in the mortar position and the reaction security force destroyed by 81s. He rifled through the pockets of the dead with precision, tossing papers aside to be lost in the wind, but pocketed many items. Orin, who accompanied him, said nothing, pulling Ed back from the top of the bunker exposed to possible fire from down below in the pass when Ed failed to recognize the danger.

Later, when Ed was finished and was heading back down to the draw he gave Orin some encouraging news.

"We're going to get an airdrop in the morning right down this pass if it's clear. Chow, ammunition." Ridgeway looked at Orin with genuine affection. "We've been in contact with our communication bird and the situation is changing. We are putting so much pressure on the Japs in this pass the 17th and the 32nd –your brother's battalion— should be able to push through by late tomorrow." He looked at Orin woefully before shaking his head, wagging his finger down the pass accusingly.

"That Williamson is a head case. He probably has less than 100 effectives left out there. We're getting the exposure cases back up to us. He doesn't have much of a battalion left, they have more frozen feet than combat wounds, believe me. So we will do one more push tomorrow and I think we're done as a fighting force!" As he spoke he looked at Orin's feet and turned serious.

"How are your dogs, Orin?" Orin shrugged his shoulders.

"Can't feel em anymore, Ed." Ridgeway stared hard, nodding his head slowly.

"I don't want you to lose your feet over this, OT," he said quietly. "Why don't you call it and join us at the draw?"

Orin smiled and slowly stood up. He picked up his Thompson and gave Ridgeway a casual salute before turning away. Ridgeway watched him trudge back up to the mortar pit and drop down into it before disappearing. From his vantage point on the rocky hogback, all Ed could see were the tops of the mortar tubes in the middle of the pit, and on one side a uncovered pile group of Japanese dead and on the other, a stacked uncovered pile of American dead. The snow was growing thicker and it was hard to tell the difference.

190

CHAPTER 22

2200 Hours, May 27, 1943, D-Day Plus 17, Engineer Hill

Jonathan Bettencourt slipped the Havana corona out of the box carefully, cushioning the remaining six cigars to protect their fragile outer leaf wrappers. Bettencourt acquired hundreds of them in Manila with about half of them in storage back at Fort Ord. He had easily 300 in the company office file boxes back on the transport, a precaution in case it was going to be a long campaign. He was only able to stuff 40 of them in his gear for the invasion, figuring like most of the troops he would be back on the ship within a week, so it was not an issue. It was an issue now, as Bettencourt loved his evening cigar. The battle for Attu seemed destined to drag on forever and damned if he would smoke cigarettes or those nasty cheap PX cigars Captain Greenley was so fond of. Resealing the box and sliding it between wool sweaters in his duffle bag, he turned down the kerosene lantern in the six-man tent he shared with Captain Greenley and the rest of the Easy Company officers and stepped outside to the twilight.

Directly in front of the tent was the back of another tent, with other tents a couple of feet on either side. The 50th Engineer Battalion (Combat) had all of the company headquarter tents stuffed in one front area on the long hogback ridge. The northern end of the ridge pointed directly towards Holtz Bay and the Sarana Valley leading to Pendergast Ridge, the small middle ridge parallel to Fish Hook Ridge. Massacre Valley was to the left and behind, and the valley leading to Chichagof Bay was to the right. The front end of the little hogback was covered with equipment or tents. The 13th Engineer Battalion (Combat) was similarly positioned a bit lower on a level plateau on the same hogback. The small, incredibly packed area was now called "Engineer Hill" once it was captured from the Japanese on May 21st.

The ridge ran completely parallel to the stream the engineers has set up as a bulldozer-ferry roadway, and it was from the streambed to the front end of Engineer Hill they had established the tow system. With most of the combat action now directly in front of the hogback in and around the Sarana Valley, the biggest challenge for the engineers from day one was coordinating and handling the constant forward flow of equipment, food and ammunition from the beach to the remote, fast moving combat troops. At the same time they were also bringing back valuable cargo, the wounded or frostbitten soldiers who were carefully shuffled from battalion aid stations to medical collection stations by litter, then finally transported via tow rope cart down to the ferrying bulldozers on their trip to the offshore hospital ships in Massacre Bay.

The whole thing was remarkable to consider—in total—if one had the time. Bettencourt rotated his Havana slowly as he lit the tip with his Zippo. Some major had scolded him a week or so back for lighting up a cigar in full view of Jap snipers at the same time of day, a curious thing to do considering the hill was festooned with lit lanterns and light systems of all kinds. Bettencourt had nodded to the major, an engineer with the 13th before tapping his ash off and walking away to light up somewhere else. Now, as then, he stepped between the tents and took his first, wonderful puff of the evening.

We have a fire mission! With that clear declaration heard all over the hill, he took another puff on the cigar and listened carefully to the noisy actions of the artillery crews 100 yards behind the HQ tents. A full regimental battery of 105 howitzers, six guns, was dug in the hogback behind them. If the HQ staff were ever in their tents the 24/7 artillery support from these guns would drive everyone mad. But they were rarely there, there was just too much to do. When they did come in, it was very late and just for a few snatches of sleep. Bettencourt had slept entirely through a half-hour fire mission once already. He heard the clanking sound of the closing of the breeches, and casually put his cigar in his mouth and stuck his index fingers in his ears as far as they would go. *Fire!*

The tent walls fluttered with each salvo, the air punching his stomach. A strange pressure vented against the sides of his skull. He was so exhausted he was unable to generate any real emotions from the interruption of his smoke by the goddamn guns. He hated them, but knew, just as he felt guilty standing behind the tent smoking his Havana, his plight was bullshit easy compared to the ground pounders out there living exposed. They were the ones who needed the fire support from these guns. Earlier in the battle when the 50th and the 13th Engineers were transporting gear to units still directly under fire, Bettencourt had taken his turn operating tractor-ferries up and down the streambed. He had carried the ammunition, the rations, the extra blankets and poncho liners up to what was the front end of the assault at the time and was glad to be turning around. What changed it for him, and every other engineer or HE operator out there trying to get the gear to the infantry, was ferrying back the wounded and the frostbite cases. It broke their hearts and made them sick to their stomach.

The streambed tractor ferry system was just a D4 bulldozer with a sled or a cart attached. Dozens of them. The streambed was comprised

192

of solid rocks, round and angular, big and small, which meant a very lumpy ride. Strapped down gear would be lost if the bulldozer operator drove too fast or did not follow the more level track coming up. Coming back, Bettencourt and the other operators would watch wounded men, on their last leg after days waiting for medical attention and then some level of basic care at the aid stations, be strapped to the cart. No medic came along with these men, just the bulldozer operator. The men, heavily sedated, would still scream, moan and cry with every jerk and bump, a constant companion for the four-mile ride down the streambed. Their eyes would bulge with shocking pain, their cries, tears and curses pitiful and merciless on the dozer operator. The ride took an hour, and occasionally a soldier would die during the journey. The operator, helpless, watched the medics gently lift the men out after he had exposed them to the most torturous pain imaginable. *You fuckin sonofabitch, you fuckin sonofabitch*, some of them called, *I'd keel ya wit ma bare hands if I could…*

Bettencourt had a few operators approach him, a strange look in their eyes, asking to be reassigned to some other duty other than transporting the wounded back. He would listen to them and tried to accommodate most of the requests. Standing there between the tents he was facing to the south where he could just make out the tiny headlight slits of the dozers coming up the stream. There was still enough light in the twilight to see fairly well, but the streambed was tricky once it got late. The trail markers became invisible and it would be easy to drop a D4 into a hole in the black water. They usually suspended the stream ferry system around 10 at night and started it up again around five in the morning.

The engineers were pretty proud of the transport system they established on Attu, and just recently completely the next phase connecting the low end of the hogback of Engineer Hill to the low end of Pendergast Ridge on the other side of the Sarana Valley. They did this by rigging another, much longer tow system between the two ridges using, again, bulldozers as cable pullers for the aerial tow carts. As the battle moved across the Sarana Valley into the mouth of the Chichagof Valley, they needed the transport system to carry over supplies and to bring back the wounded now brought from the ridgeline fights down to the Regimental Medical Collection Station. This was being done to supplement the building of a real road over the same route across the valley. Bettencourt wasn't sure about the casualty figures although he had heard some numbers that were surprising to him. The official estimates, as far as he could tell, were well off the mark considering the constant chain of evacuated men his engineers were ferrying back. It seemed to be in the thousands. He knew a high percentage were exposure and frostbite related. It didn't much matter how you become combat ineffective, he thought. You're still out of the fight.

He stayed close to the tent opening because he had a radio-telephone sitting on his bunk. Captain Greenley pulled him off a tractor earlier and ordered him to stay in the CP where *he belonged, to coordinate company shit, damnit,* he said. The temporary Easy Company CP was two tents down but Lieutenant Wheeler was there. Or was. Bettencourt wanted to be alone. Bettencourt smoked quietly thinking about the two Japanese officers he had seen a few days earlier. He found the experience still disturbing as he thought about it. As an engineer he could be expected to take a support role, but this was the Army. Anything could happen. Still, the Japanese were an abstraction to him until May 21st, when the 17th Infantry took the front end of the hogback and cleared it of all Japanese. That is, all of the ones that were *alive.*

Bettencourt and Captain Greenley had taken the tow up from the stream to the top of the hogback and walked down to the front of the ridge, where the last Japanese defenders had died, minutes after the battle was over. All of the dead were still there, both American and Japanese, sprawled about exactly as they were when they *expired.* That was the term floating in his head as he looked around, trying not to stare or appear overly concerned about the bodies. *Expired. Cancelled.* But you did stare, hard, because sometimes what you see is so foreign, so different, you could not *not stare* even if your life depended on it. The Japanese defenders had stood their ground in a number of defensive positions, some quite large and elaborate considering the hogback was essentially solid rock. The hill was so central to the support of the entire battle because it was the central high ground between the Sarana and Massacre Valleys.

In one natural hillside depression he walked up to a gun position and incomplete trench. The gunners and the Nambu light machine gun were tossed about like rag dolls, the crew obviously killed instantly by either a mortar round or a grenade. What caught his eye was what didn't seem to belong with the scene in front of him. Up ahead two young men, both in their late teens or very early 20s, were sitting side by side on a rock bench in the incomplete trench. Both were tucked back near the end of the trench where there was a small protective roof. They wore the light-colored winter tunic jackets of officers rather than the white camouflaged parka and pants of the infantry on Attu.

Bettencourt, without thinking, pulled his Colt pistol from his leather holster and held it down by his leg. He stepped cautiously into the trench to examine the two young men closer. Something was not right here. As he slowly looked the corpses over, he could see one was slumped over the other, his vertical partner had his head back, mouth and eyes wide open, almost in surprise. Bettencourt knew enough about booby traps to not disturb the bodies, but curiousity drew him close enough to see between the two men. Side by side, the one on the right had his left hand out and the one on the left had his right hand out. The outreached hands gripped one another. The one closest to Bettencourt, slumped over his companion, had a Nambu pistol in his right hand that was apparently used to shoot his companion in the upper abdomen. The other officer, the one who was shot and had his mouth open, had a Nambu pistol in his left hand but not pointed at the other officer. Bettencourt could see shrapnel had punctured the back of the shooter, possibly killing him at the instant he was killing his companion. *What the hell we got here? A couple of queers? A death pact interrupted? What else could it be?*

He had heard the stories of Japs committing suicide when they were cornered but this was the first time he had actually seen it. Or the result. Snow dusted gently on the open eyes of the officer who was shot, the flakes hovering on the eyelashes. They didn't melt or collapse because there was no body heat. Bettencourt abruptly backed up, stepping out of the trench, feeling he was somehow invading into something very personal, very private. He looked around the trench, seeing for the first time the huge piles of expended shell casings and empty box magazines from the Nambu. Somehow the two youths were apart from that. They did not belong. They didn't look like infantry officers and he noticed neither of them had sword scabbards. *Maybe already grabbed by the infantry who just took this place.*

"You want one of those Nambu pistols, First Sergeant?" Bettencourt turned, surprised to find Captain Greenley and one of the infantry officers standing next to him. He stared up at them, somehow irritated by the interruption before shaking his head.

"I'll take one," he heard Greenley say. "May never get another chance to be close to the action like this!"

Bettencourt heard the buzzer on the RT signaling someone was ringing his line. He turned into the tent and picked up the handset, squeezing the transmit button.

"Easy, Bettencourt." It was Greenley, up across the Sarana Valley on Pendergast Ridge where the other end of the aerial tow station was.

"Top, Easy Six. We got more wounded coming across from the ridge, so keep the ferry going even if they have to run all night. They're bringing guys down from the big fight up on Fish Hook Ridge and they've run out of room at the collection station, so the decision is to get them out to the ships, pronto."

Bettencourt acknowledged, wondering at this point where he would find fresh operators to drive. Most of the ones on the tractor seats had been there since about eight in the morning, when the flurry of wounded started coming down.

"Top, Easy Six," continued Greenley. "Be advised 13th Engineers have encountered some Jap stragglers and snipers down by the stream. Make sure the boys have their weapons with them, this fight ain't over yet. We can't count on the infantry to provide our security, so make sure the company is still posting guards around the clock. We've been forcing the Japs north all day, but some units are slipping away. They can be anywhere on the island."

Great. Just what we need. Bettencourt acknowledged and hung up, picking up one of the walkie-talkies, his helmet and carbine as he slipped out of the tent. To the south of the HQ tents and between the dug-in 105s were the dozens of small tents for the enlisted engineers. Jammed in between the small tents and the artillery was a battalion mess tent, so Bettencourt went directly there for a cup of coffee and a Spam sandwich before he rousted exhausted men for night duty.

It was about midnight when the last group of wounded was laboriously towed across the Sarana Valley in the aerial carts. Bettencourt knew the trip would be cold and frightening, the carts racking back and forth both from the jerking towline and the gusting wind. This group of wounded totaled about 20 men, and Lieutenant Wheeler and Bettencourt pulled together every available man to ensure they had four litter bearers each for the trip across Engineer Hill. Once across they reloaded them, one by one into the single tow cart for the quick ride down to the streambed. The wounded were set down and made as comfortable as possible as they waited for the last returning ferry group of D4s coming up from the beach. It was snowing lightly, the ground around the stream bright white, making the streambed especially black tonight. Bettencourt already had two reports of D4s dropping into deep water holes and getting stuck in the darkness. He requested replacements up from the beach motor pool through Greenley, and also received the okay, through Greenley via the battalion commander and the new ground commander, a major general, to run the D4s with full headlights.

196

On the streambed Bettencourt heard the distinct crack of rifle fire downstream in the direction of the bobbing distant headlights of the ferry dozers. This was followed a few seconds later by the *BOP BOP BOP BOP* of a Thompson submachine gun. There were a few more shots and another burst from the tommy gun, then quiet. Bettencourt waited impatiently until the first of the dozers slowly climbed up out of the streambed and stopped. He hauled himself up on the track, noticing immediately the lead operator was in bad shape. Without regard to the so-called sniper threat he flipped his flashlight on for a moment. The man had been shot through the jaw. His eyes rolled back in his head as he released his controls. He passed out cold. Bettencourt lifted the man out on the track where he was carried off by some of the other operators, a call for a medic echoed up the valley. Bettencourt sat down in the D4 and shut it down.

"Let's get these things unloaded!" He ordered. There were only eight D4s to survive the trip, so they were short two. They would have to make two more trips tonight to get all the wounded, two men to a cart, down to the ships. Once he took a complete tally, he realized they were actually short two operators, as another one had broken his wrist when his D4 slammed into a large, unseen boulder in the dark. Bettencourt asked for a volunteer among the exhausted operators to stay on the job, and reluctantly one said he would do it. Bettencourt thanked the man and reported to Lieutenant Wheeler via walkie-talkie he would fill the last empty seat himself and lead the ferry group down to the beach.

He knew the last trip up had been harrowing in the dark, and this time they would be carrying live human cargo.

"We'll go slow, and you all stick right on my tail. Go exactly where I go. Keep your weapons handy!"

The wounded were carefully strapped to the carts. It was eerie to run down the streambed in the twilight, the dark water seemed noisier, faster and deeper. It seemed much colder down on the water. Bettencourt shivered, constantly looking over his shoulder at his two patients, both big men who seemed alert and attentive. They groaned and moaned with the jerking, dipping, bouncing ride, but neither cried out. There had been reports of tow hooks separating from the carts, so Bettencourt had personally inspected each one before they started out. The sniper on the trip up was encountered in the last mile, so all of the operators hunkered instinctively behind the engines on the D4s the first 15 minutes or so. Bettencourt had his carbine strapped loosely across his chest, his eyes sweeping around up away from the water towards the light banks. *Where the hell would a Jap hide out there?* He wondered. It was flat, frozen, with no cover whatsoever.

No shots were fired. From about mile two and a half the streambed got real tricky. Areas where small waterfalls had been pushed over by the big dozers weeks before still had large holes downstream that had to be bypassed. Some were six or seven feet deep, but easy to see and avoid in the light of the Aleutian daytime. Not so easy in the dark twilight. Trying to rely on his memory from previous trips up the stream, Bettencourt instinctively stayed closer to the banks whenever there was any doubt. They also had to navigate around the two stuck D4s. The bright headlamps from his D4 bounced off of black, ice water. No sense of depth was possible. As he turned sharply right to negotiate a narrow bend in the stream, the cart lifted from the streambed and was carried sideways in an instant by the strong, downstream current, bringing it forward of the D4.

Bettencourt, glancing over his shoulder, recognized his error and turned the dozer back downstream, but the dozer's forward speed was not enough to straighten out the cart. The tow hook joining the cart to the D4 was now the top of a upside down V, with the apex or point of the V facing upstream against the current. The cart lifted up on the upstream side and continued to lift, sliding the downstream patient partially into the water. Bettencourt had no choice but to turn the D4 to the right towards the opposite bank, gunning the motor to increase speed so he could hopefully straighten out and level the cart. The scream behind him turned his head completely around in panic. The downstream patient had been sucked into the current although he was partially strapped in. The other patient was trying to hold onto the cart with one hand and his drowning companion with the other. As Bettencourt drove the D4 straight into the opposite bank something gave in the metal frame of the cart. The downstream side dropped into the water to twist up and almost completely on its back.

There was another scream and Bettencourt, already off the D4 wading towards the cart, witnessed the large body of a man, swathed in white bandages, flash downstream out of his reach into the darkness ahead. There was nothing he could do, the man was gone in an instant and out of sight. He got to the cart, realizing not only how deep the water was, but how incredibly cold it was. *Bone-numbing, strength-robbing, freezing goddamn cold.* Holding on, not knowing how much longer the cart would stay together, he felt under the dark water with his free hand until he felt what seemed to be a man's coat. He felt his way up and realized the man's head was just barely under the water. He felt for the back of his head and pushed up and up with all of his strength until the head was clear. The man, suddenly gasping and coughing, gripped Bettencourt's arm with incredible strength, pulling him down. Bettencourt stepped in closer and resisted, pressing hard against the cart.

"Don't pull, goddamnit!" He screamed weakly. *"I got ya, don't pull me down!"* The man seemed to understand, slowly releasing his dragging grip. Bettencourt, his body now about three-quarters under the current, was losing control of his muscles. His teeth chattered and his body shook uncontrollably, but he continued to press the man's head up out of the water. He could hear the sound of the other D4s drawing up and men's voices calling his name, but he didn't have the strength to respond.

Flashlights bobbed around them and Bettencourt could see some of the other operators were working around the cart, trying to stabilize it while others tried to free the wounded man. Bettencourt was so numb and cold he was having trouble breathing. The wounded man cried out, sharply and then gasped as he was brought out from below the cart and carried around Bettencourt. Two men hooked their arms around Bettencourt's shoulders and he was carried out of the water.

"Sorry sir," one of the operator's was saying to the wounded man, apparently an officer, as they wrapped him in a blanket. "I think I cut your leg when I cut the straps holding you down under the water." The man appeared to have passed out, his head tossed back with his mouth open. The same operator, now shivering uncontrollably himself now that he was soaking wet, wrapped a blanket around Bettencourt.

"Sorry Top, we couldn't find the other man. He must have washed downstream." Bettencourt didn't know what to say. He had just killed a man because of his mistake. He stared at the operator, a man named, Morrisey, with blank eyes.

"I should have known better than to turn so sharply with the current behind me. What a fuckin recruit thing to do," he gasped lamely.

Morrisey, the man who had volunteered to stay on after already working over fourteen hours, spat and shook his head.

"It's black as pitch out here on the water, and you can't see the course. This ain't your fault Top, none of us would've made this run iffen we wasn't ordered to." He glared at Bettencourt for a long moment before giving a nod over his shoulder.

"We'll disconnect that cart and get it out of the way, okay by you?"

"Yeah—fine," he chattered. "Give me a minute to warm up a bit."

They moved Bettencourt's D4 farther up the bank and disconnected the destroyed cart, pushing it to the stream bank. The big wounded man didn't have anywhere to go as there was no room on any of the other carts, but as he came to, he insisted he was more than ambulatory and would fit anywhere in the D4 cockpit. After he regained some feeling in his arms and legs, Bettencourt climbed up on this D4 and backed into the stream. He slid half out of his seat and dropped his big passenger half in the seat and half on the low quarter fuel tank on the left side of the seat. It was not very comfortable, but both men were soaking wet and they found there was a certain warmth to be found when two bodies were jammed that close together, even with wet blankets.

As Bettencourt helped his passenger up into the cab, he noticed there were soaked bandages all up his torn trousers on both legs, but he moved mechanically like the men who were frostbitten.

The big man noticed Bettencourt's look. "I really didn't need to be evacuated, I can still walk. Just shrap." he said defensively, which had Bettencourt shaking his head in wonder. He looked at the big man, who really was just a young fellow he realized under the ton of dirt and three week growth of beard. He looked closely at the collar and sure enough, upside down was a gold bar.

"Look, Lieutenant," Bettencourt said with difficulty, "I'm—real sorry about what happened. I didn't mean to do that—I do know what I'm doing."

The big guy looked at Bettencourt with level eyes. "Forget about it, Sergeant. You can't see shit out here. I feel bad about it, too. I couldn't hold em. But I almost joined him. You saved my life. I couldn't lift my head out of the water. Thanks." He sighed loudly, suddenly looking at the bulldozer and its controls with interest.

"You an engineer, Top?"

Bettencourt glanced over at his passenger and nodded. This kid was okay. He stuck out his right hand.

"Jon Bettencourt, 50th Engineers."

"Orin Craymer, Scout Battalion. Thanks for the ride. This D4 is a little more complicated than my dad's Allis-Chalmers."

"You a farm kid, Lieutenant?"

"Southwest Missouri. Stone County. More like rock scratcher than farmer. Not the best or most level land for good farming, in my opinion. But it's what we got."

"I'm from Oregon originally, Roseburg, lumber country."

The big guy's eyes closed with fatigue, coming open every now and then from the rocking, diving motion of the bulldozer.

CHAPTER 23

1900 Hours, May 21, 1943, D-Day Plus 10, Chichagof Harbor

Yoshi Nakagawa closed his eyes only to open them again, realizing the impossible had occurred. His nightmares under the morphine when he was first wounded brought the dark beasts to his consciousness only when he was asleep. The horrors of their presence receded to the corners of his mind mercifully when he awoke. The unpredictable, un-human way they moved frightened him thoroughly, stalking around like predatory animals with no consciousness, no understanding. Now the monsters were everywhere in his waking hours, walking around in Japanese Army uniforms, looking, searching, consuming those who were unable to protect themselves. He could see the monsters in the eyes of some of his fellow patients, the medical staff, and to his consternation and complete disgust, even in himself. He knew he was going mad.

He breathed deeply, pushing the air far into his lungs as if the oxygen would somehow purify him of his thoughts, of his guilt. So much had occurred in the last two days—indeed the last week—he was having great difficulty keeping it straight in his mind. Not that it particularly mattered in the long run, but his pathetic, pitiful revelation resulting in such self-loathing was both agonizing and totally unwanted. *I was a pampered child, even as a farmer's son, selected for a better life because I had a good head for numbers and quantitative thought. And here I am. Preparing, planning and waiting for my opportunity to steal the food from the mouth of a helpless, dying man because I am so hungry and because I can.*

Yoshi had recovered his memory and healed rapidly from his wounds. By the 18th of May he was walking about most of the day, asking for and receiving minor duties to assist the other patients in the tunnel hospital facility near the unfinished runway. He still received morphine once or twice a day as it gave him some temporary relief of the pain and the circumstances. Kenji, his NCO friend from the mountaintop, also remained and was pressed into service as a medical orderly. The bombing and shelling increased everyday as the Americans closed the gap and pressed the defending Japanese forces backwards towards Chichagof Harbor. Yoshi was fairly useless for any physical assistance with his right arm in a sling and his left hand, with two fingers missing, encased in a thick gauze bandage. He could, however, still manipulate the fingers of his right hand to use an abacus manual calculator for accounting duties as long as his mind stayed clear, or to make notes to maintain the meticulous personnel medical records. These sorts of duties he did willingly to simply get his mind off the growing reality of their situation, which was increasingly dire.

On May 17th, the first day Yoshi was able to move around unsupported a large part of the day, First Lieutenant Yamada, the senior medical officer, had called him aside for a private conversation.

"Lieutenant Nakagawa," he had said formally, after confirming no one was within earshot, "I know you are just now getting around on your feet, but I may need your services as a loyal Army officer." His eyes, still sunken and cold, stared without mercy into Yoshi's.

"Of course," Yoshi said cautiously. "I'll do whatever I can to help." As if to reinforce what the medical officer was about to say, the walls of the tunnel shook and reverberated from a very close shell hit. A few wounded men cried out in fear and alarm as the detonation seemed to be right at the mouth of the tunnel. Yamada seem to soften, his hard eyes losing their focus for a moment before he glanced again at Yoshi, unblinking.

"This is like nothing you have ever done before, Lieutenant, "Yamada said quietly. He brought his fingers up and made a pitched roof of his hands, pressing the peak against his nose. He signed heavily, not taking his eyes off Yoshi.

"The Americans have broken through and may be here—right here—in a hour or two. We do not have time to evacuate our patients, so I have received orders to prepare to destroy *all the patients*." Yoshi simply stared back at Yamada, not quite understanding what he had just heard. *Do what?*

Yamada's eyes narrowed, and if anything, he spoke louder and slower, as if talking to a child.

"The order may come *any minute*, and the first bit of business is to evacuate as much of my staff as possible so we can continue to support this fight *somewhere else.*" Yamada took his hands from his nose and firmly gripped Yoshi's shoulders.

"You are an Army officer so I know I can count on you." Yoshi said nothing, too confused to say anything as Yamada continued. "A few of the healthier patients we will simply put clothes on and they will walk out of here with us. The sicker patients," his eyes not leaving Yoshi's, "we will overdose with morphine, as it is something we have a lot of. Our final orders, Lieutenant, are to throw hand grenades in the

wards as we leave to make sure the job is done." Yamada took his
hands off of Yoshi, stepping back.

"I am asking *you* to talk charge of the three or four men, all
medical orderlies because I know it would be difficult for the patients to
do it to their comrades, who will do this final job with the grenades. I
want to know the job was done."

Yoshi, stunned, had no choice but to accept or he suspected, be
strapped to a bed and left as a patient to join the fate of the others to be
left behind. He was afraid of Yamada now. Yoshi didn't even
know how to throw a hand grenade properly, and certainly didn't
understand the kill radius or even how to arm the things. It just wasn't a
requirement for an engineering officer. But he also realized quite
suddenly he was not going to argue. He was just told he was one of the
survivors. He spent the next hour sitting silently by himself, waiting in
absolute horror, still not quite believing what was being asked of him.
What bothered him the most, he knew, was the realization First
Lieutenant Yamada, senior medical officer, was both willing and able to
do this assignment the minute the order came. A willingness to kill the
very patients he and the other medical staff had worked tirelessly to save
the last few days and weeks.

The order never came but a full hospital evacuation order did.
Seventy percent of the patients were to be moved immediately by litter
four miles in two stages to the surgical hospital at Chichagof Harbor. It
would take two days, with about a third of the patients dying of exposure
or shellfire in the course of the trip. The remaining 30 percent, too sick
to be transported by litter, were to be destroyed by morphine injection
immediately. Since the evacuation would take most of the night, there
would be sufficient time to confirm the morphine overdoses had done
the job and no hand grenade "cleanup" would be necessary. Yoshi
heard this last clarification from First Lieutenant Yamada himself and
walked about five paces before vomiting.

The only positive note from the sudden catastrophic turn of events
was there was never another word about a disciplinary inquiry for his
friend Kenji and the OP crews on Buchanan Ridge. Yoshi's supposed
heroism was never mentioned again either. The two-day journey
carrying the patients by litter to the new hospital at Chichagof Harbor
was a horrifying experience for Yoshi. It rained or snowed constantly,
the so-called hidden trail used was under constant bombardment from
either American 105 howitzers or naval guns. On two suddenly clear
periods on the same afternoon they were strafed by low-flying medium
bombers, injuring many of the bearers. Kenji was used as a litter
carrier and wounded himself by shrapnel. All Yoshi could do was carry

203

gravity-fed intravenous bottles in his teeth or around his neck as he walked next to a patient.   He asked for and continued to receive morphine injections and eventually was simply given a syringe kit and two-dozen vials.   He suspected he was addicted, he heard it was possible, but it was the only personal relief available to him.

What struck his heart was the fear he sensed among some of the patients now, not only for the shelling and bombing, but their fear of medical officers like First Lieutenant Yamada who quickly determined if a patient was too injured or sick to be carried on.   Some he knew were resigned to their fate, but there were others whose eyes darted from face to face anxiously as they were being treated for new wounds.   Their ears attuned to comments or the words sealing their doom.   Those patients so chosen were overdosed with morphine on the spot without ceremony and carefully laid on the cold ground and abandoned.   Litters were too valuable and were needed later, so the drugged patients were rolled off once they lost consciousness.

There was no further discussion of hand grenades on the trail, although Yoshi was hearing rumors officer patients who were alert and capable were given two hand grenades instead of a morphine overdose, as it was assumed the officers were good on their honor to complete the task.   He also found out many of the type 97 hand grenades failed to go off, hence the reason for two grenades.   *You put them side by side.* Yoshi, who heard this from Kenji, could only recoil in horror to such calm preparations for self-destruction. *I want to live. I want to live!*

He got even more physically sick when Kenji himself showed him two hand grenades he had in *his* pack—*for the end*—he said soberly. Once they arrived at the Chichagof Harbor hospital Yoshi encountered even more somber news.   Food supplies were near zero, and the commander of the garrison, Colonel Yamasaki, estimated there was only enough for the remaining troops until May 30th at one-third rations. Even these words didn't carry weight until Yoshi found out on their arrival many of the existing hospital staff had not eaten a full meal in *10 days*. *We are saving what there is for the patients or for the combat troops.* One or two rice balls were the usual daily allotment for medical staff at Chichagof.   And in nine days, there won't even be that.

The patient, an aging artillery major, had been one of the men they had carried over from the tunnel surgical hospital.   He had been wounded in both legs by shrapnel a week before and had been in solid recovery.   It seemed the cold exposure on the trail coming across plus some recent type of blood poisoning in his leg was sealing his fate. First Lieutenant Yamada removed one of his legs below the knee, but

204

the major, who had been lucid and reasonably talkative the day before, was now in and out of some delirium.   Yamada still expected him to come around and supper had arrived for him, a small thin bowl of Miso and two rice balls.   Yoshi was assigned the task of ensuring the major ate his supper if he woke up, and of course, to ensure no one else ate the meal.

His stomach growled constantly now, the cold miso still-pungent odor tantalizing to his senses as he stared at the little bowl on the side table.   Hunger did funny things to your mind, he decided, in some ways more so than powerful drugs like morphine.   Morphine dulls the senses, turning all sensory edges to either *dark dark dark* or blinding light images, none making a lot of sense and quickly robbed of clarity because you were dulled or asleep.   Hunger—hunger dulls nothing. Hunger sharpens senses to razor thin, microscopic embers to burn straight through stupid *concepts* and *philosophies* like DUTY and HONOR.   Yoshi sighed and watched the rhythmic evolutions of the major's slow breathing on his chest.   After a half an hour or so, the man's eyes opened slowly, his pupils dark and large, his brow wrinkling as he turned towards Yoshi.   He blinked without recognition, yet his brow remained wrinkled as he sniffed the air.

"Is that miso?" he asked weakly.

CHAPTER 24

1700 Hours, May 28, 1943, D-Day Plus 16, Pendergast Ridge Medical Collection Station

Ed Ridgeway demanded, cajoled, and harassed the exhausted receiving clerks at the medical collection station until a very angry regimental surgeon, a large bear of a man wearing major oak leaves threw him out. Ed tried to intimidate the surgeon by explaining he represented division intelligence, and had a *need-to-know* requirement to look at the casualty lists. The surgeon had stared at Ed with such contempt Ed knew immediately that was the wrong thing to say to this man.

"I don't give a *SHIT* about what division *NEEDS TO KNOW*! You got that, Captain?" The surgeon barked, stepping in so close to Ed's face he peppered his nose with spittle. "I have close to 60 patients we need to stabilize and evacuate, and my wore-out people are not wasting *ONE MINUTE* chasing some *BULLSHIT* after-action information for division. This regiment is still fighting and men are dying up in those goddamn mountains! *Get the fuck away from my people!"*

The surgeon stood his ground, his pent-up anger rising as he leaned in towards Ed, clearly waiting for Ed to retreat and follow his orders. Ed, who was used to this in his role as a prying intelligence officer, stepped back from the surgeon, lifting his hands in surrender. The surgeon glared and followed him as he retreated to the exit.

"I'm sorry, Major," he said evenly, "I—I was out of line." He started to clumsily lift his right arm in his sling to salute then dropped it, raising his plaster-casted left hand instead in a half wave. The surgeon just glared motionlessly until Ed backed out of the tent.

He stood outside the tent for a moment, frustrated, then moved down a couple of tents until he found the casual receiving tents. Here men who were marked for evacuation but were ambulatory waited for their turn. Some of the men had been there several days, as new more critical casualties from the fighting up on Fish Hook Ridge and the lower hills around the Chichagof Valley were taking priority. Most of the men in that situation didn't seem to care. They were out of the fight and they had survived. Everyday here is a day away from the weather exposure of Attu. They were well fed, the cots reasonably dry and warm, and they slept in sleeping bags. Most of them were in the same uniforms they were wearing when the invasion began, 16 days earlier. Their wounds or injuries were serious enough to warrant evacuation to a hospital ship and perhaps medical facilities at Adak or elsewhere, but they were ambulatory. They walked into the aid tent and walked out after treatment. Others had more serious wounds or injuries treated days earlier at battalion aid stations, where their uniforms were cut away and burned. These men were kept warm in sleeping bags and had no need for uniforms anymore.

Ed found Orin Craymer where he had left him, lying on his cot staring at the ceiling of the tent. It was, he decided, one of the saddest things he had ever experienced, sharing this fruitless search of a man looking for his brother. As a historian and an intelligence officer he was long used to a dispassionate view of the events unfolding around him. He had to. The events were interesting, even fascinating, but he was never emotionally involved to the estimates of enemy forces, potential threats, or casualties. Not until now, not ever to such an extent until he spent these last two weeks with Orin Craymer.

"No luck, huh?" said Orin quietly, his eyes still on the ceiling. All the cots were occupied so Ed kneeled down next to Orin's and slipped his helmet off.

"No," Ed sighed, "one of the docs got on my ass for harassing his clerks and I got thrown out."

"Yeah, so we all heard. Thanks for trying again, Ed. I guess I'm just not going to know until this thing is over, and now they're shipping me out." Orin slowly pulled himself up from the cot and swung his legs over to the dirt floor. To Ed it was painful to watch. Orin's dirty fatigue blouse was bulky with the bandages underneath, but his trousers were slit down on the right side to accommodate the numerous thick bandages from his buttocks to his calf and just hung there. His right hand with the human bite was finally starting to heal. His feet, marginally frostbitten, were wrapped partially in thick gauze and heavy wool socks. He fished out one of his rare cigarettes, letting Ed light it for him. Orin peered at his friend through the smoke quizzically, his exhaustion and resignation sloping his wide shoulders forward.

"Why you still here, Ed? You could have left anytime you wanted." Orin mused, casually waving towards Ed's injuries. He shook his head and smiled slowly, one of the first smiles Ed had seen on Orin's face in days. "I figured you'd catch the first boat out of this shit hole once the battalion piece was over."

Ed took the proffered cigarette from Orin's pack, lighting it while shaking his head slowly. They'd gone over this before, but Ed was starting to understand how Orin communicated his acceptance, respect and friendship. They both could have been evacuated as early as the 16th, he figured. Here it was 11 days later, Orin's wounds and a more organized medical evacuation system finally catching up with him. On the 16th Orin had let a battalion surgeon pull the shrapnel out of his arms and most of the shrapnel out of his right thigh and buttocks. A few pieces were too deeply imbedded and would need better facilities. The surgeon also noticed how Orin hobbled and insisted on looking at his feet, but the doc was somehow distracted at the time and Orin managed his first escape. He had been tagged for immediate evacuation but he tore the tag off when the staff was not looking and slipped out, returning to the remains of the Scout Battalion.

The battle for Scout Canyon as it became to be known, ended abruptly and just in time. The four-day battle down the pass to attack the Japanese defenders of the Sarana Valley ended as a success. The two-sided pressure of the 17th and 32nd Infantry coming south from Red Beach on the one hand and the Scout Battalion pressing down from the pass was too much. On the morning of the 15th, all of the remaining Japanese units in the Sarana Valley withdrew to Moore Ridge. They withdrew so quickly they abandoned precious food and ammunition stores, leading intelligence officers like Ed Ridgeway to suggest the Japanese believed they were facing a much larger force coming from the west. Captured documents and communiqués suggested some Japanese officers believed they were facing a division-sized force based on the ferocity of the attack down the pass. Captain Williamson, upon hearing this bit of information, had guffawed. When his assault force finally connected with a platoon from the 17th Infantry, he had less than 100 men still standing from his original force of 400, and not a single mortar shell left for supporting fire.

Orin, who had hoped he would be able to be part of the lead forces to hook up with the 17th and 32nd Infantry coming from Red Beach, didn't make it down to Moore Ridge until the morning of the 16th. By then the Japanese defenders on Moore Ridge were destroyed and the 17th and the 32nd had moved east towards the base of Fish Hook Ridge. Williamson ordered the Scout Battalion to stand down temporarily so they could bring out all of their wounded from the pass. Orin, knowing King Company and the 3rd of the 32nd has passed within yards of where he stood on Moore Ridge the day before, was sick with disappointment. He turned himself in to the nearest battalion aid station to get his wounds evaluated.

The success of the Scout Battalion's rearguard assault was apparently not enough to save the commanding general of the Attu assault ground force. Ed Ridgeway was surprised to hear on the 16th the island assault was considered "bogged down" and the commanding general was being replaced. Somehow it appeared the original "three days to victory" mantra for Attu had remained a firm target at the highest level of the command structure. The intelligence information received earlier suggesting the defending force was larger than anticipated was ignored. The information gleaned from the documents forwarded by Ed Ridgeway via Orin Craymer's patrol didn't seem to change anything either. The former commander's urgent request for more troops and supplies, and more time to clear the island of a larger defending force was categorized as an excuse. Appalled when he heard this intel rumor soon to be fact, Ed could only shake his head in wonder.

Normally, he spent his days as a sifter of information, looking for clues. He was always safe, dry and far from the collection point of the intelligence. For once he was a provider of information, a resource. It felt amazing to handle the information at the source and incredibly powerful to pass it on. He had no say on how the command structure used the information, of course, but never expected them to virtually *ignore* it. With the Scout Battalion finished as a combat organization by the end of the day on the 16th, Ed Ridgeway was free to evacuate himself from the island even if he didn't have a dislocated shoulder and a broken wrist. He certainly didn't report to Captain Williamson, so he was free to go and return to his world of information *sifting*.

That day he had checked in with the nearest battalion aid station and had a surgeon look his fractures over. He had seen Orin Craymer earlier grimacing as another surgeon probed his numerous shrapnel wounds, then examine the bitten hand for sign of infection. Orin looked like he was going to live and was being tagged for evacuation. The mission was over as far as Ed was concerned. He figured Orin would be evacuated at the same time he was, so he was sticking around for the surgeon to be finished with him.

His own examination earlier was less than conclusive. The surgeon had poked and probed the shoulder and his wrist. They had no working X-ray machine at the aid station that day, so the surgeon noted the obvious. Neither wound was swelling but there was the high probability of a fracture in the shoulder. Bone fragments were a real possibility, and they would need to be removed surgically. It required attention as soon as possible. The wrist was clearly broken and would not heal properly on its own. The surgeon had poked and felt around Ed's nose and removed the splint, replacing it with a big plaster bandage to remind Ed not to mess with it. That was it. Tagged for evacuation as a non-priority.

That night they had one of their very first arguments as friends. When Ed found out Orin was planning to go back to the Scout Battalion and ignore his evacuation orders, his normal unflappable demeanor turned angry. He knew Orin had missed his opportunity, due to no fault of his own, to possibly meet his brother.

"What are you talking about, Orin? What possible reason could you have to want to stay on the island? Our mission is complete. It is *over!* They are pulling out *all* of the scouts—all of them, that is, what's left of them! Williamson isn't going on, his command is gone as the mission is over." Ed, standing up and rearing up—just like the regimental surgeon he would argue with days later—threw his arms in the air in frustration.

"You can't chase your brother, Orin! The 3rd of the 32nd and the 17th infantry guys are going up Fish Hook Ridge. The Japs are making a stand up there. That's straight fucking up some 3,000 feet. You can't even walk, you dumb bastard!" Orin simply glared at Ed before standing up, demonstrating at least to Ed he was about three inches taller and wasn't about to fall over.

"I'll see you, Captain Ridgeway," he said curtly, shuffling out of the tent.

"Wait!" Ed said in frustration, following Orin and catching up with him. It was not hard to do. Orin stopped when Ed grabbed his arm with his bandaged hand. Orin grimaced but said nothing. Ed stared at Orin for a moment before shaking his head.

"You fuckin hardhead, you goddamn Okie hardhead!"

"Missouri hardhead, Ed. I'm not from Oklahoma, remember?"

"What do I have to do to get you off this island, OT?" There was no hesitation as Orin looked at him.

"Help me find my brother. I need to know if he's dead, wounded or still out there on the line. I have to do this."

So it went, Ed Ridgeway and Orin Craymer forming a strange little pact. Ed Ridgeway hooked up with some friends in regimental intelligence to find at least a place for them to stay at night while they made their search. Williamson was too busy to be bothered with Ridgeway, but he was concerned one of his wounded officers was still on the island. *He's leaving very soon, Captain.* Williamson seemed satisfied. No one asked what Ed Ridgeway was up to, although on more than one occasion he introduced Orin as a scout infantry officer temporarily assigned to Ed as an intelligence aide. Two unattached officers "working for division intelligence" never got a follow-up inquiry anyway, even from senior officers. The two of them would receive a grimace or a casual acknowledgement before they were completely ignored and forgotten.   It worked perfectly.   The only problem for Ed was his concern for Orin's wounds and frostbitten feet. He realized for once in his life he was thinking of someone beside himself and wasn't the least concerned about his own broken bones. As they searched one battalion aid station or medical collection station after another looking for casualty information, doctors would always look at both men with concern, especially if they saw Orin hobble in.

"I need to take a look at your feet, Lieutenant," they would say. After awhile Orin figured out he was better served to remain outside or nearby, out of sight.   He could not resist, however, walking through the tents and the casualty triage areas looking at each man individually. When Ed found Orin lifting the shelter halves covering the dead set outside, he drew the line and made him stop.

"This is ghoulish, OT. Knock this shit off! I can get a list of the dead, okay?   You're making yourself sick doing this!"   It was rough though and difficult to not want to look, especially the battalion aid stations close to the battle areas where the bodies were often left uncovered, their bearded, frost-covered faces all looking the same.

After a couple of days Ed had found out exactly where the 3rd of the 32nd had been and the likely aid stations used for their casualties. What he also discovered, disheartening but not surprising, was some men were carried off by other units working as litter bearers, and casualties could be found just about anywhere there was an aid station or medical collection station.   Battalions had their own aid stations but the wounded were accepted from anyplace.   Men lost their ID tags and were either unconscious when processed or possibly even died without any one actually knowing who they were.   Every aid station had a small number of men who where categorized as "unknowns".   This information drove Orin to anger and frustration, especially when they considered the earlier aid stations they had visited.   There were individuals, alive and dead they had not seen simply because they were unknown. No one had told them.

Ed did the best he could to calm Orin down.   In the long run, even in the middle of a battle, the Army was still the Army.   People— soldiers are constantly in movement, changing ranks, positions or units. Men change duty stations, change ratings, coming and going as you would expect any organization that relied so much on a constant flow of new members and had world-wide manning responsibilities.   It was because of this Ed knew, instinctively, some of the best record-keeping to be found anywhere would be by the Army, even in the middle of a battleground.

"My educated guess," he sighed one afternoon late while they picked at their fried Spam and potato dinner from a field kitchen, "is your brother Ray is still serving with his unit. He's not showing up on KIA (killed in action), WIA (wounded in action) or MIA (missing in action) reports anywhere. The 3rd of the 32nd has been a sister battalion with the 17th Infantry right from the time they landed on Red Beach. But the 17th had the lead, so the 32nd wasn't taken the casualties like the 17th. They're going up Fish Hook Ridge right behind the 17th in a day or two, so things might change, but right now, I think he's—okay. He's not wounded, he's not a frostbite casualty, and he's not—dead as far as we know. The Army is meticulous about that. If he wasn't around he would be listed as missing by now."

Orin, constantly in physical pain, looked up from his plate with dull, weary eyes. He had followed the advice of numerous medics to constantly massage his feet and keep them dry. He knew the circulation was bad and there was significant discoloration, but the feeling was coming back to his feet. It was a painful, tingling, burning feeling, yet he knew instinctively that it was a good thing, a good sign. He was very grateful to Ed for arranging a reasonably warm tent and cot to sleep in most nights, and he knew damn well Ed had set aside his own injuries to pursue this hunt for his brother. He knew. He just could not leave this island without some knowledge of his brother's fate, that's all. *I owe this to my parents, if nothing else. But mostly I owe it to Ray.*

Ed had talked briefly to one of the regimental surgeons about the issues of waiting too long to get broken bones taken care of. The surgeon had looked at him with steel eyes for a long moment.

"Are we talking about you, Captain?" Ed's eyebrows went up and down and the surgeon's eyes narrowed.

"When did they get broken?"

"Two weeks ago."

"I see. Well, we would need to X-ray them, but the shoulder, if there are pieces of bone floating about, should be no issue. The stuff will show up and the surgeon will take care of it." He looked at Ed's wrist, then smiled.

"If your wrist is not set right, and I will make a broad assumption and say it is not, the surgeon might have to break it again." Ed's eyes widened and his mouth set in a thin line.

In the face of it, Ed Ridgeway liked the way he felt. He thought of Orin Craymer and knew he was looking at a man he greatly admired and respected. But more than anything, Orin was a man who had a value system he truly believed in, and followed it. It was not something you see very often. Orin valued his duty as an infantry officer over his injuries up in the pass. He was also a man who valued his relationship with his brother more than his personal injuries, pain, or suffering. And he did it without, apparently, a soliloquy on self-doubt, or self-reflection. It was just *done*.

Ed Ridgeway had spent most of his life observing and certainly as an Army intelligence officer, *observing officially*. Such bullshit. For the first time in many years, he did not have to give some excuse for himself for why he did what he did. His shoulder hurt and so did his wrist. *I'll live.* Besides, he was still gathering information everywhere he went, information for the official division reports of the battle for Attu Island. *No matter what the outcome of the battle they would face the Japanese again very soon. It was going to be a long war.* He glanced at his wristwatch and watched Orin rub his calf muscles.

"So they got you on some evac list tonight?"

"Yep, last group of wounded coming off of Fish Hook goes across, and I'm supposed to join them late tonight." Ed lit another cigarette and rubbed his wrist.

"About time, I need to get you out of my life for awhile. You are not good for my health."

CHAPTER 25

2100 Hours, May 27, 1943, D-Day Plus 16, Pendergast Ridge Medical Collection Station

Ray Craymer was certain he had heard one of the exhausted litter bearers carrying him say it took *eight hours to bring this big goddamn sumbitch down* from the top of the ridge. He heard it, disjointed, far away as he drifted in and out of a morphine fog after a medic had injected him with the sweet, soothing stuff down at a battalion aid station. He heard the words but couldn't process it. *What big goddamn sumbitch is he talking about?* The trip down in the morning started out in a fog, his personal fog, as he was sedated heavily when Lieutenant Bowles declared their end of Fish Hook Ridge secure enough to evacuate the wounded. He felt more than saw a soldier he believed to be Bowles shake his hand. Bowles said something to him but Ray couldn't remember. It was cold, cold and snowing, and he was afraid just for a moment knowing how steep the ridge face was. There was no sky to speak of, the grey-whitish swirling snow ever present around his face until someone covered it with a part of the blanket.

He dozed off fitfully only to awaken by the constant jerking, sudden-drop, twisting and falling sensations, accompanied by the heavy breathing, gasping and cursing of the men carrying him. Somewhere down the slope as the hours passed he felt it getting warmer. At one point the blanket was carefully lifted up, waking him. He looked up at what must have been a medic checking his pulse. The dull, soothing fur of the morphine was wearing off and he was in a lot of pain. He might have even cried out, he wasn't sure, because he heard men cry out around him. He felt a stab at his arm and saw the intravenous line drift up to a bottle now being held by another soldier, then felt another poke in his arm and the soothing, furry dullness creep up his body until he drifted off again.

When he awoke he felt another stab of pain around his shoulder and tried to lift his head but couldn't. He realized suddenly he was indoors, sort of. The triage tent was the first real roof over his head in 16 days as the battalion aid station, his first stop, had only some kind of a rain fly for patients being evaluated. He found the olive drab green canvas instantly comforting as his litter was swung up across two wooden saw horses. A tall thin young man with a narrow mustache stepped up next to him without saying a word, peering at his casualty card for a long moment.   He unwrapped the wool blankets cocooning Ray to the litter, lifting sticky bandages to peer underneath, continuing to expose more skin as he did so and making Ray very cold.

He noticed Ray's eyes stayed open and were following his movements, so he glanced at the card again.   Ray sensed another litter was being placed very close to his as other medics hovered around.   Ray saw the silver railroad tracks of a captain on the man's fatigue blouse. He was wearing an apron of some kind with lots of dried blood on it. Ray stared at the blood.

"How are you feeling, soldier?"   The captain asked overly loud, not looking at Ray as he continued his examination.   When Ray didn't respond after a few seconds the captain came up to his face and waved a flashing beam across his eyes, first one and then the other.   Ray blinked, blinded and coughing, as he realized he wanted to vomit.

"What's your name, soldier?"   The captain demanded, "name of your unit?"   Ray choked back the growing bile to take a deep breath. It took him a second to answer.

"Cramer, sir, PFC.   King Company, 3rd of the 32nd."   The captain looked at the card and nodded.

"They have you marked as a sergeant.   What is it, are you a PFC or a sergeant?"   Confused for a moment, Ray remembered finally being promoted on the ridge to acting sergeant by both Staff Sergeant O'Hearn and by Lieutenant Bowles.

"I guess I got promoted on the ridge, sir, by my lieutenant."   The captain seemed satisfied with the answer and ignored Ray for the next few minutes as he probed and prodded Ray's numerous shrapnel wounds.   The captain called over a medic who helped him, very painfully for Ray, to turn him on his side so the captain could examine the wounds on his hip and thigh.   When he came across the sword wounds on Ray's thigh and knee the captain came back into view, peering at Ray with interest.

"How long ago did you get these wounds? Some are more recent than others, I assume?"   Ray had to think, think hard against the fog, trying to remember.

"Do you know the dates you were wounded, Sergeant?"   The captain asked patiently.   Ray had no idea what day it was.   He knew it was the 11th or the 12th of May when they landed on Red Beach.

"Nossir," he said groggily,   "but I think I first got hit yesterday morning."

"Okay," the captain said skeptically, "it seems some of these puncture wounds are sealed up and seem older than one day, so we need

215

to see what we got." He lifted the bandage and looked at the small bullet wound in the muscle of Ray's neck and shook his head.

"You were really lucky with this one, Sergeant, it went clean through like a hot poker, didn't hit an artery, your spine, or your windpipe!" Ray simply stared at him, not really remembering clearly exactly when he was shot in the neck. During the bayonet charge from the Jap mortar position, he guessed. Maybe.

"I've counted over 40 shrapnel punctures, Sergeant, and I'm not done! What the hell hit you up there?" The probing was starting to hurt and the nausea was overwhelming. Ray looked over at the captain and closed his eyes.

"A lot of steel and rocks, sir," he said almost as a whisper, "a lot of steel and rocks."

Ray knew he was swimming, which was not an activity he was particularly fond of, so he let the dream drift along and he hoped, the stupid hope you only get in dreams, the dream would improve and he could will it somehow to go somewhere else. It is so strange how the mind works in the subconscious, if that is where dreams reside. He swam until he came to a log—or a beach—or a raft? It was dry, and it was close and it ended the swimming so he went there. Then Linda called to him, somewhere up ahead, out in the water where it was foggy and cold. He couldn't see her at all in the fog, only hear her voice. He didn't like to dream about Linda. Linda was there—peace, quiet, safe and there. There was home. He did not want to think of her here. The stateside peace of lighted streets all night, of diners with menus a mile long, a world of warm thighs and moist lips to kiss and caress. That needed to stay there. No M1s, or hand grenades, or fucking bayonets or goddamn Japs and things that offer nothing but pain, a hard time or death. She called for him, again, her voice searching and somehow yearning. In the dream Ray knew he was safe, but he pushed off into the water, so cold, towards a voice he could no more ignore than his need for sleep or food. He swam and the water grew colder, the fog thicker, but Linda's voice remained distant as though he had swam in the wrong direction. Linda, help me, he pleaded, keep calling, because I'm getting weaker, I can't do this much longer, so keep calling.

Ray came to finding himself in a post-surgical tent lying on a stiff cot, most of his body in a mummy-style sleeping bag. He was exhausted and cold. For about 30 seconds he remembered the dream of swimming and searching for Linda, then the dream faded and vanished. He had no other recollection of anything after the initial triage inspection when he arrived. He remembered vaguely talking to some officer—a surgeon, who was hurting him as he examined him, but nothing after that.

"This is the—let's see, 28th. 28th of May, Sergeant," responded the harried medic tending to the post surgical patients to Ray's question. Ray found out he had been sedated the night before and the captain who had first examined him had cleaned up his gunshot wound in the neck, stitched up the saber wounds on his thigh and knee, and removed a great deal of the shrapnel out of his shoulders, hips, thighs and calves.

"You'll need to get the rest of it out probably in Hawaii or stateside," the medic added. All Ray knew was he hurt a lot more now than he had hurt—*was it really only yesterday?*

What made Ray's day was when he heard the *wisenheimer* jokes of Manny Torre, three cots down. There was no mistaking the New England accent when Torre talked to the medics, so when Ray propped himself up on his cot to simply stare over at Torre until Torre spotted him, he was ready.

"CRAY!" Torre bolted upright for maybe three seconds his eyes wide and incredulous until blinding pain sending him writhing and gasping for breath. "Holy shit…" he moaned, "that fuckin' hurts…"

They couldn't get out of their sleeping bags or cots so they talked across the other patients, much to the annoyance of the ones who were not so sedated they were trying to sleep. Not that it was it quiet. It was light and morning with out-going 105 fire from the battery two miles away on Engineer Hill howling as it arched over on its way to the north end of Chichagof Valley. Small arms fire, the distant, shifting *poc-poc-poc* echo of .30 caliber machine guns never went away. Groups of new wounded were still being brought in as Fish Hook Ridge was cleared from one end to the other.

Torre grew quiet as Ray confirmed the squad was gone, with Smit the only known survivor still up on the ridge as of yesterday. Torre was unconscious when the grenade had landed near the other wounded men in the trench, so he didn't know about Wallace. The color had returned to his face, but the hollow, haggard eyes and nearly three-week growth of beard still made him look like a tiny old man. His right arm was severely strapped to his chest to restrict movement of his shoulder. The huge bandage covering the slashed fingers of his left hand made his skinny little arm look like it was inside of a white boxing glove. His only option for moving around was propping himself on his left elbow, but this sent a jagged tearing stab of pain across his shoulder. It felt like the stitches were pulling apart when he did it, so he stopped.

"Oh, jeez," he said with a feeble groan, "I need a cigarette bad." He peered over at Ray, who stared at the ceiling of the tent. "If Smit is

217

still alive, then it's only us three left, ain't it?" Ray, who was thinking about Dan Cooley, looked over at him.

"That's right." He didn't notice the large man right away who blocked the doorway to the tent because people were coming and going constantly. He felt the presence of someone next to his cot so he looked up, surprised to see a wide, sling and bandage-festooned captain staring at him, a stranger. The captain was filthy dirty, but his bandages were new. He was wearing some kind of a shoulder holster rig so Ray knew right off he was no infantry officer. He leaned forward as much as he could to attempt to sit up straight.

"No—no, uh—please, don't try to get up!" The captain said quickly, his eyes peering hard at Ray, a glint of merriment in his eyes and a growing recognition of some sort. He took his helmet off, taking in Ray's visible bandages in a half of a second before returning again to his face.

"Hot damn, you two look *alike!*" He said almost to himself. His grin grew wider and he stepped in closer, his right hand out under the sling.

"I'm Captain Ridgeway, Ed Ridgeway. You have got to be Ray Craymer! You are almost the spittin image of your brother, Orin!" Ray, speechless for a second or two, leaned farther forward until it hurt to cautiously take the man's hand.

"You know my brother, Orin Craymer—sir?" He asked skeptically, without meaning to. He stared as they shook formally, but couldn't help but saying almost immediately, "he's okay, sir? Is he— here, somewhere? On the island?" Ridgeway nodded and kneeled down between the cots, drawing even closer to Ray. Ray had never seen the man in his life but sensed a great deal of familiarity in Ridgeway regarding himself and his family.

"He was on the island until late last night when they evacuated him, kicking and screaming. He's been looking for you since the day he got here, the first day of the invasion. He was with the Scout Battalion, got pretty shot up the first few days and could have been evacuated damn near two weeks ago. I couldn't change his mind so we've been looking for *you* the whole time!"

Ray didn't know what to say, his eyes welled up and there wasn't a damn thing he could do about it. He felt enormous relief, then frustration and anxiety. *Holy shit! He was right here on Attu!*

"And he's gone? You said, sir, he got shot up bad? How bad?" He could tell Ridgeway was regretting what he had said earlier and was looking for a way to say it differently. Ridgeway was looking at Ray's wounds more carefully before glancing around at the other patients in the ward, most seriously wounded.

"Serious—but not that bad," he said, almost jovially. "He got a lot of shrapnel from Jap mortars, and his feet—they got a little bit of frostbite. It was cold up in the ridges where we were.

"He's going to be okay," he added, "his feet were improving once he got them warm and dry, and all the shrapnel was in his legs and arms." Ray looked at him in obvious pain, a hundred questions in his eyes.

"How are you—Sergeant? It is Sergeant, correct?" Ridgeway asked chattily. "We've been looking for a PFC, but the WIA roster I came across had a Sergeant R. M. Cramer, and I took a chance. Well, not much of a chance, I've been here a couple of days myself when Orin was here, and even though this is a 17th Infantry medical collection station, we learned the battalion aid stations and the med collection stations take all comers when casualties are coming hot and heavy. We also learned the 3rd of the 32nd was up on Fish Hook Ridge with the 17th, and casualties were coming down from the big fight up there."

"You knew all that, my battalion, where we were?" Ray looked at Ridgeway more calmly now, his shoulders slumping with fatigue from the excitement of the last few minutes. He took in the dirty beard and uniform but couldn't help but notice the wide middle and paunch.

"You serve with my brother, sir? Are you his—company commander?" He asked hesitatingly. "He is a—officer—isn't he, sir?" The merriment returned to Ridgeway's eyes as he nodded and then shook his head sadly.

"Kinda yes, no and absolutely, Sergeant. I landed with your brother with the Scout Battalion and I did accompany them up the ridges and down the passes on the western side where we were. It was one hell of a wild trip believe you me! But I'm an intelligence officer from division, as you might have surmised, and I could barely hang on with those scout troops! I'll let your brother tell you about some of his personal adventures! He's a platoon commander, your brother, and one brave, tough hombre!" He said this with a big admiring grin, and Ray couldn't help but swell with pride to hear it.

"What about you, Sergeant? How are you? You look like you got a little shot up yourself."

"Yessir," he said quietly. "Shrapnel from grenades and mortars, not too bad." Ridgeway nodded and slowly moved his large bulk to his feet. He noticed Ray's examination of his sling and bandage, so he smiled ruefully.

"We had to sled down the top of one of the peaks and I crashed—hard!" He laughed. Glancing down at his arm he shook his head, dismissing them. "Just an out of shape fat guy who paid the price in broken bones!" He stepped back in to lean forward again, offering his slung hand to Ray.

"It is a pleasure to meet the brother of Orin Craymer. I have heard a great deal about you, Sergeant. Your brother speaks the world about you, and I can see why."

Ray didn't know exactly how to respond. He shook Ridgeway's hand again, holding on to it for a moment.

"Thank you, sir. Will you see my brother, again?"

"I don't know if we'll end up on the same hospital ship, but maybe so. Of course, the ships are still out there, and you might make it out to the same one yourself. Do you know when you will be evacuated?"

"Nossir, I don't."

"Neither do I. I'm pretty low priority and I can walk out of here, so I might be the last so-called casualty off this damned island! It serves me right, hanging out with your damned brother!" Ridgeway grinned and beamed, throwing Ray a sloppy, left-handed salute as he walked away.

"Sir!" Ray called after Ridgeway, who stopped in the doorway of the tent.

"If you see my brother before I do, tell him—tell him I am damned proud of him. Will you tell him that, Captain?" Ridgeway grew serious and nodded slowly.

"I will do that, Sergeant. You Craymers are too much!"

Ray slid back into his warm sleeping bag, sighing loudly as he wiped his eyes with his hands. He never felt better in his life. He sensed Manny Torre staring in his direction but ignored him, glowing in the warmth of the knowledge his brother had not only been on Attu, but more importantly he was now *off* of it and would be okay.

"*Sergeant? Sergeant?*" Did I hear that captain call you sergeant?" Manny mocked shrilly, his voice going up questioningly. "What did you do up there once I got bayoneted? You get visited by division officers like you are some kind of Hollywood asshole?" Ray turned slightly to his right to peer over at Manny Torre. Torre had the biggest shit-eating grin he had ever seen on the man.

"Sorry, *Sergeant*!" Torre said very respectfully, the grin even wider. "I think I just answered my own question!"

The afternoon grew colder and damper, the steady light snow replaced by a thick, sticky fog. All day casualties were being prepared for transport across the valley to Engineer Hill with the cable tow system. A few of the medics had made the run across and back and said it wasn't too bad if the wind wasn't blowing hard. The road underneath was a few days away from being complete, so Ray figured he would have to just take his chances like everybody else. The hospital was practically deserted compared to the days before when the most casualties were coming down and every cot was filled. Only 30 or 40 patients were still around, so Ray knew he and Manny would be evacuated soon. When supper time came and the medics didn't come and start to bundle them up like they had done the rest, they were disappointed and waited in frustration for their meal. It was dangerous to cross the valley on the tow carts in the dark, the medics said. The night before, one of the tractor tows carrying wounded had spilled in the stream in the darkness and a man was drowned. *Just one more day, cheer up fellas!*

Long after dinner Ray heard men coming through the medical collection station who had just returned from a reconnaissance patrol up in the middle hills of the Chichagof Valley. They were highly agitated and seemingly frightened and Ray, who was now awake more than he was asleep, was alerted to their comments.

We gotta tell the captain right now, not after some chow, goddamn it! That had ta been several hunnerd Japs getting juiced up in full combat gear! We are gonna get hit and damned if I'm gonna be around!

Ray listened as the squad-sized patrol slipped through their boundaries. The men were actually glancing over their shoulders with visible concern, looking to the north. Ray wondered how many friendly combat units were in the valley between the medical collection station and the Japs in the Chichagof Valley. He sat up, looking around, realizing not a single man was visible in the compound who was carrying a weapon. There were no guards posted. In fact, at this time at night, they rarely saw the medics come through unless there were critical patients. Ray had no weapon, not even a combat knife. Everything had been taken away from him. He heard rustling to his right in the dim light of the reduced kerosene lantern, turning to find the wide eyes of Manny boring into his.

"Did you hear those guys, Cray?" He asked quietly.

"Yeah, I sure did."

"We got Japs headin our way?"

221

CHAPTER 26

1230 Hours, May 29, 1943, D-Day Plus 18, Chichagof Valley

With the assigned hour rapidly coming up, Yoshi Nakagawa, with his friend Kenji at his side, kneeled and bowed far forward towards the shrine. They both knew these were the last few moments of privacy they would have so they came to the shrine together, to be alone. After so many sleepless nights, Yoshi had difficulty focusing his thoughts. He prayed good fortune for his parents and siblings, but could not speak the other words he was thinking. He could not, here in this shrine, say goodbye to his family and to Shikoku forever, he just could not say it.

He believed he was now consciously living in a world gone fully insane. Like many parts of his childhood and even his early adulthood, the events in his life were very orchestrated with his only role to follow along. He was always good at that, did his lessons, worked hard and was rewarded to higher levels of opportunity. He was told when he did his very best doors would open and continue to open until he had reached the highest possible level of his capabilities. He had done those things his parents and teachers had told him to do, and done them well. Nothing prepared him for the time the doors would suddenly begin to close, the spring suddenly turning to fall without the benefit and satisfaction of summer. *That's it, isn't it?* He considered in anger, *I have just started out, why must I face this now?*

Twenty-four hours earlier Yoshi witnessed numerous strange rituals among the other officers, especially those assigned to Colonel Yamasaki's command staff. These officers gathered the senior officers of the remaining garrison to read the Imperial Edict from the Emperor, the final orders from Colonel Yamasaki, and to lead them in some form of purification ceremony. Since Yoshi was no longer with his engineering colleagues, he joined the other medical officers from the combined staff from the Chichagof Harbor surgical hospital.

The Imperial Edict was not a new message, it was simply the reading of an order from the Emperor requiring all Japanese subjects, including the officers and the men who served them, to recognize their duty as Japanese soldiers. There would be no evacuation and no surrender. Their spirit as Japanese soldiers would ensure that as long as blood flowed in their veins they would fight and kill the enemy. It was their duty and their Emperor's wishes.

222

Colonel Yamasaki's message was more specific and more optimistic. There were still slightly less than 1,000 Japanese soldiers still standing on Attu. These represented all of the able-bodied forces, both infantry and support, now withdrawn from the ridgelines and concentrated in the Chichagof Valley. He believed the American forces were lax in security in the Chichagof Valley region and were assuming the battle for the island was essentially over now that Fish Hook Ridge, the only remaining known Japanese stronghold, had been overrun. Yamasaki decided that a single bold thrust up the Chichagof Valley through a weak section of the American defenses could turn the tide of the battle. With 1,000 men, essentially a reinforced infantry battalion, and his bold plan the Americans could be defeated. He believed in the initiative of his plan and the undaunted spirit of the Japanese soldier to ensure the plan's success.

A young major gave the briefing to the medical staff. Yoshi, who had never sat in on an attack briefing in his life, was amazed at the young major's enthusiasm over the plan. He didn't have a map, but stood on a table outlining the plan with his arms in swooping motions as if he were painting on a wall. *It sounded so simple, Yoshi wondered if it could actually work?* In broad terms, the major explained how Engineer Hill, the prominent north end high ground of the ridge jutting out into the Sarana Valley, had complete command of the valley. It was exactly why the Americans had placed an artillery battery there. The attack plan, to occur at night when the Americans were the least alert, would be to sweep up the Chichagof Valley like a charging *TIGER*, moving so fast in such concentrated numbers as to overwhelm the weak defenses between Chichagof and the American artillery battery.

"We will then capture the artillery battery," the major pointed with his hand, seemingly directly at Yoshi, "and turn the guns against the supply depots and troops in the Massacre Valley. If we can separate the forces," he emphasized with a fierce grin, "we can attack them and defeat them! Each of you will play a part in this great victory, because every Japanese soldier will be part of the attack!"

The medical staff, mostly doctors, nodded politely and respectfully to show enthusiasm for the plan. Their opinions and concerns, of course, Yoshi knew did not matter in the least at this point. They were medical staff, not combat soldiers. What Yamasaki wanted to convey by giving out the details for the plan was the role he was expecting them all to play.

The major, still standing on the table, looked at the doctors surrounding him with a severe, stern face.

"We will leave Chichagof Harbor at two in the morning tomorrow night and will not be returning here. All Japanese soldiers, including all medical staff officers, will leave. Every Japanese soldier who can wield a weapon and has the desire to fight, will be allowed to join us. Every Japanese soldier who is unable because of his wounds will be destroyed with morphine. Wounded officers will be given hand grenades if they so desire and they are capable."

The major stood up formally to attention and saluted sharply, before drawing his saber from his scabbard and raising it to the ceiling.

"Tenoheka BANZAI!" He screamed surprisingly loud, almost in a frenzy as he raised both arms, *"Tenoheka BANZAI!"* The medical staff, without hesitation, repeated his call. Yoshi raised his arms up and down like the rest of them, but he did not even mouth the words. He thought of the non-commissioned officers in the gun positions down near the beaches of Holtz Bay so many days ago. He remembered their shining, respectful eyes wanted to convey to him, Yoshi Nakagawa, their total willingness to sacrifice themselves to defend those beaches. Men he had to assume who had been dead and entombed in their gun positions two weeks now. His shame was so deep he could hardly stand. So many fine, incredibly devoted young men who were all gone.

"Tenoheka BANZAI!"

By midnight, every wounded patient who was not ambulatory had been euthanized. Yoshi had been asked by First Lieutenant Yamada to assist in this final procedure, standing by the beds one by one, holding the hands of some of the men or simply looking into their eyes as a final dark peace closed around them. Yamada said the wounded men had gotten used to Yoshi and trusted him, so his presence was useful in calming the men down. Yoshi, who was so ashamed of his fear he could not stand to look at himself in a mirror, accepted this assignment as fitting and something he deserved.

Yoshi devised a simply ritual that seemed to be accepted by the doomed men. He would hold their hand if they would allow him to and bow to them deeply. When he raised his head he would look them in the eyes if they were lucid, and thanked them for their service to their Emperor, to their families, and to the people of Japan. Sometimes, the eyes of these men, as the overdose was administered, would well with tears. Some would simply stare until their eyes dimmed and eventually closed. Lieutenant Yamada, who said nothing but would follow along with the ritual as long as it was done quickly, would occasionally look at Yoshi as he spoke to the patients with respectful interest. When they stepped away from the last man, Yamada placed his hand gently on

224

Yoshi's shoulder until Yoshi turned towards him. Yamada's eyes, both coldly fierce and level, softened.

"You did a good job, Lieutenant," he said gently. "That was the right thing to do for those men, and I thank you for it." Yoshi, his hands trembling, broke down in tears and rushed out of the room. Afterwards when he could, he found Kenji and talked him into the last visit to the shrine in the surgical hospital.

Outside it was cold and damp with a thick, sticky fog drifting by in waves. Troops Yoshi had never seen before were gathering near the hospital tunnel entrance. Many of them were combat troops, he could tell, by their dirty white overcoats and haggard faces. He had to assume almost all of these men were survivors and stragglers, men who had survived untold aerial bombings, naval bombardment and artillery barrages before the American troops even came close. All of them had fought in positions up in the ridgelines or on the passes until ordered to withdraw. Otherwise they were like Kenji and himself, men without units or commands. Weapons and ammunition seemed to be in extremely short supply, except for hand grenades. There were hundreds of grenades in wooden boxes. Small, deadly, frighteningly evil things Yoshi had no desire to be part of. Kenji tried to give Yoshi one but he refused, saying he would find himself another pistol instead. His Nambu, long gone since he was wounded, had not been replaced and none seem to be available.

He noticed many of the combat troops were drinking, *sake* he presumed, *part of the ritual of purification?* Yoshi was not a drinker and did not partake, noticing the increased noise and swagger of the troops the more they drank. They wanted to talk about the great victory. The officers did not seem to care, the lack of discipline more akin to a going-away party than a combat attack, but then the officers were drinking too. His morphine, dulling the senses, made more sense to him. There was nothing about this he wanted to talk about or to remember.

Units, or stray men to be formed into units, gathered in platoon-sized formations to be quickly inspected and marched away to some marshalling area. A number of hard-looking non-commissioned officers, infantry types Yoshi presumed, began coming into the hospital and forcibly gathering the enlisted medics to go outside. The medics, wearing a motley collection of uniforms to ward away the cold, were each handed a wooden pole with a bayonet attached to it. He watched in stunned silence as Kenji joined them. Yoshi couldn't believe what he was seeing. *They are going to attack the Americans with spears?* He

225

heard the NCOs explain loudly to the medics that they would be kept behind the assault troops with rifles and bayonets, but as the assault troops killed the Americans, the medics needed to capture American weapons and get rid of their spears. *When they see the ferocity of our attack, the Yankee Dogs will run like children, shitting in their pants!* The NCOs laughed at their own jokes and some of the medics joined them feebly, but most simply stared at one another, unbelieving to what was happening to them.

The worse part for Yoshi was the looks on the medics' faces when the NCOs brought the boxes of hand grenades and handed each man two of them. Kenji proudly displayed the two grenades he already had. He would not look at Yoshi at all. Yoshi did see the medic who was so kind to him the first days he was wounded and brought to the tunnel hospital near Holtz Bay, the thin young man who sang *Sakura Sakura* to himself, stare at the two grenades in his hands in disbelief. Yoshi met his eyes, seeing the sadness in them, the recognition of the finality of their own days and minutes running quickly away from them. Like the men doomed to be euthanized with morphine, the young medic stared at the grenades like they were the vials and syringes for his own passage, which they were. The medic looked up at Yoshi one more time, then slowly pocketed the grenades and moved back into formation.

Yoshi, because he was with the medical officers, was assumed to be a medical officer too. The young infantry captain who herded them outside had no use for them at this point, officers or not. He made it very clear Colonel Yamasaki expected every Japanese soldier to participate in the attack, even medical officers. *That was made plain in the briefing*, he declared coldly.

"None of you have any personal weapons," he spoke disgustedly, "and we have none to give you. But we do have these and if you charge a position hard enough, the Americans will run out of ammunition or simply run away." He held up a wooden pole with a long bayonet attached to it, and motioned to his men to hand them out. Yoshi held his gingerly in his right hand now his sling was removed. Once the spears were issued, the hand grenades were next. Deciding not to draw attention to himself, Yoshi accepted two of the devices and stuck them in his jacket pocket, planning to throw them away at the first opportunity. He watched with interest as the little 37mm anti-tank guns were wheeled along towards the marshalling area up ahead. *That is all we have left of our artillery?*

The infantry captain put his hands on his hips and slyly looked his charges over.

"Strike the striker plate on the bottom of the grenade on any hard surface to arm it. If at all possible, take an American with you!"

About 0230 in the morning the marshalling area, a well-protected wide draw at the base of Fish Hook Ridge, was filled to capacity with men. The fog drifted, hung then dissipated with a strangely regular rhythm. Yoshi couldn't believe how much alcohol was being consumed by the troops just before an attack. *Where did they keep all of this stuff, especially since we had run out of food?* When First Lieutenant Yamada brought over a bottle of *sake* and insisted Yoshi drink some of it, Yoshi had resisted for a few minutes. Yamada, drinking deeply, eyed him coldly and stuck a sharp finger into his chest.

"Do you have any idea what is going to happen to us in about an hour?" He asked distinctly, with careful enunciation. "We are going to be ordered to charge an American artillery position, which I understand is on a hill. So," Yamada took a long swig, "I may not be an infantry officer, but that means we will be attacking uphill against a well-defended position with…" he hesitated for a moment as he thought about it, *"spears!"* The grim humor of his statement made him snort. "Sure you don't want to join me for a drink, Lieutenant Nakagawa?"

At 0300 the assault formations were moved into position, the troops quieter now, their level of discipline, even when inebriated, was so ingrained they stood stock still when ordered to by the NCOs. The formations were essentially platoon-sized, led by either an officer or a senior NCO. The leading edge of the assault was comprised of platoons of infantrymen, engineers and special naval troops armed with rifles and bayonets, Nambu light machine guns and a few light mortars. The second component of the assault formation included two type 94 37mm wheeled anti-tank guns to be brought up as quickly as possible with revolving tow crews. The third component of the assault comprised of several platoons of men armed only with wooden poles with bayonets attached. Yoshi, assigned to the third group, listened to the infantry captain leading this final formation as he went over their instructions again and again. His mind was cloudy from the *sake* he had consumed or maybe it was the morphine, he didn't know. His feet were not responding well. He felt physically ill, his empty stomach racked in a knot of pain.

Speed is everything! Once we move forward, do not stop! Stay together! Your only path to victory is to stay together in a tight formation! Keep moving! Do not stop for any reason once we move forward! Then Yoshi heard it, the word passing back from the lead

227

formations, a low murmur growing stronger and stronger until the infantry captain stopped speaking. He too stood still at attention as the word rolled back to their formation, the combined voices of a thousand men strong, masculine, powerful. Terrifying to Yoshi, his heart shuddering as he heard it reverberate:

Gyokusai (spirit of glorious death)*! Gyokusai! Gyokusai!*

The orders rolled back like a garrison formation troop movement. Officers and NCOs barked the commands for marching in place, the boots slamming down on the cold ground in a solid pounding rhythm, the blood pulsing in their veins as they rocked back and forth.

Quick time, MARCH!

Yoshi, who had never marched in such large infantry formations, not even in his military classes in high school or at Osaka University, could not believe how powerful the force of the formation was. It was like being part of a huge, thundering machine. The ground beneath them shuddered as if the earth was kneeling before them as they moved forward. The air, damp and viscous, had the flavor of lead.

Left, left, left right left! Barked the NCOs marching besides them. With their spears, Yoshi thought of Roman Legions from his history books, or the Greek formations running miles with full equipment across open fields before they even encountered their enemy formations. *How far are we going? How far must we march?* He could hear the heavy breathing of the medical officers marching with him, men he knew did little physical exercise normally, but with their severely reduced diet and disrupted sleep patterns even this quick march pace could not be sustained for long.

Left, left, left right left! Stay together! Stay in formation!

The path the assault formation followed from the draw had a slight downhill slope to it, which increased their speed. Somewhere up ahead the lead platoons were spreading apart on line as they marched past a small lake and climbed up a slight rise. The valley was opening up in front of them as the fog lifted from the ground. Incredibly, as they went over the rise, they could see for the first time what appeared to be clusters of lights like small villages for miles ahead. *How bold the Americans are!* Yoshi thought, but fear suddenly struck his heart as he realized there were so many of them.

Up forward Yoshi could hear gunfire, sporadic at first, then growing in volume. The men around him, exhausted already from the quick approach march, were still silent but he could hear yelling and screaming ahead. The NCOs and officers accompanying them no longer called cadence, but pulled their sabers from their scabbards.

Steady in formation! Stay together! Stay together!

A star-cluster flare erupted in the night sky above them. The fog deck was below the flare, so it glowed in milky luminescence under its parachute, ineffective and useless until it suddenly burst under the deck at 100 feet. For one to two seconds the fields to the left were bathed in brilliant orange light until the flare landed and was extinguished. There was a roaring sound in Yoshi's head, growing in strength until suddenly his vision grew dark and he fell dizzily to the ground. Someone reached down as he laid on the ground, groggily trying to lift his arm, but he heard the infantry captain bark at the helper.

Leave him be! Stay in formation! Stay together!

After a minute or so Yoshi sat up, his head pounding sharply. Men were still running past him, but there weren't any marching formations now, just small groups of men carrying spears. An NCO pointed at him earnestly as he ran past but did not stop.

Keep moving forward! Stay together!

BOOM! BOOM! BOOM! Up ahead Yoshi recognized the reports of the 37mm anti-tank guns as he slowly got to his feet. Still dizzy, either from the *sake* or the morphine, he could not believe what he was seeing with his eyes up ahead. There was an incredible eruption of bursting shells and tracer bullets in such a concentrated place up ahead a couple of hundred yards to his left. It was like a fireworks display on the ground, a strangely moving display that seemed to climb up the side of a hillside, consuming a patch of ground before moving forward again, blanking out and blackening the space behind it. Men ran past him and Yoshi, glanced down at his feet, found his spear and followed them.

There was a cacophony of gunfire directly to his right, furious machine gun and rifle fire. Tracers whizzed past him into the darkness, up, down and suddenly right at him. He fell to the ground, the zip zip zip of the bullets seemingly apart from him and harmless, yet he instinctively stayed down. He waited a moment and started to get up when he saw in utter astonishment an American soldier, helmet-less and wearing only trousers and an undershirt, dart past him, weaponless, glancing to his left and right before disappearing into the darkness. Yoshi got to his feet and stumbled forward cautiously, moving towards what appeared to be kerosene lanterns in tents.

The tents were torn apart, shredded by shrapnel and machine gun fire, but several of the lanterns were intact, still swinging on overhead hooks. An American Army radio set, now blasted to pieces, lay on it side right next to the dead American radio operator, who still wore his headset. Yoshi stood still and took in the scene, the result of a violent attack that obviously took the occupants of the tent by surprise. Yoshi

229

counted six bloodied bodies, their personal weapons, if they had them, already gone. He stepped back carefully away from the tent, nearly colliding with another American soldier running past, a small man with a mustache whose eyes grew suddenly huge with fright before he screamed once and kept on running. Yoshi, suddenly realizing there were Americans everywhere, crouched down away from the light, moving quickly away from the tents. He did not see a single Japanese soldier around, so he headed directly towards the sound of the gunfire.

Skirting the cluster of lights where there might be other Americans, he moved silently down what actually appeared to be a road of some kind. As he moved along to the south he could hear the screams and moans of what he assumed to be wounded Americans over to his right. Creeping around a parked bulldozer with a hugh blade on it, he stopped as a group of American soldiers, walking with their arms down and without weapons, kept calling for somebody. They seemed lost or disoriented, so as they approached Yoshi carefully moved around the bulldozer keeping it between them and himself. After a few more minutes of talking to themselves, the Americans drifted off, still calling for someone or something.

Yoshi spotted a dark ditch that seemed to run parallel to the road, so he darted across the road and dropped into it. The twilight revealed only more darkness, but Yoshi sensed something was wrong and stopped moving after he had crept only a few feet.

"Who's there?" was the barked challenge in English. "Show yourself or get yourself shot, goddammit!" Yoshi could just make out some dark bundles or figures about 20 feet away in the ditch. An American carbine fired twice, both shots missing him. Yoshi turned and ran down the ditch for three or four steps before turning abruptly up the side of the ditch. The carbine fired several more times, one round tugging at his trouser leg. He cleared the top of the ditch and kept running directly towards the darkest space he could find.

His head pounding and his lungs flat out of air, Yoshi dropped to the ground when he nearly collided headlong into a darkened tent. There was no light of any kind near this tent, but he did notice there were 50-gallon drums stacked near it. He slid behind these and peeked back in the direction he had come. No one seemed to be following him. He didn't know what to do. The assault was drifting away from him, the fighting as furious as ever but moving south towards Engineer Hill and the artillery battery. He could not stay, there was nothing but confused American survivors who would shoot just about anybody. Now he was not only afraid, he was lost. He peered over the drums towards what he believed was the south, viewing the huge cluster of lights on a blackened hill a mile or so distant. Slowly drifting into grayness as the fog enveloped it. Engineer Hill. The attack was now somewhere at the base of the hill across the Sarana Valley, he could only surmise by the moving fireworks display below the lights. I need to get there, he decided, right now.

Yoshi moved as fast as he could, staying in the shadows. American troops fired sporadically into the darkness, and Yoshi realized the attack had been reasonably successful in that the assault force had covered over a mile of American held ground and was still moving forward. He stumbled across many bodies now, both American and Japanese. The American survivors were moving about cautiously, the ferocity of the attack clearly spooking them as rifle and machine gun fire erupted spontaneously in all directions. The Americans who were shooting were not getting any fire back at them, but they shot anyway.

The assault force had encountered an American infantry company standing in line for one of their open mess kitchens at 0300 in the morning. Yoshi skirted around this area very carefully, but he couldn't help but get stomach pangs from the strong smell of recent cooking. The dozens of bodies on the ground near the kitchen revealed the complete surprise of the attack on the troops in the food line. He also shifted to the east to avoid a high concentration of lights near an American field hospital the assault force had gone through. It was a narrow saddle he had to traverse, so Yoshi crept along the border of the hospital supply tents away from the lights, conscious of the much more alert and attentive armed American soldiers skulking around. He watched at a distance as a pair of Americans poked and probed dead or wounded Japanese soldiers lying around the hospital compound. He jerked involuntarily as the rifles flared when the Americans shot the Japanese at point blank range, the shots muffled and distant.

Once past the field hospital there was the open space of the Sarana Valley, mostly muskeg and foggily gray with no lights. The Americans had been working on a road across between the two hills for weeks but had a working aerial tow cart system for the interim. As an engineer Yoshi had listened to the tow system being described by infantry officers who had seen it, and was intrigued. Tonight, however, he couldn't see the tow system and worked his way on the periphery of the nearly constructed road. He slipped and fell a lot in the cold wet mulch, tempted to simply walk on the road but didn't dare. He knew there might be American guards so he moved silently only a few feet at a time, stopping to listen frequently.

The real action was at the base of Engineer Hill as the amount of American machine gun fire pouring down from the top to the base was astounding. From his valley view of the north end of Engineer Hill with the fog layer slightly above, Yoshi could count at least a dozen defending American .30 caliber machine guns laying a carpet of tracer fire down the hill. He assumed the assault force was trying to work its way up to the eastside of the hill toward the artillery battery. Yoshi, spear in hand, shivered in the cold and kept moving, shifting slightly to the east to find a way to join the assault force on the eastside of the hill without enduring the fusillade of fire at the north end.

By the time Yoshi worked his way halfway across the eastside of Engineer Hill, the sky lightened enough to be considered day. The main attack had apparently failed. Yoshi encountered some Japanese troops trying to regroup down in a small draw, or at least he thought they were trying to regroup. They drifted out of the fog as if they had suddenly materialized out of thin air. He was shocked in their condition as they stumbled down the hill. Bloodied, disheveled, and screaming incoherently among themselves with American troops apparently hard on their heels. The first unit he encountered was from the command group, and Yoshi thought for a moment he would find Colonel Yamasaki among them. He did not and the survivors, none of them officers, screamed at him that all was lost. They seemed to sense instinctively he was not an infantry officer and looked at him with both contempt and to Yoshi, sheer madness in their eyes. They cried among themselves and actually tore at their hair in bitter, physical frustration, but what made Yoshi prepare to leave was when the first one, an NCO, stepped behind a large stone and blew himself up with a grenade.

The man had been screaming at almost the top of his lungs, holding a grenade in his hand like it was a cup of tea, but when he stepped around the rock Yoshi knew and it was confirmed with the solid but muffled *WHUMP* of the explosion. Another NCO stepped around the same stone and screamed, either in pain over the loss of his colleague or he was beginning the same ritual for himself. The man came back around the rock and hurled his cap off, stomping this way and that, before pulling out his own grenade. The other soldiers were getting equally agitated, so Yoshi, seeing this, slipped away unseen up the slope, Americans or not.

The second group he came across carried spears like himself, clerks, medics or support personnel. The men were walking down the hill in single file, head down, quiet as monks crossing a mountain on their way to a remote village. There were only six of them, their faces once uplifted revealing all Yoshi wanted to know about what the attack had been like for them. They were, in Yoshi's recent experience, as dulled of feelings as those individuals he had helped euthanize with morphine.   Their eyes were flat, liquid pools of dark oil surrounded by huge white saucers, revealing nothing but fear, death, or madness.   He had no idea where they might be going.   If the attack failed there was no rally point mentioned as a fallback.   The attack could not fail.

He recognized none of these men and they certainly did not recognize him.   He stared at them but they didn't stare back.   They had lifted their heads and eyes, but the dulled pools were draining rapidly of interest.   Suddenly, the leader lowered his head and started down the hill with the others following suit immediately.   None of them looked back.   Forgotten, Yoshi stepped aside to stare at their backs, wondering what to do next.   The six men had to be visible to American units as they came down, but in the growing daylight no fire followed them. Yoshi turned around after a moment to look down but they had simply disappeared.   A single rifle shot rang out somewhere up the hill, to be followed by a fusillade of machine gun fire.   Yoshi hesitated for just a moment before started up the hill, knowing there were still Japanese soldiers up there.

CHAPTER 27

0300 Hours, May 29, 1943, D-Day Plus 18, Pendergast Ridge Medical Collection Station

When one of the senior medics, a corporal, came around to make his final evening check and ensure the tent was all buttoned tight, Ray propped himself up and waved him over. The corporal was tending the oil stove which never generated enough heat. He glanced over at Ray with a raised eyebrow.

"What can I do for you, Sergeant?"

"Do you know what units are north of us?"

"What do you mean? We have a 17th Infantry Battalion headquarters just down the hill from us, and just north of that across the big knoll is a battalion field kitchen. The kitchen has been staying open damn near 24 hours a day feeding troops rotating out of the line."

"Anything north of that, any dug in combat units held in reserve, something like that?" The corporal stood up straight closing the door to the stove. He walked over next to Ray's cot, noticing Manny Torre was awake and listening too, his manner secretive.

"You heard those guys coming back from the recon down the pass, huh?" He asked quietly, his face cracking into a sly grin. The corporal held up his hand as a pause, turning suddenly to pull open the flap and leave the tent. Ray and Torre exchanged glances but before they could say anything the corporal came back in carrying something large in a blanket. He carefully closed the tent flap behind him before unwrapping a Thompson submachine gun. It was one of the new M1A1 models with the horizontal front grip stock and no Cutts compensator.

"Got this off a captain who didn't need it anymore," he grinned. "We were supposed to have a guard detail, but they started using those guys as litter bearers hauling wounded from here to the tow ferry. What started out as a cush gig standing around our warm tents turned into a hard goddamn job, so most of those guys just disappeared. So some of us grabbed what weapons we could in case the Japs broke through." He held the Thompson awkwardly, pushing buttons and flipping levers with no clear purpose. Ray watched him for a moment with hooded eyes.

"You got any more of those things? I mean anything, M1s, carbines, even pistols?" The corporal, sensing Ray's intent, brought the Thompson down and quickly wrapped it up again in the blanket.

"Nope," the corporal said with finality, "the docs don't have personal weapons and us medics were issued carbines but those were taken away from us for our temporary guards—who are now gone. I know some of the boys have pistols and carbines they lifted from the wounded, but that's about it." He looked around the tent before backing to the door. "Patients ain't allowed to have any guns anyway. I ain't partin with that Thompson, nosirree. The Japs come here they will get a real surprise!"

"What a fuckin dumbass!" sighed Torre, shaking his head after the corporal had left. Torre gave a small whistle, turning Ray's head in his direction. He pulled up from deep inside his sleeping bag an M1 bayonet and scabbard, holding it clumsily in the white gauze paw of his left hand.

"Catch!" he called quietly, tossing the bayonet still in its scabbard across two cots into Ray's hands. He grinned as Ray gripped it and carefully unlatched the blade from the scabbard.

"I know, I stole it like a dog, but I thought I needed a weapon. I just can't use it. You have to protect us both!"

At three in the morning, Ray, who had been awake all night listening to the growing rumble of strange noises down near the harbor miles away, jerked straight up as the rumble suddenly erupted into the distant popcorn popping of gunfire at much closer range. A roar, like a cheering crowd at a football game, echoed below them, but the roar was repeated like a cheerleader section, again and again, coming closer and closer. The cacophony of gunfire increased in volume until bullets ripped through the tent walls, and the cheering roar turned into men screaming at the top of their lungs out of fear and fright. Ray looked down at his arms and pulled the needle attached to the intravenous bottle out of his vein. Other men around him were now awake and frightened, screaming or calling for help. Ray ignored them, unzipping his sleeping bag to swing his legs out, the motion ripping bandages apart. He gasped in pain and stopped for a moment until he again heard the screams of men down below them. He pushed himself up, dizzily weaving for a moment, remembering to grab the bayonet.

Stumbling around the cots he stopped just long enough to jerk the IV out of Torre's arm before turning around to slash the tent side from floor to ceiling in one motion with the bayonet. Torre, trying to unzip his sleeping bag was dragged still in the bag right off of the cot, straight out the back of the tent and across a light snow field. Ray did not stop, although he had no idea how he had the strength, until he had dragged Torre about 50 feet from the tent into the darkness. He could hear running feet but did not stop until he tripped over stacked cordwood, only there wasn't any cordwood anywhere on the island of Attu.   He didn't realize at the time the solid, stiff objects were dead bodies in canvas shelter halves.   He only knew they were dark, numerous and hard.   One of his last conscious acts before passing out was to drag Manny Torre's sleeping bag with Torre still in it right into the middle of them.   He was aware of falling right next to him, shivering from the cold.

Ed Ridgeway had asked for and received one of the now empty cots in the casual receiving tent, deciding his time at Attu was at a close and he would take the first opportunity to evacuate himself.   This was as good a place as any to stay until he left, and they kept the tents fairly warm.   He was feeling pretty good, especially after finding and talking to Ray Craymer, Orin's older brother.   If all went well, most of the wounded troops would be routed through the same in-theatre transit hospitals and there would be a good chance he would be able to link up with Orin.   Besides, he was getting good at perusing medical admission lists. He'd find him.

In the evening he had heard the comments from the small scouting party coming up from the lower end of the Chichagof Valley, so he jumped up from his cot and tried to stop them.   He was a little concerned when he realized these men had no intention of even slowing down, as they were clearly very frightened by what they had seen or experienced.   His rank stopped a couple of them, as did his obvious interest in hearing what they had to say.

There were hunnerds of em, sir—I mean hunnerds of em, juiced up and screamin!

They was screamin TEN HOOKER BANDSAWS!   TEN HOOKER BANDSAWS!   At the top of their lungs, waving sabers!   We got ta hell outta there!   We gotta report to the company commander, sir!   We gotta go!

The men literally ran away from him and the hospital compound, Ed not missing the fact some of them were still looking over their shoulders fearfully.   They were not looking at him but some unknown beyond.

Ten Hooker Bandsaw?   Of course, the Jap troops were saying Tenoheka BANZAI!   Ed sat down on his cot and lit a cigarette, wondering what to make of it.   Where would the Japs attack?   The men on the patrol were frightened, but at least two of them confirmed there were a large number of them, possibly hundreds.   These must be the survivors of the hilltop battles on Fish Hook Ridge, but really, how many Japs are still left on Attu?   Would they really choose to attack American positions at this point?

236

Ed spent a half an hour walking around the hospital compound noticing there were less than forty patients left. He also noticed there wasn't a single sentry anywhere near the perimeter. He knew of the field kitchen down below and a battalion command post for the 17th Infantry down below that. He couldn't think of any real strategic value of either of those facilities to the Japanese. But he knew he was out of the loop to the current disposition of all the troops on Attu. Maybe the Japs were considering a run at retaking the hilltop positions? That didn't make a lot of sense, but for once, the mental exercise of considering the options made him feel a little uneasy. He wasn't back in regiment or back on some ship toying around with little wooden models or stacks of paper data. He was sitting on Attu in an unguarded compound about a mile or two away from known Jap positions. Jap positions reported to be preparing for an attack somewhere.

Ed dozed for a time and woke to the strange rumbling sound down the valley. He couldn't quite place it. Getting up he was surprised to find there were no troops moving around in position to prepare for any contingency. He wasn't an infantry officer and certainly not privy to what the ground commander might be considering, but he could see nothing going around anywhere near them. Didn't they get the message? He could still hear the rumbling and it seemed to be growing stronger.

About three in the morning Ed awoke to the sound of crackling gunfire coming closer and closer in a growing crescendo. He could hear what sounded like a cheering crowd, roaring in waves, amidst the clear screams of men. Ed rolled out of the cot looking around, finding not a single person in his darkened tent. He pulled his Smith and Wesson revolver from the holster, checked the cylinder for maybe the tenth time this evening, before pulling back the door flap and peering cautiously outside. He could hear the rumbling, earth-shaking tremor of a herd of animals coming directly towards the compound. Suddenly in the light pool hundreds of men—Japanese soldiers—were rushing directly towards him out of the fog. Between those men and himself, others, American soldiers, patients in partial uniforms or thick housecoats were running in all directions. The charging Japanese closed in on the Americans and they were set upon instantly; shot, hacked, stabbed, bayoneted or clubbed to death with such vicious brutality Ed's jaw just dropped and he could not believe what he was seeing.

After a full second, his instinct for survival took over and he dashed back into the tent, darting this way and that, not knowing what to do or which direction to go. Suddenly a Japanese soldier, his rifle and

237

bayonet in front of him, charged into the tent, turning fully around until he spotted Ed. Without hesitation he charged Ed with his bayoneted rifle, clearly intending to impale Ed. Ed raised his revolver with his slung hand and fired once before he was bayoneted clear through his left lung, the charging soldier having so much momentum Ed was dragged back and through several cots before stumbling between them. The Japanese soldier, shot once through his upper cheek, was still breathing as Ed pushed him off. With his free hand still clutching his .38, he turned to his right until he felt the man's head with his bandaged hand, guiding the bore of the barrel against the skull and squeezed the trigger.

He turned on his side, unable to push the Arisaka rifle and bayonet out and off his chest. He could feel the steel stuck in bone and gristle. He had to fight to control his panic, he couldn't breathe and it hurt so much. Everywhere there were desperate screams of men as they were being bayoneted or shot in their sleeping bags, some begging for mercy. Most would be helpless patients waiting for transportation out to the hospital ships. Ed could not see any of it but the tents were close together and he could hear everything. The Japs, he noticed, were not saying much although some of them were still screaming *Banzai* as they ran through the compound. As Ed laid there partially on his back, twisting his torso so the Arisaka was lying on a broken cot and not twisting the bayonet agonizingly in his chest, he realized he had a clear view of the doorway. Several times Japanese ran into the tent, glanced about in the semi-darkness and ran back out. Finally two soldiers, one a NCO and another an officer, ran inside and stared at Ed incredulously. Ed was ready for them. The officer stepped forward, lifting his Nambu pistol and was shot instantly in the head. He did not keel over as Ed would have expected, he simply lowered his pistol and looked to be trying to sit down. He folded and fell in a heap. The NCO, however, raised his fighting sword and was shot twice in the chest.

Another group of Japanese soldiers slashed the tent walls in two and literally stepped into the tent from the opposite side, the three of them turning suddenly when they spotted Ed. Two of them raising their rifles at the same time and fired. Ed couldn't lift his arm far enough to shoot at them, feeling more than hearing a bullet striking his upper chest. There wasn't much pain at first, nothing like the bayonet twisting from his chest out his back stuck in some cot canvas. The long, heavy Arisaka rifle was a fulcrum of agony. But he heard the *WHUMP* of the bullet striking, could smell the gunpowder somehow.

The *BOP BOP BOP BOP BOP BOP* and dancing muzzle flash from the doorway came from nowhere, the three Japanese soldiers flung back as if they had been hit in the chests by baseball bats. A medic with a Thompson submachine gun stepped forward into the tent momentarily, staring at his handiwork, not once looking Ed's way before disappearing. Holy shit, Ed thought, before a black curtain sucked out the light.

CHAPTER 28

0300 Hours, May 29, 1943, D-Day Plus 18, Engineer Hill

It didn't take a genius to know something was happening, something very wrong. Captain Greenley had been standing between two of the big tents taking a cold, windy leak when he heard the first echoes of shooting a couple of miles down the Chichagof Valley. Like his first sergeant and his exec, Lieutenant Wheeler, he had crawled into his sleeping bag a little after midnight after a solid 22-hour day coordinating work on finishing the connecting road and keeping the tow systems working. He'd been drinking coffee steadily, his main diet other than the disgusting fried Spam sandwiches his first sergeant liked so much, falling into the sack totally spent knowing his bladder was full but too tired to care.

In the 30 degree, 10 mile-an-hour freezing wind he watched to the north as luminescent fog layers rolled up the valley looking all the world like slow motion gray surf as it consumed, absorbed then revealed clusters of lights as it moved forward. At the far north end he could just make out a rolling fireworks display, twinkling yellow and red tracers with small, brilliant flashes of white. A few seconds later he could hear the staccato popcorn of the small arms fire and the steady, rhythmic *BOOM BOOM* of what sounded like small cannon fire. It was coming up the valley towards them, moving fast. Holy fuckin shit!

Greenley could hear the RT in the tent next to First Sergeant Bettencourt buzzing, but being surrounded by tents filled with other company and battalion officers, a half a dozen RTs were buzzing at once and men were calling the alarm in all directions. As far as Greenley knew the only units on the south end of Pendergest Ridge were some battalion command posts, a battalion field kitchen and a big regimental medical collection station. The buzz saw he could see with his own eyes was slicing through those units like a very large, hot knife through butter. It came to him quite clearly there was nothing else between the Japanese charging up the valley and the artillery battery behind his command post but the combat engineers on the front part of the hill he was standing on.

As luck would have it for the commanding officers of the 13th and 50th Engineer Battalions (Combat), almost all of the men were back on the hill tonight. The kitchen had served supper right up to 0200 in the morning for hungry crews coming home in the dark, with most of the

240

cooks still up cleaning and preparing their stoves and equipment for breakfast in a few short hours. There were virtually no infantrymen on Engineer Hill, so the brigadier general now in charge of the engineering effort on Attu quickly organized a hilltop defense. Every cook, clerk, HE operator or medic from the administration tents, field kitchen, small aid station and road crews who could carry a rifle was being organized into small defensive units. The 17th Engineer Battalion, slightly lower on a plateau on the hogback and directly facing the Japanese assault force now perhaps 20 minutes away, started gathering every .30 caliber machine gun they could get their hands on. The engineers knew they had the tactical advantage because of the steepness of the hill, quickly dispersing the Brownings to set up very tight interlocking fields of fire.

Captain Greenley, with the help of Bettencourt and Lieutenant Wheeler, started rousting exhausted men from their tents to join in the defense of the northwest side of the hill, as were other companies from the 50th Engineer Battalion (Combat). Bettencourt had spotted the crates of hand grenades near the CP tent and distributed them in large numbers to all of Easy Company. *What do we do with these, Top? Shit, when they start coming, throw them down the hill!*

Bettencourt heard the artillery officers order the elevation of half of their guns to be ready to rain shot and shell on the attacking Japanese, and the other half lowered to the horizon ready to fire canister rounds point blank if the Japanese broke through the engineer defenses. That was a sobering thing to hear and to think about. But the artillery stayed silent for the present because they believed the attacking Japanese force was now thoroughly mixed with American units down in the valley.

Colonel Yamasaki, for his part, was totally heartened when he discovered the intelligence on the American road connecting Pendergast Ridge and Engineer Hill was correct, the road was almost finished. The attack was so far a complete success, the Americans caught by surprise, the pathetic defensive efforts disorganized and easily overcome. He considered the dry road straight to Engineer Hill divine providence and a clear sign of impending victory. Energized with the thought of his target, the artillery battery, now less than a half a mile away, he led his command group straight down the road at a dead run.

The fog conditions made the use of star cluster flares virtually useless but a few were fired overhead anyway. The fog was rolling around like thick pouring cream a few hundred feet below the top of Engineer Hill, the flares illuminating blindingly back off the pure white of the top layers. For the engineers on the hill, it was like waiting for an unseen herd of stampeding animals. The overwhelming urge was to turn tail and run in the opposite direction. They could hear the Japanese

241

coming up the hill before they could see them, the concerted foot pounding running of a thousand men at once, with the screams of *BANZAI BANZAI BANZAI* eerily coming up from the white soup. It was even more frightening because they sounded so damned close.

First Sergeant Bettencourt was running around the big staff tents to get out in front of them when a 37mm shell popped through both sides of a tent in front of him. The shell hit two men running side by side next to the tent, vaporizing both of them and decapitating an officer as he emerged from another tent. Bettencourt stumbled, stunned, not believing what he had just seen, until another 37mm popped through the same tent and kept on going. He took a deep breath and stepped around the gore in front of him knowing the next one might land right where he stood. He ran forward in a crouch for about 50 yards before dropping to his knees next to his men. He changed his mind to fall on his stomach as bullets started coming up the hill. He crawled forward just as a star-cluster flare erupted high to his right on the 13th Engineers side of the hill, illuminating a scene he would never forget.

Japanese soldiers were emerging out of the fog layer as if they were running out of the sea, the long tendrils of fog still shrouding around them as they charged forward, hundreds of them, the flares twinkling and reflecting on their long bayonets and sabers. The Japanese were charging straight up the steep hill, screaming like an out-of-control mob right into the solid wall of tracer-filled lead coming from a dozen .30 caliber machine guns mounted on the top of the hill. The gunners were holding down their triggers, the narrow interlocking paths of lead overlapping, scything down the Japanese like a huge saw, cutting bodies literally in half with the concentrated fire. Incredibly, despite the virtual wall of lead being poured down on the attacking troops, Bettencourt could see some of the troops were managing to get very close to the top of the hill before they too were shot down.

Here they come! Bettencourt spun around to see Japanese troops emerging out of the fog in front of the 50th Engineers sector, where they had fewer machine guns. As the machine guns started their staccato tattoo on the lead troops coming up the hill, Bettencourt saw one of his platoon sergeants stand up, a hand grenade in each hand, with a another dozen men following suit. *Let em fly boys!* Two-dozen grenades were hurled in two quick tosses right into the line where the fog ended and the Japanese continued to emerge. A few seconds later the grenades exploded *BANG BANG BANG* almost as one, in two waves, just as a new group of Japanese troops were coming out of the fog. The engineers repeated the feat two more times, two-dozen grenades at a time. The effect was so devastating to the troops attacking the hill the

242

machine guns eventually stopped firing because they ran out of targets. No more Japanese emerged out of the fog in a concerted mass attack, just an occasional group of two or three, or even an occasional single soldier, all to be shot down in seconds.

Bettencourt realized the same thing had happened to the hill defended by the 13th Engineers, the machine guns had stopped firing from the lack of targets. What was strange was the fact it wasn't quiet, they could all of them still hear Japanese voices, loud and screaming, down below in the fog. It was disconcerting and confusing, with everyone on the hill looking at one another nervously. Gunners changed ammunition belts and engineers on Bettencourt's side of the hill prepared more hand grenades.

A sudden flurry of gunfire very close to the extreme flanks on both the 50th and 13th Engineer positions, almost behind them, caught Captain Greenley's attention. He ordered a platoon of Easy Company engineers to back away from the line and shift south around the hill in case the Japanese were coming behind them. It was a sound move. As soon as the platoon was in position Greenley could hear gunfire behind the tents on the hill. Like every other engineer on the front side of the hill, Greenley began to worry the artillery crews with the lowered 105s might think the position was overrun and would fire canister rounds in their direction. He had the foresight to bring along an RT and a cable reel and was on the horn immediately with the 105 fire director. He was reassured the 105s would remain secured, but was advised Japanese troops were reported on the hill as artillerymen had killed a half a dozen already. Greenley did not like the idea of Japanese troops behind him so he called Lieutenant Wheeler for a conference.

Wheeler came up the hill in a low crouch, a strange look on his face. Bettencourt saw him coming and stepped from the line to join them. Greenley pulled them back a few yards so they could talk when Wheeler raised his hand to interrupt him.

"Sorry, sir," he apologized, "but do you hear that?" Bettencourt, who had been hearing the same thing, nodded in affirmation. He heard it too. Greenley, who had been on the RT with the 105 fire director, had not. They all crouched on their heels in silence, listening. *Whump... whump... whump... whump... whump.* A few seconds would pass, and then another muffled series, *whump... whump... whump.*

"What the hell is that?" asked Greenley, almost to himself. "Sounds like—grenades?" Bettencourt shrugged his shoulders.

"Beats the hell out of me, sir. It's right down there below us in the valley in the fog where the Japs are."

243

Wheeler cocked his head before shaking it slowly in dismissal. "I just don't know what it is, it's sounds like—well, either underground detonations or dynamite detonated underwater. It's—muffled, somehow." Both Bettencourt and Greenley nodded in agreement.

"Well," Greenley said finally, "we'll find out soon enough." He nodded towards Wheeler, his face grim. "The artillerymen have killed Japs right behind us, so some of them are getting though. I want you and Bettencourt to take 10 men and sweep all the tents behind us to make sure we don't have any of them Banzai sons of bitches waiting for us with a grenade. No prisoner bullshit, shoot em on sight, clear?"

Wheeler and Bettencourt broke the 10 men into two groups, each of them taking five men. Almost every single large tent still had a kerosene lantern burning in it, so there was surprisingly a lot of light between the tents. They stayed way back from the line of testy, nervous, trigger-happy engineers on the line encircling three-quarters of Engineer Hill, and far from the very nervous artillerymen, concentrating instead on the two acres where most of the tents were. Splitting the encampment in two, the two groups separated to quickly inspect each tent in their assigned area. Two men searching each tent with the other three right outside covering. After three quarters of an hour, they had searched each of the more than 60 tents on the hill without finding a single Japanese soldier.

Gunfire still erupted behind them occasionally, and engineers on the front side fired machine gun and rifle fire, but it was sporadic now. The sky was lightening, so Wheeler ordered the 10 men back to the line to join Captain Greenley. Wheeler and Bettencourt went to the Easy Company CP tent and Wheeler called Greenley on the RT, letting him know they found nothing and the 10 men were on their way back.

"We found out what the noise was, Easy, over," said Greenley, once Wheeler completed his report.

"Easy Six, Easy, what was it?"

"Japs were killing themselves with their own grenades. On the 13th Engineer side some of the Japs were coming right out of the fog and blowing themselves up in plain view. Same sound. They would stick the grenade to their stomach and—well, it was that strange sound."

"Jesus," was all Wheeler could say. "I mean, roger, Easy, over." He turned to pass the information on to Bettencourt, but he had already stepped outside of the tent.

Bettencourt went into his tent and pulled out the last Cuban he had. He knew the battle was not over, but he knew it was over for him. He could hear the transmission from Greenley because he had stepped outside and stopped just on the other side of the tent. He shook his head and clipped his cigar.   These sons of bitches are crazy.   Their attack fails and they blow themselves up!   He stepped outside of his tent to be away from the light, looking out to the south.   No tow tractors were running this late and he couldn't see the river.   Bettencourt lit the cigar carefully, rolling it around to light it evenly.   He didn't know what he was going to do now that his supply was gone.   He could only hope they could get back to the transport ship and he could get into the company lockers to find his stash.   Otherwise, he was shit out of luck.

In the flame of his match he thought of the major scolding him about lighting up. Grinning to himself, he lowered his cigar and walked around the tent to the other side not visible to the south.   Might as well be safe.   This would be one hell of a night to get picked off by a Jap sniper.   He took his first luxurious puff and lowered the cigar, his hair rising on the back of his head when he spotted the shadow of a man between the tents moving his way before suddenly stopping.   From the subdued lantern light cast through the tents on each side, Bettencourt could see the man was wearing a khaki outer jacket and trousers.   He was small, slight and thin, and he was carrying a—spear. A fucking Jap officer!

Bettencourt had left his carbine on his bunk inside of his tent, but his .45 Colt pistol was in its leather holster on his right hip.   His heart in his throat, he dropped the cigar to fumble for the flap button on his holster, expecting the Japanese officer to rush him. Bettencourt stepped backwards and drew his pistol in one motion, knowing the piece was cocked and locked with a round in the chamber.   He thumbed off the safety in the same motion and leveled it the Japanese officer's head.

The Japanese officer seemed visibly distressed with the pistol pointed at his face, his eyes wide and blinking.   He stopped, then very slowly raised his free hand as he leaned forward, motioning he was putting the spear on the ground.

"DON'T MOVE!"   Bettencourt barked, his finger already starting pressure on the trigger of his pistol.   The Japanese officer, when he moved forward in the light between the tents, revealed a thin, youthful face.   He had a frightened, confused, but determined expression on his face.   He kept one bandaged hand up and the other holding the spear half on the ground.   He remained motionless until his eyes widened as he glanced up at something behind Bettencourt.   The *BOP BOP BOP BOP BOP* was practically in Bettencourt's ears, deafening him, the muzzle flame from the Thompson reaching to his elbow.   The youthful Japanese officer was punched from groin to forehead with the heavy slugs and jerked backwards off his feet, falling instantly motionless.

Bettencourt, who had jumped nearly a foot himself, spun around in surprise and anger at Lieutenant Wheeler, who still had the Thompson in his shoulder, the muzzle of the old-style Cutts Compensator curling smoke a foot from Bettencourt's right shoulder.

"What were you waiting for, Sergeant?" Wheeler said accusingly, lowering his Thompson slowly. "I came out of the CP and spotted this Jap sneaking past, so I came around to cut him off and damn near killed you in the crossfire. You had him covered! What the fuck were you doing?"

Bettencourt slowly lowered his pistol, his wrist shaking now. After a long pause, he holstered the pistol and retraced his steps to find his Cuban. "I was smoking a cigar." Brushing his cigar off, he stared at Wheeler before pointing at the corpse.

"This guy didn't have a weapon, except a fuckin spear. I think he was trying to put his—spear down and raise his hands, but I don't know for sure."

Wheeler glared at Bettencourt and brushed past him roughly, kneeling next to the body. He rifled through the pockets carefully and almost immediately came up with two grenades in the outer jacket. He slowly turned around and approached Bettencourt, holding the grenades close to his face.

"Well look at this, Bettencourt," he said coldly. "The son of a bitch would have pulled one of these on you and blown your shit away. You heard Captain Greenley, no prisoner of war shit, not with these fuckers." He lowered the grenades, turning them around in his hand. Bettencourt knew it was the situation Wheeler had been looking for. Wheeler put the grenades in his field jacket pocket and watched Bettencourt relight his cigar.

"You don't fool me none, Bettencourt," he sneered, "you've got Greenley in your pocket, but I got your number. You may be the best heavy equipment operator in the Army and you're a good first shirt, but you ain't much of a soldier." He stared at Bettencourt until Bettencourt blew cigar smoke in his direction, intentionally. Infuriated, Wheeler stepped forward to speak then apparently thought better of it. He turned on his heel and walked away. Still shaking with anger, Bettencourt stood where he was for several minutes. He looked down at the youthful Japanese and he remembered the two young officers or cadets he had discovered in the gun pit right here on Engineer Hill days before, the two who seemed to have had some kind of suicide pact. This boy—and he looked younger every minute he laid there on the ground, was of the same kind as those two, he decided. Definitely not infantry. Not warriors in the normal sense of what we have come to understand Jap

246

soldiers to be. But the kid was on this hill, which means he made that long charge up from the Chichagof Valley and up the firestorm of machine gun fire, and only armed with a spear and a couple of hand grenades. He intended on doing something.

Bettencourt stepped closer and kneeled next to the boy, not touching him, not looking at his horrific wounds, but wondering what was going through his head when he was running through the tent area. Was his intention to surrender? To stab some American officer with his spear? Whatever his plan was, he changed his mind when he saw me. Or did he? Maybe Wheeler was right. Bettencourt also considered those last moments before Wheeler stepped in and killed him. What were you going to do, Bettencourt?

The time for the cigar was gone so he laid it down on the ground a few feet from the body. The sky was much lighter now. Gunfire was very sporadic and distant, but this time Bettencourt knew it was over. He looked over at the body one more time then walked around it to the other side of his tent. He picked up his carbine and went looking for his company.

CHAPTER 29

1600 Hours, May 30, 1943, D-Day Plus 19, Engineer Hill

The hilltop battle for Engineer Hill ended it for the Japanese defenders of Attu. The mass suicide killings continued all morning long until the fog dissipated and infantry could see the few survivors wandering around, dazed and disoriented right out there in the open. Machine gunners mowed them down if they were in range, as well as did carefully placed 81mm HE rounds. By noon, infantry slowly closed around the Sarana Valley in front of Engineer Hill to sweep it from one end to the other. It was tough going and the muskeg was thick. There wasn't much thought given to producing prisoners so Japanese who suddenly popped up were shot on the spot. Those who were wounded were executed before they were searched.

Jonathan Bettencourt reorganized Easy Company schedules to become an engineer outfit again, assigning crews to their original job— moving supplies up to the troops all around the Chichagof Valley, bringing wounded troops back across the Sarana Valley gap between Pendergast Ridge and Engineer Hill on the tow carts, keeping the tractor ferry system down the stream going and placing as many men as he could spare on the almost-completed road. Bettencourt focused on his work, getting his schedules neat and tight so he wouldn't have time to think about what they had just gone through. He wanted more than anything to be away from Attu, to get stinking drunk and smoke a Cuban and forget about the whole goddamn mess.

Japanese bodies were buried in mass graves via bulldozer from the front of Engineer Hill. With combat operations essentially complete on Attu there was a full-scale effort in getting the remaining American wounded off the island. Hundreds of American soldiers were killed or wounded during the Banzai attack from the bottom of the Chichagof Valley to the top of Engineer Hill, so the medical collection station on Pendergast Ridge was cycling men through as quickly as the tow and ferry system could handle them. *Get them out to the hospital ships, pronto!* His engineer HE operators on the dozers were exhausted, so Bettencourt wrote himself on the schedule to drive wounded down the stream to the hospital ships.

On the third trip down for the afternoon, Bettencourt waited at the head of the stream for the wounded to be loaded on the tow carts. He sat in the seat of the D4 eating a cold fried Spam sandwich and smoking one of those nasty Roi-Tan cigars Captain Greenley had given him, ruminating on his own personal exhaustion.   He no longer looked at the wounded as they were being loaded because they all looked the same.   Pathetic, dirty, and out there.   Sure, they could still talk or scream at you, but they were no longer on Attu Island and they had ceased being regular soldiers.   Ever since the drowning incident a few days earlier he had avoided the stream ferry detail, but it couldn't be helped now, they needed every man.

"Jeez," the medics complained behind him, "this guy is heavy!" Bettencourt peered over his shoulder as they loaded a large, heavy-set man up over the edge of the cart and set his stretcher in place.

"Easy, now..." said the senior medic, harried and exhausted himself, "he's got a bad lung wound."   The newest stretcher rigs had the IV fluids secured on poles above the stretcher, and there were two bottles attached to this man.   Bettencourt glanced over at the man's face, plump, pasty gray and unshaven—and climbed down off the tractor.   He walked over to the number two D4 in line and nodded to the operator.   He watched as they lifted the two wounded for this man's tow cart and did a double take when he recognized one of them.   He waited until they had set the two stretchers in the cart before walking up to the back of it and peering in to make sure.   He looked carefully at the big man on the left and shook his head in disbelief.   The wounded man, who was awake, sensed Bettencourt's presence and stare.   He looked up at him, a puzzled look on his face as he watched Bettencourt shake his head and grin at him.   He seemed to know him, but he had never seen the man before in his life.

"Damn, Lieutenant," Bettencourt said with wry amusement, "I don't know how you did this!   How did you manage to get yourself back on the island—and then how'd you imagine to get shot up again! Incredible!"   The big man stared at Bettencourt for a long moment until some realization came to him and he started to nod his head slowly. Bettencourt was catching on something was wrong, and stepped in closer, concerned the poor guy had a head injury or something.

"You do remember me, don't you, sir?   I hauled your ass down this stream just a couple of days ago and damned near drowned your ass! It's me, Jonathan Bettencourt, 50th Engineers!"

Ray Craymer, who had an extra tight compress bandage on his throat for his neck wound, coughed and stared straight ahead.   Manny Torre, the wounded man in the right side of the cart, peered over at Ray dully, not quite understanding what was going on.

Ray, who was also so laced with morphine he couldn't quite tie his thoughts together, tried to say something to the sergeant who seemed to know him but the drug took over and he simply closed his eyes. He was so exhuasted he just needed the blackness, the peace. Bettencourt stood there for a few seconds, a little confused, before deciding to just let it go. *The guy probably just flat out doesn't remember me. Well, he came back even with all those shrapnel wounds, what did you expect? He's got be a looney case in any event to want to come back to this place!*

Bettencourt went back to his D4 and glanced in his tow cart. There were now two men in it, one swathed in bandages and laying very still, and the other one, the large one, had his eyes open. The eyes followed Bettencourt so he stopped and nodded at the man, noting he had captain's bars on the collar of his very bloody field jacket.

"Afternoon sir," he said, "I'll try to keep the ride as comfortable as possible." The captain, obviously in considerable discomfort, blinked but there was a twinkle in his eye. He tried to grin.

"Well, Sergeant," he wheezed weakly, "I knew of this—ferry system of yours, but never figured I would be a customer." He turned his head to examine Bettencourt more closely. "You are the chauffeur for the afternoon? I have heard the ride can be—interesting."

Bettencourt thought just for a moment of the man rushing past him in the dark water, and the other man now back in the number two cart who had almost drowned due to his driving error.

"I'll do the best I can, sir. It won't be comfortable, I won't lie to you. It will take about an hour and you'll be fit to be tied when we're through."

Ed Ridgeway looked at Bettencourt thoughtfully as he realized the man was dead serious.

"Damn, Sergeant, you don't have to sugar coat it for my benefit." Bettencourt seemed pained as he nodded and walked away. Ridgeway listen to Bettencourt fire up the D4 and check in with the other drivers with his walkie-talkie. The medic had pumped him full of morphine just a few minutes before and he was starting to feel the effect. Morphine made him sick to his stomach but the deep, throbbing agonizing pain from the bayonet wound through his lung and both sides of his body just hurt so much, there was no way he could explain it to somebody.

The sky above was gray, but he saw a long, wispy slash of blue far up through several tiers of clouds. This place, he thought, this island was like nothing any of us had expected. He was very glad to leave it. Combat was not what he had expected it to be either. It came to him, oddly at this time because he had not considered it once in the last 24 hours, he was personally responsible for the death of three men. He could see the faces of all three clearly, the common soldier who had bayoneted him, the officer he had shot in the head and the NCO he shot in the chest. He had seen their faces for just fleeting seconds, but all died under his hand and he was cursed with a memory lodging the distinct images forever in his consciousness. They would never leave him those three, none who had shown the least hesitation in trying to kill him. What a place to live. What a horrible place to die. We all came a long ways to do that.

CHAPTER 30

0600 Hours, June 29, 1943, D-Day Plus 48, San Francisco

Summer had come to the city gently, the flowers encouraged by the spring rains spread all over the brick trellises of the old house on Ashbury Street. The sun was just starting to cast a golden glow over the rooftops as Linda Wong made her tea. Her roommates were also early risers, invisibly going about the business of preparing for another school day. They had seen the envelope for the letter and knew Linda was keeping to herself about the contents. Linda was such a cautious, careful, and thoughtful individual, and her roommates guarded her secrets and her treasures as if they were their own.

Ray had told her not to expect much mail once they shipped out for the Pacific, but he would try to keep her informed if there wasn't an invasion blackout. A couple of times in early April he had called the house and left a message, but there was no number to call back to. He was restricted to post like all of the 7th ID soldiers prior to shipping out, and would call later. In mid-April she did receive the one other letter, post-marked Monterey, California, letting her know he would be leaving soon and would not be able to come up to see her. All this they had already discussed, but she found the words on the one page letter comforting somehow. His tightly packed, half-script half block letters were so masculine but yet so boy-like to her, she found the smudged ink on the page more endearing than the words themselves. Writing looked like such an effort for him; she knew he selected each word carefully. It made her think of her students, the ones who hovered so tightly over the page as they labored over the words.

She poured her tea and opened the latest letter again, pressing the neatly folded page flat so she could read it with both hands on her cup. This letter was different as the handwriting was less legible. Ray apologized for it explaining he had been injured and holding a pen was difficult. Not to worry, he said, he was recovering fine and nothing was "missing". The postmark on the letter said something, Missouri, which gave her a double-take. Fort Leonard Wood, Missouri. He spelled it out for her, Fort Leonard Wood was about 130 miles from St. Louis and about 90 miles from Springfield, the closest real town near his parents' home.

Ray made a brief reference to having been involved in an invasion in the Aleutian Islands, which meant nothing to her. What he did say was he had finally hooked up with his brother, Orin, and both of them served in the same campaign, both were wounded and sent home to Fort Leonard Wood to recover from their wounds. Orin, he said, was an officer and was in much worse shape than he was, but he too would recover. They were in a big hospital on the post and were being well taken care of. Included in the letter was a small photograph of the two brothers, both in dark bathrobes sitting close together in deck chairs. Linda was amazed at how much they looked alike. She carefully pulled out another photograph, a small head and shoulder shot she had taken of Ray in Golden Gate Park in the fall. Her heart sagged and tears welled in her eyes as she compared the sheepish grinning figure in one with the gaunt face and sad eyes in the other.

You found each other, she thought, *at least you found each other.* I know you missed your brother terribly and worried about him. Linda turned both pictures down on the table and continued reading the letter. Ray's enlistment was coming up and he was talking about possibly being discharged by the Army after he recovered. He wasn't sure, it depended on how much longer the war might last. He said his wounds were not serious and there didn't appear to be any permanent damage, but he had a lot of them and the Army decided he needed to recover close to home. He even talked about maybe going back to school.

Linda took a deep breath and paused before reading the last paragraph, her eyes welling with tears again. She daubed them with her fingers before forcing them back onto the page. Ray asked her to come to St. Louis on the pretext to see her family, and then come down to Fort Leonard Wood to visit him. A soft smile waned as she read his description of a vague life together, of how he realized her importance to him. She paused and read his plans again. How could she explain to him how it would never work? How her parents would never accept him, or how Americans would never accept their relationship? St. Louis, Missouri was not San Francisco. This was 1943 in the middle of a war with an Asian nation. He seemed to have forgotten what was happening in the country. What difference did it make to Americans on the street whether you were Chinese or Japanese? You were only another Asian face, the face of the enemy. She thought again of her mother and grandmother. *Europeans all look alike.*

Linda Wong washed her tea cup and dried it before putting it away. She glanced up at the big clock on the wall realizing she would be late for school if she didn't hurry. In her bedroom she carefully placed the two photographs side by side, looking at them with focused intensity. After a moment she opened her jewelry box and lifted out the wooden tray, placing the letters and the photographs neatly underneath.

She quickly dressed and brushed her long black hair. Seeing herself in the mirror she stopped to stare, examining her face and delicate features. With her hand she reached up slowly under her breast to feel her heart beating, closing her eyes because she was not able to visualize his face the way she wanted. She let the tears come, finally, and didn't try to hold them back. *Someone*, she thought, *should cry for us*.

ABOUT THE AUTHOR

Jerry Coker lives in Northern California with his wife and dog, sharing time between the Sonoma Coast and the Sacramento Valley. During 1968-69 he served as a U.S. Marine rifleman with the 2nd Battalion, 26th Marine Regiment in South Vietnam until he was wounded and medically retired.   Returning to school, he earned degrees from the University of California, Davis, and Brown University.

In May of 1943 his father Roy Coker served as a Regular Army infantryman with the U.S. Army's 7th Infantry Division during the invasion of Attu Island, earning a Bronze Star for Valor for his actions on Fish Hook Ridge.   Roy Coker continued serving with the Seventh ID during a number of Pacific campaigns until he was wounded and sent home to recover.

www.ingramcontent.com/pod-product-compliance
Lightning Source LLC
Chambersburg PA
CBHW011352010726
47494CB00008B/2279